The Secret Wife

LINDA KAVANAGH

Harlequin MIRA is a registered trademark of Harlequin Enterprises Limited, used under licence.

Published in Great Britain 2014.
Harlequin MIRA, an imprint of Harlequin (UK) Limited,
Eton House, 18-24 Paradise Road,
Richmond, Surrey, TW9 1SR

© 2013 Linda Kavanagh

ISBN 978-1-848-45305-0

60-0914

Harlequin (UK) Limited's policy is to use papers that are natural, renewable and recyclable products and made from wood grown in sustainable forests. The logging and manufacturing processes conform to the legal environmental regulations of the country of origin.

Printed and bound by
CPI Group (UK) Ltd, Croydon, CR0 4YY

The Secret Wife

ACKNOWLEDGEMENTS

Sincere thanks to editor Sally Williamson and all the team at Mira, to my wonderful agent Lorella Belli, for her support and belief in me, and especially to all my readers who have already made my previous novels bestsellers in Ireland.

CHAPTER 1

'I'm getting married!'

Laura Thornton looked the picture of happiness as she held out her left hand so that her friend Kerry could admire her engagement ring.

'Congratulations!' Kerry said, hugging her, and trying to appear happy for her. But she was worried. She didn't like the man Laura was planning to marry. Okay, so he was charming and handsome, a stockbroker who seemed to have a knack for making money. Yet there was something profoundly needy about him. Not that being needy was wrong – it just wasn't what you expected to find in a mature, successful man. Nevertheless, Laura seemed convinced that she'd found a man who genuinely cared about her.

'So when is the wedding?'

'Next month – we saw no reason to wait, since we want so much to be together!'

So soon! Kerry experienced a frisson of fear. It looked as though Laura was being her usual impulsive self.

'It's going to be a very small wedding – I mean, since neither Jeff nor I have any family. But I'd really like you to be my bridesmaid.'

Kerry nodded. 'Of course. I'd be delighted.'

Nevertheless, she was disturbed at the haste with which Laura was marrying this man, whom she hardly knew. Although aware that her friend was impulsive, Kerry suspected that Jeff was the one pushing for this rush into marriage.

Kerry and Laura had met Jeff one evening in a pub. The bar had been crowded, and Laura had been trying desperately to catch the barman's eye. Jeff had witnessed her attempts and, being tall, he'd gallantly ordered the drinks for her, then insisted on paying for them. Laura had been impressed by the good-looking, blond-haired man, and they'd spent the rest of the evening chatting to each other.

Kerry had disliked him on sight. She'd recognised a smooth-talking chancer, but Laura had quickly fallen for his superficial charms. Before long, Laura could hardly frame a sentence without bringing Jeff's name into it, and Kerry knew that it was pointless to urge caution. Laura was already head over heels in love with him. Instinctively Kerry knew that, if she raised any objections to Jeff, Laura would interpret it as sour grapes on her part, and she'd be the one to lose Laura's friendship. Already she could sense that Jeff was keen to loosen the bonds between the two women. He'd demand total loyalty, and that loyalty would require him to be the centre of Laura's universe. Would Laura allow that to happen?

'Oh, Kerry, I'm so excited!' Laura said, her face wreathed in smiles. 'I never thought I'd meet anyone like Jeff – and that he'd want to be with me, too! He's the most wonderful man I've ever met and I just feel *soooo* lucky to be marrying him!'

Kerry smiled, although she felt that her face was in danger of cracking from the effort, and quickly steered the conversation away from any further discussion of Jeff's merits. 'So what are you going to wear? Have you picked a dress yet?'

'No, so you'll have to come shopping with me!' Laura said, grinning. 'We can find a dress for you, too. How about something in burgundy? It would look wonderful with your dark hair…'

Kerry nodded. She didn't really care what colour she wore. It was Laura's day, so she'd wear whatever dress Laura chose for her. But there was something she urgently needed to find out. She'd need to raise the subject as delicately as possible with Laura, and sooner rather than later...

Kerry made a special effort to share Laura's enthusiasm for her approaching big day. Together, they trawled the dress shops during their lunch hour and, with Kerry's approval, Laura blew a month's salary on a gorgeous cream taffeta dress with a detail of tiny pearls.

Kerry's dress proved to be a simple and straightforward purchase. She readily agreed to a deep burgundy chiffon dress that Laura discovered in a small boutique, thinking how contrasting the two of them would look at the wedding – Laura's blonde hair and cream dress versus her own dark dress and dark brown hair. Kerry also opted to wear a simple matching flower in her hair, whereas Laura was thrilled to find a glamorous pearl and feathered fascinator that was an exact match for her dress.

As they relaxed over a coffee in a city-centre café after their shopping expedition, Laura was still giddy with excitement. Kerry looked at her – it was time to ask Laura the question that had been preying on her mind. She took a deep breath.

'Laura, have you told Jeff about the money?'

Laura looked up from the cream doughnut she was slicing. 'Not yet – there's never been the right time, what with all the preparations for the wedding. But I'll tell him as soon as we're married.'

Inside, Kerry sighed with relief. Thank goodness. But how on earth could she delicately point out to Laura that she needed to protect her huge inheritance?

'Look, love, I think you should wait a while before telling

him,' Kerry ventured. 'You can't be sure how things will go – none of us can – but what if you ended up divorcing Jeff? He could probably claim a lot of your money.'

Laura bridled. 'You seem to be implying that there's something devious about Jeff! That's a horrible thing to say about a woman's fiancé just before she gets married!' Her eyes filled with tears. 'He's the best! Poor Jeff's survived a violent childhood, with dysfunctional parents – yet despite such an awful start in life, he's become hugely successful. I'm so proud of him.'

Kerry nodded, as though to agree with Laura's estimation of Jeff's abilities, but to her it was yet another red flag. Jeff was looking dodgier by the minute.

She reached across the table and took her friend's hand. 'Love, I'm only looking out for you! By all means tell him when you've been together for a year or two – but wait a while, just to be sure. Please?'

Laura looked sullen and offended.

'Look, Jeff has a comfortable home and both of you have jobs you love,' Kerry pleaded. 'You can live happily as you are for the time being. Then when you eventually tell him, you'll have proved that he's the man for you.'

Laura's expression became angry. 'I know *now* that Jeff's the man for me! Are you implying that I don't know my own mind?'

Kerry raised her hands in appeasement. 'Of course not! I'm just concerned for you. I'm sure you'll be perfectly happy with Jeff. I just don't want you losing any of your fortune.'

Laura nibbled a piece of her doughnut, then looked at her friend and sighed. 'Sorry, Kerry – I know you mean well. I really do appreciate your concern, but Jeff and I…well, we're in for the long haul. But I don't want you and me to fall out, so I'll hold off telling him for a while.' She looked at Kerry with a triumphant look on her face. 'Then you'll realise that Jeff truly is the man for me – I know he loves me, no matter what my financial situation is.'

Kerry nodded, relieved that the fortune Laura had inherited on the death of her parents and brother was safe from Jeff. She was convinced that if he knew what was in Laura's bank account, there would be little money left by the time she discovered what he was truly like.

She shivered, wondering briefly if Jeff could already know about the trust fund that had been set up for Laura, and which she'd received several years earlier, on reaching the age of twenty-five. Maybe their meeting in the pub hadn't been accidental after all?

Putting on a smile, Kerry turned to her friend. 'How many guests are you having altogether?'

'At the last count, about twenty.'

Laura had invited around a dozen colleagues from the Sociology Department of the university where she was a lecturer, a few of Kerry's colleagues from the engineering company where she was a partner, and a few friends of Jeff's from his badminton club. Kerry wondered uneasily why no one from other areas of Jeff's life would be attending – even though he'd no family, surely he had work colleagues who were friends? In her opinion, there was definitely something odd about him, but she was not about to start pointing out his deficiencies, since Laura was clearly annoyed with her at the idea of keeping Jeff in the dark about the money she'd inherited.

'You'd better stay with me the night before the wedding,' Kerry said, smiling, as they gathered up their booty and left the café. 'It's supposed to bring bad luck if the groom sees you before you get to the registry office.'

Laura nodded, her eyes now sparkling again with excitement. She'd already given up her own rented flat and moved in with Jeff, since they'd decided to make their home in his sumptuous Islington apartment. 'Well then, we'll also have to make that our hen night!' she said, smiling. 'Since Jeff and I wanted to get married as quickly as possible, there hasn't been time to do a lot of the normal stuff.'

Kerry shook her head sternly. 'There'll be no hen night for you on the eve of the wedding, madam – I don't want you nursing a hangover on your big day!'

Kerry suspected that Jeff probably wouldn't want Laura having a hen night anyway, since it would mean she wouldn't be focusing all her attention on him, and he'd see danger in the combination of alcohol and male strippers that was usually on the menu. In essence, Jeff wouldn't want Laura having any fun if he wasn't there to share it. Or control it.

The day of the wedding dawned bright and sunny, and Laura was already up and in the kitchen when Kerry padded out of her bedroom in dressing gown and slippers.

'Oh, Kerry, I'm so excited!' Laura squealed, jumping up and down, then hugging her friend as Kerry tried to switch on the kettle. 'Here, let me get you some breakfast – I'm far too nervous to eat anything myself!'

'You've got to eat something,' Kerry warned her, managing to put two slices of bread in the toaster. 'Otherwise, you might faint during the service, and that wouldn't look great on your wedding day!'

Laura nodded. Her friend was right, as usual. But there were butterflies in her stomach, and she couldn't sit still. Before leaving her room she'd checked and checked again that her shoes, bouquet and fascinator were all lined up and ready. Thrilled, she'd touched the hem of her wedding gown that was hanging on the back of the bedroom door, wrapped in tissue paper. She couldn't wait to be Jeff's wife.

'Here – eat this,' Kerry said, pushing a slice of buttered toast across the table towards her. 'I'm not letting you leave this apartment until there's something in your stomach!'

Nodding, Laura took the slice of toast and began chewing obediently. She couldn't even taste it because she was so nervous and so excited, but she knew Kerry was right, and was only looking out for her. She had to eat something. Otherwise, she might keel over just as she was taking her vows. And nothing was going to stop her from saying 'I do' to her beloved Jeff.

Swallowing the toast, she smiled at Kerry. 'Can I ask you one more favour? Just in case I get a bit tipsy today, will you make sure Jeff doesn't eat any wedding cake? I'm just worried in case he'll forget, after having a few drinks himself. The hotel people know to prepare his meal separately, but I didn't have time to organise a peanut-free cake.'

Kerry raised an eyebrow. 'What do you mean?'

Laura grimaced. 'Jeff has a severe allergy to peanuts. Even a whiff of a peanut in his food could be enough to kill him.'

Kerry looked sceptical.

'It's true – if he accidentally ingested any, he'd immediately go into anaphylactic shock. That's why he has to carry an adrenaline pen with him at all times, so that he can inject himself if he has a bad reaction, or someone else can inject him if he collapses.' Laura took a deep breath. 'So you can see why I worry.'

Kerry smiled warmly at her friend. 'Of course I'll keep an eye on him! But if his problem is so severe, I'm sure he's well aware of it himself.' Smiling, she patted her friend's arm. 'So the only nuts at your wedding will be your friends!'

Laughing, Laura led the way into the bedroom. At last it was time to get dressed.

As Kerry helped her into her cream taffeta dress, Laura's expression abruptly changed to one of sadness. 'I really wish I had my parents and my brother here with me today,' she said wistfully. 'I'm missing them so much right now!'

Her eyes filled with tears, and Kerry hugged her.

'You're the only family I have left,' Laura added. 'I mean, you're all alone too, since your mum died, so we only have each other.' She brightened. 'But Jeff and I will have kids eventually, so we'll create our own family over time. And I'm sure you'll have kids some day, too. I hope they'll be good friends like us.'

Laura brushed away her tears and concentrated on putting on her fascinator and matching pearl earrings. She'd never got over the death of her parents and brother in a tragic car accident when she was almost twelve. All she had left of them now was a few precious photographs, which she kept in her bedside cupboard. She regularly took them out and looked at them – it enabled her to remember that she'd once been part of a happy family. And she blamed herself for what happened. She'd gone to check on an injured bird that morning, so she'd missed the planned trip to get new school uniforms for her and her brother Pete. After waiting in vain for her daughter to appear, her mother had final-ly decided to set off with Pete, and at the last minute her father had chosen to take a lift in her mother's car. Laura was well aware that if she hadn't delayed her mother, they might never have crashed, and her father would never have taken a lift be-cause they'd have left for town already. Ever since then, Laura had carried around the guilt like a huge weight on her back.

Laura wiped away another tear. As Laura's close friend since childhood, Kerry, too, had been devastated by what had happened, and, sadly, Kerry's mother had died of a suspected heart attack while both young women were still at universi-ty. Without a doubt, the early loss of both their families had brought her and Kerry even closer.

'Come on, dry those tears – you'll ruin your mascara,' Ker-ry said briskly. 'There's no time for sad memories today. This is a happy day, and I want to see you smiling.'

Laura obliged, giving Kerry a winning smile. Then she picked up her bouquet of freesias and roses, surveyed herself in the mirror, and gave a contented nod. She was pleased with what she saw. Looking back at her was a woman who had the clear eyes of someone in love, who was just about to marry the man she adored.

'I'm ready,' said Laura, taking a deep breath.

CHAPTER 2

*E*llie Beckworth rode her bicycle home from work, sensing that there was something definitely wrong with the front wheel. It was wobbling too freely, and she decided that at the earliest opportunity she'd take it to the village bicycle shop. Perhaps it needed a new tyre, or possibly the wheel frame had become slightly bent. There were so many stones on this stretch of the road, all of them waiting to snare unwary cyclists...

Widowed a year earlier, Ellie was employed as a chemist in the laboratory of the local canning factory. Her job had proved a lifeline after John's sudden death, since the small pension from his job didn't come near to covering her mortgage payments. Besides, returning to work had occupied her mind and distracted her from the loneliness that had enveloped her since John had passed away.

She and her husband had moved to London only a year before his death, when he'd been offered a partnership in a small accountancy firm in the city. They'd left the north of England behind, intent on making a new life, and hoped to raise a family in the London suburbs. They'd even found the house of their dreams, near a village on the outskirts of London but within commuting distance of the city – a small house called Treetops, with a huge three-acre woodland garden, just made for half a dozen kids. But no children were forthcoming, and now there never would be.

Deep in thought, she didn't hear the car approaching until it *was almost level with her. It gave her such a fright as it swept past that she and the bicycle wobbled dangerously, teetering for a few seconds before veering sideways and crashing into a ditch.*

'Aaagh!' Covered in debris, and with her bicycle clearly beyond repair, Ellie surveyed the mess. Her clothes were dishevelled, and she was having difficulty extracting the twigs that had become knotted in her curly hair.

'Are you okay?' said a voice, and Ellie found herself looking up into a pair of dark brown eyes.

'Does it look as though I'm okay?' she retorted. 'I don't usually choose to dress in muddy clothes, and wear half a tree in my hair!'

As she struggled to extricate herself from the muddy ditch, a hand gripped hers firmly and pulled her up. Ellie recognised the owner of the factory where she worked – Alan Thornton, or 'Mr Alan' as the employees called him.

'You're Ms Beckworth from the laboratory, aren't you?'

She nodded, raising her eyebrows. 'I'm surprised you know who I am. I mean, you've got hundreds of employees.'

'Who couldn't help noticing you? You're gorgeous,' he said, smiling.

'Well, I'm not exactly at my best right this minute,' she said tartly, continuing to pick leaves and debris from her hair and clothes. 'But then again, I don't usually make a habit of spending my time in ditches.'

Alan smiled down at her, and she noticed how very tall he was. 'I'll pop your bike in the boot, and give you a lift home,' he said, effortlessly hoisting it out of the ditch. 'It's the least I can do. I feel responsible for what happened – it's obvious that I drove too close to your bike and gave you a fright.'

'Thank you,' Ellie said, climbing into the front passenger seat and telling him her address while hoping she wouldn't leave too much debris in his pristine car. The interior was magnificent, and

*she looked appreciatively at the leather seat covers and the elabo-
rate walnut-and-chrome dashboard. 'Very nice,' she said, running
her hand along the edge of her seat. 'How the other half live, eh?'*

He laughed. 'It's not mine. All the company cars are leased.'

*'Well, I'd be happy to drive something like this, even if it wasn't
technically mine,' she replied, trailing her hand along the dashboard's walnut fascia. 'Right now, I don't even have a bike!'*

*'Don't worry, I'll take care of that,' Alan said, starting the en-
gine and pulling out onto the road. 'I'll order a replacement bike
right away.'*

*'Well, if you're feeling generous, maybe you'd get me a lease-
hold car instead of a bike?' Ellie said, smiling impishly at him.*

*He laughed. 'The fall doesn't seem to have affected your brain,
does it? You've still got all your wits about you!' He smiled at
her kindly. 'How are you managing? It's about a year since your
husband died, isn't it?'*

*Ellie nodded, surprised once again that he knew so much about
her. Then she remembered that she'd seen him at John's funeral,
and had considered it a nice gesture that the company's owner
had bothered to attend a mere employee's husband's funeral.*

'I'm fine, thanks,' she told him. 'Anyway, work keeps me busy.'

*Alan darted a glance in her direction. 'If the fall's genuinely
shaken you, please don't hurry back to the laboratory tomorrow,'
he told her.*

*Ellie gave him a scornful look. 'Do I look like some ridiculous-
ly dim damsel in distress? It would take more than a fall off my
bike to wind me!'*

*'Yes,' he said softly, 'I can see that now. You strike me as quite
a remarkable woman.'*

*As Alan turned in off the road and drove up Ellie's driveway, he
whistled in admiration. 'Wow, I'd no idea there was a house tucked
away in here – it's so secluded! And you've quite a bit of woodland
behind the house, too. It's lovely! I really like the veranda, too.'*

'Thank you.' Ellie smiled sadly to herself, remembering that she and John had bought the house with a future family in mind.

As the car drew up outside the front door, Ellie hesitated, unsure what to do.

'Would you like some tea?' she asked.

'Yes, please.'

In the kitchen she filled the kettle, knowing that Alan was watching her. It made her feel intimidated and excited all at once. To have such a powerful and attractive man looking at her was a strange yet heady feeling. At the same time, she felt embarrassed at her untidiness, and hurriedly tucked a stray stand of hair behind her ear. She knew she must look a fright.

'Here – there's a bit of grass stuck behind your ear.'

Suddenly, he was beside her, removing the offending grass and placing it in her outstretched hand. It seemed such an intimate thing to do, as though they'd known each other for a long time.

'Oh, thanks.' Flustered, she took the piece of grass and dropped it into the bin beside the worktop. 'I must look a mess,' she said self-consciously. 'Excuse me, I'll just go to the bathroom and tidy up – '

She felt his hand on her arm, restraining her, and it seemed to sear through her skin.

'You don't need to do anything. You look lovely the way you are,' he said softly.

His eyes searched her face, and she felt herself drowning. When he reached out and touched her face, she felt as though her whole body was on fire. He seemed to know it, because he said softly, 'I'm married,' as though waiting for permission to advance his suit.

She nodded. 'I know,' she said, trying to smile. 'All the best ones are usually taken.'

'It doesn't stop me wanting you.'

He didn't remove his hand from her arm, and she didn't move from where she was standing – so close to him that she could feel his breath. She shivered with excitement. It had been so long since a man had touched her. In fact, she'd never wanted any man to touch her as much as she wanted this man to touch her. Desire raced through her like a forest fire.

'I want to kiss you,' he whispered, and she had no time to reply before his lips found hers and she was kissing him back.

It was as though that first kiss ignited a raging fire in both of them. Her hands were suddenly all over his body and his were on hers, and she was aching for more. Like two people possessed, they began tearing off each other's clothes, leaving a trail of garments across the kitchen and hall as she led him upstairs to her bedroom.

In a frenzy of desire, they kissed and explored each other's naked body, unable to get enough of each other. And each time he took her, she reached a shuddering crescendo of pleasure.

Later, as they lay sated, their bodies drenched with sweat, they looked at each other and smiled shyly.

'I'm not going to apologise,' he said, kissing her nose. 'You are the most exciting woman I've ever met, and I want to make love to you over and over and over again…'

'Then I'll have to make sure I fall off my bike more often!' she said, smiling.

Suddenly, his voice was husky again. 'Please tell me I can visit you again tomorrow?'

'Yes,' she whispered.

'In fact,' he said, leaning towards her, 'I don't think I can wait till tomorrow.'

As he reached for her, desire coursed through her again. And even though she was exhausted from their earlier coupling, he brought her to ecstasy once more.

The following evening, just as she arrived home from work, a delivery van arrived and deposited a shiny, new, state-of-the-art bicycle with five-speed gears at her front door. An envelope was taped to the front basket and as soon as the deliveryman had gone, she tore it open with shaking hands, pulling out the note inside. It read: 'I'm so glad you came crashing into my life yesterday. I can't wait to see you again.' He'd signed his initial at the bottom.

Clasping the note to her chest, she felt a surge of joy running through her body. Yesterday clearly meant as much to him as it had to her. All day at work she'd been thinking of him, and when she'd caught a glimpse of him in his office as she walked by, her heart had leaped in her chest with joy.

Because of her excitement, Ellie didn't give much thought to the fact that this was a seminal moment in her life. There was still time to alter its course. But she silenced the warning bells that reminded her he was married, and the father of a young son. The excitement she felt – the feeling of being more alive than she'd ever felt before – negated everything else.

CHAPTER 3

In a sumptuous room off the hotel lobby, the champagne reception was in full swing. Laura smiled appreciatively at her new husband, who was talking to some friends of his from the badminton club. Jeff looked so handsome in his dress suit, his blond hair curling over his ears, his eyes a little glazed from all the champagne he'd been drinking.

'Congratulations – you look radiant, Laura!' her lecturer colleague, Maria, said, giggling as she emptied her champagne glass and deftly grabbed another from a passing waiter. 'Jeff's such a handsome guy – and a stockbroker to boot! Some women have all the luck!'

Laura nodded. She couldn't be happier, and she loved being surrounded by all her colleagues on this very special day. She smiled as she watched Timmy, another lecturer from the Sociology Department, trying to impress Greta, the department secretary, with his version of the moonwalk, which wasn't an easy feat, given the amount of champagne he'd already consumed. Several of Kerry's colleagues from Sea Diagnostics, the engineering company where she was a partner, were also hovering around the bar. Laura waved across the room to Kerry's colleagues, Norma and Jack, who were involved in some kind of shot-drinking competition. She suspected there would be quite a few hangovers needing a cure the following day!

She glanced across at Jeff, who was now talking to Kerry

– she was glad that her best friend and husband seemed to be chatting together happily. It was so important to her that they got along. She was well aware of Kerry's initial apathy towards Jeff, but she'd noticed that Kerry had been making a real effort to be friendly towards Jeff, and she silently applauded her for it. Her best friend was bound to feel a little left out – after all, they'd been friends since childhood, separated only during the six years immediately after Laura's family died, when she'd moved away to live with her grandfather. But they'd always kept in touch, and had eventually managed to attend the same university. Their lives had been closely linked for many years, which meant that Laura's marriage would undoubtedly bring about a change in their friendship, although she intended making every effort to ensure that Kerry didn't feel left out.

Professor Darren Coyle, head of the Department, sidled up and slipped an arm around her. His thick glasses were askew, his normally neat, dark hair was falling untidily over his forehead and he was inebriated from the champagne. Laura felt a surge of affection for him as they hugged. She was pleased to have him with her on such an important day.

'You look the picture of happiness, Laura!' he slurred, planting a kiss on her cheek. 'I hope you won't let Jeff take you away from us? You know how much we all love working with you!'

'Of course not!' Laura told him, smiling. 'I love my job too much.'

For a moment, Darren looked puzzled. 'Oh. I thought Jeff said something about you giving up work – '

Laura shook her head. 'Definitely not! It'll take more than marriage to prise me away from all of you!'

On the other side of the room, Jeff was still in conversation with Kerry.

As he looked down triumphantly at her, he raised his glass of champagne. 'Now Laura's mine – all mine!'

Kerry smiled. 'Congratulations to you both!' she said, choosing not to let him know that she'd got his message. In effect, he was telling her that he'd soon see to it that he became the centre of Laura's universe, and that his new wife would have little time left to spend with her friend.

Kerry kept the smile on her face as she walked across to the bar to top up her champagne glass. She'd be there when Laura needed her, as she suspected she eventually would. Kerry had no doubt that Jeff would soon reach his sell-by date. But Laura would be the last to realise it.

After a pleasant reception, a delightful wedding meal and a cheery send-off from their friends and colleagues, Jeff and Laura returned to Jeff's luxurious apartment.

'I just wish my family had been there today,' Laura said wistfully, as she closed the front door. 'That would have been the icing on the cake…'

'You're lucky to have no family!' Jeff retorted angrily. 'My parents beat me constantly, so I'm grateful that *they* weren't there!'

Laura was stunned and more than a little shocked by his remark. It seemed particularly thoughtless to dismiss the loss of her parents and brother so insensitively. But she supposed he himself was hurting and hadn't realised how cruel it sounded. Hers had been a loving family, whereas Jeff had only ever known violence.

Suddenly, being back in the apartment seemed such an anti-climax after all the excitement of the wedding.

'Did you say anything to Darren about me giving up work?'

Jeff shrugged his shoulders. 'I might have mentioned that

we'll be starting a family soon, and then you won't have time to work.'

Laura looked at him incredulously. 'Jeff, whether I work or not when we have kids will be a shared decision! I'll probably prefer to keep up my lecturing, and use the university crèche for our children. Anyway, we'll decide that together when the time comes, won't we?'

Jeff said nothing, then he turned to her eagerly. 'But you're going to take my name, aren't you?'

Laura looked at him in surprise. 'Well, no, I wasn't intending to. I mean, I'm known in my profession as Laura Thornton – I'd rather not confuse things.'

Jeff looked hurt. 'But I want us to be a single, loving family unit! Won't it be odd for our children if their parents have different names?'

Laura smiled mischievously. 'Well then, why don't you take my name? Then we can all be Thorntons!'

Jeff scowled. 'Maybe I should just change my name to "hen-pecked" and be done with it!'

Laura smiled. 'Why is it okay for a woman to change her name, but not a man?'

Jeff shrugged his shoulders, but didn't answer. Then he began hassling her again. 'Seriously, wouldn't it be better if we were all called Jones?' he wheedled.

He looked so earnest that Laura had to smile. 'Look, I'll think about it,' she replied. 'But I really don't see why it's so important – '

'Well, if it's not so important to you, why don't you just agree, since it matters so much to *me*? Laura, I just want us all to share the same name, and be a real family!'

Knowing Jeff's history, Laura relented. If creating their own little family unit was so important to him, then maybe she should be willing to give way on this one. After all, wasn't marriage all about compromise? Besides, his insistence made her feel cherished – he was obviously looking towards a long and happy future together.

'Okay, then. I'll become Laura Jones.'

'Oh, love, you don't know how happy that makes me!' Jeff said, his eyes alight with joy. 'I feel as though you're really going to be mine now! Oh, Laura, I love you so much! Let's hope we'll have lots of little Joneses as well!'

Laura smiled as he hugged her tightly. It was really such a small thing to do, yet it made Jeff so happy. And she was pleased that she could make him feel good. After his awful childhood, she wanted so much to make up for it and to help him build a wonderful future with her.

CHAPTER 4

As they curled up together in Ellie's bed, Alan stroked his lover's cheek tenderly. They'd been seeing each other daily for several weeks now, and each bout of lovemaking was just as exciting as the last.

Even going to work each morning was proving exhilarating. Ellie felt like a teenager in the throes of first love, and she lived for occasional glimpses of Alan in his office. He, too, had started coming to the laboratory on flimsy pretexts, and Ellie feared that someone would soon notice how deeply she blushed whenever he entered the room.

'This has got to stop,' Ellie begged him. 'Someone is going to notice before long. I just want to touch you all the time.'

Alan agreed with her. 'But I can't stay away from you! We're going to have to find a way of spending more time together.'

And now Alan felt he'd found it.

'If you were to leave the factory, I could visit you any time – at lunchtime, in the afternoon, in the evening – and no one would ever know.'

As she opened her mouth to protest, he silenced her with a kiss. 'I could continue to pay your wages, so you'd maintain the same lifestyle as before. But we could then spend much more time together. What do you think?'

Ellie pretended to consider his offer, but already her mind was made up. Why be employed if she could pay her mortgage with far less effort? She'd be able to devote her life to loving Alan full-time. Because, by now, she'd admitted to herself that she was deeply in love with him.

Luckily, she'd never made any close friends at the factory. The laboratory staff were few in number, and contact with the factory workers was limited to the times when she collected batch samples for testing. During her marriage to John, she'd gone straight home after work rather than going to the factory social club or local pub. Now all that could work to her advantage. Other than factory manager, Tony Coleman – who clearly fancied her – the other workers left her more or less alone. If she gave up working at the factory, she wouldn't need to worry about a trail of visitors to her home to disrupt her secret relationship with Alan.

'Okay, I'll do it,' she said, her eyes shining. 'I'll leave the factory.'

Alan hugged her. 'Oh, Ellie, it's going to be wonderful! We'll be able to create our own little world at Treetops, where no one else can touch us.'

Everyone at the factory was surprised to hear that Ellie was leaving. She smiled glibly as she lied about her plans for setting up a home tutoring business, providing one-to-one private lessons in science subjects for students.

Tony Coleman was clearly disappointed. He'd always tried to create opportunities to talk to her when she visited the factory floor to take batch samples for testing in the laboratory. He seemed to view these chats as some kind of proof that they were ultimately destined for each other. Which was never going to happen, as far as Ellie was concerned!

On the day of her leaving party, Alan was among the first to arrive at the social club. He bought drinks for everyone before making a short speech about Ellie's value as an employee, how much she'd be missed, and wishing her well in her new business venture. After a round of applause from all her colleagues, Tony claimed her for a dance as the small combo in the corner began playing. Soon, the small dance floor was crowded, but Ellie could feel Alan's eyes on her as she and Tony jived. She knew he'd be trying his best not to look at her, but he'd be unable to help himself.

Tony was particularly attentive as they made their way back to the bar after their dance. 'Where exactly will you be tutoring the students?' he asked. 'If you need to convert a room into a classroom, maybe I could give you a hand – '

'Thanks, Tony, but it's all sorted,' Ellie told him, smiling. Although his attentions were irritating, she was glad Alan could see that another man obviously found her attractive.

Everyone was buying her farewell drinks, and Ellie knew she was drinking far more wine than she should, but this was her special night, and she was excited at being on the threshold of a new and wonderful life.

As the combo switched tempo and began playing jazz, Tony appeared again and dragged her onto the dance floor. Although Alan was talking to a group of his factory workers, Ellie knew he'd still be watching her. She was enjoying the heady sensation of being the focus of two men's attention, and she was now deliberately flirting with Tony as he whirled her around the dance floor. She wanted to make Alan jealous. She wanted him to know that she could be with other men if she wanted to, but that she'd chosen to be with him instead.

As Ellie returned to the bar, with Tony still hovering eagerly in the background, Alan was suddenly by her side. His expression was bland, although she knew from the intensity in his eyes that he wasn't feeling quite as calm as he appeared.

'You've no idea how jealous of Tony I am!' he whispered in her ear. 'He seems to be monopolising all your time tonight, and there's nothing I can do about it.' He smiled mischievously. 'But

I can't fault his taste in women!' Then he spoke more loudly for effect. 'Can I get you another drink, Ms Beckworth?'

'Thanks – a glass of white wine, please.'

Having procured the drink from the barman, Alan handed it to Ellie.

'You shouldn't be looking so happy,' Ellie whispered teasingly. 'After all, you're losing a valuable employee!'

'Sorry,' he said regretfully, although it was clear he wasn't sorry at all. 'It's just that I'm starting a whole new secret life with the woman I love. I'm finding it hard to hide my excitement.'

Just then, Tony muscled his way to the bar again, and seized Ellie for another dance. Laughing ruefully, she allowed him to lead her out onto the floor. She could see that other groups of workers were nodding towards her and Tony. She could guess that she and the factory manager were now pegged as a potential couple.

Buoyed up by other people's observations and several pints of lager, Tony chanced placing a kiss on her cheek. Ellie was beginning to regret flirting with Tony earlier, because he seemed to be assuming that there was now some connection between them. And since she and Alan had agreed that it would look better if she left on her own, she'd have to avoid any offer from Tony to share a taxi home.

Professing exhaustion, Ellie left Tony on the dance floor and unsteadily made her way back to the bar. It was now getting late, although there was no sign of the party winding down.

'Can you order a taxi for me?' she whispered urgently to Alan. 'And make sure I'm not sharing it with Tony?'

When her taxi finally arrived, Ellie slipped quietly out of the social club without saying goodbye. It was easier that way. In the warmth of the taxi, she sat back and hazily considered her future. One segment of her life was finally ending, but another much more exciting one was just beginning.

Chapter 5

Darren looked at her uncertainly. 'You're changing your name?'

Laura nodded. 'Yes. Now that I'm married, I want to be known as Laura Jones.'

Her boss chewed his lip as he studied her across his vast desk. 'Isn't that a bit drastic? I mean, you've been lecturing here for what – nearly ten years? Everyone knows you as Laura Thornton. Why would you change it?' He fiddled with his pen. 'Surely you can keep your professional name separate? Can't you just be Mrs Jones in your private life?'

'I'll never be "just" Mrs Jones!' Laura said hotly. 'I'm proud to be changing my name. Jeff and I will eventually start a family, so it'll be best if we all share the same name.'

Darren grimaced, hearing echoes of Jeff's words at Laura's wedding. He cared about Laura very much. She'd always been a strong, independent woman – a little impulsive, but an efficient and valuable member of his staff, and he wasn't at all happy about what was happening to her. Her whirlwind courtship and hasty marriage was anathema to his own careful nature. He didn't like Jeff either, although he had to admit that no one would ever be good enough for his Laura.

He made it clear that he wasn't pleased. 'But you've always said you'd never change your name – don't you remember all those chats we had in the canteen? You were always so ada-

mant that, as the last Thornton of your generation, you wanted
to keep your family name alive, even if you got married.'

Flushing, Laura nodded, annoyed with Darren for having
reminded her, and feeling guilty for abandoning her family's
identity. 'Well, I've changed my mind. Life changes, people
change.'

Darren grimaced. 'This is going to involve quite a lot of
paperwork,' he muttered. 'It might take me quite a while to
get it all done.'

'It's not that big a deal, Darren. If the passport people can do
it, why can't you?' she replied.

Laura was growing more and more annoyed at having to
defend her decision. She'd encountered surprise and incredulity when she'd announced her change of name to colleagues
and friends. In fact, several people had made veiled sugges-
tions that the decision hadn't entirely been hers. It made her
very hot under the collar. Surely it was no one's concern but
hers and Jeff's? Okay, so she'd always sworn that she'd never
change her name, and she wouldn't be doing it now except
that it seemed to mean so much to Jeff. Making him happy
seemed a small price to pay for the niggling guilt she was feeling at abandoning the Thornton family name. Kerry had given
a derisive laugh when told of the name change, then had tried
to cover it up by changing the subject, and now Darren was
making her feel as though she was abandoning her late parents
and brother as well.

Laura wished everyone could just be happy for her. She and
Jeff were building a life together – she was simply changing
her name to show her commitment to him and to their future.

Darren adjusted his glasses. 'Have you told the others in the
department yet?'

'I mentioned it to Maria, and I saw Timmy in the canteen – '

'What did they think?'

Laura felt embarrassed and angry all at once. She didn't need to justify her actions to anyone. 'They're happy for me – what else would you expect?'

In fact, both her colleagues had been surprised, and clearly disapproving. Timmy, at least, had had the good grace to try and hide it. 'What does Darren think?' he'd asked, and Laura had felt annoyed with him. Since when did she need to consider how Darren felt about her personal decision to change her name? 'I haven't told him yet,' she'd replied angrily, and had been surprised at the brief flicker of sadness she'd detected in Timmy's eyes. Maria had been more direct: 'W – haaat?' she'd screeched. 'Are you losing your marbles, Thornton? Oh, sorry, I mean "Jones"!'

Darren grimaced. 'Well, Laura, I guess it's your decision.'

'Yes, it is,' she said evenly. There was no point in getting annoyed with her boss, because he was the best in the world and she loved working with him. He'd come around before long.

With a deep sigh, Darren began shuffling papers around on his desk. 'Well, I'm always here if you ever want to talk.'

Laura could feel the anger rising inside her again. 'About what?' she asked sharply, knowing full well what Darren meant.

'Anything,' he said, looking straight at her. 'My door is always open.'

As Laura left the room Darren sighed, finding that a Shakespearean quote summed up his feelings exactly: 'The lady doth protest too much, methinks,' he muttered, as he heard the door close. He was worried about Laura, and furious with Jeff. What kind of man would urge his new wife to abandon her family name, especially when it meant so much to Laura and represented so much of what she had already lost? Didn't Jeff understand her at all? If *he*'d been in that lucky position – of being married to the adorable Laura – he'd want her to treasure her memories. They were part of who she was, not something to be discarded for the sake of Jeff's ego.

He sighed. Before Jeff had blundered into Laura's life, Darren had allowed himself to imagine elaborate scenarios in which Laura had eventually realised that the man she truly loved was sitting at his big desk, right under her nose…But the vivacious Laura would never have looked at a plodder like him anyway. Sighing, he reached for the file containing the department's accounts. There was nothing like a pile of boring paperwork for distracting him from pointless daydreams…

As Laura made her way down the corridor to her own office, she felt annoyed and unsettled. She was only changing her name, for heaven's sake. Why did people seem to think it represented a whole lot more? Clearly no one was happy about it. Except Jeff.

As she thought of her new husband, her heart soared with joy. They'd prove everyone wrong. She'd immediately order a new plaque for her office door that would read: '*Dr Laura Jones*'. Eventually she and Jeff would have several little Joneses, and they'd all live happily ever after. At last she'd be part of a family again.

CHAPTER 6

'Ellie, are you in?'

Annoyed, Ellie recognised the voice – it was Tony Coleman from the factory. She'd been going to ignore the knocking on her front door, until she remembered that she'd left her new bike outside. He'd know that she was in.

Ellie opened the front door. 'Yes, Tony? What can I do for you?'

His face red, Tony shifted from one foot to the other. His hands were behind his back, but Ellie could see that he was holding a bouquet of flowers.

'Just checking to see that you're okay, now that you've left the factory,' he mumbled. 'Everyone misses you, and since I was out for a stroll during my lunch break, I thought I'd call and see if there was anything you needed – '

With a sigh, Ellie stepped aside and gestured for him to step inside. It would be bad manners to leave him standing on the doorstep, although she hoped his visit would be brief. He was clearly moving his interest in her up a notch, and she knew she'd eventually have to tell him she wasn't interested. She ushered him into the open-plan living room.

'Would you like a cup of tea, Tony?'

He nodded, his face suffused with relief. He wasn't being evicted straight away. He might be given enough time to explain his intentions.

In the kitchen, Ellie turned on the electric kettle, wondering how quickly she could get rid of him. She suspected that Tony was about to launch into some kind of declaration, and she wanted to make her position clear before he did, thus saving him from any embarrassment. She intended claiming that she was still grieving for her late husband, but she suspected that Tony would still try to persuade her that an occasional visit to the cinema with him would lift her spirits and couldn't do any harm...

Ellie checked her watch. Alan would be calling by in the early afternoon, and she needed time to take a shower and get changed into something sexy before he arrived. She needed to get rid of Tony as quickly as possible.

As she carried a tray laden with tea and biscuits into the living room, Tony was immediately on his feet, trying to help, dropping the flowers and only succeeding in getting in the way. Ellie silently poured the tea, anxious not to give him any encouragement. She had to admit that she was guilty of flirting with him at the party in the social club in order to make Alan jealous, so she'd brought this unwelcome intrusion on herself.

Tony cleared his throat, the mug of tea undulating in one trembling hand, the bouquet of flowers now clutched in his other hand. 'Ellie, you know that I really like you – '

Ellie's heart gave a jolt. Through the window behind Tony's head, she could see Alan's car turning in at her gateway and heading up the drive, and there was no way she could warn him. Tony was babbling on about how much she meant to him, but she was no longer listening. Her heart was beating wildly at the thought of their affair being uncovered. How ironic to be unmasked after she'd actually left the factory! Ellie was having nightmares at the thought of an unsuspecting Alan entering the house and calling her darling, making some sexual comment or starting to take his clothes off in the hall, as he often did in readiness for their lovemaking.

As Tony continued to waffle, it occurred to Ellie that if she could get him outside onto the veranda, Alan would have a chance of seeing him before he got out of his car. Although he couldn't now avoid speaking to Tony, it might give him time to think up some excuse as to why he was there.

'Tony, let's take our tea outside onto the veranda,' she said brightly, trying not to let her anxiety spread to her voice, and steering him outside before he had a chance to object. 'It's a lovely day, isn't it? Oh, goodness!' she added brightly. 'That looks like Mr Alan's car! I wonder what he's doing here?'

By then, Alan's car was pulling up outside, and Ellie waited, terrified, to see how things would unfold.

'Oh, hello!' Alan said pleasantly, as he stepped out of the car. He didn't look in the slightest bit embarrassed, and he smiled first at Tony, then at Ellie. 'Great weather today – I hope there's a heat wave on the way!' he said, coming up the steps onto the veranda and shaking both their hands.

If anyone was ill at ease, it was Tony. He looked down at the bouquet of flowers he was still clutching, and his face turned red, since his intentions towards Ellie were now perfectly clear.

Alan turned to Ellie, took an envelope from his pocket and handed it to her. 'I brought the balance of your wages, and the holiday pay you're owed, Ms Beckworth.'

'Oh, thank you, Mr Alan – that's very kind of you,' said Ellie, grateful that he'd quickly assessed the situation and slipped into 'boss' mode. 'But, really, there was no need for you to bring it in person.'

'No trouble at all,' Alan said smoothly. 'I knew I'd be passing by on my way back from the company solicitors in London, and I thought I could save you the journey to collect it.'

'Would you like some tea?' Ellie ventured, aware that they were both performing for Tony's sake, yet sensing that it would sound polite to make the gesture.

'No thanks, Ms Beckworth – I've got to get back to the factory for a meeting, so I need to be on my way.'

'Well, thank you once again,' Ellie said, glancing at Tony to see how he was reacting.

He was still standing there as though frozen, looking awkward, and still holding the bouquet of flowers.

'Tony, can I give you a lift back to the factory?' Alan asked, rather pointedly.

Tony was torn by indecision. He looked from one to the other and, seeing no encouragement on Ellie's face, he sighed, silently handed her the flowers and nodded to Alan.

'Okay, thanks, Mr Alan,' he said, defeat written all over his face. He turned to Ellie, with a tortured look. 'Goodbye, Ellie – maybe I'll call to see you again?'

'Thank you for the flowers, Tony – they're lovely,' Ellie said, ignoring his query and smiling noncommittally. Tony seemed to accept that he'd lost the battle. Sighing again, he followed Alan out to his car.

After giving Tony a lift back to the factory, Alan returned, carrying a large bouquet – a much bigger and more expensive one than Tony's had been.

'Here are the flowers I couldn't give you earlier, my love,' Alan said, grinning. 'I had to leave them in the car and tell Tony that they were for my wife! Luckily, I had a few unused wages envelopes in the glove compartment, and I was able to stuff one of them with the other envelopes to create a bulky package – were you impressed by my ability to improvise?'

Laughing, Ellie hugged him. The close call added even more passion to their lovemaking. Without any preliminaries, he took her with a ferocity that delighted her – he seemed to be re-establishing his right to her body. 'You're mine, all mine,' he whispered repeatedly, as though he could wish away Tony's intentions towards her.

Afterwards, they laughed at how well they'd performed their

roles, and how close they'd come to disaster. Then Alan looked serious.

'I can understand why Tony fancies you – what man wouldn't?' he said, his voice husky with desire. 'But if he starts calling regularly, it could make things difficult for us.' Then his face clouded over. 'Unless, of course, you fancy him? *If you do, I'll back off. After all, Tony is a good man, and a hard worker – '*

Ellie smiled at him tenderly, feeling cherished by his concern. 'Don't be silly, love – you're the only one I want,' she confirmed, tweaking his nose as they cuddled up together. 'Besides, we'll be together eventually, won't we?'

He nodded, still looking worried. 'Sometimes I feel bad that I can't give you what you want,' he said sadly. 'In fact, I can't promise you anything for quite some time. I've incurred huge debts just to keep the factory going, and it'll be a while before they can be cleared. Worse still, my debt is to my wife Sylvia's father. Tony could at least offer you marriage straight away. Are you sure you want to wait? I'll understand if you don't – '

'I'm sure,' she replied, kissing him passionately.

Now that she'd found the man of her dreams, every breath she took seemed to be just for him. The loss of her husband just over a year ago had seemed like the greatest tragedy at the time, but his death had inadvertently given her another chance to find Mr Right. And she'd definitely found him in Alan.

She smiled to herself as they snuggled up together, watching Alan as he dozed. No other man could dazzle her the way that her beloved Alan could. When he'd repaid the loan to Sylvia's father, he'd be free at last. Then they'd be together forever.

Chapter 7

Kerry was surprised to hear Laura's voice over the apartment intercom, and instantly buzzed her in.

'I've brought the wedding photos,' Laura told her as she reached Kerry's apartment. 'I collected them on my way home from work, and they're great! Everyone seems to have had a good time.'

'Well then, let's get a bottle of wine opened!' Kerry declared, heading for the kitchen. 'I don't think I could cope with all those pictures of you and Jeff drooling over each other without at least a glass of wine to fortify me!'

While Kerry went to get the wine, Laura took out the photographs. She was looking forward to sharing the memories of her wedding day with her closest friend. Without Kerry, she'd never have survived the death of her family and the upheaval of moving away to live with her grandfather. Although the pain of loss was always there, she'd learned to come to terms with it. Now, she was on the threshold of a new and exciting life with Jeff. Laura felt a surge of affection for her friend.

She smiled, noticing the small, plastic model of the Eiffel Tower on Kerry's mantelpiece, alongside a collection of iridescent shells they'd acquired on holiday together two years earlier. How well she remembered both those holidays, but for very different reasons…

When Kerry entered the room again, carrying an opened

bottle of wine and two glasses, Laura pointed to the plastic Eiffel Tower.

'I'm amazed you've kept that old thing – it's awful, isn't it? But I was only eleven when I brought it back for you.'

Kerry smiled. 'I remember missing you so much while you were away with your family, and wishing I could be there too.' She grimaced. 'I suppose it's also a symbol of happier, care-free times…'

'Yes, that was the last family holiday Mum, Dad, Pete and I ever had,' Laura said softly. She glanced at the shells. 'And I'll never forget that scuba diving holiday either – if it hadn't been for you, I'd definitely have drowned.'

Kerry shook her head, looking slightly embarrassed. 'It was nothing – anyone would have done what I did.'

'Well, thank goodness you were there – I don't know why I suddenly felt so weak and disoriented that day, but if you hadn't realised something was wrong, and guided me back up to the boat, I wouldn't have survived. You saved my life.'

Kerry smiled, sitting down on the sofa beside her. 'Well, that's what friends are for. Anyway, what's made you feel maudlin all of a sudden?'

'I don't know,' Laura admitted. 'I have this uneasy feeling that I just can't shake off – maybe I'm afraid that something's going to happen to Jeff. I love him so much, Kerry! I'd die if anything happened to him.'

Kerry smiled, hoping to lighten the atmosphere. 'Maybe those rose-tinted spectacles of yours are over-developing your psychic abilities,' she teased. 'I can just see you – Madame Laura, the world's greatest psychic! Perhaps you should give up the day job and get yourself a crystal ball instead?'

Laura grinned, leaning across to give her friend a playful dig. 'Very funny. Okay, I'm probably just being paranoid but, as the saying goes, that still doesn't mean they're not out to get me!'

Kerry looked suddenly serious. 'I'm sure that fear is part and parcel of being in love with someone,' she said gently, thinking uncharitably to herself that if Jeff vanished off the face of the earth, it would be the best thing that ever happened to Laura. But she didn't dare give voice to her opinion.

Noticing tears in Laura's eyes, she reached out and hugged her. 'Oh, cheer up, you old worrier,' she said affectionately. 'Nothing's going to happen to Jeff! Why not look forward to the meal he's taking us for tomorrow night? By the way, I'm wearing my new red dress, so don't you dare wear anything that'll clash with my outfit!'

Laura nodded, making a visible attempt to cheer up. 'Okay, I'll wear my blue dress. And yes, I'm really looking forward to Chez Jacques – it's Jeff's favourite restaurant. They're aware of his allergy there, so he can depend on them to make sure his food is peanut-free.'

'It's pricey too, isn't it?' Kerry said, grinning. 'But then, I guess stockbrokers make lots of money! I love a night out when someone else is paying!'

'Well, Jeff wants to thank you for all the help you gave us organising the wedding,' Laura told her. 'You've been a marvellous friend, and Jeff really appreciates your kindness, too.'

Does he now, Kerry thought sarcastically to herself. She was well aware that Jeff didn't like her any more than she liked him, and it would have been Laura who'd urged him to make the gesture. But she accepted the compliment as Laura intended. 'I was glad to help,' she replied.

Pouring wine into the two glasses, Kerry passed one to Laura. 'Now, let me see these wonderful wedding pictures – I hope the photographer didn't catch me in any compromising situations?'

Laura smiled. 'I wish he had – I'd be delighted to think you'd met someone to be in a compromising situation with!'

Kerry smiled mischievously. 'Well, one of the waiters *was* rather cute – '

Smiling, Laura unwrapped the pile of printed photos and spread them out on the coffee table. With their glasses now full, Kerry leaned forwards, clinking glasses before they began. Within minutes, both women were laughing and happily reminiscing over the events of Laura's special day.

In the restaurant the following evening, Jeff was at his most charming. 'I'm the luckiest man in the world, being here with two beautiful women!' he purred. 'And I'm happily married to this gorgeous creature beside me – '

As he leaned across to kiss Laura, his insincere flattery was not lost on Kerry. But she could see that Laura was lapping up the attention, her cheeks pink with pleasure.

As the headwaiter approached their table to take their order, Jeff beckoned him to come close and spoke softly in his ear. 'I presume I don't need to remind you about my allergy – '

The little man smiled obsequiously. 'Of course, Monsieur Jones. As a regular, esteemed customer, you can be assured we will always take the very best care of you.'

Jeff nodded, looking pleased. He seemed to be enjoying the familiarity with which the waiter addressed him, and the idea of having a top restaurant knowing who he was. He looked over at Kerry, happy that she'd witnessed the exchange.

Having selected their main courses, all three sat back and sipped their wine. The restaurant was full, with tables in a semi-circle around a small dance floor. Behind the dance floor, on a small dais, a trio of musicians played a mixture of jazz and blues. The lighting was subdued and romantic, changing colour with the tempo of the music. A few couples were already on the dance floor.

By now, Jeff had removed his jacket and hung it on the back

of his chair, clearly intending to take to the floor. As the combo began to play a slow set, he looked at Laura, a question in his eyes, and as one, they stood up. 'Do you mind if we leave you?' Laura asked, looking guilty at Kerry.

'Of course not – you go ahead,' she replied cheerfully. 'I've got two left feet anyway – I'd rather sit here and watch you two make idiots of yourselves!'

As Jeff and Laura stepped out onto the small dance floor, Jeff leaned down and pressed his cheek to his wife's. As Kerry watched, she wondered about their future. As far as she was concerned, Jeff was a loose canon, and the sooner Laura got rid of him, the better. But despite her misgivings, she had to concede that they made a very attractive couple, both willowy and blond and clearly besotted with each other.

After a while, the slow numbers ended and the tempo of the music increased, and Jeff and Laura returned hand in hand to the table. At that precise moment, the waiter arrived bearing their main courses. With a flourish, he placed their chosen dishes in front of them. Laura and Kerry had both ordered a chicken dish, but Jeff's steak looked a great deal bigger and more appetising.

'Ooh, yours looks nicer than ours – can I steal one of your chips?' Kerry asked Jeff, as his plate was placed in front of him. Nodding, he allowed her to lean across and take the biggest chip on the plate. As Kerry munched, she closed her eyes in sheer delight. 'Hmm, this is gorgeous! Jeff, I think you made the wisest choice this evening!'

Jeff seemed flattered that Kerry approved of his choice of main course. She also suspected that he wouldn't have been quite so eager to let her take a chip from his plate if Laura hadn't been present to witness his generous gesture.

As the women began eating, Jeff topped up their wine glasses and re-filled his own. Then he began to tackle his enormous steak, and both women paused politely, waiting to hear his opinion of it. As he chewed the first piece, he nodded to them enthusiastically. 'Lovely,' he murmured. 'It's done exactly as I like it. The texture is – '

Suddenly, his eyes started bulging, and Kerry was instantly reminded of the film she'd seen of *The Incredible Hulk*, in which the man's appearance altered drastically right before the viewers' eyes. The same seemed to be happening to Jeff – he was now clutching his neck, and his lips and face were swelling rapidly. He seemed to be gasping for breath as he thrashed about, overturning several chairs as he fell to the ground.

'His pen, his pen!' Laura screamed, jumping up from the table and overturning the bottle of wine. The red stain spread all across the white cloth as she frantically grabbed Jeff's jacket and began searching in the pockets. 'I can't find it!' she screamed, 'It's not there!'

'Here, give me that – '

Kerry snatched the jacket from her and began searching the pockets. But the pen wasn't there. 'Maybe it fell to the floor –' she told Laura, who was now screaming at the staff to do something to help.

But no one seemed capable of doing anything. Everyone seemed rooted to the floor in shock and terror as Laura cradled Jeff's head, simultaneously screaming and crying. Crawling beneath the table on her hands and knees, Kerry began searching around in the near-darkness, but without success. There was no sign of Jeff's adrenaline pen.

By now, Laura's screams had penetrated the music and the laughter, and other people were beginning to realise that something was amiss. The music came to an abrupt halt as Laura continued to scream for help. 'Get an ambulance – please!' she cried. 'He'll die if we don't get him adrenaline quickly – '

A man pushed his way through the crowd and eventually

managed to reach Laura. 'Adrenaline, did you say? Has he an allergy?'

As Laura nodded through her sobs, the man pulled an adrenaline pen from his pocket, 'Look, this is my own pen – I'm allergic to wasp stings, but it should help – '

Snatching it from him, Laura quickly ripped off the protective cover and rammed the needle into Jeff's thigh through his trousers. Almost as quickly as he'd collapsed, Jeff began to come round. There were sighs of relief from the people milling around him as he sat up, disoriented but alive. His lips were still swollen, but his eyes were no longer bulging. He was clearly confused, and didn't seem to know where he was.

The headwaiter was beside himself with guilt. 'Monsieur Jones, I don't know what happened! We are always so careful – '

Laura brushed him aside, eager only for Jeff to have enough space and fresh air to recover. Tears of relief were now running down her face. 'Thank you, thank you!' she sobbed, addressing the man who had supplied the adrenaline pen, clutching his sleeve as though she never wanted to let him go.

In the distance, the shrill sound of an ambulance could be heard. As the sound got nearer, Laura grabbed Kerry's arm. 'I'm going to the hospital with him. Can you get yourself home?'

Kerry nodded. 'Of course. Don't worry about me – Jeff is your priority now,' she said warmly. 'The restaurant will call me a taxi.'

Within moments, the restaurant doors were flung open and several paramedics made their way across the restaurant to Jeff's table. Having explained to them what had happened, and that another diner had supplied an adrenaline pen, Laura began to sob quietly with relief. Her face tear-stained, she was still clutching Jeff's hand as he was carried outside to the waiting ambulance. Diners and curious passers-by had now gathered on the pavement outside, and Kerry had to fight her way through the throng to say goodbye to Laura. After the two women silently hugged, Laura stepped into the waiting ambulance.

Kerry stood watching in the darkness until the ambulance disappeared into the night.

CHAPTER 8

*A*s the months slipped by, Ellie's life developed a pleasant daily routine. Every workday afternoon, Alan would leave his office for a late lunch, and they'd make love in her bedroom for most of the afternoon. They simply couldn't get enough of each other.

But Ellie became more and more jealous of the woman who wore Alan's wedding ring. And she became increasingly unhappy about his vague promises to leave his wife and young son when the time was right.

'Look, love – my wife's father's money is the only reason that I still have the factory,' Alan assured her as they lay in bed one afternoon. 'If I divorce her now, her father will pull the plug and I'll lose everything.' He looked at her tenderly. 'Then I won't be able to pay your bills either. We just have to wait until the market's more stable – then it won't matter if they withdraw their capital. I'll be able to keep the business afloat on my own by then. Just have patience, love – please.'

Ellie sighed, laying her head on his shoulder. She didn't have any other choice – he meant everything to her, and she'd wait as he asked. After all, she was lucky to have someone who truly loved her, even if that love couldn't be publicly acknowledged yet.

But Alan had a surprise for her. Reaching into his jacket pocket, he took out a little box and presented her with a thick, stylish gold band inset with a huge diamond. On the inside there was an inscription: 'Alan and Ellie forever'.

'Now you're my secret wife,' he told her, sliding off her old wedding ring and slipping on the new. 'This ring can be an engagement and wedding ring combined. I doubt if anyone else will notice the difference – but you and I will know what it signifies.'

Ellie gazed at the ring, her heart full of love for him. 'Of course people will notice – this ring is gorgeous! Thank you, my love – wearing your ring will mean so much to me,' she whispered fervently, raising her lips for his kiss. The ring made her feel a lot more confident about waiting for him now. As she gazed at her left hand, moving it about to let the large diamond catch the light, it seemed to confirm the intensity of their love. Some day soon he truly would be hers.

She did feel guilty about Alan's wife, and for that reason she always kept her distance when she saw her in the nearby village, wheeling her young son in his buggy. Sylvia had tried several times to engage her in casual conversation – usually about the weather – but Ellie always made an excuse to get away. It was obvious that Sylvia was just trying to be neighbourly, but Ellie didn't want to be forced into an introduction. Nor did she want to acknowledge Alan's child, since the boy would only remind her that another woman had been able to give him something she never could.

Besides, she wanted to keep their own little world separate and private. She didn't want to be part of this other life that Alan lived. In a way, she feared that acknowledging the contrasting circumstances between his other life and hers might make her bitter. Although they only lived within half a mile of each other, his wife and family lived in a world of opulence compared to hers – no doubt they had crystal chandeliers in their drawing room and two cars in the garage. They dined in expensive restaurants and attended gala dinners. Although she knew he hated every minute of these events, she longed to be the woman by his side, greeting the mayor, dressed in the latest fashions and having all the other women envy her. Nevertheless, after these events, he'd hurry back to her little house as often as he could and she'd take him in her arms and make everything right again. But then, afterwards, he'd have to head home to the woman who rightly expected him to be in her bed every night.

Now, he kissed her forehead. 'Some day soon, I'll show you off to the world, dressed in the finest clothing money can buy,' he whispered.

It was the waiting for these glory days that was so painful. But for now, the beautiful diamond and gold ring had given her new confidence in their future together.

CHAPTER 9

The following morning, Laura awoke alone in the apartment she shared with Jeff. Sitting up in bed with a jolt, she recalled the events of the night before, remembering that her husband had been kept in hospital overnight, after the near-tragic incident at the restaurant.

Jumping out of bed, she quickly showered and dressed, wondering if her strange feelings from the day before yesterday had been a genuine portent of what was to come. She shivered. The incident had been one of the most horrific in her life – and that was saying something, given that she'd already endured the tragic loss of her family, been uprooted and sent to a new home and school, and then nearly died underwater two years earlier.

Munching toast in the kitchen, Laura went over what had happened. She was mystified – given his health problem, surely Jeff wouldn't have been so careless? His adrenaline pen was a lifesaver, and would have been more important to him than anything else. How could he have mislaid it?

Abandoning her second slice of toast, Laura decided to turn detective, heading into their bedroom once again and specifically to the wardrobe, where Jeff would have taken out his best suit and transferred the pen from his workday clothes. Finding nothing in the pocket of the jacket he'd worn during the day, she surveyed the wardrobe from top to bottom, checking the shirts stacked on the shelves at the side, the tie rack drawers on the bottom.

As her eyes scanned the floor of the wardrobe, they alighted on Jeff's shoes, all expensive leather, all neatly in a row. And there, sitting in one of them, was his adrenaline pen.

Laura grabbed it, feeling angry at what she considered to be Jeff's appalling carelessness. Hopefully after what had happened at the restaurant, he'd start to take his health issues seriously in future! He must have thought that he'd slid the pen into his pocket, but it had missed, falling instead into one of his shoes on the wardrobe floor. To test her theory, Laura stood exactly where Jeff would have been, and deliberately dropped the pen. When it fell silently into one of his shoes, she felt vindicated. She'd confirmed that the shoe's soft leather would have dulled any sound that might have alerted Jeff to what had happened.

Leaving the bedroom, she headed back to the kitchen, and made a quick call to Greta, the Sociology Department's secretary, explaining what had transpired the night before, and asking her to get another lecturer to cover for her that morning. With assurances from Greta that she didn't need to worry, Laura hung up.

It also dawned on her that since Jeff wouldn't be going to work that day, she ought to ring his place of business and let them know what had happened.

Normally, she contacted Jeff by mobile phone, and she was embarrassed to admit that she didn't actually know the phone number for the stockbrokers where he worked. In the study, she scanned the phone book, but she couldn't find any entry for Denham, Goodwood & Clayton. She then turned on her computer and typed the name into a search engine, but there didn't appear to be a listing for any company with that name.

Could she have put the company names in the wrong order

– perhaps it was Goodwood Denham & Clayton? Typing in the names in this order, once again she came up with nothing. And the phone book again didn't yield any company of that name either. Even trying the names in several different combinations didn't yield any useful information.

Puzzled, Laura bit her lip. There had to be a very good reason why this was happening. Perhaps the company had changed its name, and Jeff had forgotten to tell her? It sounded rather far-fetched, but Laura was prepared to consider anything. After all, Jeff went off to work every morning. If he didn't go to Denham, Goodwood & Clayton, where on earth did he go? And where did he get the money they lived on? They had an expensive flat in a prestigious part of the city, filled with beautiful, antique furniture and a state-of-the-art kitchen – all originally owned and paid for by Jeff.

Checking her watch, she grabbed her car keys and headed out of the apartment. It was time to collect Jeff from the hospital and bring him home.

In the hospital, Jeff was already dressed when Laura arrived.

She hugged him fiercely. 'I'd thought I'd lost you!' she told him, tears in her eyes.

'I was a bit worried myself!' Jeff admitted. 'What the hell happened to my adrenaline pen?'

'I found it this morning – in one of your shoes,' Laura told him, taking out the pen and handing it to him. 'You must have *thought* you were putting it in your suit pocket, but it fell to the floor instead.'

Jeff's face darkened. 'But I know I brought it with me! I remember checking that it was in my pocket while we were in the taxi, on our way to the restaurant!'

Laura kissed his angry face. 'Well, you were obviously wrong,' she told him. 'Anyway, let's hope nothing like this ever happens again. I couldn't bear to lose you –' her cheeks dimpled '–especially now that there might be a new addition to our family…'

Jeff's face lit up. 'What? Are you telling me you're pregnant?'

Laura smiled. 'Well, I've missed my period this month, so I think it's quite possible.'

Jeff kissed her enthusiastically. 'That's wonderful news!'

Laura silenced him with a finger to his lips. 'Let's not jump to any conclusions yet,' she urged him. 'I'll make an appointment with the doctor, and get one of those pregnancy testing kits. I want to be sure before we tell anyone.'

Jeff nodded, but he was unable to contain his delight. 'I'm going to be a father!' he whooped. 'We're going to be a family at last!'

Back at the apartment, Jeff was still in a state of excitement at the news Laura had imparted to him. 'I'm going to be a father!' he kept repeating, a smile of incredulity on his face.

Laura was feeling upbeat too, and a new and exciting future was beckoning. Soon, she'd tell Jeff about all the money she'd inherited. After all, it didn't feel right to keep such information from the man she loved. Kerry was worrying unnecessarily.

'By the way, I tried to ring your office this morning,' she told him. 'I thought it only fair to let them know why you wouldn't be in today. I looked them up in the telephone book, and Googled Denham, Goodwood & Clayton. But they weren't listed anywhere.'

Jeff grimaced. 'Ah,' he said, looking at the floor.

Laura stared at him expectantly. There was definitely something amiss, and she was suddenly frightened. The silence from Jeff seemed to confirm her worst fears.

He began pacing up and down the room. Then he thought better of it and sat down, lowering his voice as he spoke.

'Look, I'm going to have to trust you. But if you ever tell this to anyone, you could be putting my life in danger. And yours, too.'

Laura's heart began to thud painfully.

Jeff glanced around the room, as though to ensure that no one could hear what he was about to say.

'Look, the truth is – I'm not a stockbroker. I work for MI5.'

Laura's mouth dropped open. 'What? Are you being serious, Jeff?'

'You probably wondered why I didn't have any work colleagues at the wedding,' Jeff explained. 'Now you know. Undercover agents can't risk having their cover blown.' He looked at her angrily. 'You must never tell anyone what I've told you.'

Laura nodded. 'Of course not. But surely you could have told me? I'm your wife!'

'No, I couldn't – lives depend on the kind of work I do. I had to sign an oath never to tell anyone.' He raised an eyebrow. 'No MI5 operative ever tells their family. I'd never have told you if you hadn't gone digging. And now that I've trusted you with this confidential information, you must never discuss it with anyone, not even me.'

Laura nodded, chastened. She was shocked. Clearly his job required him to keep others in the dark about his life. She felt upset at being kept out of such an important part of his life, but she could also acknowledge that there would be good reasons for him to keep quiet. A talkative wife, or a nasty ex-wife, could compromise an agent's position, destroying years of credibility that he'd built up. And already Jeff had trouble trusting people.

'W – what if I need to contact you?'

'You already have my mobile number. But only ever call me in the direst of emergencies.'

Having assured her that he was well enough to go back to work, Jeff left the apartment.

After he'd gone, Laura began mulling over all that her husband had told her. She felt a frisson of delight at the thought of Jeff doing such important work for national security. He was her very own personal James Bond! It seemed such a glamorous – and also dangerous – life, and now she was part of it. Had she been secretly vetted herself? No wonder Jeff always seemed tense and worried lately. He obviously had a lot of responsibilities that she knew nothing about. She'd be kinder, and more supportive, and eventually she'd prove to him that he could trust her.

Laura also felt a sense of relief. She *had* wondered why Jeff only had a few acquaintances at the wedding, and didn't seem to have any close friends with whom he socialised. She hadn't voiced these thoughts to anyone else, but she suspected that Kerry had been wondering about his lack of friends, too. Now she finally understood why.

Unable to contain her excitement, Laura was in the pub early, and had already brought their drinks to the table by the time Kerry arrived.

'How's Jeff?' Kerry asked anxiously as she settled into the cosy booth. 'Really, I'd have been just as happy if you'd cancelled, and stayed home to look after your husband.'

Laura laughed. 'Oh, Jeff's fine,' she said. 'He even went back to work this afternoon, and he's working late this evening, too!'

Kerry looked at her friend in surprise. She could also see that Laura was giddy with excitement, and bursting to tell her something.

'Come on, I know that look of yours!' Kerry told her, smiling. 'What's happened? You're like a hen on a hot griddle – out with it!'

Jeff had warned her not to tell anyone, but Laura knew she could trust her best friend. She looked all around her. Assured that there was no one sitting near enough to overhear, she turned to Kerry and lowered her voice. 'You must promise me that you'll never repeat this to anyone – '

Kerry nodded, looking intrigued.

Laura looked around again before speaking, then she beckoned Kerry to come closer. 'Jeff's not actually a stockbroker – he works for MI5,' she told her. 'That's why he couldn't tell me the truth – because the work he does is top secret!'

Kerry raised an eyebrow. She didn't believe a word of it. But if Laura chose to be gullible, it wasn't up to her to disillusion her. MI5 indeed. She wondered what exactly Jeff *was* up to. She'd been meaning to do some research on Mr Jones – now it was definitely time to do so. She was still worried that Jeff might be after Laura's fortune.

'Of course, I'm sworn to secrecy, so promise me you'll never mention this to anyone!' Laura added worriedly. 'I'm only telling you because you're my closest friend.'

'My lips are sealed,' Kerry said noncommittally.

CHAPTER 10

Ellie was excited. Today was the day that Alan was going to end his marriage.

'I'm going to ask Sylvia for a divorce,' he'd told her determinedly as they'd lain together the afternoon before. 'This morning I paid off the final instalment of the loan from Sylvia's father, so I don't owe Dick Morgan anything any more. I've approached the bank for working capital, so it should all be plain sailing from now on.'

Ellie's heart had soared with joy.

'I'd also prefer to split from Sylvia sooner rather than later,' Alan added. 'It'll be easier for Pete to adjust while he's still too young to understand what's involved.'

'But you'll make sure to see him regularly?' Ellie asked, more than willing to make this small concession, now that she was gaining a much bigger one.

'Of course,' Alan replied, flashing her a grateful smile.

As he held her close, she revelled in his nearness, his smell, his masculinity. She was so excited to think that soon he'd be hers completely!

Excited, Ellie watched from the window as Alan's car drove in at the gate and up the driveway. As it disappeared from view, she waited anxiously while he parked it out of sight, behind the house. It was just occurring to her that, from now on, he wouldn't need to hide his car any more. They'd be a proper couple, and they could be seen together at last. They could shop together, eat out together, go to the theatre together ...

Briefly, she thought of Tony Coleman, who was still inviting her to the cinema every time she met him in the village. There had been times when she'd actually considered saying yes. The nights when Alan wasn't around were long and lonely, and sometimes she longed for some adult company. Besides, a trip to the cinema would have served as cover for her affair if she'd been seen publicly with Tony. Now, of course, there would be no need for any cover ever again! In fact, she couldn't wait for everyone to know that she was about to become Mrs Thornton!

She felt a brief pang of guilt for poor Sylvia, who must, by now, be reeling in shock. But Ellie couldn't afford to feel sorry for anyone – it was her special time at last, and she couldn't wait to tell the world that she and Alan were finally going to be together.

Anxiously, Ellie hovered at the door, wondering why Alan was taking so long to come inside. Today, of all days, she'd expected him to come bounding through the door, since he was finally coming to her as a free man. Usually there was an urgency in his stride, since both of them would be anticipating the joys of making love together.

But something was different today. As Alan stepped into the hall, his shoulders were slumped and he seemed reluctant to face her. She had a horrible feeling in the pit of her stomach.

He gave her a sad smile as they embraced. 'Oh, my darling, darling love,' he whispered, as he held her tight.

'What's wrong?' she asked, almost afraid to know the answer, but needing to know it anyway.

'It's the factory,' he answered, and she was relieved that it wasn't an accident.

'Well, if no one's dead, it can't be that bad,' she said, smiling to lighten to atmosphere.

He looked grave. 'But I'm afraid it's bad news for us,' he replied. 'My negotiations with the bank have fallen through – I thought they were happy with my business plan, but they've refused point blank to lend me the money I need for expansion. So I'd no other option but to go to Sylvia's father again for another large cash injection.'

She bit her lip, knowing exactly what that meant.

'I'm sorry, love – I can't possibly ask Sylvia for a divorce now. Not while I'm taking her father's money.'

Ellie buried her face in his jacket so that he couldn't see her tears. She knew how difficult things were for him, and she didn't want to add to his burden. But her own dreams were being put on hold yet again.

'I know this is awful for you, love, but please remember that I'm torn too,' he whispered. 'Although I'm not in love with Sylvia any more, I do care about her, and I respect her.' He kissed her nose. 'But none of us can help who we fall in love with. That first day I met you, I instantly fell head over heels for you.' He held her away from him and gazed at her earnestly. 'Can you wait, love? It won't be for ever, I promise. I'm expecting to sign a contract with one of the largest wholesalers in the country very soon. I'm hoping the bank will reconsider its position when it sees the substantial increase that the contract's going to make to our turnover.'

Ellie nodded, glancing down at the gold and diamond ring that confirmed Alan's love for her.

'I also have to go away on business for a few days,' he told her gently. 'I need to meet with some of our biggest fruit and vegetable suppliers. Unless we can negotiate a better price for their produce, we could have another serious problem on our hands.' He smiled at her sadly. 'I know this wait is disappointing for both

of us. But we still have each other, and we'll eventually manage to be together for good.' He kissed her tenderly. 'You'll be okay while I'm away?'

Ellie nodded. 'But I'll miss you terribly,' she whispered.

'Good,' Alan whispered back. 'I couldn't bear it if you didn't!'

CHAPTER 11

'For God's sake, what happened?'

Laura looked embarrassed and defensive as she walked into Kerry's apartment.

'Nothing – I hit my head on one of the kitchen cupboards.'

'No, you didn't! Did Jeff do this to you?'

Laura glared at her. 'No, of course not! Why would you think that?'

Kerry ushered Laura into the kitchen, urged her into a chair, and turned on the kettle to make coffee. As she took down two mugs from the rack above the stove, she surreptitiously surveyed her friend, noting the livid patch, already turning blue, and the large black circle under her left eye, which Laura was trying to hide by pulling her blonde hair across it. Kerry was well aware that no accidental bump would inflict such a huge amount of damage.

Placing a cup of coffee in front of her friend, Kerry sat down beside her. 'Laura, you're a strong woman – you don't have to put up with this!'

At first, Kerry thought her friend was going to continue denying what had happened, but her kind words seemed to cut through the wall Laura had initially tried to build around herself. Suddenly, she was sobbing, and Kerry put her arms around her, saying nothing, just letting her friend cry. Gently, she patted Laura's back in a gesture that might be used to soothe a troubled child.

'You know what you have to do, don't you?' Kerry said at last.

Laura rested her head on Kerry's shoulder. 'I can't leave him! He's been so cruelly treated by his family in the past – I'm his family now, and anyway, I love him. If I leave him, that will just prove that he can't trust anyone!'

Kerry shook her gently. 'But you can't let a man hit you – once they start, it gets worse each time. And there will be another time, believe me. And another. You must get out now, love – before something really bad happens to you.'

Laura looked at her earnestly. 'I can't, Kerry, I just can't. I made my vows for better or worse. Jeff's just a bit stressed at the moment – I think he's under a lot of pressure at work – and I want to help him through this rough patch. It will be okay, I promise. Nothing bad is going to happen. Jeff and I will get through this. All I have to do is prove to him that I love him and won't leave him. Then things will settle down.'

Kerry grimaced. 'People don't hurt the ones they love. This shouldn't be happening to you, Laura.'

Wiping away her tears, Laura looked defiant. 'I've made my choice – I want to be with Jeff! He's my husband, and I intend spending the rest of my life with him. It was nothing – just a silly argument, and now I'm sorry I said anything to you about it.'

'What exactly happened?'

'Oh, nothing really. I wasn't feeling well – I've been feeling a bit queasy in the mornings – and I hadn't squeezed the oranges for our early morning juice. He got annoyed with me, and one thing led to another.'

'So he hit you.'

'No, it wasn't like that – I complained about being asked

to do it, and Jeff just over-reacted. He was very sorry afterwards.'

Kerry was well aware that Laura was giving her a tightly
edited version of the truth, but she saw no point in pushing it.
Her own imagination could fill in the gaps. But she was instantly alert to Laura's mention of being sick in the mornings.

'You're not pregnant, are you?'

Laura blushed. 'Why do you ask?'

'You mentioned getting sick in the mornings, so I was just
a bit worried – '

Laura bridled. 'Why would you be worried?'

'Well, it might be better if you didn't get pregnant immediately, at least until you've sorted things out between you and
Jeff. Because if you have a child now, you'll be tied to him for
ever.'

Laura looked annoyed. 'But I *want* to be tied to him for
ever! Jeff wants kids and so do I. He'll settle down once we
have a family.'

'And if he doesn't? Jeff seems to be repeating his father's
version of what family life is.'

Laura bridled again. 'That's not fair! Anyway, since when
did *you* qualify in psychology?'

Kerry grimaced. There was only so far she could go in criticising Jeff before she would alienate Laura. Maybe she'd
crossed the line already. But she was well aware that things
were more likely to go downhill rather than improve. If a marriage wasn't good at the beginning, there was little hope that it
would improve later.

'Well, you know that I'm here for you, day or night. If anything goes wrong, pick up the phone and call me. On second
thoughts, forget the phone – just get out and come here straight
away.'

Laura shook her head vehemently. 'It wasn't like that –

you're making a mountain out of a molehill. Look, I'm going home. Thanks for the coffee.'

Kerry smiled, trying to lighten the atmosphere. 'No need to say thanks – you didn't even drink it.'

CHAPTER 12

*A*s Tony Coleman made his final nightly check on the machinery in the factory, ensuring that everything was turned off and the safety switches turned on, he wondered yet again how he might advance his suit with Ellie. Perhaps he should make another attempt at asking her out. After all, a widow must get lonely, and he was comfortably off and could give her a good time.

He'd fancied Ellie ever since she'd arrived at the factory, but back then she'd been married, so he hadn't given any serious thought to a relationship with her. But after her husband died, he'd begun looking at her in a very different way. She was gorgeous – any man could see that, but she'd never shown any interest in him. His heart had plummeted when he'd heard she was leaving the factory, but then it had occurred to him that he was being handed an even better opportunity. If he offered to help her establish her new business, he might gradually worm his way into her affections...

Ellie didn't seem to go out much – he'd never seen her socialising in any of the local pubs. Then again, perhaps he should be relieved that she wasn't out and about, since undoubtedly she'd have been snapped up by now. She was a stunning-looking woman, with those luscious lips, big blue eyes and the figure of a goddess. Perhaps he should make another move soon, before some other guy set his beady eyes on her. Surely his position as factory manager must count in his favour?

From time to time, he'd seen Ellie shopping in the village, and he always made a point of stopping to chat. Several times, in a roundabout way, he'd invited her to the cinema, but she always seemed to avoid giving him a direct answer, or suddenly found some reason why she had to rush away. Perhaps she was shy? Just because a woman was beautiful didn't mean that she was supremely confident. In fact, he liked the idea that Ellie mightn't realise just how gorgeous she was! Or maybe she was playing hard to get?

As he shut the main door of the factory, turned on the alarm and headed for his car, he decided to make another attempt at winning Ellie's affections. He'd call on her again and invite her to see the latest blockbuster, which had received wonderful write-ups in all the newspapers. Perhaps a 'softly softly' approach would work best – by initially suggesting an occasional cinema outing together, he'd gradually manage to turn a series of companionable outings into something more...

He smiled to himself as he got into his car. Ellie was a prize worth winning; there was no doubt about that.

Tony nursed a pint – and his bruised ego – in his local pub, as he tried to come to terms with the earlier events of the evening.

He'd risked calling on Ellie, and had been surprised when she'd accepted his invitation to the cinema. But after going out of his way to drive her home, he'd been sent packing with a flea in his ear!

He felt aggrieved and angry at being treated in that way. After all, he'd paid for the cinema tickets and used his own petrol to drive her home!

He supposed he'd only got himself to blame – he should have played it cool and taken his time in courting her, like he'd planned to do. It was never a good idea to declare yourself too eagerly where women were concerned – they walked all over any man who was decent enough to let them know how he felt. Tony was also peeved because Ellie had always maintained that she was single. Yet he'd got the distinct impression that there might be another man somewhere in the background...

Tony took a final swig of his pint angrily, then slammed down his empty glass. Maybe Ellie Beckworth was putting it about for someone else – if so, then she definitely wasn't the kind of woman he was after. All in all, he'd probably had a lucky escape. It would be a long time before he bothered with Ellie Beckworth again...

CHAPTER 13

A week later, a radiant Laura arrived at Kerry's apartment, after work. 'I've got wonderful news!' she told her friend. 'I'm pregnant!'

'Congratulations!' Kerry said, hugging her tightly.

'Jeff is over the moon!' Laura told her. 'He couldn't be nicer to me – he's treating me like a queen! He brings me breakfast in bed and the morning newspaper before he leaves for work. I couldn't be happier either – I feel cherished and very special.'

Kerry smiled noncommittally.

'That business earlier – it was just a silly mistake,' Laura whispered. 'Please forget about it, Kerry. Jeff never meant to hurt me.'

Surreptitiously studying the side of Laura's face, Kerry could see that the bruising had more or less healed, and there was little evidence of Jeff's handiwork any longer.

Nevertheless, Laura could see her friend looking, and felt a pang of remorse. She wished she hadn't told Kerry about what had happened, but she'd been feeling vulnerable and shocked at the time, and had needed the support of someone who cared about her.

Jeff hadn't meant to hurt her that day when he'd lost his temper. She loved him so much, and she wasn't going to let one silly little fight ruin their future together.

Kerry hugged her again. 'I'm so happy for you, love. Are you hoping for a boy or a girl?'

Laura gave her a dazzling smile. 'I'd love a little girl, but Jeff wants a boy. But I'll be happy just as long as it's a healthy baby.'

Smiling, Kerry nodded. Perhaps she was being uncharitable, but she couldn't help wondering how Jeff would react if he didn't get the son he wanted. For Laura's sake, the baby had better be a boy.

Darren received the news of her pregnancy with equanimity.

'Well, congratulations, Laura,' he said, but there was no delight in his voice, and she felt oddly deflated by his response.

He stepped out from behind his big desk and hugged her, but she had the feeling that it was a sympathetic hug rather than a celebratory one, and she felt decidedly disturbed by it.

'I hope you'll be staying on?'

'Of course!' Laura assured him. 'You know I love my job, and as long as you're willing to keep me on, I'm happy to be here!' She smiled, willing him to smile back. 'And when I come back after maternity leave, I'll be able to use the university crèche.'

Darren nodded, but there was no smile forthcoming. 'I wish you well, Laura,' he said solemnly. 'I hope that everything works out according to plan.'

He wished he could appear more enthusiastic, but there was a lump in his throat that he simply couldn't dispel. He'd already seen the bruises on her face, and Timmy had approached him with his suspicions too, wondering if there was anything they could do. Now Laura's pregnancy was another unwelcome surprise, and Darren was finding it impossible to be anything other than worried. Lately, Laura seemed to be rushing headlong into life-changing situations without much thought.

Or was it simply because he was jealous of the man who'd had the courage to woo and win her?

No matter how hard Darren tried to dismiss it, the quotation: 'Faint heart never won fair lady' kept circling around his brain. Maybe, if he'd had the courage of his convictions, Laura would now be safe, and expecting *his* baby, not another man's.

Laura looked at her boss tentatively. It was clear that Darren had terminated their discussion, and she felt disappointed by what she sensed was his disapproval. Why couldn't he be happy for her? Why couldn't everyone be happy for her?

As she left his office, she felt tense and stressed. It wasn't supposed to be like this. People were supposed to be pleased when someone became pregnant. But even Maria, Timmy and Greta had been less than enthusiastic when she'd told them in the canteen a little earlier. Was it because they suspected that Jeff had hit her? She'd explained away her bruises as an accident, but she'd seen the knowing looks on her colleagues' faces, as though they'd seen straight through her lie.

She sensed that Kerry had reservations, too. Well, she'd prove them all wrong! She and Jeff would live happily ever after, and this child of theirs would put the final seal on their happiness.

Returning to her office, Laura sat down at her desk and surveyed the pile of essays that needed marking. Try as she might, she couldn't focus her mind on them. She managed to struggle through the first few papers before deciding that it wasn't fair to the students since her mind was on other things.

She turned to the window in her office and gazed out across the campus to the sports fields in the distance. She felt very much alone. Somehow her marriage and pregnancy were isolating her from her colleagues; yet, in another sense, she'd always felt alone, ever since the death of her parents and brother.

But then she smiled, patting her belly. 'At least I have you, little person,' she whispered. 'So I'm not really alone any more.'

CHAPTER 14

Sylvia Thornton was emptying the pockets of her husband's suits as she prepared to take them to the dry cleaners. Suddenly, her fingers closed around a rolled-up piece of paper. Curiously, she opened it, and discovered that it was a receipt from a well-known firm of London jewellers, and the item purchased had been a very expensive diamond and gold ring.

For a moment, Sylvia's heart stood still, and she found herself considering, for the first time ever, if Alan could be having an affair. The thought of him with another woman was sheer torture – surely he'd never do such a thing to her?

Since she and her husband maintained a glittering social calendar, and every day he was at the factory, she'd assumed he'd have little time for dalliances elsewhere. Now she wondered just how naïve she'd been.

Clutching the receipt, Sylvia mentally ran through the list of her friends...well, if she was honest, they were really only acquaintances – women from the same wealthy circle whom she joined at charity luncheons and on visits to health spas or nail bars, or at the golf or tennis club. Could Alan be having an affair with one of those women?

Sylvia's eyes narrowed. Perhaps it was with that minx, Janette Walker. Whenever she and Alan encountered Janette and her husband – the permanently inebriated Matthew – the woman was always quick to slip her arm through Alan's, and flirt outrageous-

ly with him, regardless of Sylvia's presence. On the other hand, could it be someone from the factory? And if so, did the rest of the staff know? Her face reddened with shame at the thought of such duplicity on Alan's part, and such humiliation on hers.

But then, with a feeling of enormous relief, Sylvia remembered that her own birthday was only two weeks away – no doubt the ring was intended as a gift for her! Smiling, she replaced the receipt in one of Alan's other jackets. She wouldn't spoil the surprise by letting him know that she'd discovered what he'd bought her.

On the morning of her birthday, Alan was already up by the time Sylvia awoke. Slipping on her dressing gown, she padded downstairs to the kitchen, where she could hear Alan whistling as he prepared breakfast.

He was smiling broadly as he greeted her. 'Good morning, love. Happy birthday!'

'Thanks – I didn't expect to sleep quite so late.'

Warily, she eyed the breakfast table. Alongside the morning papers, Sylvia could see two gift-wrapped boxes. She guessed that the bigger one was a gift purportedly from young Pete to his mummy. A smaller box stood beside it, and Sylvia's heart did a quick somersault. Thankfully, it looked exactly like the kind of box that would contain an expensive gold and diamond ring. Relief flooded through her. She'd been silly to worry, and everything was going to be fine.

Smiling, Sylvia sat down at the table, just as Alan began singing 'Happy Birthday' as he carried two plates of scrambled eggs and buttered toast to the table.

Leaning forward, he kissed her. 'I'm hoping we might manage to have breakfast together before Pete wakes up.' He looked at her expectantly. 'Go on – open your presents!'

Taking a deep breath, Sylvia picked up the bigger gift box, the one whose label read: 'To Mummy from Pete xxx'.

She smiled as she unwrapped a pair of pretty gold filigree earrings, ornately shaped in the letter 'S'.

'Obviously, I had to help him,' Alan joked. 'I mean, he hasn't learnt his alphabet yet!'

'They're lovely,' Sylvia replied, standing up and crossing to the mirror where she slipped on the earrings and stared at her reflection.

'Aren't you going to open my *present?'*

'Yes, of course.'

Returning to the table, Sylvia's heart was beating so wildly that she felt certain Alan must hear it. She smiled as she lifted up the small box. All she had to do now was open Alan's present, find the ring inside, and all would be well again. She could abandon all her silly suspicions and enjoy the rest of her birthday. Flowers had already been delivered from Daddy, and she knew he'd slip her a cheque later that evening when they all met for dinner. It would be for a generous amount too but, right now, all she was concerned about was the contents of the box she held in her trembling hand.

Her fingers shook as she tore off the gift-wrapping, and her heart sank like a stone as she gazed at the bracelet lying on a bed of soft tissue paper inside.

'Oh!'

'Don't you like it?' Alan asked anxiously.

'Yes, yes – of course. I love it,' Sylvia assured him. It was beautiful, but it wasn't the ring she'd been expecting.

'Are you sure you like it, darling? If not, I can change it for something else, you know that.'

Although her heart was breaking, Sylvia reached up and kissed her husband's cheek. 'It's perfect!' she told him. 'It'll go beautifully with the new dress I'm wearing tonight. What time have you booked the restaurant for?'

'Eight-thirty. I've booked a table for six – and I've arranged for the table you like. You know, the one by the window.'

Sylvia raised her eyebrows. 'Six? Who else is coming?'

'Janette and Matthew.' Alan grinned. 'Janette was most insistent that they be present to wish you a happy birthday!'

Sylvia's heart gave a jolt. Janette, with her red mouth and long talons, and the woman she considered most likely to be having an affair with her husband! Surely Alan wouldn't invite his mistress along on his wife's special day?

'Must we have them there?' she answered peevishly. 'After all, it's my *birthday! Shouldn't I be the one to choose the guests?'*

'Sorry,' Alan said sheepishly. 'I thought you'd enjoy their company – your father and aunt aren't exactly livewires, are they? And you know what a madcap Janette is. I thought she'd add a bit of fun to the occasion.'

Sylvia grimaced. 'I suppose there's nothing that can be done about it now – but I wish you'd asked me before inviting them.'

'I didn't actually invite them – I bumped into Janette as I was coming out of the jeweller's, carrying your gift bag. She wanted to know what was inside, and who it was for.'

Sylvia bit her lip angrily. Janette had probably been with *him at the jeweller's – no doubt the beautiful ring had been bought for her.*

'When I told her the gift was for your birthday, Janette invited us for drinks at their house,' Alan added. 'I explained that we were having dinner at La Strada with your father and aunt, and she insisted that she and Matthew join us.'

Sylvia bit her lip. She felt like crying. Her birthday was already ruined.

In La Strada, the wine flowed freely, the conversation was lively and everyone seemed to be enjoying themselves. It was impossible to fault the restaurant. The table Alan had booked was situated exactly where Sylvia liked it, the waiters were attentive, the food delicious. As expected, her father had given her a cheque as soon as they arrived at the restaurant, and even Sylvia had been surprised by the large amount. Her father had seemed pleased by her reaction, and Sylvia wondered if he'd somehow guessed that she needed cheering up.

Aunt Maud had knitted her a sweater, in a hideous yellow colour that Sylvia instantly disliked. But she assured her aunt that it was a colour she adored. Her aunt's face was pink with pleasure, and Sylvia could feel the tears forming as her heart filled with affection for the older woman. It was good to be surrounded by people who would never hurt you. But as she glanced across the table – at Alan and Janette, who were engrossed in a private conversation – her heart contracted. She'd always believed that Alan would never hurt her. Now she wasn't so sure.

Sylvia glanced around the restaurant. Every other table was full, and all the other patrons seemed to be enjoying themselves. As the waiters delivered the several extra bottles of wine that Matthew had ordered, Sylvia wondered how long she'd have to endure the proceedings. But, as the guest of honour, she could hardly leave before the party cake was brought out and she was forced, child-like, to blow out her candles. Her only hope of surviving the evening was to get drunk.

This was something she usually avoided, believing that her position as Alan's wife demanded a certain level of decorum in public. But to hell with Alan tonight, she thought. Let him dare comment!

Sylvia sneaked a glance at Janette's husband. Clearly Matthew had a head start on her – he was already well oiled, and pontificating to anyone who would listen about some theory of his for converting water into fuel. Then her gaze moved to Janette again. Or more specifically, to Janette's left hand. The woman was wearing what looked suspiciously like the ring listed on the receipt in Alan's pocket!

Sylvia took a deep breath and leaned across the table. 'I love *your ring,' she said loudly, and was gratified to see Janette blush. She glanced quickly at Alan, but he was already deep in conversation with her father, and didn't appear to have heard her comment.*

'Oh, thanks,' Janette said off-handedly, then quickly changed the subject, seizing the nearest bottle of wine and topping up Sylvia's glass. 'Do you like this St-Emilion?' she asked eagerly. 'It's a nice wine, isn't it? Personally, I prefer a Châteauneuf-du-Pape, but Matthew always orders what he likes, regardless of what I want. Before we left home this evening, I made him promise to go with my choice this evening, but, oh no, he has to start showing off his knowledge of wines every time!' She smiled at Sylvia as she took a gulp from her glass. 'Although I can't fault him on this one – although I'd never let him know that!'

Sylvia was both embarrassed and relieved when the birthday cake finally arrived. She felt embarrassed because all eyes in the restaurant had turned towards her, and relieved because the candle-blowing episode signified that the evening was drawing to a close. Sportingly, she blew out all her candles in one go, and was rewarded by a round of applause from her own table, and catcalls from inebriated diners across the room.

At the end of the night, as Alan helped her put on her coat, Sylvia watched carefully for any interaction between her husband and Janette. But other than a perfunctory kiss on the cheek, they had no further contact before Alan steered his wife outside to the waiting taxi.

'I haven't seen you drink so much in a long time,' Alan said mildly as they settled into the back seat of the taxi.

Sylvia arched her eyebrows. 'So?'

Alan laughed, holding up his hands in appeasement. 'I didn't mean anything by it – I'm just glad to see you enjoying yourself.'

Sylvia said nothing. If Alan thought she'd enjoyed herself tonight, he was very much mistaken. But maybe, when a man had eyes for only his lover, he could hardly be expected to notice that his wife was suffering.

The following morning, Sylvia was surprised to receive a phone call from Janette.

'Hey, birthday girl, how are you feeling today?'

'A little hung over,' Sylvia admitted. In fact, she had a monumental hangover from all the wine she'd drunk. But it had helped her to get through the otherwise intolerable evening.

'Look, about the ring – '

'Sorry?'

'You admired my ring last night – '

'Did I?'

'Yes, and I'm sorry I changed the subject so quickly. But Matthew doesn't know I've bought it. I mean, he got me the new Merc convertible last month and I didn't want him to think I was ungrateful. But when I saw the ring – well, I just couldn't resist it. So I put it on my gold card – '

'I'm sure you did,' Sylvia said dryly, remembering the night before, when she'd watched Janette coquettishly whispering in Alan's ear while Matthew swayed drunkenly in his seat, waffling incomprehensibly.

'You won't mention it to Matthew, will you?'

'Of course not,' Sylvia replied, unable to think of anything else to say. But now she no longer believed a word that Janette – or Alan – told her. And she surmised that the mistress was now cleverly asking the cuckolded wife to help keep knowledge of the affair from the mistress's own husband!

'Let's do lunch some day soon – ?' Janette added brightly.

'Of course, that would be lovely,' Sylvia replied, thinking to herself: 'Over my dead body.'

'I'll call you, okay?'

'Okay.'

CHAPTER 15

Laura looked pale as she lay in her hospital bed. She was just beginning to doze off when Kerry burst into her private room.

'My God, Laura – are you all right? Is the baby okay?'

Laura sat up. 'I'm fine, and so is the baby. It was a false alarm – I had a show of blood last night, then another at work today, and my colleague, Maria, drove me to the hospital. But the doctors say that everything's okay.'

Kerry gave an exaggerated sigh of relief. 'I was worried sick when Maria texted me! She just said that you'd been taken to hospital, so I didn't know what exactly had happened.'

Laura smiled apologetically. 'Sorry, love – I didn't have time to give anyone a detailed account of what was happening.'

Kerry looked worried. 'I assume you've contacted Jeff?'

Laura nodded. 'Yes, he'll be in later.'

She felt too ashamed to tell her friend that Jeff had hit her again the night before, and that his aggressive behaviour during sex might well have been a factor in her threatened miscarriage. Despite claiming that he longed for the baby, Laura feared that Jeff's erratic behaviour was starting to put her pregnancy in jeopardy. Lately, his temper had seemed to flare up in an instant. It was making Laura miserable, but she didn't know what to do.

Stifling a sob, she turned it into a cough as Kerry looked at her. She couldn't understand why her marriage had suddenly gone sour. They were married such a short time – wasn't this meant to be 'the honeymoon period'? Or did Jeff feel that having won her and made her pregnant, he could now revert to being the man he truly was? And what kind of man was that?

After Kerry had gone – with promises to ring later and bring in anything she might need – Laura lay back on her pillows and awaited her husband's arrival. She'd chosen to text rather than to speak to him, since she didn't relish another explosion over the phone. Perhaps he was having a difficult time at work? Yet she didn't dare ask him about it, since he'd told her that she couldn't. Perhaps his recent brush with death in the restaurant had made him more fearful for his life? He'd been adamant that he'd brought the pen with him to the restaurant, and Laura realised by now that Jeff hated being wrong about anything. So she'd said nothing further about the matter. She longed to be able to help him, but Jeff seemed determined to keep his problems and insecurities – whatever they were – to himself.

'Hello, love,' Laura said warmly, as Jeff arrived at her bedside.

'Is the baby all right?'

Laura nodded, deflated that he hadn't enquired about her own health or given her a hug. She didn't like to admit it, but she'd become sadly aware that Jeff's charm and warmth had disappeared very soon after they were married. It was as though he didn't feel the need to please her any more.

'Yes, it's fine,' she replied. 'Hopefully, I'll be home in a few days.'

'What happened?'

'I don't really know – I'd just finished giving a lecture when I suddenly developed cramps. Then I discovered I was bleeding, so Maria drove me straight to the hospital.'

Laura realised guiltily that she was giving Jeff an edited version of what she'd told Kerry, by avoiding any mention of the bleeding the night before. When Jeff had taken her in anger, she'd known that something was wrong, and a visit to the bathroom afterwards had confirmed it. But right then she didn't want to draw any attention to his involvement, since that might precipitate another burst of anger, which would somehow end up with her being blamed.

Laura also avoided mentioning that she'd phoned Kerry, and that her friend had already been in to visit her. She was gradually coming to realise that it was safer to avoid any mention of Kerry when Jeff was around. Despite Kerry's attempts to be nice to Jeff, her husband wasn't making a similar effort. Nor had she told Jeff about her night at the pub with Kerry. Since he'd been out himself that night, she'd felt it wiser not to draw his attention to it. Let him think that she'd been at home, waiting for him. He seemed to like her best in the role of acquiescent wife.

'So my son is definitely okay?'

Laura nodded, exasperated. 'The *baby* is okay, Jeff – we don't know whether it's a boy or a girl yet. The doctor said that everything seems fine. I'm just supposed to take things easy for the next few weeks.'

'Then maybe you should give up work?' Jeff said hastily. 'Standing at a lecture podium all day can't be doing our child any good.'

'Jeff, I only give two lectures a day, and they're less than an hour each,' Laura protested. 'The rest of the time is spent giving tutorials or correcting exam papers – all of which are done sitting down. Anyway, the doctor says that I can continue working.'

This last bit was a lie – the doctor hadn't expressed any opinion – but Laura wasn't planning on spending her pregnancy lying on a couch and being bored. She loved her job too much to stay at home.

CHAPTER 16

When she missed a period, Ellie paid little attention, since it never crossed her mind that she might be pregnant. As she'd never conceived during her marriage, she'd assumed that becoming pregnant wasn't ever going to happen for her. But when she missed a second period, she was excited and frightened all at once. Since she was now in her late thirties, she wasn't going to miss the opportunity of having this child. And having this baby would tie her to Alan in a way that even a marriage certificate couldn't. Giving Alan a child would put her on a par with Sylvia.

Ellie was bubbling with a mixture of excitement and tension as she waited for her beloved Alan to arrive. She'd now passed the first trimester, and since her pregnancy was no longer in doubt, she'd decided that the time was right to let him know. She'd been anticipating this moment all day. In her own mind she'd played the scenario over and over like a continuous newsreel, and in it he'd expressed his delight and excitement at her revelation. She'd gone through the scene so often that she felt certain it would play out exactly the same way in reality.

As she watched his car coming up her driveway, she felt her heart thumping uncomfortably in her chest. She seemed to be waiting for an eternity as he parked his car behind the house, gathered up the bouquet of flowers he often brought her, and stepped into her hall.

She'd planned to wait until they were in bed before telling him, but she was so nervous that she blurted it out the minute he arrived. 'I'm pregnant!' she announced, watching his face closely to gauge his reaction. She'd hoped to see delight, but instead she saw confusion, followed by a look of guilt as he struggled to say something appropriate.

'B – but I thought...' he said at last.

'You thought I was taking precautions?'

'Well, yes, I assumed...'

'I never managed to conceive during the years that John and I were together, so I assumed I wasn't able,' she told him, disappointed by his initial reaction. But she wouldn't give up this child, even if he begged her to. She looked at him from under her eyelashes. 'You don't mind, do you?'

'No, of course not!' he said quickly. 'If that's what you want – ? If you do, then that's wonderful!'

'But is it what you want? To have a child with me?'

'Yes, yes, it's just that – '

He took her in his arms, but since she knew him so well, she was aware that something was definitely wrong.

'What is it?'

'You know I can't leave Sylvia yet.'

Ellie nodded, relieved that this was all that was bothering him. 'Of course I understand. But this pregnancy was totally unexpected,' she assured him earnestly. 'I don't want you thinking I'm putting a gun to your head. I know our time hasn't come yet. But this impatient little person – ' she patted her stomach tenderly '– has moved things up a notch.'

He still didn't look convinced.

'I know I must wait for you,' she whispered, slipping into his

arms. 'But this may be my only chance to have a child...I'm not getting any younger, you know.'

He kissed her forehead tenderly. 'You'll always be young to me,' he said.

'So you're happy for us?'

'Of course.'

Ellie allowed him to hold her in silence, aware that it would be financial suicide for her to try to rear this child alone and without his support.

He seemed to read her thoughts. 'Your child will want for nothing,' he whispered. 'I'll make sure that you have everything you could possibly need.'

Deflated, she said nothing. He'd referred to 'her' child – already he seemed to be distancing himself from the baby she was carrying.

He smiled as though to placate her. 'Don't worry, I'll love this child just as much as – '

She silenced him by resolutely placing a finger on his lips. 'Don't say it. I don't want to hear you refer to this child as the illegitimate one.'

'I wasn't going to – !'

She bridled. 'Well, then, how were you going to refer to it? By referring to your other child as legitimate, you'd be implying that this child isn't!'

'Oh, love, please don't split hairs – I know this complicates things, but we'll get through it.'

She sighed, her dream now slightly tinged with sadness. She'd hoped and dreamed of a more positive reaction from him. If only the three of them could be a family! But she'd decided long ago that it was preferable to have a small amount of time with someone she loved rather than a whole life with someone like Tony Coleman.

'Well, I'm not prepared to live on the fringes of your life. I want this child – ' she touched her belly *'–to have all the advantages* her *child will have.'*

'Of course – anything you want,' he said, kissing her gently.

With that, Ellie had to be content. She knew he'd ensure that her child would have the best of everything. After all, she'd now forged a lifelong connection with him.

CHAPTER 17

Kerry found it astonishing that Laura trusted Jeff so implicitly, and didn't need to check up on the man with whom she'd rushed into marriage. Unlike her, Laura was a trusting and gullible soul, taking people at face value and just assuming they were who they said they were. Kerry accepted that Laura's naïvety was largely due to losing her parents at such a young age, and not having the normal family support structures in place while she was growing up.

Kerry was also still worried that Jeff might have known in advance about Laura's fortune, and have targeted her specifically. Without telling Laura, she decided that she was going to follow Jeff one morning as he left their apartment, and see where he went. She doubted that he'd go anywhere near Whitehall, where she knew that most of the covert services were located. Of course, if Jeff *was* telling the truth, she'd never be able to prove it anyway, but she didn't believe for one minute that Jeff had anything to do with the secret service. He was too volatile, for starters. Agents would need to be capable of staying calm in difficult situations and, in her opinion, Jeff would never have got past the first interview.

She also thought back to what Laura had told her about Jeff's violent parents, and found herself wondering if there was any truth in that story either. Violent parents wouldn't look very good on a CV for special ops and, even if he'd lied in his application, M15 wouldn't have been long in sussing out the truth. No, Jeff was definitely up to something, and she intended finding out the truth.

The following morning, Kerry was lurking outside Laura and Jeff's Islington flat by eight o'clock. When the alarm had gone off at six, all she'd wanted to do was turn over and go to sleep again, but she reckoned it would be easier to follow Jeff while Laura was still safely in hospital. She'd wondered if he'd bother to leave the flat at all – since Laura wasn't there, he didn't need to pretend that he was going to work.

After forty-five minutes spent shivering in a doorway opposite their flat, Kerry watched as Jeff stepped outside and closed the door. Keeping a safe distance behind him, she followed, thinking yet again that if he truly was a secret agent, he wasn't a particularly good one, since he didn't seem to realise he was being followed.

As she tried to keep up, she hoped that he wouldn't suddenly sprint for a bus, since she was already having trouble matching his long strides. She had some hope of following him if he took the Underground, although even there it would be easy to lose someone on a crowded platform.

Luckily, Jeff headed down to the tube and Kerry was able to hide herself among the people waiting for the next train. She'd taken the precaution of wearing a hooded jacket and had altered her hairstyle and make-up, so she felt confident that Jeff wouldn't notice her. If he did, she'd have to make up some excuse for being there. In theory, her job as an engineer entitled her to be anywhere, so she could claim to be on her way to meet a client to discuss one of Sea Diagnostic's projects.

As the train roared into the station, Kerry kept her eye on Jeff, managing to get into the same carriage, although she made sure to stand behind other commuters while watching to see where he'd get off.

Jeff made one change of train. To Kerry, who was still close behind him, it seemed that he was heading into the centre of the city. But when the train got there, and the crowds began to thin out, Jeff didn't get off. The carriage had become decidedly empty, so Kerry quickly sat down and tried to partially cover her face. She began to worry about her situation, since without the protection of other bodies, Jeff might notice her before long.

Fortunately, when he stood up to get off two stations later, Jeff moved to the forward doors of the carriage, so Kerry hung back until he'd left the train, leaping off just before the doors closed. By now, Jeff was making his way up the escalator, and Kerry followed, her hood pulled up, poised to look away in case he turned and looked back down the escalator.

They were now in the Docklands area of the East End, and Kerry held back as Jeff headed towards a large modern hotel and entered the foyer. As she lurked outside, peering in through the heavy glass doors, she saw him enter the dining room at the back. Taking a deep breath, she lowered her hood and followed him inside.

Luckily, staff at the reception desk were dealing with guests arriving and departing, and she was able to walk straight past them without being queried. Outside the dining room she paused, trying to spot Jeff inside. Finally, she saw him sitting at a corner table with another man. Luckily, Jeff had his back to the door, but Kerry frowned as she looked at his companion. He was a tall, well-dressed man, and Kerry knew she'd seen him somewhere before. Who on earth was he?

As the man caught her eye, Kerry quickly looked away, embarrassed. It was time to get out of there, before the man drew Jeff's attention to her presence. Hopefully, she just looked like a hotel guest in search of her breakfast companion. She hurried back to the foyer and left the hotel, still puzzled.

She'd definitely seen or read about this man quite recently. Could he be a politician?

Hurrying back to her apartment, she changed into more suitable work clothes and headed off to the Sea Diagnostics offices. She'd research the situation further just as soon as she got the chance.

CHAPTER 18

*E*llie caressed the soft material lining the bassinet. It was a glorious wickerwork creation lined with oodles of soft, luxurious fabric and trimmed with lace. But a cot would undoubtedly be better value. On the other hand, Alan had told her to spend as much as she liked on whatever items she needed – he'd said that only the best was good enough for their baby. 'And have it all delivered,' he'd insisted. 'I don't want you carrying anything in your condition.'

Already she'd been wandering around the baby section of the big department store for most of the afternoon, and she still hadn't managed to see all the items on offer. It was astonishing how many beautiful cots, prams, car seats and clothing were on display, and how much money you could spend on a tiny baby!

She suddenly thought of her late husband, John, and wondered what he'd make of her present situation. It was a very different life from the one she'd envisaged. Strange that she should think of death when she was in the process of creating new life.

Feeling that someone was watching her, Ellie suddenly turned and found a pair of gentle brown eyes looking into hers.

'Oh, hello,' said Sylvia Thornton. 'I thought it was you. You're Ellie Beckworth, aren't you?'

Ellie nodded, perturbed at this unexpected encounter. 'And you're the factory owner's wife.' She couldn't bring herself to mention Alan by name.

'Yes, I'm Sylvia. I've seen you at staff parties before you left the factory, and I sometimes see you shopping in the village when I take Pete out in his buggy. But we've never had a chance to talk before now.'

Sylvia was delighted to make Ellie Beckworth's acquaintance. It was comforting to think that here, at least, was a woman she didn't have to view as Alan's potential mistress. Ellie was clearly too independent to rely on any man, certainly not one married to somebody else. Besides, Alan had always made a point of never socialising with his employees, except for the annual Christmas party and staff retirement parties. He said it wasn't good for business, and that the boss needed to maintain a certain distance if he was to keep his employees' respect.

Ellie felt self-conscious about her growing belly, especially when Alan's wife made a point of looking down at it.

'How far on are you?' Sylvia asked.

'Six months,' Ellie murmured.

'You look the picture of health,' Sylvia said approvingly.

Ellie tried to smile in acknowledgement, all the while wondering how quickly she could make her escape.

But Sylvia seemed determined to chat. 'The stock here is wonderful, isn't it?' she said, fingering a tiny hat and matching mittens that hung on a display panel beside them. 'I'm hoping for a girl this time – there are so many pretty dresses available!'

She smiled warmly at Ellie, who suddenly felt dizzy and feared she was going to faint.

'Y – you're pregnant?' Ellie whispered.

'Yes!' Sylvia replied. 'I'm only three months gone, so nothing's showing yet. And we've no idea what sex it is.'

Ellie could feel her eyes welling up and she turned away, pretending to cough so that Sylvia wouldn't see her tears.

'I really shouldn't be browsing,' Sylvia added, unaware that Ellie's world was collapsing all around her. 'After all, most of *the baby stuff we bought for Pete will be usable again. But I simply couldn't resist buying something!' She smiled, delving into a shopping bag bearing the shop's logo. 'If I have a girl, I'll be guilty of stereotyping, because I couldn't resist buying this gorgeous little pink outfit!'*

She waved the little dress and matching socks in front of Ellie, who longed to reach out and throttle her.

Sylvia suddenly noticed Ellie's white face. 'Are you all right?' she asked, alarmed. 'Do you need to sit down? Look, they have a coffee shop on this floor. Let's get you over there immediately.'

Leaning on Sylvia and feeling ridiculous, Ellie allowed herself to be led into the coffee shop, where Sylvia found her a chair and asked the woman behind the counter for two coffees.

'Would you like something to eat?' Sylvia asked anxiously. 'I find that I'm always ravenous when I'm pregnant.'

Ellie shook her head, unable to speak because of the huge lump in her throat. She felt betrayed by Alan, and winded by what she'd just heard. At the very moment when Sylvia had revealed her pregnancy, something inside her had died.

Ellie had never asked Alan about his sex life with his wife, but it had always been there, hanging over their relationship like a dark cloud. Perhaps the same issue hung over every illicit relationship. What lover didn't want to be the only one in their beloved's life?

Logically, Ellie had always known that Alan and his wife must have some physical contact – otherwise Sylvia's suspicions would be aroused. Now, as she looked at Alan's wife across the coffee-shop table, she was having to confront his other life head-on. She'd never allowed herself to consider that the logical outcome of their occasional sexual activity could lead to another pregnancy.

Suddenly, Ellie realised that Sylvia had been talking to her, but she hadn't heard a word.

'P – pardon?'

Sylvia looked embarrassed. 'I'm sorry for loading this on you, but I've no one else I can talk to. I really need a friend right now, and somehow I feel that I can trust you.'

Ellie nodded, since it seemed the easiest thing to do.

Sylvia took a deep breath. 'I think my husband's having an affair,' she said softly.

Ellie gasped, wondering for a split second if Sylvia knew about her and was about to confront her.

'Yes, I knew you'd be shocked,' Sylvia said, looking miserable. 'I was shocked, too. I've no idea who it is. Well, actually, I did suspect someone we socialise with, but now I'm not so sure and, anyway, I've no idea what to do about it.' She looked imploringly into Ellie's eyes. 'You seem to be the kind of strong, independent woman who'd be worldly about this kind of thing. Have you any advice to offer me?'

Ellie felt as though she'd stepped into an alternate universe.

'N – no, not really,' she managed to say at last, but her voice sounded strangled and totally unlike hers. 'I mean, it's probably best to do nothing,' she added lamely.

Sylvia nodded, seeming to hang on Ellie's every word.

'It'll probably blow over,' Ellie added again, trying to sound helpful. 'These things usually do.'

Sylvia grasped Ellie's hand gratefully. 'Thank you,' she said, a look of relief on her face. 'You've no idea how relieved I am to hear you say that.' She suddenly looked guilty. 'I hope you'll keep what I've told you to yourself – '

Ellie nodded, unable to speak. She felt she was suffocating, and she found it impossible to drink the coffee that had suddenly appeared in front of her. She began to stand up from the table, knowing that if she stayed there any longer, she was in danger of breaking down.

Sylvia looked startled. 'Are you feeling sick? Are you sure you don't need something to eat? I could ask the waitress to get you something – '

'No, I'm fine, thanks,' Ellie said, stumbling from the table. 'But I have to go – it was nice meeting you.'

'And you, too.' I've embarrassed her, Sylvia thought to herself. Although I hardly know her, I've crossed the line by unfairly involving her in my problems. But I was desperate for some honest, womanly advice. No wonder she doesn't want anything more to do with me.

'Goodbye,' Sylvia said sadly, desperately wishing that Ellie could have stayed longer 'Good luck with your pregnancy.'

'And you with yours,' Ellie replied. Then she rushed out of the coffee shop and down the escalator as fast as she could. She desperately needed to get out of the department store. She was overwhelmed by the need for fresh air...

In the local park, Ellie sat down on a bench and cried. She felt totally betrayed by Alan. He'd known for at least a month, maybe even two, that Sylvia was pregnant, and yet he'd said nothing. He'd led her to believe that her own pregnancy was the most exciting thing that was happening in his life – whereas he was also having another baby with his wife!

As long as she hadn't actually met Sylvia, Ellie had been able to imagine her as a vain, controlling, selfish woman, worthy of her hatred. But having discovered how genuinely nice she was, Ellie felt wretched at being the one who was cheating with her husband, and also bearing his child behind her back. Sylvia seemed so innocent, so genuinely interested in Ellie's pregnancy, and Ellie had the impression that she'd have liked to make a friend of her. But there would be no way she would bear to maintain contact with the woman she was deceiving.

The meeting also made her angry and insecure about Alan. How could he not love such a nice woman as Sylvia? He clearly liked his wife enough to have sex with her. Maybe it was Ellie he was deceiving, and that he had no intention of ever leaving his wife. Insecurity rose up inside her like bile.

Yet how could she claim to be a decent person herself, when Alan's wife was the innocent victim of their appalling deceit?

CHAPTER 19

Kerry sat on the edge of Laura's hospital bed, holding her hand sympathetically.

'How do you know all this?' Laura demanded, tears in her eyes. 'You couldn't possibly find out so much by simply following Jeff!'

'No, you're right – when I got home after work this evening, I checked through the last few weeks' newspapers online, because I'd a hunch that I'd seen a picture somewhere of the guy who was with Jeff. And there he was, smiling as he left court after his acquittal. He'd been prosecuted for importing and supplying Class A drugs, like heroin, and cocaine.' Kerry grimaced. 'But the informer who was to testify against him disappeared – presumed dead – so he got off.' She reached into her pocket and took out a folded piece of paper. 'Here – I printed off the page, so you can see for yourself.'

Laura looked at the picture of the smiling man, but it meant nothing to her. She definitely didn't recognise him.

Kerry looked at her earnestly. 'What worries me is why Jeff would be meeting a guy like that?' She took a deep breath. 'Aren't you worried that whatever he's doing, it looks decidedly dodgy?'

Laura could feel anger building up inside her. 'You've no business following my husband while I'm here in hospital!' she said hotly. 'I'm sorry now that I told you about his real line of work – he's clearly on some kind of mission. He probably has to deal with these people for reasons of national security!'

Seeing how angry Laura was, Kerry quickly backtracked. 'I'm sorry, love – I accept that maybe I shouldn't have followed him. But I'm worried about you, and I just want you to be safe and happy.'

Laura looked slightly less angry, so Kerry decided to tell her what else she'd looked up.

'I also Googled Jeff's father's name. There were lots of old newspaper reports about his family at the time of his parents' deaths. The coroner ruled that Jeff's mother had been murdered by his father, and then the father hanged himself.'

Laura turned pale with shock. 'Oh God! I knew his parents were violent, but I'd no idea his father was a murderer! Poor Jeff – that explains so much.'

Kerry grimaced. 'I just thought you should know. You'd have been livid with me if you found out later that I'd known all this and hadn't told you.'

Laura nodded. 'Okay, I get that. But Jeff can hardly be blamed for his awful parents, can he? It's not his fault that his father was a murderer. I know Jeff is scarred by his childhood – he probably didn't tell me all that because he's embarrassed by it.'

Kerry squeezed her hand apologetically. 'Promise me you won't let him know that I've told you all this?'

Laura looked at her truculently. 'Of course I won't! He'd be so humiliated. You know how insecure Jeff is! Besides, he's my husband. I signed up for better or for worse, and I'm expecting his child. So I have to make a go of it.' She looked at Kerry defiantly. 'Besides, I love him.'

Kerry smiled sympathetically. Still gullible. Still seeing the best in her husband, despite the fact that he'd hit her, and told her a pack of lies from day one. Love truly *was* blind.

When Kerry had left, Laura lay alone in her bed feeling shell-shocked and very vulnerable. No, Kerry had to be wrong. But this new information of Kerry's – that he'd been having breakfast with a well-known criminal – was certainly worrying. Undoubtedly he was doing it as part of his job for MI5. Jeff was probably working on some kind of sting. No doubt his recent violent outbursts had just been a reaction to all the dangerous work he was doing. He hadn't really meant to hurt her, and all would be well just as soon as this difficult assignment was over. She'd just have to be patient until then.

Feeling exhausted by it all, Laura lay back and patted her belly. At least the baby was okay, so she could look forward to the family that she and Jeff were creating together. Her number-one priority was this little person growing inside her. She owed it to this child to make the best of her marriage, and to create a happy home environment for it to grow up in. If she was to start questioning everything her husband did, she'd have no marriage left. Jeff had to be allowed to do his job without her interference – hadn't he told her that she wasn't ever to question him about what he was doing? Presumably that was for her own protection. Jeff wouldn't want any of the unsavoury characters he dealt with intruding into his family life. She felt a warm glow of contentment. He was only trying to keep her safe. Feeling relieved, she picked up a magazine and began flicking through the pages.

CHAPTER 20

Laura was relieved to be going home at last, despite Jeff off-handedly informing her that he wouldn't be available to collect her the following day, and that she'd have to take a taxi home on her own.

After he'd left her hospital room, Laura hadn't been able to stop the tears. She had felt wretched, and hurt that her husband couldn't be there for her. She assumed that the demands of his job were keeping him away, and she suddenly wished Jeff had an ordinary, nine to five job. Other people had offered to bring her home: Darren was first to offer, then Maria, followed by Kerry. But she'd turned them all down – pretending that Jeff was collecting her – because she couldn't bear to see the pity in their eyes.

Once back in the apartment, Laura looked around at all the magnificent fittings, state-of-the-art kitchen and sumptuous furnishings, and felt her heart almost break. On the surface, she and Jeff had everything. But where it mattered, they seemed to have very little. Laura wondered if she was lacking somehow. Maybe Jeff needed a much more dynamic woman than she was. Clearly, she wasn't enough to make her husband happy. Was Jeff as disappointed with their marriage as she was? Nevertheless, she was expecting a baby with him, so she'd make the best of it in order to create a good home environment for their child. And she'd try to be the best mother she possibly could. Hopefully things would get better.

The following day, Laura returned to work. Her colleagues were surprised to see her back so soon and urged her to take it easy. They all volunteered to ease her workload, or bring her coffee or food from the canteen. Their kindness overwhelmed her, and she felt a sense of peace in her work surroundings that she never seemed to feel at home. Why couldn't Jeff express those same caring feelings? He was supposed to love her, whereas her colleagues, who were simply acquaintances, had shown more humanity and kindness to her than he ever had.

Darren fussed and flapped like a mother hen, urging her to put her feet up at every opportunity, and insisting that for the rest of the week she only give her afternoon lecture, and that he'd give the morning one. It felt good to be pampered, but Laura was keen to pull her weight and get back to her full-time schedule as soon as possible.

'I'll be staying on at the university this evening,' Laura told Jeff, as she tidied up after their lunch and got ready to leave for her afternoon lecture. 'There's a debate organised by the students of the Literary and Historical Society at eight o'clock, and Darren has asked me to attend. All the staff in the department will be going, to give moral support to our students.'

Jeff shrugged his shoulders as he sat back and drank his coffee. 'What's the debate about?'

'That drugs should be legalised by the government.'

Jeff looked up, his eyes narrowing. 'How could anyone be so stupid?'

'It's only a student debate,' Laura said mildly, not sure what exactly he meant by his comment. But she felt that it was safer to avoid any further discussion.

Yet Jeff suddenly seemed keen to keep the conversation going.

'What's your opinion?' he asked, and for a second Laura hoped they were about to have an adult discussion about it.

'Well, I'd favour legalisation,' she said, smiling. 'Governments have been fighting the drugs war for years without any success. Like Prohibition, once you forbid something, it goes underground. If drugs were legalised, it would reduce crime, and save taxpayers the money that's currently being spent on keeping people in prison. The quality of the drugs would be better, too – they wouldn't be cut with dangerous substances.'

Jeff was getting angry. 'I might have known you'd feel that way,' he said disgustedly. 'That's what you lefty, university types always think. Drugs should never be legalised!'

'Jeff, it's only a debate!' Laura said quietly.

She could see how agitated he was becoming and touched his shoulder in a calming gesture. She could guess why Jeff would oppose decriminalisation – his parents had probably been drug-users as well as being violent psychopaths.

'I'll be back about ten tonight.'

Jeff looked truculent. 'Your lecture is over by five. Why aren't you coming home first?'

Laura smiled to lighten the tension that she realised was building. 'It's hardly worth it – I'd barely be here for half an hour before I'd be leaving again. I'll just grab something to eat in the canteen before it closes,' she finished, avoiding mentioning that all the lecturers were meeting there before heading off to the debate.

Jeff became angry if he knew that other men would be in her company. It was ridiculous that she had to watch everything she said – it was like being a teenager again, and needing parental permission to go anywhere.

By now Jeff had risen to his feet and, too late, Laura recognised the manic gleam in his eyes.

'Are you saying I'm hardly worth spending half an hour with?' he asked, his voice deceptively gentle.

'No, no – of course not!' Laura said anxiously. 'I love spending time with you.'

'Then why are you going to this stupid debate?'

'Because Darren asked all the lecturers to attend,' she explained anxiously.

Jeff's voice was low and menacing. 'So what Darren says is more important than what your husband wants?'

'No, of course not!'

'Then stay here, with me, tonight.'

'Jeff, be fair! I promised Darren I'd go – '

'And we can't break a promise to good ol' Darren, can we?'

Laura was torn by indecision. She shouldn't have to beg, but she was actually afraid. In fact, she was suddenly terrified.

'Jeff, it's part of my job! I have to be seen to support my own students – '

The blow, when it came, was almost a relief – she'd been expecting it for several minutes. She was momentarily blinded by its impact. At first, she thought her neck had been dislocated, but as the pain receded she found she could still move her head. Her hand reached up and felt a deep gash along her cheek. Already it was beginning to throb.

'Why do you make me so mad?' Jeff screamed. 'You're the most infuriating and self-centred woman I've ever met! The only thing that matters is what *you* want!'

Laura longed to verbally retaliate, but she was too terrified. Jeff was blaming her for his own behaviour. Touching her stomach, as though to reassure the child within, she rushed into the bathroom. Immediately locking the door, she surveyed her pale, red-eyed face in the mirror over the sink, and watched as blood dripped from the open gash and ran down the length of her cheek.

There was no way she could give her afternoon lecture or go to the debate now. Luckily, her phone was in her jacket pocket, so she dialled Timmy, claiming that something had urgently come up, and asking him to give the lecture for her. His immediate agreement, and concern for her well-being, was her undoing.

Tears filled her eyes, blurring the image of her face in the mirror. She felt so tired that she hadn't even the energy to open the bathroom cabinet and find ointment and a dressing. As she rang off, her legs gave way, and Laura sank to the floor and wept.

CHAPTER 21

'*W*hy didn't you tell me?'

'Tell you what?'

'That your wife is also expecting your baby!' Ellie spat out the words venomously, hardly waiting until Alan had stepped inside her front door before verbally assaulting him. Her eyes were red from crying, and she looked as though she wanted to tear him limb from limb.

Alan had the grace to look embarrassed. 'How did you find out?' he asked. When there was no reply forthcoming, he sighed and looked at her uncertainly. 'I just didn't know how to tell you,' he said. 'I'm sorry.'

'Sorry you slept with her or sorry I found out? I thought you told me you didn't find her attractive?' Ellie said angrily. 'Then how the hell is she three months pregnant?'

He licked his lips nervously, unable to find any words that would make sense. 'Look, you know I have to sleep with her occasionally,' he whispered, reaching out to stroke her back as though soothing an upset child. 'But it's never like the way it is with you.'

Swatting his hand away, Ellie folded her arms and said nothing.

'Ellie, you know her father holds a huge stake in the company now –'

'To hell with you and your damned factory!' Ellie shouted.

*'What about me? What about the child I'm carrying? It'll be
born three months before your precious wife gives birth, but I
doubt if there'll be any fanfare of trumpets for us, will there?'*

*'You know the score!' he protested. 'I thought you said it was
enough just to be pregnant! I thought you were happy about it –* '

*'I was, until I found out that your wife is pregnant too! It makes
a mockery out of all your declarations, doesn't it?'*

*'Don't be ridiculous!' Alan replied, angrily now. 'You know I
love you, and you also know I'm looking forward to our baby. But
you have to accept I have another life as well!'*

*'Oh, go to hell!' she shouted, pushing him out the front door
and slamming it behind him.*

It was the first time he'd left without making love to her.

*Sylvia sighed, looking across at her husband who was reading
the newspaper after dinner. She should be feeling elated about
this pregnancy, but instead she felt flat and uninvolved, as though
it was happening to someone else. If she felt anything, it was resentment. This should be a joyous time, but her continual worries
about the ring – which seemed to point to Alan having an affair
– had taken away any pleasure she might feel. It was ironic that
despite their rare and loveless coupling, nature had intervened
with a plan of its own.*

*Sylvia wished she had the courage to confront Alan about the
receipt. But every time he looked at her so openly and unflinchingly, her courage failed her. On the other hand, did she really
want her suspicions confirmed? As long as they could keep up
a seemingly happy demeanour with each other, it was probably
easier to maintain the lie that all was well between them. Ellie
Beckworth was right – if he was having an affair, it would eventually fizzle out. Surely the other woman would finish with Alan anyway, when she discovered that his wife was pregnant? Although
if it was Janette, she'd probably enjoy the situation and use it*

to her own advantage, flaunting her tiny waistline in contrast to Sylvia's thickening one.

Sylvia looked across at her husband. 'Alan...' She hesitated. 'Are you genuinely happy about this pregnancy?'

'Of course I am!'

Abandoning his newspaper, he crossed the room to where Sylvia was clearing the table, slipping his arms around her. 'Are you happy about it, Syl? Is it too much for you – I mean, I know Pete's birth was difficult – '

'I'm fine,' she said firmly. 'I just needed to know that you were pleased to be having another child.'

'Pleased? I'm delighted!' he said tenderly.

His show of kindness brought tears to her eyes. Maybe she was wrong about his affair – how could he look at her so caringly if he was involved with another woman?

Breaking away, he looked at his watch. 'I've got to check something at the factory,' he told her cheerfully. 'I'll be back in an hour or two, okay?'

When he'd left the room, Sylvia sighed to herself. They hadn't been intimate since the baby had been conceived, and she wondered, yet again, if some mistress was satisfying him instead. She had briefly considered the possibility that Alan's trips to the factory could be a cover for an affair, but decided she was wrong. He was never gone for more than an hour or two – surely it would be impossible to conduct an affair in such a short time frame?

Crossing to the window, she watched as he got into his car and drove away. She always detected something in his demeanour before he left for the factory – there was usually a spring in his step, and an air of excitement about him, as though he actually enjoyed dealing with all the problems.

Sylvia sighed as she headed to the nursery to check on Pete. In a way, she envied Alan his devotion to his career. She just wished that he could have that same gleam in his eye when he was coming home to her.

Alan left Greygates and hurried to Ellie's house. But when she opened the door and saw him on the doorstep, she burst into tears and tried to close the door on him. But he ignored her protests and pushed past her into the house.

'I'm so sorry, love,' he said, trying to take her into his arms. 'I just couldn't find the right words. But we'll make this work, won't we?'

'How could you treat us both so badly?'

'I never intended to hurt either of you,' Alan said guiltily. 'And I'm genuinely excited about our baby.' He patted her stomach gently. 'I never lied to you about that.'

'But what about Sylvia? She's really nice!'

'Of course Sylvia's a nice person,' Alan said gently. 'I just don't love her the way I love you.' He sighed. 'It's very much a marriage of convenience – but you know all this already.' He kissed Ellie's tear-stained face. 'I'm grateful to Sylvia for her family's money, but my heart and my body belong to you.'

'But you still sleep with her!'

He kissed her forehead. 'I haven't slept with her for ages. But I can't afford to fall out with her, since it's her father's money that keeps the factory going.'

Tears pricked Ellie's eyes. 'It's always about money, money, money! Why can't you be happy just to live here with me?'

Alan looked at her bleakly. 'Love, whether you like it or not, I already have a son – and now two more children on the way – all of whom I'll love and protect. I want them all to have a good upbringing and a good schooling.' He looked at her angry face. 'If there's no money, then it won't be possible to look after you, pay your mortgage and give them a decent education. And if the factory closes, hundreds of people will be out of a job. Is that what you want?'

'Don't you dare make me responsible for people losing their jobs!' she retorted, stomping out of the room. She hadn't told him about Sylvia's worries over his affair – she felt a peculiar loyalty, or perhaps it was guilt, towards his vulnerable and insecure wife. In fact, she felt totally confused about everything that had happened.

As she stood alone in the kitchen, Ellie wondered if she was a fool, and if it was time to take back ownership of her life. Perhaps it would have been better accepting the attentions of Tony Coleman. At least he could have offered her marriage. On the other hand, she deeply regretted accepting his invitation to the cinema that night when Alan had been away – she should have guessed he'd only see it as encouragement. But sometimes she simply craved adult company, since the loneliness of loving Alan was almost too much to bear. Of course, she hadn't mentioned her cinema trip to Alan – there were some things better kept to oneself.

Ellie sighed. Anyway, it was Alan that she loved, and it always would be. As she gazed, unseeing, out the window, she felt the fluttering of the child in her belly, and knew that there was no greater joy than knowing she'd soon fulfil her dream of becoming a mother.

She heard Alan coming into the kitchen, but she didn't move until he pressed against her and slipped his arms around her. She could feel the tension in his body, and she knew that there was something else he needed to say to her.

'I can't possibly leave Sylvia at the moment,' he said, holding her tight. 'Pete's birth was difficult, and she'll probably need medical intervention this time, too. It would be cruel to leave her now.'

She longed to scream at him: But what about me? I'm pregnant too! Why is it acceptable to leave me all alone? But she said nothing, allowing herself to be held as she considered what all this meant for her own future, as well as that of her unborn *child. His wife's pregnancy felt like a huge betrayal, yet who was betraying whom?*

Ellie sighed, surrendering to her fate as she turned to face him, acquiescing by resting her head on his shoulder.

CHAPTER 22

The following morning, as Laura hurried along the university corridor, hoping to sneak into her office unnoticed, her heart sank as she saw Darren approaching from the opposite direction. It would be churlish to ignore him so, keeping her head slightly tilted, she gave him a cheery wave before quickly unlocking her door and stepping inside. She'd covered the new gash on her cheek with make-up as best she could, but it was still obvious, and she didn't want anyone commenting on it, least of all Darren, who never missed a thing.

Fortunately, due to Darren's kindness, she didn't have to give a lecture until the afternoon, and she hoped that by then any swelling would have gone down. That morning, she intended staying in her office and getting on with all the papers she had to correct. Hopefully, she could do that without having to see anyone.

But it was not to be. Laura cursed silently as she heard the rap on her door. Briefly, she considered ignoring it, or pretending she hadn't heard it. But she was meant to be a professional, and in a work situation she couldn't simply ignore it.

Turning her head to hide the wound, she pretended to be studying a pile of papers as she called out: 'Come in!'

Her heart sank as Darren stepped inside and closed the door.

'Laura, I noticed that Timmy gave your lecture yesterday afternoon, and you weren't at the debate last night. Are you okay?' he asked anxiously. 'You were holding your head rather oddly out in the corridor – '

He gulped as she turned to face him. 'Oh, my God! What happened?'

'I – I walked into a door.'

'Ah.'

He said nothing more, and Laura could feel tears stinging her eyes. He didn't believe her. But he was allowing her to save face, and that made her feel even worse.

They stared at each other, Darren unsure what to say next and Laura almost daring him to say anything else.

His brown eyes clouded with concern as he crossed the room and silently took her in his arms. His kindness and support was Laura's undoing. The floodgates opened and she wept, her tears soaking the shoulder of his jacket.

'Was the door's name Jeff?' Darren whispered.

Laura was about to shake her head, but then she realised it was pointless. It was obvious to anyone with half a brain that a door couldn't have inflicted an injury like that, and her tearful demeanour wasn't helping either. She was finding it hard to pretend that everything was okay when it clearly wasn't.

'It was an accident,' Laura told him.

'Yeah, they're always accidents,' Darren added dryly. 'Is there anything I can do? I think you should go home – you're in no state to give lectures today. In fact, you shouldn't have come in at all.'

Laura shuddered at the thought of going home. That was where it had happened. And even though Jeff wouldn't be there, just being in the apartment would make her jumpy and insecure.

Darren rubbed her back affectionately. 'Look, I'll get Maria or Timmy to take over your lecture this afternoon. In fact, they or I can take over your lectures for the rest of the week.'

'No, honestly – '

'That's an order, Thornton – sorry, Jones – and it's not nego-
tiable.' He suddenly grinned. 'It's occasions like this that make
me love being the boss!'

Laura couldn't help smiling back through her tears. Darren
was such a sweet guy, and always so kind to her.

Then his face darkened. 'If you don't want to go home, I can
give you the keys to my place,' he said. 'You can stay there as
long as you need to – '

Vehemently, Laura shook her head. 'I'm okay. Thanks, Darren – I'll go home.'

Darren released her from his embrace and stood back, looking at her sadly. 'Are you sure that's wise? Maybe a break for
a few days would be a good idea.'

Laura shuddered. She could only imagine Jeff's reaction if
she told him she was staying in another man's apartment.

'No, it'll be fine.'

Darren studied her injured face. 'Have you seen a doctor?
Just in case you've broken your cheekbone. Or I can drive you
to the hospital – '

'No, no. Thanks, Darren,' Laura said firmly. 'I'll take your
advice and leave the lecturing to you, Maria or Timmy. But I'll
stay on here and get the students' essays corrected – '

'Don't even think of it, Laura. You need to rest, and give
yourself a chance to heal.'

Laura nodded, overwhelmed by his kindness. 'All right.
Thanks, Darren – I'm really grateful. But I'm going to insist
on taking the essays with me.'

'Okay, but take it easy for as long as you like,' Darren said
gently. 'I don't want you back here until you feel fit and well
again. And if there's anything I can do – just pick up the phone.
You know I'm always here for you.'

Nodding, Laura turned away. Darren's kindness had brought

tears to her eyes once again. It was good to know that somebody cared, because she felt terribly alone and vulnerable.

'Laura – '

She stopped in her tracks, but didn't turn back to face him,
knowing what was coming.

'You don't have to stay with him just because you're pregnant,' Darren said softly.

Laura didn't answer, because she didn't know what to say.

CHAPTER 23

The following week, Laura returned to the university. Although her cheek was healing, she still felt overwhelmed by sadness. She'd done as much as she could to help Jeff cope with his demons, but she seemed powerless to lessen his pain. Even when he'd been rude and offensive, she'd bitten her tongue, hoping that by refusing to react, he'd calm down and realise that she wasn't his enemy. Jeff had a gigantic chip on his shoulder, and it seemed to be getting bigger. Blithely, she'd believed that marriage would give him the security he craved – and which she craved too – but nothing seemed to pacify the monster within him.

She was also becoming frightened by his sexual demands – what she'd initially believed to be passion had degenerated into a form of violence. But she was too embarrassed to discuss his demands with anyone else. Not only did it seem like a betrayal, but also her own pride was preventing her from admitting that her marriage was less than perfect.

She was also deeply worried by what Kerry had told her. Her friend seemed convinced that Jeff was involved in some kind of criminal activity because she'd seen him with a drug-dealer. But Jeff hated drugs – he'd already made that very clear to her, so he couldn't possibly be involved in selling them. She preferred to believe that his bad humour resulted from the precarious and dangerous situations in which he had to work.

On one occasion he'd come home in a temper and, despite her efforts to cheer him up, he'd turned on her once again. 'What do you know about problems?' he'd sneered. 'You haven't got a clue!'

'Well, that's because you won't tell me anything!' she'd retorted, angry that he could negate her own suffering so offhandedly. She'd lost her entire family, yet he treated that monumental event as though it counted for nothing.

'You know I can't tell you!' he'd roared, lashing out again with his hand, catching her across the cheek with his wedding ring. As she reeled from the blow, she had felt wet on her cheek, and her fingers had found blood as she touched the broken skin. The gash from his previous attack had split open again.

Storming out of the room, Jeff had slammed the door and retreated to the TV room.

Laura's eyes filled with tears. Was it always going to be like this? She was carrying his baby, yet even that didn't seem to affect his attitude to her. Why wasn't she one of those lucky women whose husbands cherished them during their pregnancies? Her heart was breaking, but still she wasn't prepared to give up on Jeff. If only she could break through the wall of pain that surrounded him, she felt sure that all would be well.

Later, he'd grudgingly apologised, although he hadn't attempted to examine her injury, or offer any help. Laura had said nothing when he'd mumbled his apology. There didn't seem to be anything worth saying.

Later that night in bed, he'd turned to her, and she'd hoped their coupling would bring them emotionally closer, and help to heal some of the damage that Jeff's temper was doing to their relationship. But he'd taken her in anger again, not heeding her cries of pain. It was as though her confusion and pain turned him on, or satisfied some terrible need deep within him.

When she'd screamed and begged him to stop, he'd held her down, ignoring her protests.

'Shut up! Don't think I won't kill you, too!' he'd muttered, as he continued to thrust violently into her.

Despite the pain, Laura's mind was buzzing. What did he mean by 'too'? Had he killed someone before? She didn't dare raise the issue with him – she was too terrified. She was seeing a side of Jeff that she didn't know at all. Kerry had tried to warn her but, as usual, she'd been stubborn and wouldn't listen. Could Kerry be right?

Afterwards, as she lay beside her husband while he slept, wide-awake and unable to sleep, she had rationalised it away as something he'd simply said in anger, on the spur of the moment. Nevertheless, his threat didn't augur well for their future. She wondered what demons were chasing him, and whether he could run fast enough to get away from them.

A tear rolled down her injured cheek, and she wiped it away as gently as she could. Then she touched her belly, as though to assure the little baby within that she'd look after it, no matter what the future held.

CHAPTER 24

When Ellie experienced the first few contractions, she wasn't unduly worried. She'd read all the books and faithfully attended her antenatal classes, so she knew these were probably Braxton Hicks contractions – the ones that sometimes happened in the weeks preceding the actual delivery. It was as though the womb was in training for the big event, and was flexing itself in preparation. Besides, she wasn't due for another two weeks, and it couldn't happen now anyway, because Alan was away, and he'd promised to spend as much time as he could with her during her labour. He was planning on telling his PA, and anyone else who needed to know, that he'd be attending important meetings all that day. Since the midwife wouldn't be needed for most of her labour, Ellie was looking forward to long periods in Alan's company while she waited for their baby to be born.

She hadn't slept very well the night before, probably due to the thunderstorm that had raged outside. But now all was calm, and it was a bright summer's day again, although some of the trees in the garden had been divested of branches and the ground outside was strewn with debris.

'Ow!' A jolt of alarm shot through her as a really severe contraction rendered her breathless. Fifteen minutes later, it was followed by another one just as strong, and Ellie wondered if it was time to phone the midwife.

Making her way to the phone in the kitchen, she looked in vain for the address book where she'd written the midwife's number. Dammit! She now remembered that she'd taken it upstairs the night before, and left it on her bedside table beside the telephone extension. How could she have been so stupid as to leave it there at such a critical time?

She began crawling up the stairs on her hands and knees, pausing to puff after every few steps because the pains were becoming more regular and severe. Ellie experienced a wave of panic. If she went into labour upstairs, how would the midwife manage to get through the locked front door?

Crawling back down again, Ellie sat on the bottom step. When another strong contraction gripped her, she knew she had to get help urgently. But there was no one she could phone and ask to go upstairs on her behalf, because she had no friends. She'd given up everything to be Alan's secret wife, and now she feared that she and her baby might suffer because no one was on hand to help her. Why on earth did Alan have to be abroad just when she desperately needed him?

Resolutely, Ellie stood up and staggered towards the phone in the kitchen. She'd ring directory enquiries and ask them to locate the midwife's number. As a last resort, she could ring for an ambulance, but she was still intending to give birth at home. She was determined to out-do Alan's wife by giving birth without any medical intervention.

Leaning against the kitchen cupboards, Ellie picked up the receiver and began to dial. But there was no sound from the phone at all. Not even a dial tone. Puzzled, Ellie looked at the receiver, then shook it. Why wasn't it working? What was wrong? Then it hit her like a ton of bricks – the heavy storm the night before must have caused a local cable to come down. Now she had no way of contacting anyone. She was all alone and about to give birth, and she was terrified.

She cursed the isolation of her house – its private and tran-

quil setting meant that no one was likely to hear her, even if she screamed at the top of her voice. There was only one thing she could do – she'd have to make her way down the driveway and out onto the road, where hopefully she could flag down a passing motorist or pedestrian.

Leaving the house, Ellie made her way gingerly down the driveway through the fallen branches, stopping every few minutes as another contraction gripped her. Never had her driveway seemed so long, or help so far away...

She sighed with relief as the gate and the road came into view. All she needed was for a kind Samaritan to come back to the house, locate the address book and then phone the midwife from a working phone.

She gasped as another contraction winded her. These were no Braxton Hicks contractions – these were the real deal. Panic set in as she contemplated having her baby by the side of the road.

As she faced the oncoming traffic, Ellie wondered how she was supposed to attract attention. Should she stick out her thumb like a hitchhiker? A few drivers looked at her curiously but drove on, and Ellie concluded that she wasn't far enough out on the road to get their attention. She must look a sight – eight and a half months pregnant and flailing her arms by the side of a very busy road. Maybe people assumed she was a madwoman, and best avoided. Yet if she stepped out any further, she risked being struck by the cars speeding by.

Ellie was crying quietly in desperation when a large car drove by, then slowed and pulled in a few hundred yards further down the road. The driver's door opened and Ellie's heart plummeted as Sylvia Thornton climbed out and hurried back to where Ellie was standing, her own pregnancy now clearly evident.

'Are you okay?' she asked, a concerned look on her face. Ellie quickly explained the situation, relieved to have help, but wishing it could be anyone but Alan's wife.

'Let's get you back to your house, then I'll drive home and ring your midwife from there,' Sylvia said briskly. 'Here, lean on me – I can see you're having a contraction. How far are they apart?'

Ellie explained how increasingly close they'd become, gratefully clutching Sylvia's arm as they made their way slowly back up the driveway of Treetops.

As they reached the front door, Ellie experienced a sudden jolt of fear. There would be evidence of Alan's presence all over the house! Since there had never been any need for him to hide his belongings, his shaving kit and aftershave were in the en-suite bathroom, his dressing gown was hanging on the back of the bedroom door! But there was no time for any further reflections as another contraction seized her just as she was opening the front door.

Inside, Sylvia helped Ellie to the sofa in the open-plan living area, then looked around her. 'Now, Ellie – where exactly is your address book?'

Ellie bit her lip. There was no way to avoid letting Sylvia go upstairs to the bedroom where she and Alan had made love only two days earlier. She was also thinking of the beautiful ring Alan had given her – lately her finger had become too swollen to wear it, so she'd left it on the dressing table. If Sylvia saw it and read the inscription on the inside, their secret would be out and there would be hell to pay. Hopefully, she'd put it in the drawer of the dressing table and not left it on the top, but she couldn't be certain where exactly it was...

'It's in my bedroom – on the bedside table.'

As Sylvia headed upstairs, Ellie was filled with trepidation. What would she do if Sylvia found the ring, or something else incriminating, and came down the stairs screaming at her? She could hardly expect her help after that. Ellie also didn't want to leave her address book in Sylvia's possession, even briefly, since Alan's phone numbers were in it, and Sylvia might accidentally –

or curiously – look through it. Frantically, she looked around for a piece of paper and a pen, so that she could write out the mid-wife's number for Sylvia when she came back downstairs. Ellie was quietly freaking out, especially as Sylvia seemed to be taking an awfully long time...Had she spotted something incriminating up there? Alan used a particularly expensive brand of aftershave and if Sylvia spotted it, she might start to put two and two togeth-er...

As Sylvia began descending the stairs, her demeanour looked normal enough, and Ellie held out her hand for the address book. 'Here – let me write the midwife's phone number on this piece of paper for you,' she said brightly, producing the pen and paper she'd located on a nearby bookshelf. 'That'll make it more con-venient, won't it?'

Sylvia nodded, handing over the address book, and Ellie sighed with relief at having it in her possession once again. Hav-ing looked up the number, she wrote it down and handed the piece of paper to Sylvia.

Sylvia tucked it into her pocket. 'If I can't contact your mid-wife, shall I call an ambulance?'

Ellie shook her head. Although it was probably foolhardy, she was still determined to give birth at home.

Sylvia bit her lip. 'I don't like leaving you here on your own... Why don't you just come back to my *house? Then I wouldn't need to keep asking you where everything was – '*

'No!' Ellie had to stop herself from shouting, but the thought of having Alan's baby in Alan's house was like being in some al-ternative nightmare.

Sylvia nodded apologetically. 'Sorry, I should have realised that you'd much rather be in your own home. I'll gladly stay with you, but Pete will be finished at the crèche by three, so I'll need to collect him then.' She looked at her watch. 'But that's not for several hours yet. I'm sure the midwife will be here long before

I need to leave.' She smiled impishly. 'Hopefully, you might be holding your baby by then!'

Ellie nodded through the pain of another contraction. Sylvia really was such a nice woman.

'I'll be back as quickly as I can,' Sylvia assured her. 'Is there anything I can get you? Any treats you'd like me to bring back?'

Ellie shook her head. Even if she'd been desperately craving for something, she couldn't have borne the guilt of having Sylvia bring it to her.

When Sylvia had left, Ellie tried to make herself as comfortable as she could. She'd be relieved when the midwife arrived, at which point Sylvia could leave and Ellie would have one less thing to worry about. She wondered if the strain of coping with Sylvia's presence and her own combined guilt and fear were causing her contractions to become even more severe.

Fifteen minutes later, Sylvia was back.

'Our phone line is down too, so I had to go into the village to make the call,' she told Ellie. 'Unfortunately, two of your midwife's other clients are also in labour, so she's notified another midwife on your behalf. But it seems that the second midwife is already delivering a baby over on the other side of the village – but she'll get here as soon as she can.' Sylvia smiled apologetically. 'I'm afraid you're stuck with me, for a while, anyway. Thank heavens I'm not due for another few months myself. You seem to have chosen a very popular time of year to deliver, Ellie!'

While Ellie rested between contractions, Sylvia busied herself in the kitchen, making tea to accompany the freshly baked scones she'd brought back from the village bakery. Initially Ellie had refused to eat, but hunger and the delicious smells wafting from the kitchen eventually got the better of her. It felt bizarre to be eating food supplied by her lover's wife, and she wished, yet again, that Alan's wife was anyone but Sylvia. Then she could have a guilt-free friendship of her own as well.

As Sylvia collected the plates after they'd eaten, she cleared her throat. 'Look, I'm sorry for – well, for pouring out my troubles to you when we last met. It was unfair of me – but I really was grateful for your advice. You were right, too. All I needed to do was sit it out.'

Ellie tried to look nonchalant as she spoke. 'Really? I mean, do you think the affair is over?' She felt a total hypocrite. But she was also avid for any information about her lover's marriage. If Sylvia was happy, what did that mean for her own future with Alan?

Sylvia shrugged her shoulders. 'I'm not sure – there are times when I'm still convinced he's having an affair...but he's a lot calmer lately. You were right when you advised me to say nothing. It's true what they say – "Least said, soonest mended".'

'What made you think he was having an affair?' Ellie asked, hardly daring to ask, yet keen to find out how Alan had slipped up, so that they might ensure it didn't happen again.

'The usual way, I suppose. I was sending his suits for dry-cleaning, and I discovered a receipt in one of the pockets for a very expensive diamond and gold ring. I was expecting to be given it for my birthday, but it never happened.'

Ellie's blood ran cold. If the ring wasn't on her bedside table, had she left it somewhere else where Sylvia might yet come across it? She must also warn Alan to be more careful.

She also felt sick at the thought of Sylvia uncovering her own duplicity. For some reason, she didn't want to disappoint this woman, whom she liked very much. And it was clear that Sylvia would also like their tenuous friendship to continue. But Ellie knew she'd have to cut off any contact with Sylvia as soon as her baby was delivered. She felt dreadful at the thought of using Sylvia, then discarding her. The poor woman was actually helping to deliver her own husband's baby!

'Is there anyone you'd like me to contact?' Sylvia asked. 'I can *easily drive into the village and use the public phone again. What about your – I mean, your child's father?'*

'He's away.'

Sylvia smiled. 'Men, eh? They're never around when you need them! My husband is away too, and I really wanted him to come with me for my check-up tomorrow.'

'Will you mind terribly if you have a second boy?' Ellie asked.

'No, not as long as the child is healthy,' Sylvia answered. 'But a girl would be nice this time.' She grinned. 'Well, you know that already, since you've seen the gorgeous pink outfit I've bought!' She looked closely at Ellie. 'What are you hoping for?'

'Like you, a healthy child.'

'And your – I mean, the father of your child – would he prefer a boy or girl?'

'Aaaagh!' Ellie groaned suddenly and gripped Sylvia's hand. She hadn't expected to be glad of a contraction, but the severity of this one prevented her from replying to any more personal questions.

'Can I get you some more cushions?' Sylvia asked, as Ellie's contraction eventually subsided. 'They might help to ease the pressure on your back.'

'Yes, please,' Ellie replied gratefully. 'You'll find some in the drawing room – just out of the door and to the right.' She suddenly froze. Ellie had just remembered that she'd taken delivery the previous day of a beautiful floral arrangement from Alan, and it was on the drawing-room table! Had she removed the card that came with the delivery? Luckily, Alan had only signed his initial, but the message had been quite racy.

Returning with several cushions, Sylvia placed them behind Ellie's back. 'I see you've got a beautiful array of flowers in there. Clearly someone cares for you very much.'

Ellie's mouth was dry, so she nodded, too nervous to say anything.

'I see your man friend has the same initial as my husband,'

Sylvia added, smiling at Ellie, whose heart was now in her mouth.

'Er, umm, yes – his name is A-A-Anthony.'

Sylvia gave her a triumphant look. 'Aha – I guessed as much! He wouldn't be called Tony for short, would he?'

Relief flooded through Ellie as she realised that Sylvia thought Tony Coleman was the man in her life! What luck that she'd picked the name Anthony. It had simply been a spur-of-the-moment choice, but it had worked out perfectly. She smiled noncommittally, hoping to create the impression that Sylvia was right.

But Sylvia's expression had now darkened. 'But surely he should be here – with you? I didn't realise that his job involved travel...'

Ellie feigned a contraction, hoping she could distract Sylvia from probing any further. She was genuinely feeling very uncomfortable, and desperately wishing that the midwife would hurry up so that Sylvia could leave.

'Do you think I could have another cup of tea?'

'Of course!'

Sylvia rushed into the kitchen and Ellie lay back on her pillows, relieved to have even a few minutes on her own, without having to continuously play a role. But it wasn't long before Sylvia was back, and this time she wore a big smile on her face.

'The phone's working again!' she told her. 'What a relief!'

Ellie nodded in agreement, until it suddenly dawned on her that this reconnected phone could cause her even more problems. What if Alan rang and Sylvia answered? They'd managed to fool Tony Coleman in the past, but it would be impossible to think up some excuse that would fool Sylvia.

As Ellie drank her tea, she found that her hands were shaking. She felt out of control and on the brink of disaster. Where the hell was the midwife?

As a series of severe contractions ripped through her, Sylvia came and sat beside her, holding her hand, rubbing her back and mopping her brow and, for a while, Ellie managed to forget the peculiar relationship that existed between them. But anger towards Alan welled up inside her. Why wasn't he here when she needed him? No doubt he was off wining and dining clients while she was struggling to bring his child into the world.

'Have you ever helped anyone to give birth before?' Ellie asked, as she tightened her grip on Sylvia's hand during a particularly strong contraction.

Sylvia shook her head.

'Well, I think you might be about to have your first experience – ' Ellie roared at the top of her voice as she felt a sudden urge to push. 'Oh God, I can't stop – '

She felt a burning sensation, followed by a feeling of total relief. Sylvia stared in astonishment at the tiny baby who had just appeared, then she galvanised herself into action. Turning the child over, she gently tapped its back. As it began screaming, she handed it to an exhausted Ellie.

'Congratulations – you have a beautiful daughter!' she said, her face a picture of wonder and delight.

It was a strangely intimate moment, and the women smiled at each other, each of them experiencing a gamut of emotions.

Instinctively, Ellie opened her blouse and held the baby girl to her breast, and she began suckling almost immediately.

'Have you chosen a name for her yet?'

'Yes, I – we – are going to call her Kerry.'

'What a lovely name!' Sylvia said enthusiastically.

Just then the midwife arrived, and the spell was broken by her cheery, no-nonsense attitude.

'Well, I can see that you two have managed perfectly well without me!' she said cheerfully, cutting the cord and checking Ellie and the baby thoroughly. 'What a fine healthy baby!' she added. Then she glanced at Sylvia's stomach. 'I can see you'll be next,'

she said, smiling. 'How nice for you two friends to be pregnant at the same time! When are you due?'

'In three months,' Sylvia replied, smiling back.

'Well, you've done a great job here today, but now it's time for you to go home and rest,' the midwife told her. 'You've had enough excitement, and I don't want another early birth on my hands!'

Sylvia looked at her watch. 'My goodness – it's almost time to collect my son from the crèche!' She took Ellie's hand in hers. 'Are you sure you're okay?' she asked earnestly. 'Is there anything else I can do for you before I go?'

Cradling her baby, Ellie shook her head. 'You've been wonderful,' she said, tears in her eyes. 'I don't know what I'd have done without your help.'

Blushing, Sylvia shook her head in rebuttal, but Ellie could see that she was pleased to have her role in Kerry's birth acknowledged.

'And the midwife's right,' Ellie added. 'After you collect your son, you need to go home and take it easy.'

'Well, if you're sure there's nothing else – '

'Thank you – for everything,' Ellie whispered fervently.

The following day, a floral arrangement of lilies and pink carnations arrived for Ellie. The card accompanying it was signed: 'Congratulations from Sylvia and Alan Thornton.'

How ironic, Ellie thought, that Sylvia should be the one to send it.

So far, there had been no word from Alan. But after the stress of the previous day, Ellie was content to nurse her daughter alone. She didn't want visitors as she bonded with her baby. She'd fulfilled her dream of having a child, and she didn't need anything more. Except Alan, of course. She longed for his arrival, and to see the joy in his eyes when he held his baby daughter in his arms. Now they were a family at last.

She thought once again of John, her late husband, wondering what he'd make of the present situation. He'd always known how much she longed for a child, so perhaps he wouldn't be too shocked by what she'd done.

As Ellie thought of Sylvia, she was aware – more than ever – of how awkward the situation would be between them now. Since she had played such an intimate and important role in Ellie and Kerry's life, it would appear churlish to cut her off without even a backward glance. Yet she had no other choice. At least she could rely on Alan to support her in keeping her distance from Sylvia.

But it made Ellie sad. More than ever now, she longed for the friendship of someone with whom she could share the milestones in her child's life, and chat about the important and the inconsequential things that were part and parcel of motherhood. Much as she loved Alan, Ellie was well aware that his eyes would glaze over if she tried to tell him about the minutiae of her daily life.

But such a friendship with Sylvia could never be. She'd sacrificed that comfort and support for Alan's love and a child of her own. And it was a price she was more than willing to pay.

CHAPTER 25

'Sea Diagnostics is having a reception next week, and we're invited,' Laura told her husband enthusiastically. 'Kerry's very excited because one of their design teams has won a contract to develop a new type of sub-sea cable. Isn't that great?'

Laura glanced at Jeff, who stared back at her impassively. He wasn't showing any enthusiasm for this very important event in her friend's life.

'Well, I'm going anyway,' Laura said, when she got no reply. 'Everyone at Sea Diagnostics is thrilled, and I want to be there to wish them well.'

'What are you planning on wearing to the reception?'

Laura smiled, pleased that Jeff was beginning to show some interest.

'I was thinking of the green dress – you know, the one with the embroidered flower detail around the neck. What do you think?'

Jeff grimaced. 'Isn't the skirt a bit short? Why don't you wear your maxi dress?'

Laura raised her eyebrows. 'Are you serious? I was going to donate that old thing to a charity shop – it's terribly drab and conservative. I don't know why I ever bought it.'

'Well, I love it,' Jeff said. 'You look very ladylike in it.'

Laura raised her eyebrows. She hadn't heard anyone use the word 'ladylike' in years. It had a distinctly sexist feel about it.

'I have no wish to look "ladylike", as you call it,' she replied sharply.

'Well, since you're my wife, and going to have my baby, I expect you to dress accordingly,' Jeff said stubbornly. 'I don't want the woman I chose to be regarded as a slut.'

'Jeff!' Laura was appalled. 'Why would anyone think that?'

'I'm a man, for Christ's sake! I know how men think! You're my wife, so I have to protect you.'

Briefly, Laura thought how ironic Jeff's comment was – right now, the only man she seemed to need protection from was him. Luckily, her cheek had almost healed by now, and all that was left was a small scar.

'Jeff, I don't need protection – and certainly not from someone's thoughts!'

'Well, there's no point in giving them the opportunity to think about you in that way,' he said sullenly. Then he brightened. 'Tell you what – why don't I buy you a new dress for the occasion! I'm free this afternoon if you are. Let's go shopping!'

Laura was pleased to see that Jeff's mood had changed for the better. Luckily, she had no lecture that afternoon, as she'd swapped with Maria who needed the following morning off. There were only end-of-term papers to correct, and they could wait.

'Okay,' she said cheerfully. 'Let's hit the town!'

The reception was in full swing when Laura and Jeff arrived.

At first Kerry didn't recognise her friend in the distance – she didn't look remotely like the Laura she knew so well. At the earliest opportunity, while Jeff was queuing at the free bar, Kerry sidelined her friend and gave her a long, hard look.

'Where on earth did you get that brown dress? It's certainly not your usual style,' she said, trying to be diplomatic.

'Don't you like it?' Laura said, disappointed. 'Jeff chose it for me.'

Kerry raised her eyebrows. 'I didn't know Jeff was interested in women's fashion.'

Laura blushed. 'Well, he wanted me to have something nice for the party tonight.'

'But you never wear anything like that.' Kerry took a deep breath. 'If I'm honest, it's downright frumpy. You usually wear much more glamorous stuff.'

Laura looked at the floor, her cheeks red. 'Well, Jeff doesn't like me to look too sexy – he says that other men will think I'm cheap. He doesn't want his wife being looked at in that way.' It was clear that she wasn't overjoyed about the situation either.

Kerry said nothing. Jeff was clearly a control freak.

As Jeff rejoined the two women, carrying two glasses of wine, Kerry gave him a cursory wave and then hurried off to greet some new arrivals.

'What did *she* want?' Jeff muttered, staring sourly after her retreating back as he handed his wife a glass of wine.

Laura sighed. It was unlikely that her husband would ever warm to her best friend.

'She wanted to make sure that we were enjoying the reception,' she said evenly.

As they stood among the throng of guests, Laura was trying her best to look happy. But it was proving impossible, because Jeff was now criticising everyone's clothing, the food being served and the product being launched, although he knew absolutely nothing about sub-sea technology. Laura felt on edge in case anyone overheard the remarks he was making.

Jeff took a sip from his glass and made a face. 'God, I hate this cheap stuff – I'm going to the bar outside to get us a proper drink,' he muttered, dumping his glass of wine on a side table and walking off.

Laura said nothing. Although she'd never admit it to anyone else, she was glad to have a few minutes alone without Jeff's snide comments about everyone else at the reception. She wished she'd been able to come alone, but Jeff had insisted on accompanying her. It was tiresome having to reassure him all the time that she wasn't looking for opportunities to be unfaithful. She genuinely loved him, but he seemed to have great difficulty in believing her.

As she stood, deep in thought, Norma, one of Kerry's colleagues, appeared with a pleasant-looking man in tow.

'Hello, Laura. I hope you're enjoying the evening?'

'Yes, it's great!' Laura replied enthusiastically. 'Thanks for inviting us – we're having a wonderful time!' If only that were true, she thought sadly, thinking of Jeff's permanently miserable frown. 'And congratulations to you all,' she added. 'We're thrilled about your success!'

'Thanks,' Norma replied. 'But since there are so many industry people here tonight, I thought you might be finding it a bit boring. Paul here is a trauma counsellor, and you're a lecturer in sociology, so I figured you two would be bound to have something in common.'

'Hello, Paul.' Smiling, Laura extended her hand, and Paul smiled back as they shook hands.

'Well, I'll leave you two talking,' Norma said, smiling. 'I see someone arriving whom I've just *got* to talk to.'

Rushing off, she left them smiling at each other.

'Your job sounds rather intriguing,' Laura added, more out of politeness than interest.

'Well, that's one way of putting it, I suppose!' Paul said. 'But dealing with people's tragedies can be quite draining.'

Laura tried to look interested. But she was edgy, and concerned about Jeff's bad mood. Somehow, he always managed to ruin social gatherings. And she was worried that he'd see her chatting with another man. That would be a sufficient cause for the outbreak of World War Three.

'Is yours a nine to five job?'

Paul shook his head. 'Unfortunately not. I work with problem families – and a lot of domestic violence takes place after hours, primarily fuelled by alcohol. If someone is injured, I may need to liase with police and the courts.'

Laura suddenly perked up. 'You deal with families where there's a history of violence?'

Paul nodded.

Laura quickly glanced around. There was still no sign of Jeff. 'Paul, could I ask your advice – on behalf of a friend of mine?' she asked nervously.

Paul nodded. 'Of course. What do you want to know?'

Laura took a deep breath. 'This friend is married to a guy who hits her. Her husband says he loves her – and she loves him – but she doesn't know how she can get him to stop.'

Paul grimaced. 'I'm afraid she's the last person who can stop it,' he replied. 'A violent man usually comes from a violent family. He doesn't know how to love any other way – his only experience of love has been from people who've been violent to him. Love and violence are inextricably linked in his mind – he can't separate intimacy from abuse.'

Laura's hands were now shaking. 'Is he genuinely capable of loving anyone?'

Paul nodded. 'Oh, yes – even men who dominate their wives and girlfriends are very emotionally dependent on them. They hit them because they've been taught that controlling the people they love is the best way to ensure that they themselves won't get hurt.'

Laura hesitated. 'Can they change?'

Shaking his head, Paul gave her a cynical smile. 'Empty promises tend to be the stock-in-trade of violent men. They swear they'll change, but it rarely happens because they must actually *want* to change. And mostly they don't.' He looked directly at her. 'Anyway, treatment usually requires years of therapy – too long for your friend to risk sticking around. Violence begets violence, so the next generation become victims too.'

Laura shuddered. It all seemed so bleak.

'Does your friend have any children?'

Laura shook her head, guiltily touching her belly at the same time.

'Good. Now's the time for her to break the link.'

Laura shivered. 'It seems awful to condemn someone like that…Even murderers can experience remorse, so why do you say these people can't?'

Paul gave a sad smile. 'People who are abusive have a remarkable sense of entitlement – they need to be gratified straight away, so they yell, scream, hit, slap and punch, and blame other people for the way they are. They carry a lot of pain inside, but it never excuses what they do to their victims.'

Laura bit her lip. Based on Paul's description, Jeff had all the characteristics of a classic case.

Paul looked directly at her, and Laura suspected that he was well aware that she was the one dealing with a violent partner. His eyes seemed to be boring into the small scar that was still visible on her face. 'I presume your friend's husband hasn't shown any inclination to change?'

'Well, er, sometimes he apologises after he hits m – her…'

Paul smiled sympathetically. 'Tell your friend to get out.'

'But I – she – loves him!'

'And he may love her too. But that's not a good enough reason for her to risk her life. These situations invariably get worse over time.'

In the distance, Laura could see Jeff making his way back through the throng of guests. 'Paul, it's been nice talking to you. But if you'll excuse me – '

'Of course.' He patted her arm just before he left. 'I wish your friend good luck – and I hope she makes the right decision.'

As Paul moved away to join another group, Laura was left reeling as she walked in Jeff's direction. Risk her life? Surely that suggestion was a bit over the top? She shivered. On the other hand, hadn't Jeff also said that he'd 'kill her too'?

Just then, Jeff arrived at her side with their drinks.

'Who was that?' he asked, studying Paul's retreating back.

'Oh, just someone Norma introduced me to.'

'But I saw him touching your arm before he left. Why was he doing that?'

Laura shifted uncomfortably. 'I don't know – maybe he was just one of those touchy-feely guys.'

'What were you talking about?'

'I don't really remember – the weather, I think?'

'Well, it looked a lot more intimate than that!' said Jeff angrily. 'Anyway, I don't know why you needed to talk to him – you're supposed to be talking to me!'

'Jeff, stop being ridiculous!' Laura hissed. 'You weren't here!'

'I was getting you a glass of decent wine, in case you hadn't noticed!' he retorted.

'Well, you can hardly expect me to ignore someone I've been introduced to! That would be intolerably rude. People go to parties and receptions to chat to other guests as well, you know. Otherwise we might as well have stayed at home.'

Jeff was sullen, and Laura felt a wave of sorrow for him. He was so terribly insecure. Maybe, when he felt more confident about her love, he'd stop this silly behaviour. She particularly remembered Paul's comment that there was a lot of pain in people like Jeff, and she longed to be the one who would help him to leave his troublesome past behind. Perhaps when he became a father, he'd feel more confident.

But Paul's other words were still ringing in her ears. Surely it couldn't be true that people like Jeff were unable to change – weren't there exceptions to every rule?

Smiling, she tucked her arm into her husband's. 'Jeff, you're the only one I want to be with.'

'Then let's go home. This place is boring.'

Laura bit her lip. She didn't really want to go, but the evening had lost its magic by now anyway. And somehow she didn't even feel like herself in the awful dress that Jeff had insisted on buying.

'Okay,' she said dully.

But Jeff wasn't even listening any more. Already, he'd disengaged his arm from hers and was striding towards the exit.

Abandoning her drink, she followed him out of the door.

Later that night, Jeff was vigorous and demanding in bed, and seemed interested only in his own pleasure. He didn't seem to care that he was hurting her – in fact, Laura's cries of discomfort seemed to add to his enjoyment and drive him into a greater frenzy. Perhaps he was angry with her for talking to another man at the party. Or maybe he just hated having to attend the party in the first place. Whatever it was, Laura was left feeling particularly sore and violated.

When he fell asleep afterwards, she lay awake clutching her stomach in discomfort and feeling very worried. Something didn't feel right. Creeping to the bathroom, she noticed several spots of blood on her nightdress.

Climbing back into bed, Laura lay quietly beside her husband, studying Jeff's face as he slept. Never had she felt so alone. Right from the beginning of their relationship, her husband had seemed to enjoy rough sex in which he subdued her. At first it had been exciting – a sign that he loved and needed her – but, as time went by, she realised that he didn't even seem to be present when they made love. He was in a fury of passion that had nothing to do with her. It was as though he saw her simply as a means to his own release, not a person in her own right or an equal participant in the act of lovemaking. He seemed to be in some other place from which she couldn't bring him back.

She longed to reach out and soothe him, but she didn't dare. Jeff's insecurities were becoming impossible to handle.

CHAPTER 26

The following morning, Laura didn't feel well, but she got up nonetheless and went through the motions of getting ready for work. She felt a dragging sensation in the pit of her stomach, but she didn't want Jeff to start fussing, so she said nothing. Instead, she made toast and coffee for them both, and chatted as pleasantly as she could manage while they had breakfast together. Then, with a brief, absent-minded grunt, Jeff gathered his keys and briefcase and headed out of the door.

As soon as she was certain that he'd gone, Laura sank down gratefully onto the couch. She didn't think she could go to work today, although she'd agreed to take Maria's lecture as well as her own. But the dragging sensation had turned into severe pain. Gripping her middle, Laura rocked from side to side, hoping that the pain might ease if only she could distract herself. She longed to take a painkiller, but she didn't dare in case it would have a detrimental effect on the baby. Maybe if she tried to read...Grabbing the previous day's newspaper from the coffee table, Laura tried to focus her mind on the headlines. But she felt light-headed, the print seeming to dance before her eyes. And the pain wasn't easing. If anything, it was getting worse.

Now she was really beginning to worry.

Reaching for her phone, Laura called Darren, explaining apologetically that she wasn't well enough to come in that day, but that she was due to give Maria's morning lecture in addition to her own. Perversely, she wanted Darren to bite her head off, but as usual he was kind and concerned, urging her to take as long as she needed to get well. There was no problem, he assured her. He'd give both lectures himself, and ask Maria to take over her other lectures until she felt well enough to return to the university.

Laura had tears in her eyes when she came off the phone. He was such a sweet, kind man. Why on earth couldn't Jeff be a bit more like Darren?

A little while later, as severe pains began ripping through her abdomen, Laura grabbed her mobile phone and rang Kerry. She hated imposing on her friend and taking her away from her job, but there was no one else she would trust to help her. Right then, she needed Kerry's calm authority to help her get through whatever was happening to her.

When Laura heard Kerry's voice over the intercom, she could barely struggle to her feet to press the entry button, and by the time her friend reached the apartment, she'd collapsed onto the sofa again.

'Christ, you look awful!' Kerry whispered, as she hugged her friend. 'What can I do for you? Shall I make you a cuppa?'

Laura nodded, glad for some semblance of normality in her life, since right now everything else felt totally alien. As she listened to the familiar sounds of tea-making coming from the kitchen, she was grateful for Kerry's presence. Maybe the tea would help to ease the terrible cramps, which seemed to be getting worse.

When Kerry returned from the kitchen with two mugs of tea, a sudden look of dismay crossed her face as she placed them on the coffee table.

'Laura, you're bleeding!'

As Laura leaned forward to look, Kerry urged her to lie down again, and rushed off to the bathroom to get some towels.

'Listen, love, I think we'd better call an ambulance,' Kerry said, as she slid several towels under her friend.

Laura could detect the panic in her friend's voice, although she was trying to hide it. 'Do you think I'm having a miscarriage?' she whispered, pleading for a negative answer. But in her heart she already knew.

'I-I don't know, but something's definitely not right,' Kerry said, as she dialled the emergency number. 'You need professionals who'll know what to do.'

Giving all the relevant details to the dispatcher, Kerry disconnected the call and sat down again beside Laura on the couch.

'It won't be long now, love – the paramedics will be here in a few minutes,' she said reassuringly.

But Laura already suspected that it was too late the save the baby. A tear rolled silently down her cheek.

'Would you mind getting me a wet cloth from the kitchen?' Laura asked anxiously. 'I need to get the blood out of the sofa and the carpet – '

Kerry looked at her incredulously. 'Stop worrying about the damned furnishings, Laura! I'll do my best to clean it up once the paramedics have taken you to hospital. Do you want me to call Jeff?'

Laura shook her head. 'Let's see what the medical people say first. There's no point in bothering him until we know what the verdict is.'

'But he'd want to be with you.'

Laura looked at her unflinchingly. 'Well, I don't want him there. He'd only fuss. Besides, he doesn't like me to ring him during the day.'

Kerry raised an eyebrow. 'Well, I think, under the circumstances, he'd expect you to call.'

'Too bad,' Laura snapped. She was beginning to feel angry with Jeff, feeling certain that his violent sex the previous night had been a contributory factor in this already fragile pregnancy.

Kerry said nothing, aware that this was the first time since her marriage that Laura had openly acknowledged that her husband might be less than perfect. It seemed that she was becoming a bit more realistic about Jeff.

The intercom rang, and Kerry leaped to her feet.

'That'll be the paramedics,' she announced, her voice suffused with relief.

As Laura lay resting in her private hospital room, the door burst open and Jeff was suddenly at her bedside.

'Why didn't you phone me?' he screamed, furious. 'Why the hell did you ring that so-called friend of yours? It was *my* baby you were having! I should have been there!'

Laura closed her eyes. She was too tired for arguments. In fact, she was too tired for anything. After the trauma of her miscarriage, she just wanted to go to sleep.

'Jeff, please – I'm not in the mood for an argument,' she said quietly. 'There are times when only another woman can understand what you're going through, that's all. Please don't take everything so personally.'

A tear slid down Laura's cheek as he sat down in the chair beside her bed. Jeff hadn't even asked how she was feeling. All he could think of was his own loss. Well, she was devastated too. According to the doctors, there was no specific reason why she'd lost the baby, and they felt certain she'd carry any future baby to term. So that was good news really, although right then she just felt bereft and alone. She wished Jeff would put his arms around her and ask how she was coping. She wished they could share their pain with each other, and support each other through it. But instead it felt as though Jeff saw her as his enemy rather than his ally. She wondered if his aggressiveness was due to guilt – perhaps he, too, was remembering his vigorous sexual activity the night before.

Laura's eyes filled with tears. 'They told me it was a little girl,' she said softly.

Jeff said nothing, but Laura could see that he was making a supreme effort to control his temper. He was too clever to lose it in the hospital.

'When are you coming home?'

Laura shook her head. 'I don't know yet – the doctor will be around later, and she'll give me her verdict then.'

Jeff nodded, rising to his feet. 'Well, phone me on my mobile when you find out,' he said curtly, before leaving the room.

Alone in her bed, Laura could feel the tears coming, and she angrily brushed them away. It was as though Jeff was punishing her for losing the baby. He hadn't even brought her flowers – then again, flowers were for celebrations, and they had nothing to celebrate. Suddenly, she couldn't stop the tears any longer, and they poured down her face as she sobbed bitterly. Since the very beginning of her pregnancy, she'd loved the baby she was carrying inside her. She'd dreamed of holding it in her arms – now, she'd never have a chance to tell it how much she had cared.

CHAPTER 27

*A*s Alan left the airport and hailed a taxi to take him home, he felt hugely relieved that the business week was over. He'd finally managed to get the contract with a new tin supplier signed, and on very favourable terms, too. But he was tired from all the negotiations. He'd had to bluster and make endless objections to their initial proposals before eventually hammering out a very satisfactory deal – one that augured well for the future of the factory.

In the back of the taxi, he patted his briefcase, where he'd stored his gifts for Sylvia, Pete and Ellie. He'd also managed to pick up a very expensive Lladró figurine at a knockdown price, and he was feeling very pleased with himself. He'd been collecting Lladró for many years, and always enjoyed adding new pieces when he had the time to browse.

He yawned, wondering how Sylvia and Pete were. And Ellie – he was longing to see her, too. If anyone could make him forget how tired he was, it was she. He felt himself hardening at the very thought of her. Even though she was close to giving birth, and her bump made it awkward to get close, they still made love at every opportunity. He adored that woman, and he was looking forward to being there to support her during the birth of their child.

'Hello, darling. Did you have a good trip?'

Alan nodded as he kissed Sylvia's cheek. 'Yes, everything went *well. I eventually got the deal I wanted, but it was hard work getting there!'*

Pete appeared from the playroom, and ran into his father's arms.

'Hello, little man!' Alan said affectionately.

'Toy for me, Daddy?'

Alan grinned, producing a package from his briefcase. Despite Pete's tender years, he already understood all about presents! As the child ripped the gift-wrap from the plastic fire engine his father had brought him, Alan presented Sylvia with a pair of diamond earrings. Thanking him, she slipped them on, but he could see she was bursting to tell him something.

'What is it, Syl?'

Sylvia looked at him, her eyes shining mischievously. 'You're not going to believe what I did this week – '

Alan nodded, encouraging her to go on.

'I helped Ellie Beckworth to give birth!'

Alan could feel his heart almost coming to a standstill; yet on some level, he was conscious that outwardly he had to appear calm and in control.

As he stood silently, unable to speak, Sylvia assumed he needed reminding about whom she was talking about.

'She's that nice woman who lives half a mile away at Treetops, and runs a tutoring business from home – she used to work at the factory?'

Alan nodded slowly, needing to call on all his reserves of control. 'Oh, yes, I remember now,' he said at last. 'She worked in the laboratory, I think.' He took a deep breath, not sure how the play the situation. 'She's had a baby, you say?'

Sylvia laughed. 'Oh, Alan dear, you're so unobservant! You must have seen her around – she was very big towards the end! When women carry all to the front, it usually means they're going to have a girl. Well, now she has a beautiful little daughter – and I helped her deliver it!'

'So, you've taken up a new career as a midwife,' Alan said lightly. 'How did that come about?'

Keeping a tight rein on his facial expression, he listened as Sylvia talked, her eyes alight as she explained what had happened. All Alan could think of was how close he and Ellie had come to disaster, but it was obvious that Sylvia hadn't suspected a thing. Nevertheless, his two separate lives had come too alarmingly close for comfort.

'Well, since you seem to know so much about these things, do you think we're having a boy or girl?' he asked, eyeing Sylvia's bump and hoping to move the discussion away from Ellie.

Sylvia looked at him coyly. 'Well, what do you think? I'm getting rather large in the front, aren't I? So I'm betting on a girl.'

Alan took her in his arms and hugged her, so that she wouldn't see his expression. He was afraid his excitement might be showing. He had a daughter! He was longing to see Ellie and this new child of his.

'Well, I'll be happy with either a boy or a girl,' he told her, wondering how soon he could slip away to visit his secret wife.

At Treetops, Ellie was waiting eagerly for Alan's visit. He'd phoned briefly while Sylvia was feeding Pete in the kitchen, and had promised to call later that evening. As soon as she saw his car coming up the driveway, she had the door open and was waiting for him to step inside.

'Come and meet your daughter!' she said proudly.

'You're wonderful!' he whispered, kissing her hair as he held her close. 'I'm so sorry I wasn't here for you when you gave birth.'

'Don't worry – your wife was,' Ellie said, giving him a cynical smile. 'I presume she's told you all about it?'

Alan nodded, stepping into the living room, and Ellie proudly led him over to the cradle in the corner where young Kerry was sleeping.

'She's beautiful!' Alan whispered, gazing in awe at the tiny baby sleeping peacefully. 'But I wish you hadn't had to go through all this without me. How did it happen?'

Ellie explained about her early labour, the disconnected phone line and how his wife had stopped to help. Now that the stress of Sylvia's involvement was over, she was able to laugh about her initial fears. 'I never expected to have your wife in my home,' Ellie told him, smiling. 'There wasn't time to hide anything incriminating, so I was terrified she'd spot something belonging to you!'

Alan shuddered. Just thinking about what could have happened gave him palpitations.

'But I'm also deeply grateful to her,' Ellie added humbly. 'Without her, I don't know what would have happened. She may well have saved our baby's life.'

Smiling, they slipped into each other's arms. Their relationship was different now, and they both acknowledged it. They were a family, albeit a family that couldn't proclaim itself in public.

Ellie then told him about the flowers and how, on the spur of the moment, she'd used the name Anthony to explain away his initial on the accompanying card: 'I hope Sylvia doesn't snub Tony Coleman, because I managed to give the impression that he might be the father,' she said. 'It made Sylvia very annoyed on my behalf – she thought Tony should have been present at the birth.'

Alan chuckled. 'Luckily, Sylvia is too polite to behave badly in public, so I don't think we need worry on that score.' Then he suddenly remembered the gift he'd bought for her, and produced a package from his pocket. 'Thank you for my adorable baby daughter,' he whispered, as she unwrapped a magnificent diamond pendant. In the glow of the light overhead it sparkled as Ellie lifted it out of its box.

'It's beautiful!' she told him, turning her back to him and urging him to fasten it around her neck.

'No, you're the one who's beautiful!' he whispered, nuzzling her neck as he fixed the clasp. She felt the quickening of desire, and knew he was feeling it too.

Suddenly, the peace was broken by the sound of crying from the cradle. 'It's feeding time!' Ellie announced, smiling. 'Kerry and I have already established a routine – every three hours she wakes up hungry, she feeds for fifteen minutes, then goes off to sleep again.'

As Ellie lifted the baby out of the cradle, and brought her back to the sofa to breastfeed, Alan couldn't help eyeing Ellie's beautiful breasts, now bare and tantalisingly full of milk, as his tiny daughter began suckling contentedly. He marvelled at Ellie's beauty.

Ellie smiled, knowing exactly what he was thinking. She always knew when Alan was ready to make love. Which was nearly always. They could never get enough of each other, and giving birth hadn't changed those feelings one iota. If anything, she wanted him even more now.

When the baby eventually fell asleep, Ellie gently extricated her and laid her back in her cradle. When she approached Alan, making no attempt to cover her breasts, she could see his erection straining through his trousers.

His expression was a mixture of tenderness and excitement as she stood provocatively before him.

'Ellie, I'm not sure if you realise what you're doing – '

But her wanton expression told him that she knew exactly what effect she was having on him.

'Please, Ellie, don't make me want you so much – '

As she kissed him, Alan groaned.

'Stop, Ellie – '

But she didn't stop, and her hands became even more adventurous.

'Isn't it too early?' he whispered. 'I mean, I'm longing to make love to you again, but are you sure you're ready?'

She could feel his erection pressing against her.

'I'm sure,' she whispered, taking his hand and leading him upstairs.

CHAPTER 28

When Jeff collected Laura from the hospital a few days later, they drove home in silence. Already, Laura had a headache from the sheer dread she felt at being alone with her husband. The silence in the car was oppressive, the atmosphere loaded with tension. She darted a glance at Jeff's profile, and could see that his lips were tightly pressed together and he was frowning – a sure sign that there would be hell to pay when they got home.

Then her anger reasserted itself. She hadn't done anything to provoke his ire! She hadn't lost the baby deliberately. If anything, Jeff should be consoling her and showing her some kindness. Losing the baby had been a horrible and devastating experience, and her husband should be capable of understanding that.

When they reached the apartment, Laura fully expected Jeff to come round and open the passenger door for her, given that she was still a little unsteady on her feet. But Jeff remained in the driver's seat.

'You'd better get out,' he told her. 'I'm putting the car in the lock-up.'

Biting her lip, Laura gingerly alighted from the car. This wasn't the homecoming she'd been hoping for, although perhaps it was the one she should have expected.

Alone, she let herself into the silent apartment. Instantly, she longed to be back in the hospital, where the medical and nursing staff had been kind and caring.

When Jeff entered the apartment a few minutes later, Laura heard him cursing as he threw down his keys on the hall table. He was clearly in a temper. She felt too tired to cope with his mood, and hoped he'd either go back to work or go into the TV room and just leave her alone.

As she lay on the couch in the living room, Laura longed for a cup of tea. But she didn't dare ask Jeff, and she didn't feel well enough to make it herself.

To her relief, he disappeared into the TV room, but before long she heard the sound of things being thrown about. When she heard something large hitting the wall, she feared it was the TV set – or could it be her computer?

Struggling to get to her feet, Laura called out. 'Jeff – what's wrong? Do you want to talk about it?'

The door of the TV room was suddenly thrown back on its hinges. As Jeff strode over to the couch, his face was like thunder, she sat down again. 'Talk about it? Of course I want to talk about it! I was trying to restrain myself, but if you want me to talk, I'll talk!' He stared down at her, rage and contempt in his eyes. 'You stupid bitch, you couldn't even manage to hold a child in your belly! Other women manage it, so why can't you? What sort of woman are you, anyway? And not only that – you had to carry a female child when you know I want sons!'

Laura was shocked by the venom in Jeff's voice, and by his totally irrational views. She felt weak and very tired, and all she wanted to do was sleep.

'Can we save this discussion until I'm feeling better?' she whispered.

'No, we can't! Anyway, you're the one who suggested we talk about it! So what the hell *is* wrong with you?' Jeff shouted, standing over her. 'Did the doctors say why it happened?'

Laura was annoyed now. 'Why do you assume it's *my* fault? The doctor said that these things happen sometimes – if there's something wrong with the foetus, nature decides to get rid of it, so it's for the best in the long run.'

She was tempted to suggest that his recent violent sexual behaviour might have been a contributory factor, but the look on his face made her quickly change her mind.

Jeff's eyes narrowed. 'I hope you're not implying that my genes are faulty – '

'No, of course not – '

The blow caught her across the side of her head, and suddenly she was seeing stars. What had just happened? Laura found herself on the floor from the impact of the blow, and when she put her hand to her mouth, blood came away on it. She felt something gritty inside her mouth, and realised that part of a tooth had broken off. Her head and her mouth were throbbing, and she realised that Jeff had hit her. Again.

As he stormed out of the room, Laura continued to lie on the floor, in pain and disbelief. She felt too lethargic to get up. Her insides hurt, and she wondered vaguely if she'd started bleeding again. The doctor had told her to rest for the next week, and to allow her husband to pamper her. Laura felt tears forming – the doctor couldn't possibly imagine the kind of relationship she really had.

She must have passed out, because suddenly she opened her eyes to find Jeff smiling down at her tentatively, a mug of tea in one hand, a wad of tissues in the other.

'I'm sorry, love,' he whispered, placing the mug on a small table beside her, and helping her up off the floor. Gently guiding her back onto the couch, he began dabbing her bleeding mouth with the tissues. 'I don't know what came over me – I suppose I was just so disappointed. But we'll try again, won't we, love? And you'll give me a son next time, won't you?' He gave her a wheedling smile. 'Isn't there a test that can tell what sex it is early on in the pregnancy?'

Laura wished that a giant hole would open up in front of her and that Jeff would disappear into it. Right now, she didn't want to be anywhere near him. Because she knew that it wouldn't take much for his violence to flare up again.

'Of course we'll try again,' Laura lied, 'but I need time to recover before then. The doctor said I must heal before I can become pregnant again.'

In truth, she had no intention of ever making love to this man again, if indeed her experiences with him could be called lovemaking – their sex life had always been on his terms. She had just made up her mind to leave him, but she didn't dare tell him, because she knew what the consequences would be.

Although her lip and tongue were hurting badly, Laura took the proffered mug and downed the contents, enduring the pain rather than risk displeasing him.

By now, Jeff was kneeling down in front of the couch, weeping and begging her to forgive him. 'It's just that I felt so disappointed,' he sobbed. 'But I shouldn't have taken it out on you, love. I'm so sorry.'

Laura said nothing. Everything felt weird and out of synch. It was like living in a real-life Punch and Judy show, where she was in favour one minute and out the next, and there was no rhyme or reason as to why she was being punished.

'Do you want to tell me what else the doctor said?' Jeff asked, gently lacing his fingers through hers.

Laura shook her head. The last thing on earth she wanted was to discuss her miscarriage with Jeff. Or anything else, for that matter. 'Not now, if you don't mind,' she said dully. 'I'm feeling very tired – '

Suddenly, Jeff's mood reverted to anger again. 'But I'll bet you've discussed it all with your so-called friend!'

Laura sighed, no longer caring how he reacted, because as far as she was concerned, her marriage was now over. 'If you're referring to Kerry, yes, of course I talked to her about the pregnancy – and since she came to the hospital later, naturally she knew that I'd lost the baby.'

'You mean, *we* lost the baby! And how dare you discuss our relationship with that – that – *creature*!' He glared at her. 'I suppose you've told her about our arguments, too?'

Laura grimaced, aware that yet again Jeff was refusing to accept responsibility for anything he'd done. 'Arguments' implied equality between the participants, whereas Jeff was always the angry one, and the perpetrator of the violence that inevitably followed.

'Yes, Kerry did notice the bruises, and asked me about them.'

Jeff snorted. 'How dare you tittle-tattle to someone else! It demeans our relationship! That's what my mother used to do – she'd run to the neighbours, humiliating Dad in his own street!'

Despite her injuries, Laura no longer felt afraid of expressing her own anger. 'But your father hurt her! She needed to get help!'

'My mother deserved it,' Jeff said, his voice dangerously low, before leaving the room, slamming the door after him.

Shortly afterwards, Laura heard the door of the apartment slam, and she was relieved that he'd gone before his anger boiled over again. But she wasn't going to be his victim any longer – otherwise, she might end up dead, just like his mother.

At last she was facing the unpalatable truth. She wasn't free to say anything she wanted, or have an opinion that was contrary to his. Everything she said had to be passed through a filter in her brain, in order to ensure that it wouldn't offend him and result in her being battered.

Kerry and Paul the counsellor were right – it was time to get out. She'd tried to be the woman Jeff wanted – she'd done her best to restore his faith in human nature by being there for him, through thick and thin. But defending his father's violence didn't augur well for their future together. And if she had children with Jeff, she'd still be trapped, because even if she left him, the courts would award him visitation rights, and she'd never be free of him. Now was the time to go, before another pregnancy linked them together for ever.

Mopping her bleeding lip, Laura picked up her phone and made her way to the bathroom, locking the door behind her in case Jeff should return.

Kerry answered immediately, listening as Laura told her that she was leaving Jeff.

'I feel guilty about going – I vowed to stay through sickness and health, and now I'm abandoning him, and leaving him to his demons!' Laura whispered, a tremor in her voice.

'Forget about Jeff, and get out this very minute!' Kerry urged her. 'Shall I come over and help you pack?'

'No – I don't want to risk another confrontation,' Laura whispered. She could imagine Jeff's fury when he found out she'd left him. He'd see it as a massive betrayal, and he'd never forgive her. 'Besides, I have a better idea,' she added.

Laura explained to her friend what she intended to do, and Kerry reluctantly agreed.

'I'll make up your bed in the second bedroom,' she replied. 'And I'll be over first thing tomorrow morning – after Jeff's gone for the day – to put the first stage of your plan into operation.'

'Thanks, love,' Laura whispered, tears in her eyes. As always, her dear friend was there for her when she needed support.

CHAPTER 29

'You sneaky bitch!' Jeff hollered down the phone. 'You moved your clothes out bit by bit, so that I wouldn't notice! You planned this whole thing with that so-called friend of yours!'

'I'm sorry, Jeff, but there was no other way,' Laura said, gripping her mobile phone tightly. 'If I'd told you face to face that I was leaving, you'd have tried to stop me.'

'Damn right I would've!'

Laura felt brave enough to state her case now that she was in the safety of Kerry's apartment.

'I can't live in fear all the time. I really did love you, but I couldn't keep letting you hit me. You need to get help.'

There was a pause at the other end of the line. 'Will you come back to me if I get help?'

Laura sighed. 'No, Jeff – I'm sorry. You've made me so afraid that all the love I had for you got pushed out of the way.'

She could hear him crying in the background, and her own eyes filled with tears. It would be tempting to run back to him and try to soothe his pain, but it would never work.

'I love you, Laura – more than I've ever loved anyone. I'm so sorry for what I've done to you – I'll get help immediately. But please come back to me.'

Laura wiped away a tear. She could hear the anguish in his voice. She could picture the little boy, terrified of his parents' wrath, but who had nevertheless absorbed their violent way of dealing with problems.

'Sorry, Jeff – I can't. I wish things didn't have to end this way, but I don't want to be scared any more.'

She heard a sob at the other end of the phone.

'Please, Laura – give me another chance.'

He sounded so contrite and, momentarily, Laura caught a glimpse of the old Jeff, the man who'd been charming, tender and affectionate when they first met. He'd been so anxious for things to go right, and she'd needed to assure him that she genuinely liked his company and wasn't going to drop him. But as soon as they got married, the boot was suddenly on the other foot, and she'd learnt how quickly he could switch from being nice to being nasty.

'No, Jeff – it's over,' she said firmly. 'I can't risk anything else happening to me. We haven't even been married a full year yet – what state would I be in if I stayed with you for another year? Accept it, Jeff. It's over.'

CHAPTER 30

*S*ylvia sighed as she bent to pick up the trail of toys that Pete had left in his wake. He was now having his afternoon nap, and she intended dozing in a comfortable chair while she had the chance. She could be sure of an hour before he was likely to wake up again.

After placing the toys in the toy box, Sylvia eased herself into one of the club chairs in the living room. She felt large and cumbersome, and even the slightest exertion winded her. But she was coming to the end of her pregnancy, and for that she was grateful. Soon, the tiredness and the bloated ankles would hopefully be a thing of the past.

In the silence of the room, Sylvia tried to relax, hoping that the birth would be quick and hassle-free this time. Pete's birth had been difficult, and her doctor had already warned her that she might need a Caesarean section. She patted her bump. As far as she was concerned, it was definitely a girl, because this pregnancy felt decidedly different from her last, and she was carrying all her extra weight to the front. Hadn't she made that very comment to Alan, about Ellie Beckworth?

As her thoughts turned once again to the enigmatic woman who lived only half a mile away, Sylvia shook her head in mystification. She'd hoped that by helping Ellie to give birth, she might manage to forge a bond with the other woman. Afterwards, she'd hoped that an invitation to tea might be forthcoming, or even a *phone call to suggest they meet for a cuppa in a local café. But Ellie had retreated into her shell again, and Sylvia was left feeling that she herself was somehow to blame.*

As she lay back in the chair, Sylvia reviewed her behaviour while in Ellie's house, concluding yet again that she hadn't done anything to warrant being dismissed so summarily. The only conclusion she could reach was that Ellie Beckworth was simply a very private person, and didn't need or want friends.

Sylvia sighed as she contemplated her final visit to the obstetrician the following day, when decisions would be made about the type of birth she would have. She wished she had a friend to accompany her, because Alan was taking the afternoon off to mind Pete. It would have been nice to have Ellie there, reassuring her that all would be well. Alan did his best to be supportive, but a man couldn't possibly empathise in the way that another woman could.

A wail from the nursery broke the peace of the afternoon, and Sylvia struggled to her feet. Pete had woken much earlier than usual. She wondered if somehow he was aware that changes in their family dynamic were imminent, because the more she longed to rest, the more he seemed to demand her undivided attention.

In the nursery, Pete was standing at the bars of his cot, his face red on one side from sleeping, his curls matted with sweat. His mouth was open in the rictus of a scream, and Sylvia tried to comfort him as she lifted him out of his cot. His nappy was wet and he seemed to weigh a ton, and Sylvia wished she'd accepted Alan's offer of a live-in nurse during the latter stages of her pregnancy. But she'd been determined to be independent, hoping it might cast her in a more favourable light with her husband. Since she looked so ungainly and always felt tired, there was no other way she could hope to compete with the mystery lover whom she still feared that Alan had taken. She continued to hope that the news of her pregnancy might have dispatched the other woman, but she had no way of knowing if her rival was even aware of it.

As she placed Pete on the changing mat, Sylvia gave a start. Had she just had a contraction? She wasn't due for another week! As Pete continued to cry, Sylvia felt her patience snapping, and she experienced what definitely felt like another contraction as she removed the child's soiled nappy. She felt a moment of panic – she was alone with a crying baby, and feeling as though she'd definitely started labour.

After putting a clean nappy on him, Sylvia placed her screaming son back in his cot, despite his very loud protests.

Hurrying into the hall, Sylvia lifted the phone and dialled the factory.

'Alan,' she told him peremptorily, 'you'd better come home. My labour has definitely started.'

When Alan arrived at Treetops the following afternoon, he tried to hide his elation, but Ellie could see how secretly thrilled he was. 'Sylvia had a seven-pound baby girl by Caesarean section,' he told her, trying to sound unconcerned out of respect for Ellie's feelings, but he was finding it impossible to stop smiling.

'So I heard – congratulations,' Ellie replied, trying to keep the note of sourness out of her voice. The birth was already being talked about in the village. She'd been told all about it that morning, by a woman whose husband worked at the factory.

Alan sighed. He knew how jealous and hurt Ellie was feeling about his other life, and he was anxious to keep her as content and even-tempered as possible.

Ellie looked at him defiantly, daring him to show any sympathy for Sylvia. She felt decidedly jealous of this new child – the one born on the right side of the blanket – who was now heralded with gifts and welcomed into the community at large. The workers at

*the factory had already made a collection and bought a gigantic
teddy bear for the little girl. Needless to say, there had been no
such gifts after the birth of her own daughter.*

'*What are you going to call her?*'

*Alan hesitated, not wanting to seem too excited and involved
with this new child of his.* '*Sylvia wants to call her Laura.*'

Ellie nodded. '*That's a nice name,*' *she said stiffly.* '*I think I
should send Sylvia some flowers – after all, she sent me a bouquet
when Kerry was born.*'

*Alan nodded. He supposed Ellie had no other choice. He knew
Sylvia would be pleased to receive them – he just hoped she
wouldn't see them as an opportunity to reconnect with Ellie.*

'*Wouldn't you like to see your eldest daughter?*' *Ellie said tartly, reminding him that he already had a female child.*

'*Of course! That's one of the reasons I'm here,*' *Alan replied,
chastened. He was well aware that Ellie's nose was out of joint,
and that he needed to appease her.*

*In the living room, young Kerry was sleeping in her cradle.
Alan caressed her cheek as she slept, then bent down to kiss her,
aware that Ellie was watching his every move. He felt as though
he was on a tightrope, caught between the two women in his life.
One wrong move and he could plummet to unimaginable depths.*

'*Will you be visiting us later this evening?*'

*Alan knew he was being tested. If he spent too long with this
latest child of his, there would be hell to pay from Ellie. But he
had to spend time with Sylvia and baby Laura in the hospital.
Sometimes he found it difficult to manage these two very separate
lives.*

'*I can't manage tonight, my love, but I'll be here tomorrow
afternoon. Is that okay?*'

*Ellie nodded, relieved that at least he wasn't forsaking their
usual arrangement. But it was clear that she was far from happy. Alan made a mental note to buy her a special gift – one that*

would make her feel cherished and appreciated – and something for Kerry. If he forgot a gift for the child, his head would be on the block.

Much to Ellie's chagrin, Alan left shortly afterwards. This was the second time they hadn't made love the minute he arrived, and Ellie knew that he was controlling his passion for her out of respect for Sylvia.

Damn the woman, Ellie thought, as Alan's car drove out the gate. She now felt diminished by Sylvia's ability to produce the perfect family – a boy and a girl – for Alan. In her daydreams, Ellie had imagined Sylvia having a second boy, while she would have a daughter, who'd therefore have a special place in Alan's heart by virtue of being his only female child. But now, her child was effectively ousted by this new, tiny interloper.

CHAPTER 31

'Stay here for as long as you like,' Kerry told her, as she and Laura sat in the kitchen of Kerry's apartment. 'Don't even think of moving into a place of your own yet. You need time to get your head together – I mean, it must all have been a terrible shock. And after the miscarriage, too, you're bound to be feeling down, and in need of some TLC.'

Laura smiled gratefully. 'Thanks, love – I really appreciate all your support. But I can't impose on you indefinitely – '

Kerry laughed. 'Hang on, you've only been here for a few days! When you've been here for a few months, I might think about throwing you out!'

'Seriously, I feel I should start making plans. I don't want Jeff thinking that I'm a weakling who can't stand on my own two feet.'

Kerry frowned. 'You're still letting him rule your life. He's gone, so to hell with him. You must do what's best for you.'

'Well, I still think it's best if I get my own place. You know what they say about guests and fish!'

Kerry laughed. 'By all means start checking out places. I'll gladly look at apartments with you, but there's no rush.' She squeezed her friend's arm in an affectionate gesture. 'You don't want to push yourself too hard. You've been through so much lately, and I actually enjoy having you here.'

Laura shivered. 'Thank goodness I never told Jeff about the

money – you were right as usual, and I've been such a fool! I could have made such a mess of things if you hadn't suggested I delay telling him – '

Kerry patted her shoulder. 'There's no point in stressing yourself about it now. You did the right thing, and that's all that matters.'

Laura nodded, looking at the bare third finger of her left hand. Before leaving the apartment she'd shared with Jeff, she'd taken off her wedding and engagement rings and left them in an envelope. Then she grimaced, remembering the wedding presents she'd had to leave behind in the flat.

'I'm sorry about leaving that fabulous coffee machine you gave us,' she said ruefully. 'It was a lovely gift, and I know you went to a lot of expense. But I don't ever want to set foot in that flat again, and I doubt if Jeff will surrender it willingly.'

Kerry hugged her. 'Don't give it another thought – a coffee machine is nothing compared to your safety. There are plenty of coffee machines in the world, but there's only one you. Look, you're safe, and you're a free woman again,' Kerry said equably. 'It could have been a lot worse.'

Laura nodded. 'How was I so easily fooled? You saw through him early on, but I was such an idiot.'

Kerry grinned. 'Jeff's a good-looking fellow, and he *did* more or less sweep you off your feet.'

Laura nodded sadly. 'How could I have thought you weren't happy for me?'

'I *wasn't* happy for you – I was certain that you were making a terrible mistake, and in my own clumsy way, I tried to tell you so. But there's only so far that a friend can interfere – I mean, it's your life. I just hoped that you'd delay the wedding for a while, so that you'd discover what Jeff was like before you actually married him.'

Laura laughed ruefully. 'And, of course, I didn't listen – I couldn't wait to sign on the dotted line! But how did you know what he was like?'

Kerry shrugged. 'I didn't, but there was just something about him – a kind of possessiveness that I didn't like. But for all I knew, that might have been a trait you admired. No one can ever know what goes on in someone else's relationship, so I just had to hope that you knew what you were doing.'

'Well, I think you've proved conclusively that I didn't,' Laura said, grimacing. 'I really did love Jeff at the start, and I genuinely thought we'd be happy together. I suppose I identified with his pain – he'd lost his parents too, so we had a lot in common. I think we were both lonely, and longed to create our own family unit.' She sighed. 'I'm embarrassed to think that I fell for him because he seemed so needy – I thought I could give him the stability he craved, and that in return he'd never leave me. Now I know that we couldn't have been a worse combination.'

In retrospect, she'd realised how quickly Jeff had spotted her vulnerability. Then like a heat-seeking missile, he'd honed in on her own neediness, and her desperation to be part of a family had blinded her to the reality of their situation. She'd never again allow a man to bowl her over like Jeff had. Perhaps her emotional journey would take her to true love next time – if she ever bothered with another man, that is. Now, at least, she knew what she *didn't* want in a man.

She turned and looked searchingly at her friend.

'Why on earth did I stay with him after he'd hit me? I'm an intelligent, independent, educated woman, for Christ sake!'

Kerry looked away. 'Probably because you're still riddled with guilt over the deaths of Pete and your parents. I think you probably let Jeff punish you for it.'

Laura bowed her head. There was a ring of truth in what Kerry said – she'd always felt responsible for her family's deaths, because if she hadn't delayed her mother that fateful morning, their journey might not have led to such catastrophic consequences.

Kerry stood up and went to make coffee. 'Let's stop talking about Jeff right now – he's in the past, and you don't ever have to see him again. He doesn't deserve any more space in your head.'

Laura nodded. 'Let's go out on the town tonight – there's a new bar open on Flower Street, and I'd like to give it a try. What do you think?'

Kerry punched the air. 'An excellent idea! Let's paint the town red!'

The new bar on Flower Street was already packed when they arrived. There was a pleasant air of camaraderie among the customers, and the staff seemed efficient and friendly. There was a range of introductory drink offers written up on boards, and a group of young men were standing near the counter and downing shots in some kind of drunken competition.

'This place could become our local,' Laura said approvingly, as she sipped her gin and tonic. 'There seems to be a nice crowd here, and it's within walking distance of your place, Kerry. If I get an apartment near here too, we could meet up for drinks after work on Fridays.'

Kerry nodded, glancing around. 'Yeah, I like the design and layout of the place. They've made the best use of the limited space, and I love the way they've disguised the reinforced steel joists holding up the mezzanine floor over the bar – '

'Can't you ever stop thinking about how things work?' Laura said, exasperated. 'There are some nicely built guys here, too! Needless to say, I'm off men myself for the foreseeable future!'

Kerry suddenly gasped. 'Oh, Christ, no! Don't look now, but Jeff has just come into the bar!'

'Then we're leaving!' Laura said resolutely, downing her drink in one gulp. 'I don't want to be anywhere near that – that – '

But it was too late. Jeff suddenly materialised beside them.

'Well, hello!' he said, smiling at them both. 'What an amazing coincidence!'

'We're just leaving,' Laura said abruptly.

Jeff looked hurt. 'There's no need to go on my account,' he said, using his most reasonable voice. 'I'll stay at the other end of the bar if that's what you want. Can I get you both a drink?'

'You have to be kidding! I don't want anything from you, Jeff – just for you to leave me alone,' Laura replied, angrily.

'I understand, Laura, but we do have some things to sort out. Can't we talk about things over a drink? I wanted to ask you what you wanted to do about our stuff, all the wedding gifts we have. Would you like to have the coffee machine and the dinner service back? I feel it's unfair for me to keep all our wedding gifts. I could drop them off for you at Kerry's place – '

Laura found she was unable to speak. How weird that Jeff should be thinking about the very same thing that she and Kerry had been discussing earlier!

'No, thank you, Jeff,' she said at last, her voice trembling. 'I don't want you anywhere near Kerry's apartment. You can keep them.'

Jeff looked crestfallen.

Kerry grabbed Laura's arm. 'Come on,' she said firmly. 'We're leaving.'

Strong-arming Laura out of the bar, Kerry marched her along the street, still holding onto her arm tightly, as though trying to control a recalcitrant child.

As they turned a corner, Kerry finally let go and the two women stared at each other.

'Is it always going to be like that?' Laura whispered. 'Am I going to keep bumping into him everywhere I go? I feel sick.'

'Don't worry,' Kerry said firmly. 'I'm sure he was just as surprised as we were. Besides, what else could he do but say hello?'

'But he came right over to us!'

'Well, he wanted to ask you about the wedding gifts.'

'If he'd just stayed at the other end of the bar – '

'Look, maybe that bar isn't the best place for us to make our local – I mean, it's quite near to where you and Jeff used to live, so he could turn up there at any time.'

Laura was shivering. 'Don't you find it strange that we were talking about Jeff hanging onto the wedding gifts, then he turns up and offers to return them? It's as if he could read our minds…'

Kerry smiled, linking her arm through Laura's. 'Now you're really becoming paranoid!' she said. 'Come on, let's go over to the Irish bar in Cook Street.' Kerry glanced behind her. 'Hopefully, Jeff will stay in Flower Street tonight, but you've got to face the fact that you're bound to bump into him from time to time.'

CHAPTER 32

The man stood in the shadows as Kerry left the offices of Sea Diagnostics and began heading for home. He glanced at the photo again. Yes, it was definitely her. There could be no doubt about the likeness.

He followed at a safe distance, comfortable in the knowledge that she had no idea who he was. Even if she turned around, there would be nothing suspicious about him being there.

As she reached the entrance to the Underground, Kerry began to experience a prickly sensation running up her spine, and she got the distinct impression that someone was watching her. Swinging around quickly, she was just in time to see a man ducking into the shadows of a shop doorway.

As she continued on down the steps to the Underground, Kerry couldn't resist another quick glance back. No one seemed to be following her now, and she sighed with relief. Maybe she'd just imagined it. After all, there was no logical reason that anyone would be following her. She'd been working so hard lately that her brain was probably fried, and she was letting her imagination run riot. On the other hand, this wasn't the first time lately that she'd felt someone was following her. For some time now, she'd been experiencing the same uneasy feeling as she'd left work, and on several occasions,

172   LINDA KAVANAGH

when she'd been alone in her apartment, her phone had rung. But when she'd answered, no one had replied, although she'd got the distinct impression that someone was on the other end of the line.

Kerry glanced around her, but none of the other passengers on the platform seemed remotely interested in her. She sighed with relief as her train clattered into the station and she got on board. *Was* she imagining it, or had that man genuinely been following her? Maybe it had simply been a coincidence that he'd chosen that precise moment to step into a doorway. She was being ridiculous. But it gave her the creeps to think that someone might be spying on her.

Even though she was in a public place, with people all around her, Kerry suddenly felt very scared.

Outside the Tube station, the man was feeling very annoyed with himself. By stepping into the doorway, he'd only drawn attention to himself. But when she'd turned around so decisively, he'd been worried for an instant that she might be about to challenge him. He'd have to be more careful in future. He wasn't ready to make his move yet. He slipped into the shadows once more, deciding to abandon his mission until another night.

Laura was watching TV when Kerry arrived home. She jumped up, concerned, when she saw Kerry's slumped shoulders and worried expression.

'Are you okay?'

'I'm fine,' Kerry replied abruptly. She no longer wanted to talk about what had happened. She just wanted to go to bed and seek the oblivion of sleep.

'You look a bit – '

'I'm just tired,' Kerry lied. 'We had a lot of meetings today.'

'You poor love, let me make you a cuppa. Have you eaten this evening? Let me cook something for you – '

'Stop fussing – I ate earlier, with Norma and Jack,' Kerry lied. 'I'm just going to have a bath and an early night.'

Laura looked anxious. 'Are you sure I can't get you anything?'

Kerry shook her head. 'Right now, I just want some peace.'

Laura got the message, and left her friend alone.

As Kerry lay in the bath, letting the warm water wash around her, she was annoyed with herself for not making more of an effort to hide her distress from Laura. Her friend was clearly aware that something was wrong, but Kerry didn't want to be quizzed about it. She saw no point in telling Laura about the man until she'd assessed the situation for herself and decided what to do about it.

Kerry wondered if Jeff could have arranged for someone to follow her. Perhaps he'd actually spotted her that day when she'd followed him to the Docklands hotel. She was also well aware that, by showing her support for Laura, Jeff would see her as a threat to his chances of getting back with her. Equally, Jeff's drug-dealer breakfast companion might have alerted Jeff to her presence in the hotel that morning, and she suspected that neither of them would have been happy that she'd spotted them together. Perhaps they were giving her a warning. Kerry shivered, remembering the newspaper cuttings she'd looked up. Lots of the people who had been due to testify at the drug-dealer's trial had conveniently disappeared...

Kerry climbed out of the bath and reached for her towel. She wasn't going to let anyone unnerve her! And if it was Jeff, how dare he or his drug-dealing friends think they were going to intimidate her...

The following morning, Kerry arrived, bleary-eyed, at the Sea Diagnostics offices.

'You look as though you've had a rough night,' Norma said, surveying her colleague's look of exhaustion as she headed for the coffee machine.

'I didn't sleep a wink,' Kerry admitted. She hadn't intended to say anything to her colleague about the events of the previous evening, but she was so on edge that the words suddenly came tumbling out. 'I was followed last night,' she blurted out. 'When I left here, some man was hanging about, and he followed me as far as the tube station!'

Norma grinned. 'Oh, don't mind him – he's always hanging around outside. He's a bit weird, but I think he's just lonely. He's pretty ancient, and totally harmless.'

Kerry's eyebrows shot up. 'What? Then why haven't I seen him before?'

'He only comes out in the evening. You're only seeing him now because you stayed late to work on the project.'

Kerry's heartbeat was returning to normal. She felt rather foolish now – after all, she was a woman of the world, not an innocent schoolgirl. It was an immense relief to discover that there was a simple explanation for her concerns, not the complicated scenarios she'd been envisaging in the early hours when she couldn't sleep. She was almost feeling affectionate towards the old guy now.

'You're such a fusspot!' Norma said affectionately, mussing her colleague's hair.

Kerry laughed good-naturedly as she poured herself a cup of coffee. She was also relieved that she hadn't said anything to Laura the previous evening – if she'd unburdened herself to her friend, she'd now be left with egg on her face. And that was something Kerry could not abide. She always took pride in being sensible and fearless. At least now there was no longer any reason for her to worry.

CHAPTER 33

'*Oh, hello, Ellie. Do you mind if we join you?'*

'*No, of course not. How nice to see you!' Ellie tried to hide her discomfort as she saw Sylvia, with baby Laura in her arms, looking down at her. She was sitting in the busy village café, with Kerry balanced on her knee, awaiting the arrival of her coffee and scone after doing her weekly shopping.*

Sylvia pulled her buggy in alongside Ellie's, lifted Laura out and sat down facing her. The two women smiled at each other.

'*It's rather crowded in here this morning, isn't it?' Sylvia said. 'It must be the miserable weather that's brought everyone inside!'*

Ellie nodded, unsure of what to say next. Since she'd only just ordered, she couldn't exactly get up and leave, yet she dreaded having to spend half an hour making small talk with Alan's wife. She owed the woman a huge debt of gratitude, but she hadn't banked on spending any further time with her. Now Ellie would have to make the best of a difficult situation.

'*Your daughter is lovely,' Ellie said lamely. 'And so big for – six months?'*

Sylvia nodded, pleased that Ellie had remembered the child's age. 'Yes, doesn't the time just fly? It seems only yesterday that you and I – '

This unintentional reference seemed to highlight the length of time since they'd last seen each other and increased their mutual embarrassment. 'How is Kerry doing? She looks the picture of health!' Sylvia said, smiling at the serious, dark-haired baby on Ellie's knee.

Kerry gave her a disdainful look, and turned her attention to Laura, whose blonde curls seemed to fascinate her. She reached out her chubby little arm, but Ellie deftly moved her before she could lean across the table and grasp the younger child's hair.

'Yes, she's doing great.'

'And her father – is he helping out?'

'Yes, of course.'

Sylvia flushed, wondering if she'd overstepped the mark by mentioning this unknown man in Ellie's life. She still wasn't certain if it was Tony Coleman, and she seemed to be always putting her foot in it where Ellie Beckworth was concerned.

By now, Ellie's coffee and scone had arrived, and the busy waitress had taken Sylvia's order for tea and a pastry.

'Please go ahead,' Sylvia urged Ellie. 'Otherwise your coffee will be cold by the time my tea arrives.'

Nodding, Ellie took a sip of her coffee, suddenly realising that Sylvia was bound to notice her magnificent gold and diamond ring. It was so distinctive, and normally she loved showing it off. But she didn't want to risk Sylvia commenting on it.

Luckily Sylvia was smoothing down Laura's hair and didn't notice as Ellie deftly twisted the ring around so that the diamond was no longer visible. From the back, it simply looked like a broad gold wedding band.

'I presume your son's at his crèche?' she asked, hoping to find a neutral topic they could discuss with relative ease.

Sylvia nodded, smiling mischievously. 'Yes – having him out of the way for a few hours gives me the chance to bond with Laura, because when Pete's around, he's terribly boisterous, and demands lots of attention.'

'How does he get on with his new sister?'

'Oh, he thinks she's wonderful! It's just that he doesn't realise

how fragile she is. I have to watch him in case he might whack her with one of his toys. He's too young to understand the harm he could do.'

Ellie smiled. If only she could keep this topic going...

'Have you noticed much difference in your children's person- alities?' she asked, sussing that Sylvia was happy to chat about Pete and Laura.

'Oh, yes. Even though Laura is only six months old, I can see already that she's very impulsive. And in some ways, she's more outgoing than Pete – he's a more demanding child, but hopefully that will change as he gets older.'

Sylvia looked at Kerry. 'And your daughter? What traits have you seen developing?'

'Well, she loves concentrating on things, and is very deter- mined,' Ellie replied. 'If she decides she wants to do something, she'll see it through, no matter what. If her building blocks top- ple, she'll keep going until they're all stacked up again, even if it takes hours. She just won't give in. It seems an odd trait in a child so young, but it does keep her occupied for ages!'

She and Sylvia shared a conspiratorial smile. They both knew how nice it was to get an occasional break from the unending task of minding of a small child.

Sylvia smiled eagerly. 'I've been dying to ask you about the business you run. I admire any woman who can set up on her own – I'd be hopeless at anything like that.'

She seemed to be waiting expectantly, and Ellie racked her brains to think of something plausible to say.

'Well, actually, I sold the business a while back,' she said at last. 'It was doing well, and I was offered a good price for it. And, of course, my late husband left me with a good pension.' All of which was totally untrue, but she could hardly tell Sylvia that her own husband was keeping Ellie and her child in comfort!

'I think you're amazing,' Sylvia said, looking admiringly at El-

lie, who blushed, feeling a total fraud. 'It must have taken great courage to leave the factory, where you had a secure and permanent job. I'm so glad it all went well for you.' She laughed deprecatingly. 'Luckily, I had a rich father, and I found a rich husband as well!'

In the silence that followed, Ellie felt that she should really ask Sylvia about the details of Laura's birth. It would be the caring, womanly thing to do, since it was a topic that united women everywhere. But she was afraid that by asking about the details of her Caesarean, it would re-establish that earlier bond they'd shared when Sylvia helped her give birth to Kerry. And she couldn't allow that to happen.

By the time Sylvia's tea and pastry arrived, Ellie had almost finished her coffee and scone. She was dying for another coffee, but that would mean staying in Sylvia's company even longer. Maybe the time was now right to extricate herself and leave the café on some pretext.

Sylvia almost seemed to read her mind. 'Shall I order you another coffee? You're not in any rush, are you?'

'Actually, I am,' Ellie said apologetically, as she stood up from the table. 'I have to meet a friend. I'd better get going, or I'll be late.'

As Ellie strapped Kerry into her buggy, Sylvia began reaching for the bills that the waitress had left on the table.

'No, I'll get these – it's my treat.' Ellie snatched the bills off the table, and Sylvia conceded defeat.

'Thank you,' Sylvia said, smiling. 'My treat the next time, okay?'

As soon as the words were out, Sylvia knew she'd said the wrong thing. Ellie had frozen, as though the idea of another coffee in Sylvia's presence would be intolerable.

'Yes, of course,' Ellie said eventually, but the gap had been too long for Sylvia to believe her reply.

When Ellie had paid and left the café, Sylvia gestured to the waitress for another pot of tea. As she bounced little Laura on her knee, she gazed sadly out of the café window, watching as Ellie wheeled Kerry's buggy towards her car. She was always on edge when she met Ellie Beckworth, sensing that there was some undercurrent she didn't quite understand. She liked Ellie, but there seemed no way of breaking down the shell that seemed to surround the other woman.

Sylvia wondered if Ellie's distant manner could be because she was embarrassed about having a child outside marriage. But did anyone care these days? Well, Sylvia didn't care a damn – as far as she was concerned, it was no one's business but Ellie's. And, presumably, Tony Coleman's. But it would be difficult to make that point to her without embarrassing them both.

CHAPTER 34

Laura had an appointment at her local dental surgery the following morning. She'd asked Darren for a few hours off, explaining that she'd broken a tooth, but not telling him how it had happened. As always, her boss was understanding, and he'd agreed that Maria could give her morning lecture instead.

She was anxious to get her tooth fixed, because its jagged edge was cutting the inside of her lip, and proving extremely painful when she ate or drank. In the waiting room, Laura flicked through a series of out-of-date magazines before abandoning them. There were two other people in the room – an elderly woman and a man who was hidden behind the folds of his newspaper.

Laura instantly felt a flicker of fear – could it possibly be Jeff? She felt that he was capable of turning up anywhere she went. When the man put down his newspaper, she was relieved to find herself facing an extremely attractive, dark-haired man who appeared to be in his mid-thirties. They smiled at each other as the elderly woman was called into the dentist's surgery.

As they sat together, the man ventured a remark: 'Nice day, isn't it? What a pity we're stuck in here while the sun's shining!'

Laura nodded. 'Nevertheless, I was very grateful to get an

appointment today – I've broken a tooth, and it's really irritating. What are you having done?'

'Just a filling – the old one fell out and I've been meaning to get it sorted for ages.' He grinned. 'It took a really bad toothache to get me here!'

The receptionist popped her head around the waiting room door.

'Mr Rudden? Dr Brady is ready for you now.'

The man seemed disappointed to be called so soon. 'Best of luck with the tooth!' he said, smiling at Laura as he left the waiting room.

'And to you, too,' she said, smiling back. She also felt a pang of disappointment as he left the waiting room. She'd been surprised and pleased to find herself enjoying another man's company, and it was a relief not having to censor everything she was going to say. After all she'd been through with her husband, it seemed a positive sign.

'Are you sure you feel able to take on the second years for statistics?'

Laura nodded as she sat in front of Darren's desk in his office. She was glad of the opportunity to help him out, since he'd been more than good to her over the previous few months. In fact, he'd been looking out for her for years.

Darren looked at her unflinchingly. 'And how are *you* feeling? You coping okay?'

Laura nodded, knowing that this was Darren's oblique way of referring to her miscarriage. He'd been kind and supportive all through her ordeal, and she was glad of the chance to return the favour by taking Timmy's classes.

'Are you sure you'll be okay standing for so long?' he added. 'I can always bring in another lecturer – I don't want you to tire yourself unnecessarily.'

Laura nodded, her heart filled with affection for this generous and caring man.

'It's no problem, Darren. In fact, I'll enjoy doing it.'

Darren smiled, nodding his approval. 'It'll only be for two weeks. Thanks, Laura. I really appreciate your help.'

'No problem.'

'How's the tooth?'

'It's fine, thanks. Luckily, it just needed to be filed down a bit, and a filling put in.'

As yet, she hadn't told any of her colleagues that she and Jeff had parted. The break-up was so new to her that she still woke up in the mornings with a feeling of dread in her stomach, until she realised she was safe in Kerry's apartment.

She was also embarrassed about how short her turbulent marriage had been, although she guessed that most of her colleagues had been well aware of Jeff's unsuitability long before she had. Right then, she couldn't quite face the thought of proving them right. She knew they'd all be relieved for her, but that didn't make her feel any better.

Darren took off his glasses and wiped his eyes. He looked tired, and Laura's heart went out to him. She was deeply fond of him, and wished he could meet someone special. He was such a wonderful man, and it would be a lucky woman who finally snared him. But he seemed to devote all his energies to running the department.

'If there are any other courses you need me to cover, just let me know,' she said. 'I have plenty of time on my hands.' She could see a question forming in Darren's eyes, but she quickly deflected it. She didn't want to entertain any queries about Jeff right now. 'I'm giving first and second-year sociology lectures every morning next week,' she added, 'but I can fit in extra lectures in the afternoons, if you need me to. Or if anyone needs a break.'

'Thanks, Laura – I might just take you up on that offer.' He looked at her shrewdly. 'And you're definitely okay?'

Laura gave him a convincing smile. 'Of course. But *you* look tired,' she added, deflecting attention away from her own situation.

Darren wiped his eyes again. 'Yeah, I'm a bit tired right now. Running this show can be a headache sometimes.' He put on his glasses again. 'Are you *sure* everything's okay with you?'

For a moment, Laura almost decided to tell him that she'd left Jeff, but then she changed her mind. 'Darren, I'm fine, honestly,' she said airily. 'Just let me know if you need any more help.'

Leaving his office, Laura headed down the corridor towards her own room. As she opened the door to enter, she glanced with distaste at the plaque adorning it. At her own insistence, it read '*Dr Laura Jones*'. How she longed to rip it off the door and throw it in the bin! But it would have to stay there until she decided to inform her colleagues that her marriage was over.

CHAPTER 35

During her lunch break, Laura decided to stock up on some food at the supermarket. As she wandered through the aisles, she filled her trolley with the various items on her list, then she heard a voice behind her.

'Well, hello again!'

Laura turned to see the good-looking, dark-haired man to whom she'd spoken in the dentist's waiting room.

Her heart gave a little jolt and, smiling, she returned his greeting. 'How's the filling?' she asked.

'Oh, fine – I don't know why I left it so long,' he replied, patting his cheek. Then he grinned cheerfully. 'But I wouldn't have met you otherwise!'

Laura's cheeks turned pink with pleasure.

'I presume you got your broken tooth fixed okay?' he asked.

Laura nodded, pleased that he'd remembered. 'Yes, thanks – it's a relief to be able to eat without feeling that my mouth is full of pins.'

He smiled. 'Speaking of eating, I'm planning on going to the café across the road as soon as I've finished my shopping. Why don't you join me if you're free?'

Laura felt a bubble of happiness welling up inside her.

'Thank you, I'd like that.'

The man gave a pleased grin. 'Okay, I'll see you there in, say, fifteen minutes?'

'Okay – great.'

In a pleasant daze, Laura continued with her shopping, hardly able to concentrate on what she was supposed to be buying. She smiled to herself. Wouldn't Kerry be surprised to hear that she'd already got a date! Well, a date of sorts. Lunch was a neutral, getting-to-know-you sort of date. Laura laughed to herself – she was only going to have lunch with a nice guy, and there was nothing more to it than that. Nevertheless, it seemed to augur well for the future – Jeff was firmly in the past, and some day soon she'd have a very different and hopefully better life.

After putting the groceries in her car, Laura quickly checked her appearance in the driver's rear view mirror, locked the car then crossed the road to the café.

The man was already there, and he waved to her as she made her way to his table.

'By the way, my name is Steve Rudden,' he said, as she sat down.

Shaking hands, Laura introduced herself and took a seat opposite him. They both spent a little time consulting the menu, before giving the waitress their order. When she'd left, they caught each other's eye, and both laughed.

'Okay, I'll go first,' Steve said. 'I run a small accountancy business, I'm single, I live in Hammersmith and I like football, tennis and vintage cars. I own a 1929 Rolls-Royce, which is my pride and joy. I nearly got married once, a long time ago, but she met someone else and dumped me. I grew up in Yorkshire, and my parents and sister still live there.' He looked expectantly at her. 'Now it's your turn,' he said.

Briefly, Laura summed up her own life, explaining about her career, the death of her parents and brother in a car crash, her plan to move into a new apartment after her brief but unsatisfactory marriage. She didn't mention Jeff's violence. It didn't seem appropriate to tell someone she barely knew.

At which point their food arrived, and they both tucked into it with gusto.

Laura was enjoying Steve's company, and secretly marvelling at how easy it had been to meet another man. She'd had no intention of dating again for a very long time, but fate seemed to have deposited Steve at her door. Of course, Steve might not want to see her again, but she was already starting to hope that he would.

Her phone rang, and Laura grimaced. She glanced at the number – Jeff was hassling her again. She rejected the call and continued with her meal, but she noticed Steve watching her closely.

The café was beginning to fill up with lunchtime diners, and so far they hadn't been expected to share their banquette. But knowing they could be joined by other people before long, Laura decided to tell Steve about Jeff before they acquired an audience.

'My ex is proving tiresome,' she confessed. 'That was him on the phone just now. He can't forgive me for leaving the marriage – he keeps ringing me all the time. I don't answer any more, because when I do he just starts being abusive.'

As if to prove the point, Laura's phone rang again. They both looked at the screen.

'I guess it's time to change your number,' Steve said seriously.

Laura nodded, wondering if she would ever be free of Jeff.

Steve picked up the bill just as Laura reached for it. 'I asked you, so it's my treat,' he said, smiling. 'But if you really feel I've compromised your dignity as an independent woman, you can always invite me to lunch another day – ? Or maybe a meal? I know a great Italian restaurant. It's old-fashioned and basic, but with marvellous food.'

Laura nodded, smiling back at him. She liked the idea of seeing Steve again. 'I'd really like that.'

CHAPTER 36

*O*ne little dark-haired girl and one blonde-haired girl eyed each other as they queued for the tuck shop on their first day at prep school.

'I know you. You live in Greygates, don't you?' the dark-haired girl ventured.

The blonde girl nodded, looking surprised. 'How do you know that?'

'I live not far from there. Do you know where Treetops is?'

The other girl nodded. 'Isn't that the house hidden behind all those big trees?' Then she grinned sheepishly. 'I suppose that's why it's called Treetops!'

Nodding, the dark-haired girl smiled back. 'I've built a platform up in one of the tallest trees – you can see for miles from up there. I can even see your house!'

The other girl raised an eyebrow in disbelief. 'Wow! That sounds amazing. Did you really build a platform on your own?'

The dark-haired girl nodded. 'I'm pretty handy at things like that,' she said, without a trace of modesty. 'I can build a platform in your garden too, if you'd like me to.'

'Would you really?' The blonde girl was in awe of her new friend.

The dark-haired girl nodded. 'You can come and play in my garden any time you want,' she said. 'By the way, my name is Kerry.'

'And mine is Laura.'

The girls looked at each other shyly.

Kerry smiled. 'Your dad owns the canning factory, doesn't he?'

Laura nodded 'What does your father do?' she asked.

'I don't have one – my mum's a widow. My father died before I was born.'

'Oh.' Laura was puce with embarrassment, but Kerry didn't seem bothered. In a way, not having a father seemed to lend her an air of mystery, and it occurred to Laura that having one less parent would mean a great deal more freedom, since there would be one less pair of eyes scrutinising everything you did.

By the time the queue reached the tuck-shop counter, the girls had discovered that they'd be sharing most subjects.

'If you like, you can come to my house and play with my dolls,' Laura said generously. 'I've got about a hundred.'

'Eeuch!' Kerry wrinkled her nose. 'I hate dolls. I'd rather play cops and robbers up in the trees, or pirates, or go on my skateboard.' She looked at Laura's disappointed expression. 'I'll show you how to skateboard, if you like. It's much more fun than dolls! You can go really fast, and you can even learn to flip the board over, and do all kinds of exciting things – it just takes practice.'

'Okay,' Laura said tentatively, warming to the idea the more she thought about it. Skateboarding sounded like fun. The large courtyard behind her house would be perfect for practising in. Wouldn't Pete be surprised – and jealous – if she could demonstrate some clever moves? As the younger sibling, she was always trying to outsmart her brother, and this might be the very opportunity she was waiting for.

'Will you really teach me to skateboard?'

'Of course. It's easy – just a matter of balance. You won't be long getting the hang of it.'

Laura smiled, her eyes alight. 'Thanks, that's great. I'll ask Mum and Dad for a skateboard for my birthday.'

'When is your birthday?'

'Next month. I'm having a party – will you come?'

Kerry nodded. 'Yes, please! How old will you be?'

'I'll be eight,' Laura announced.

Kerry smiled triumphantly. 'That means I'm three months older than you! But don't you have to be eight already before starting prep school?'

Laura lowered her voice confidentially. 'I know, but my parents asked the principal to make an exception for me, since I didn't want to wait another whole year.'

Kerry nodded matter-of-factly. 'People always make exceptions for those with lots of money.' She squeezed Laura's hand. 'But I'm glad they made an exception for you – because I think you're going to be my very best friend!'

As the family finished dinner, Laura decided to bring up the subject of her new friend.

'Mum, there's a girl in my class that I'd like to invite to my party.'

Sylvia nodded approvingly. 'Of course, darling. I'm glad you're making new friends. What's her name?'

'Kerry.'

Alan's head shot up. 'Did you say Kerry?'

Laura nodded. 'And the great thing is – she lives near here, too.'

'Really?'

Laura nodded again. 'Yes, she lives at Treetops. She's such fun!'

Sylvia looked hesitantly at her husband, realising that Kerry had to be Ellie Beckworth's daughter.

Sylvia still wondered if Tony Coleman was the father of Ellie Beckworth's child, although she'd never dared broach the subject with Alan, since he'd say she was simply being a busybody. She *also remembered how, all those years ago, Alan hadn't been keen for her to befriend Ellie. Nor had Ellie responded to her overtures either. Now, ironically, their daughters seemed to have taken matters into their own hands.*

Sylvia still felt a deep affection and gratitude towards Ellie. It seemed strange to think now that while she and Ellie had both been pregnant with their daughters, she'd been convinced Alan was going to leave her for someone else. Sylvia gave a little involuntary shiver. But for Ellie, she might have confronted Alan, perhaps with dire consequences, since he'd have abhorred her lack of trust, and it would have permanently damaged their relationship.

Sometimes she wondered if she'd misread that receipt for the diamond and gold ring. Could Alan have simply had second thoughts about giving her the ring, and exchanged it for another expensive item of the same value? Perhaps the jeweller hadn't felt it necessary to issue a new receipt. Nevertheless, she'd always wonder…

'I'm sure it's very nice for you to have a friend who lives so near,' Sylvia said to her daughter, glancing at Alan to ensure his approval. It was one thing to discourage an adult friendship with Ellie, based on their differing social positions, but it would be unfair to discourage Laura, who needed to learn about the give and take of friendship. She looked at her husband. 'It'll be nice for Laura, won't it, dear? Having someone nearby to play with?'

Alan nodded, trying to look absent-minded, but his feelings were far from vague. He supposed that since the girls were attending the same prep school – both paid for by him – it was inevitable that they'd discover they lived within half a mile of each other. He should have insisted that Kerry be sent to a different school, but Ellie was adamant that her daughter would receive exactly the same standard of education that Laura did.

Hopefully, the girls would discover that they were like chalk and cheese, and they'd outgrow their friendship with the passing of time.

'So can Kerry come to my birthday party, Mum?'

Sylvia darted another glance at her husband, but didn't wait for his approval this time. 'Of course, darling – what a lovely idea!'

CHAPTER 37

That evening in Kerry's apartment, Laura couldn't stop smiling.

'He's really nice, and he's even got his own accountancy business. I like a dynamic, independent man, don't you? When I met him in the supermarket, Steve asked me to have lunch with him – and he's invited me out next Friday evening!'

Laura was in a bubbly and animated mood, and Kerry was amazed that she'd come through her tragic marriage with her happy and impulsive nature still intact.

Taking their pizza out of the oven, Kerry grimaced at her friend. 'I'm pleased for you, love, but promise me you won't be rushing down the aisle again for a while yet? I don't think I could handle two weddings in less than a year!'

Laura laughed as she placed cutlery and plates on the table. 'Don't worry, I'm just going to have fun. Anyway, I need to apply for a divorce from Jeff first. But, more importantly – ' she grinned mischievously '–I'm sure Steve has some nice friends, and maybe we can find one who takes *your* fancy.'

Kerry gave her a sarcastic look. 'Let's find out what this Steve fellow is like before you start fixing me up with one of his friends!' she said.

'Oh, he's really great!'

'I seem to remember you saying the same thing about Jeff,' Kerry added dryly.

Laura looked guilty. 'You're right. But, honestly, I'm only going out for a meal with this guy. I'm not going to rush anything.' She looked sincerely at Kerry. 'I mean, I wasn't even looking for anyone, but fate seems to have intervened.'

Kerry looked doubtful as she nibbled a wedge of pizza. 'Fate produced Jeff as well. Please be a bit more careful this time, won't you?'

CHAPTER 38

Laura surveyed the clothes she'd hung in the wardrobe in Kerry's spare room. She was trying to decide what she'd wear for her second dinner date with Steve. As she flicked through the hangers, Laura grimaced as she remembered the brown dress that Jeff had insisted she wore to the Sea Diagnostics reception. She'd left both the brown dress and the maxi dress in the wardrobe of his apartment. Shuddering, she wondered how she'd ever let him dictate what she should wear. She never intended wearing anything like those frumpy things ever again!

Suddenly her mobile rang. Without checking the number she answered it, assuming that it might be Steve. A second later, she bitterly regretted her decision.

'You fucking whore!' Jeff screamed down the phone. 'You couldn't wait to get your knickers off for another man, could you? You seem to have forgotten you're still my wife – I'll kill you for this!'

'Jeff, please!' Laura was horrified. 'We didn't – ' She stopped. She would not demean herself by answering his accusations. The fact that she and Steve hadn't had sex was irrelevant. She'd left her marriage and was a free agent as far as she was concerned. She'd told Jeff it was over, so it wasn't as though she was sneaking around behind his back.

'You never intended staying with me, did you?' Jeff raged.

'You're a liar and a cheat, just like every other bloody woman I've ever met!'

'Jeff, that's not fair!' Laura replied angrily. 'I expected to spend my entire life with you, but you wrecked our marriage with your violence! Now, I'm hanging up. Please don't call me again.'

No sooner had she ended the call than her mobile phone rang again. Looking down at Jeff's number again, Laura suddenly lost her temper. 'You bastard, Jeff!' she screamed, answering his call. 'I am sick to death of you – don't make me do something I'll regret! You're nothing but a pathetic loser!'

Exhausted from her outburst, she turned off the phone and flung it across the room. Hopefully Jeff would now realise that she meant what she'd said. There was no going back for them as a couple, and the sooner he accepted that, the better.

Laura was shaking as she entered the kitchen.

'What's wrong?' Kerry asked, looking concerned. 'I thought I heard you shouting – '

'Jeff just phoned,' Laura said, her voice trembling. 'Oh, Kerry, he called me a whore!'

The tears came, and she wept as Kerry held her tightly.

'He said I was still his wife, and that he'd kill me for dating someone else – but how on earth did he know I'd been out with Steve?'

Kerry bit her lip. 'He must be watching the apartment.'

Laura's tears were now replaced by anger. 'The nerve of him! Anyway, when he rang back, I gave him as good as I got. I told him to take a hike, so maybe he'll realise that I'm not meek little Laura any more!'

Kerry could see that Jeff's behaviour was seriously distressing her friend. 'It was probably just bad luck that he was watching when Steve collected you last night,' she said reassuringly.

'Maybe, but it's the not knowing that's so frightening,' Laura said angrily. 'He wants me to be on edge all the time, and he's succeeding.'

CHAPTER 39

Laura's party was going well, and the magician hired to amuse the children had proved very popular. Afterwards, the youngsters had descended on the food like a plague of locusts, and only a few sandwiches remained, now well-trodden into the floor. Alan smiled. He had to hand it to Sylvia – she really did seem to know what kids liked. The children attending the party were a mixture of their friends' children, the sons and daughters of his factory workers, a few of Laura's new classmates – and, of course, Kerry.

The downstairs of the house looked as though a bomb had hit it. Gift-wrap lay everywhere, abandoned by Laura as she'd excitedly opened her presents. She was so thrilled to be eight! Toys, jigsaws and birthday cards littered the living room. Her new skateboard held pride of place in the middle of it all. She'd been so excited as she'd unwrapped it earlier that morning at the breakfast table.

Since the weather was still warm for October, the children were now running wild in the gardens, and everyone seemed to be enjoying themselves. As Alan joined Sylvia outside, he slipped an arm around her. 'You've done brilliantly,' he told her. 'Laura's having a ball!'

But Sylvia looked worried, and Alan followed her eye-line to where Kerry was playing at the swing. Some of the other children were trying to push her off.

'Oh, dear, she's rather a tomboy, isn't she?' Sylvia said anx-

iously. 'Kerry's actually taken the seat off the swing and is now hanging from the top by her arms! Surely she'll hurt herself? And if the other children start copying her – well, I'm not sure what to do.'

Alan laughed. 'Don't worry – she looks as though she knows what she's doing.'

'But if she falls, how could I ever face her mother?'

Sylvia's comment made Alan realise that a calamity like that would mean contact between Sylvia and Ellie, so he strode over to Kerry and peeled her hands from the top of the swing and placed her on the ground.

Had he imagined it, or had she just tried to kick him?

Hands now on her hips, Kerry glared at him with a mixture of anger and contempt. 'Why did you do that?'

'Because you might fall, and I don't want to have to explain to your mother that you broke your arm or leg at our party.'

Kerry looked at him scornfully, and he had to hide his smile. She looked exactly like Ellie did when she was annoyed. The child was becoming a replica of her mother!

Alan smiled at her, trying to diffuse the tension. 'Laura tells me you're brilliant at skateboarding. Any chance you could show me how you do it?'

Kerry's fierce expression was disbelieving at first. 'You really want to watch me?'

Alan nodded, pleased when her face brightened.

'Okay – c'mon. I've left my skateboard over in your courtyard.'

Without hesitation, Kerry took his hand and they began walking towards the courtyard behind the house. Sylvia smiled quizzically at him as he went by, clearly grateful that he'd managed to distract the child from her daredevil antics.

In the empty courtyard, Kerry collected her skateboard and stepped on it.

'This is where I'm going to teach Laura,' she told him.

Alan nodded approvingly. 'She's really looking forward to it. Is it true that you travel everywhere on your skateboard?'

Kerry nodded. 'Yes, it's a really fast way of getting around. When I'm older, I'll probably get a bike. But Mum says I'm too young for one yet.'

As Kerry demonstrated her ability around the courtyard, Alan marvelled at her skill. She really was good at it! He could see the determination on her little face as she concentrated on her moves, particularly her back flip, clearly keen to impress him.

'Bravo! You really are talented!' Alan said, clapping as she came to a stop in front of him.

Kerry looked at him shyly. 'Thanks,' she said. 'Laura could be just as good as me – if she sticks with it, that is. She starts something but doesn't always finish it.'

'Well, with such a good teacher as you, she's bound to succeed,' Alan told her, and was pleased to see her face flush with pleasure.

As they walked back to the garden where the party was in full swing, Alan had a sudden thought.

'Kerry, would you like me to teach you how to ride a bicycle?'

The little girl looked quizzically at him. 'But I haven't got a bike!'

Alan smiled down at her. 'Well, I could teach you when you do get one.'

It was an impulsive idea, but the more he thought about it, the more he liked it, and the more he wanted to do it. He welcomed the idea of spending some one-to-one time with his secret daughter.

Kerry nodded, but in her own mind she dismissed his offer as just another of those empty promises adults made and later forgot about.

'I really mean it,' Alan said, looking down at her sceptical expression. 'But don't tell Laura, because she might be jealous.' He

grinned. 'Anyway, since she's three months younger than you, she can learn to ride later.'

Kerry looked pleased that the three-month age difference had been acknowledged, and Alan smiled to himself, knowing how much even a few months mattered to a small child.

He also suspected that Kerry was shrewd enough to appreciate the value of secrecy. But even if she did eventually tell Laura about the lessons, while he'd be disappointed in her, it wasn't as though the sky would fall. He'd simply tell Sylvia that he'd felt sorry for the girl and had spent a few afternoons helping her.

As they walked back to the party, Alan was filled with resolve. He really did want to teach Kerry to ride a bike. Perhaps he wanted a little time to bond with his secret daughter, and he knew Ellie would be pleased.

'Bye, Mr Thornton,' Kerry said, as she ran off to join the other children.

Alan smiled, watching as she and Laura quickly singled each other out, Kerry taking her place in the game beside Laura. They were so different, yet they seemed to get on very well.

As the party ended, the usual chaos ensued as over-excited children rushed to their parents' cars, clutching their goodie bags.

'It's been fun, but I'm very glad it's over!' a relieved Sylvia whispered to her husband.

It had been arranged that Alan and Sylvia would each drive the few remaining children home. Alan made sure that Kerry was one of the children who got into his car – he didn't want Sylvia and Ellie meeting again. Similarly, Alan made sure that Kerry was the last child to be dropped off, so that he could manage to have a brief word with Ellie.

'Thanks, Mr Thornton,' Kerry said, as Alan deposited her outside the front door of Treetops.

'You're welcome, Kerry,' he called, waving as the child rang *the doorbell.*

   As the door opened, Ellie stepped outside. 'It's very good of you to drop her home – thanks, Mr Thornton.'

   Alan nodded. 'No problem, Ms Beckworth.'

   By now, Kerry had disappeared inside, and Ellie risked crossing to the car, leaning in and quickly kissing him.

   'Careful!' Alan whispered. 'That child of ours is very bright. Let's not rock any boats just yet!'

   Although he felt a surge of desire, he quelled the instinct to sweep her into his arms and make love to her on the spot.

   'I have an idea,' he told her. 'I think it's time we got Kerry a bike.'

Chapter 40

The following day, Laura's mobile phone continued to ring every hour on the hour until finally she turned it off. Since she was meeting Steve again that evening, she'd wanted to keep her phone on in case he needed to contact her. But Jeff made it impossible. She really did need to change her number.

She felt a surge of excitement as the time when Steve would arrive was drawing near. To hell with Jeff if he was watching – what could he do but make more abusive phone calls? Which she wouldn't answer.

On the dot of eight, Steve arrived in his magnificent, black, 1929 Rolls-Royce. As she stepped out of the apartment lobby and into the street, Laura was blown away by its sleek lines and impressive finish. 'Wow! It's fabulous!' she told Steve, her eyes shining. 'I can't believe I'm about to travel in such style!'

Steve was clearly pleased by her response and, smiling, held open the passenger door for her. Casting a glance around the street, Laura was relieved that there was no sign of Jeff. She settled herself in the passenger seat, and they were off. Laura was equally impressed by the car's interior. She loved the smell of the old leather seats and the crafted walnut dashboard.

As Steve drove along, Laura found herself gradually relaxing with each mile. She glanced at his profile. He really was a good-looking man. She wasn't really looking for a serious relationship yet, but there was no harm in seeing what might happen between them.

The restaurant proved every bit as delightful as Steve had claimed. The French cuisine was wonderful, and the maître d' was both efficient and flirtatious towards Laura. She was amused by his gallantry and banter, and Steve didn't seem to mind that he kept kissing Laura's hand at every opportunity. It crossed her mind that if Jeff had been with her instead of Steve, his reaction would have been very different.

During the evening, Laura's phone rang and, glancing at the number, she cursed silently. Reaching into her handbag, she turned it off. She wasn't going to let Jeff ruin her dinner.

After a beautiful meal and a bottle of wine between them, Laura was feeling full and happy. As Steve paid the bill and they prepared to leave the restaurant, she tucked her arm through his. 'Thanks for a really lovely evening, Steve,' she said warmly. 'Next time, it'll be my treat, okay?'

Steve smiled back. 'I'll hold you to that,' he said, kissing her lightly.

Laura felt content and at peace with the world. It sounded like he intended seeing her again. Things could only get better between them...

As they strolled arm-in-arm through the car park, Laura wondered about her evening with Steve. She did really like him. He was a lovely guy, and she was growing more and more fond of him...

'*Holy shit!*'

Laura was awakened from her reverie by a roar of anger from Steve. They'd reached the Rolls-Royce, and she could hardly believe her eyes as she stared at the vehicle. The word '*Whore*' had been scrawled across the sleek, black bonnet in some kind of white paint.

Her heart beating wildly, she looked all around her. She knew who had done this. Rage filled her heart.

Now he was destroying her future as well as her past.

Steve was already on the phone, talking rapidly to someone, but Laura had no idea who. Although the evening was warm, she was shivering. Probably from shock, she thought, unable to believe that Jeff would go this far.

When Steve finished his phone call, he walked around his car, caressing it as though it was a wounded person whom he was reassuring. It was obvious that the car meant a lot to him, and Laura felt overwhelmed by guilt as she watched his stunned expression and haunted eyes.

Eventually, he left the car and ventured over to where Laura was standing. In silence, they looked at each other. Laura felt shaky and miserable, and couldn't believe that anything she could say would help the situation, or make Steve feel any better.

At last Steve spoke. 'Look, I like you, Laura, but there's clearly something weird going on here, and I don't want to be part of it.' He shrugged his shoulders. 'If you haven't already gone to the police, you should do so now. Your ex is a psycho, and I don't want to end up injured or dead because your ex doesn't want you dating anyone else. So I'm out of here. Sorry.'

'Oh, Steve, I'm the one who should be sorry for what's happened to your car,' Laura said humbly. 'Please let me pay for the repairs – '

Steve's smile was bitter. 'Forget it, Laura. It's not your fault, but you'll have to go to the police. Otherwise this guy will keep ruining your life.'

Laura nodded, feeling awful.

Steve took out his phone, called a taxi and, when it arrived, paid the cab driver and helped Laura in.

'Goodbye, Laura,' he said sadly. 'I'm sorry it had to end this way.'

Feeling numb, Laura wept quietly as the taxi drove off. It wasn't just the loss of such a nice guy that bothered her so much, but the fact that Jeff was still ruining her life. She'd do what Steve had suggested. It was definitely time to contact the police.

CHAPTER 41

When an emotional Laura arrived back in the apartment, Kerry hastily threw on her dressing gown and joined her in the kitchen, as Laura angrily told her friend what had happened.

'Why won't Jeff leave me alone?' she shouted. 'How dare he interfere in my life! How dare he think he can still tell me what I can do, or who I can go out with!'

'He's not just interfering in your life – he's wrecking it!' Kerry said grimly. 'I presume your guy Steve will report the damage to the police?'

Laura was looking miserable. 'He said he would. Unfortunately, he's not "my" Steve any longer – Jeff's made sure of that! I'd just assumed that Jeff was still venting, and that eventually he'd stop his stupid carry-on. But what if he doesn't? What if he keeps hurting anyone connected to me? Even you could be next!'

Kerry nodded, unable to think of anything to say.

Laura sat staring into the cup of coffee that Kerry had just made, her anger mounting. 'How on earth could Jeff know where Steve and I were tonight?' she whispered angrily. 'Even if he was standing outside the apartment and saw us leave, he wouldn't know where we were going. He'd have needed luck to get a taxi straight away...'

Kerry grimaced. 'Maybe Jeff's employing other people to do his dirty work?'

Laura nodded. 'Yes, I think you could be right. I'm positive he wasn't outside the apartment when Steve and I left here to-night. So maybe he arranged for someone else to follow us – '

Kerry gasped and Laura turned quizzically towards her. Kerry quickly pressed a finger to her lips, then grabbed a piece of paper and wrote hastily on it before passing it to Laura. Then it was Laura's turn to gasp. Kerry was suggesting that there could be a listening device in the apartment.

In total silence, and using only hand signals, the two women began checking behind clocks and ornaments, in drawers and beneath cupboards, and in between books and CDs.

Eventually, Kerry located a small device with a tiny, blink-ing light attached to the underside of the coffee table in the living room. Gesturing to Laura to follow, she headed for the kitchen, where she dropped the device into soapy water in the washing-up bowl. The blinking stopped immediately.

'Now you can't hear us any more, you bastard!' Kerry hissed. Then she turned to a horrified Laura. 'So that's how lover-boy knew we'd be at the bar in Flower Street! And that you were annoyed with him for hanging on to the wedding presents. He'd also have known about your date with Steve, because we sat at that very coffee table talking about it!'

Laura shivered. 'How on earth did he manage to put it there?'

'He must have done it the night you were both here for dinner,' Kerry replied. 'Remember he was alone in the living room for about ten minutes – that would have been more than enough time to attach it.'

Laura let out a groan. She was still finding it hard to take in the enormity of Jeff's deceit. 'But why would he want to bug *your* flat? It doesn't make sense. He and I were still together then!'

Kerry grimaced. 'Obviously, being married didn't stop him

wanting to spy on you,' she reasoned. 'He must have wanted
to find out what you and I were talking about.'

Laura cradled her head in her hands. 'How could anyone
stoop so low?' she whispered.

'You said he was insecure – I guess men like him can't bear
their women to be independent of them. And after you'd broken up with him, the device he'd planted here was even more
useful, since he could now find out everything about your new
life.'

Laura shivered. 'Why can't he just let me go? I'm never
going back to him.'

'I don't think Jeff can accept that you rejected him. He's
convinced that you'll come back to him if he just pursues you
enough. Either that, or – '

Kerry hesitated.

'Or what?'

'Or he's deliberately trying to drive you out of your mind.'

Laura stared at her. 'Why would he want to do that?'

'Because if he can't have you, he wants to make sure you'll
never be happy with anyone else.'

Laura gave a heartfelt sigh. 'I've been a fool, haven't I?
Why did I try so hard to make it work with Jeff? I guess it
was because I wanted somewhere to belong, and someone to
belong to. I've been so lonely since I lost Pete and my parents.' She looked earnestly at Kerry. 'Our families give us our
identity and history, don't they? I suppose I thought that Jeff
could give that back to me. By starting our own family, we'd
be building a family history of our own.'

Kerry nodded. 'Thanks goodness you didn't!'

Laura was still reeling from all the bizarre events of the
night. 'One thing that Steve said was that I should contact the
police myself,' she said.

Kerry looked worried. 'I see the logic, but I'm beginning

to wonder if that's a good idea,' she cautioned. 'Jeff might become even more violent if you report him.' She put her arms around her friend. 'I just don't want anything bad to happen to you.'

Laura said nothing, feeling overwhelmed by Jeff's vindictiveness.

Kerry injected some positivism into their discussion. 'Look, it might just be enough to change your mobile phone number. Tomorrow, you should definitely contact your service provider.'

'Yes, you're right.'

Kerry squeezed her friend's arm. 'Cheer up, love – before long, Jeff will get fed up with pursuing you. Hopefully, by this time next year, we'll hardly remember his name!'

Laura smiled weakly. She knew Kerry was trying to rally her but, deep down, she wondered if Jeff would let her go so easily. I won't allow him to get under my skin, she vowed. He's not going to win.

Chapter 42

'Oooooh!' Kerry wobbled uncertainly and the bicycle juddered for a few seconds, then she fell headlong into a flowerbed.

Alan ran to her and helped her up. 'Are you okay? You did really well!'

Grimacing, Kerry wiped the dirt from her hands. Her knees were stinging, and she felt certain she'd skinned them both. But she was determined not to cry. She was relishing every minute of her time with Mr Thornton. It was almost like having a dad of her own.

She'd been astonished and thrilled when Mr Thornton had kept his promise. He'd arrived at Treetops one afternoon after school with a new bike in the boot of his car, and it had been exactly the right size for her. 'But you mustn't tell Laura, or anyone else, about the bike or the lessons,' he told her sternly.

That very afternoon, she'd had her first lesson.

'It's all about confidence,' Alan told her, as he helped her to brush the mud off her knees. 'You were doing fine until you got a fit of nerves, right?'

Kerry nodded.

'Now, hop up on that bike again, and let me see what you can really do.'

Kerry grinned, climbing on, determined to show Mr Thornton that she was a worthy pupil. He'd already spent ages running alongside her, holding on to the bike as she pedalled up and down

Treetops's driveway. It was only when she'd realised that he'd let go, and she found she was actually cycling on her own, that she'd got such a fright and ended up in the flowerbed. At least the ground there was reasonably soft. So far, she'd managed to veer away from the holly bushes near the front gate.

As Kerry got on the bike once more, Alan held the back carrier and ran alongside her as she pedalled. 'Keep going, Kerry!' he shouted, as she cycled down the driveway. 'You're really getting the hang of it now!'

Kerry smiled as the bike wobbled. She knew he'd just let go, but she was managing to keep steering straight ahead. Then she cycled around the grass in a circle, and came to a neat stop in front of him.

Alan's face was wreathed in smiles. 'You were great that time! You've got amazing balance!'

Kerry's little face was aglow as she wallowed happily in his praise. She so envied Laura having such a great dad! She was enjoying their secret meetings, and her mum definitely liked him too, because they were always whispering and laughing when they thought she wasn't listening.

However, Kerry had also worked out that once she learnt to ride, Mr Thornton wouldn't need to spend time with her any more. So she was actually taking a lot longer to learn than was strictly necessary. The pain of a few bruises and scraped knees were worth it in order to have his undivided attention.

'I'm definitely getting the hang of it,' she told him. 'But I still need a few more lessons – '

'Yes, of course. I'll see you here at the same time next week – ?'

As she nodded, Kerry's face was a picture of happiness. She had more of his visits to look forward to, and maybe she could fake a bad fall next time, to stretch out the lessons a little longer.

Alan was also enjoying the time he was spending with his secret daughter. Throughout the winter months and into the spring, he'd been giving Kerry a lesson once a week. Having spent the earlier part of the afternoon with Ellie, he was able to claim that he'd 'just arrived' at Treetops when Kerry got back from school.

He was well aware that the child had already become a perfectly competent cyclist, but he didn't mind her little deception – he was flattered that she wanted to spend time with him. He'd also come to appreciate Kerry's determination and her courage, and he realised that she, too, was benefiting from their time together. She was a hardy little thing, so unlike Laura, yet their differences seemed to have cemented a surprising friendship between them.

Kerry's mother appeared at the door. 'Would you like a cup of tea before you go, Mr Thornton?'

'Yes, please, Ms Beckworth – this is thirsty work out here!' Alan replied amiably. 'But Kerry is doing brilliantly. She'll be a really competent cyclist by the summer!'

Leaving Kerry to put away her bike, Alan headed inside to Ellie's kitchen, glad of the opportunity to spend even a few minutes alone with her. Seeing her, but not being able to hold her, was torture. And soon, their time together would be even more limited – summer was approaching, and the children would be on long holidays from school.

Alan sighed at the thought of not being able to see Ellie every afternoon. For years, he'd led a charmed life, slipping away from the office for a late – and long – lunch with Ellie almost every working day. Sylvia assumed he was at work all day, and during the evenings and weekends he'd been able to tell her that he had urgent factory business to attend to. But now that Kerry was growing older, things weren't quite so easy. Already he was unable to visit Ellie at weekends, and during the week he had to leave Treetops long before Kerry returned from school.

'I don't know how I'll cope if the school holidays get any longer,' Alan grumbled, giving Ellie's hand a surreptitious squeeze. 'As

Kerry gets older, maybe we can send her to one of those summer camps for a week or two?'

Ellie laughed. 'Luckily, she's old enough to join the junior tennis club this year, and she's really looking forward to it.' She smiled at him. 'That takes place every weekday afternoon for most of the summer.'

Alan winked conspiratorially at Ellie. 'Then I'll buy her the best tennis racquet money can buy. After all, the more she likes tennis, the more she'll keep playing!' He sneaked a hand up Ellie's sweater. 'And the more time we'll have to spend together!'

Alan was pleased. Maybe the school holidays wouldn't be such a problem after all.

When she saw Laura's little face appearing at the front door, Ellie thanked her lucky stars that Alan had left ten minutes earlier – it would have been a catastrophe if the child had spotted him teaching Kerry to ride her new bike.

'Hello, love,' Ellie said, addressing Laura warmly, more out of relief than anything else. 'Kerry's upstairs getting changed.'

She glanced out of the window. Thankfully, Kerry had put her bike away, so there was no evidence of her daughter's clandestine activities on display. 'What brings you here today, Laura?' Ellie asked. 'Don't you usually have ballet classes on Fridays?'

Laura nodded. 'Class was cancelled today, so I thought I'd come over and see if Kerry wanted to play.'

Just then, Kerry came downstairs and greeted Laura warmly.

Ellie smiled at both girls, who were by now sitting at the kitchen table. She produced two tall glasses and filled them with juice from the fridge.

Laura studied Ellie's left hand as she put one of the glasses down in front of her. The diamond in the gold ring she always wore was enormous, and it sparkled as it caught the light. Laura had always been enchanted by its beauty – she'd never seen anything quite as stunning in her whole life. It looked like a ring that should belong to a queen who lived in a palace, rather than a widow who lived in a very modest house.

'Your ring is gorgeous,' Laura ventured.

For a split second, Ellie hesitated. 'Why, thank you,' she said, smiling. 'I love it too.'

'Did your husband give it to you?' Laura ventured, suddenly realising how cheeky her query sounded. Her mother would be furious with her for being so blatantly rude. Her cheeks burned, but it was too late to take back her query now.

Ellie smiled. 'It was given to me by someone very special,' she said softly, holding the ring up to the light.

Laura nodded, relieved that Ellie hadn't chided her for her rudeness. It was only later that she realised Ellie hadn't actually answered her question. But with a child's lack of interest in anything that didn't directly concern her own life, she quickly forgot about it.

But Ellie didn't.

CHAPTER 43

Having changed her mobile phone number the following day, Laura felt a lot more secure. She was still smarting from the events of the previous night, and the fact that Steve had effectively dumped her, but had decided that the best way to get over the ignominy was to throw herself into her work with a vengeance.

As the week progressed, she began to feel a lot calmer, and was relieved that there were no further calls from Jeff. She hoped that he'd realised that the daubing of paint on Steve's car had been a step too far and had finally decided to leave her alone. She'd also put off going to the police, reasoning that she didn't want to antagonise Jeff if he'd already decided to leave her alone.

By Friday, as her students left Laura's office at the end of her afternoon tutorial, she was looking forward to going home, showering and getting ready for her night out with Kerry and her colleagues. She then had the whole weekend ahead, and she intended to do some serious relaxation.

As she switched her phone back on, it began to ring. Laura guessed it was probably Kerry, phoning to see if she'd left work yet. She picked it up off her desk and was just about to press the call button when she looked at the caller ID. She froze. It was Jeff's number.

Quickly she pressed the red button and rejected the call.

How on earth had he managed to get her new number already? She'd had it for less than a week! Anxiously, Laura looked all around her office, as though Jeff was likely to pop up from behind her desk or suddenly materialise beside her. She was shaking and furious. The gall of him, daring to contact her after what he'd done to Steve's car! Did he really think she'd ever want to speak to him again?

In a fury, Laura locked her office and proceeded down the corridor. Her excitement about the night ahead had already waned considerably, and she wondered if she should give the planned outing a miss.

The door to the office of the department's secretary was still open, and Greta waved to Laura as she hurried past.

'Goodnight, Laura. I hope you and Jeff are planning an exciting weekend!' she called.

Laura stopped in her tracks and had a sudden thought. 'Greta, did you give out my new phone number to anyone?'

The department secretary looked vague. 'No, I don't think so.' Then she brightened. 'Oh, yes, I'd forgotten – but then, I don't suppose your husband counts! Yesterday, he rang to say he'd accidentally deleted your new number, and could he have it? He said he felt such a fool.'

Laura nodded, feeling annoyed. 'So you gave it to him.'

'Of course. Why wouldn't I?'

Laura bit her lip. Greta was right – under normal circumstances, there would be no reason not to. So far she'd avoided telling anyone in the department that she and Jeff had broken up. She hadn't wanted people's sympathy in case it made her to burst into tears. Now that reasoning felt so childish and stupid.

'Well, I'd be grateful if you wouldn't tell him anything more about me,' Laura said gently. 'Jeff and I have broken up, and he's being difficult about it.'

Greta's eyes widened. 'Oh, Laura, I'm so sorry!' she said, looking surprised and guilty at the same time. 'If only I'd known – '

Laura nodded ruefully as tears threatened to form. 'It's my own fault – I should have told you all before now. But I feel such a fool! I'm not even married a full year yet, and my marriage is over already.'

'Well, I'm sure you've made the right choice,' Greta said supportively. 'Marriage isn't for everyone, you know.' She looked at Laura grimly. 'But I think maybe you need to change your phone number again.'

Leaving Greta's office, Laura turned and went back down the corridor. Since she'd told Greta that her marriage was over, she felt it was only right to let Darren know as well. He was her boss, and as a matter of courtesy he should really have been the first to hear it.

Knocking on his door, Laura waited apprehensively. She hoped he wouldn't be overly kind to her, since she was likely to break down and cry if he did. Entering at his call, Laura stood in front of Darren's desk, feeling awkward.

'Sit down, Laura – take the weight off your feet,' her boss urged. 'How did you get on with those statistics lectures?'

'Fine,' said Laura dismissively, as she sat down. She never had any problem with her teaching schedule. It was in other areas of her life that things weren't going so smoothly.

'Well, then, is this a social call?' he asked, smiling.

Laura sighed. She couldn't put off telling him any longer. 'Jeff and I have split up,' she said.

Darren's expression was grave. 'I'm very sorry, Laura. But perhaps it's for the best.'

Laura knew that there wouldn't be anyone in the Sociology Department who'd be sorry to see Jeff out of her life. Most of her colleagues had already made it clear that he wasn't their favourite person, and she couldn't blame them either. If anyone was to blame, it was her for being so stupid. Why hadn't she left him the first time he'd raised his hand to her?

'Do you want to take some time off?' Darren asked softly. 'If you feel you need some space, I'm sure Maria could delay her break for a week or two.'

Vehemently, Laura shook her head. 'That's the last thing I need,' she said. 'I was going to ask you if I could do some extra hours – work is probably the best thing for me right now.'

Darren nodded. 'Well, I can't deny that I'd be delighted if you could take the second years for their social cohesion module. I'd been thinking of bringing in a substitute lecturer, but if you're sure you feel up to it – '

'Of course I do,' Laura told him briskly.

Darren suddenly grinned, and Laura could see that his eyes were twinkling. 'I presume we can now take down that dreadful plaque on your door?'

Nodding, Laura blushed.

'Good,' Darren said briskly. 'Can you take over from Monday week? That'll give you time to revise and update your lecture notes for the course. But don't worry about the first year tutorials – I'll handle them myself.'

Laura nodded. 'Thanks, Darren,' she said, rising to her feet. She was grateful that he hadn't gone all maudlin on her, or tried to wheedle the details of the break-up from her. Right now, sympathy would be her undoing, but Darren seemed to know that instinctively.

'Laura – ' Darren took off his glasses and polished them on his handkerchief. 'Please don't forget that we're all here for you.'

Laura nodded, a lump in her throat as she left the room and closed the door.

When she'd gone, a big smile appeared on Darren's face, and he punched the air in jubilation. At last, he'd got his Laura back.

Chapter 44

After several more phone calls from Jeff over the weekend – none of which she had answered – Laura accepted that her ex-husband wasn't going to give up, and that it was time to approach the police about his behaviour.

During her lunch break on Monday, Laura stepped into the local police station and hurried to the front desk.

'Officer, I want to report my ex-husband's unreasonable behaviour.'

The grumpy-faced policeman looked bored as he sat behind a mound of papers. 'Hold on, I'll see if someone is available to talk to you.'

After an eternity, he returned with an officer in tow, who gestured for her to follow him into a dingy office down an equally dingy corridor.

As they sat down on opposite sides of a table marked with cup rings and scuffmarks, the officer gestured for her to begin.

'I've recently left my husband because he turned violent after we got married,' she explained, the words tumbling out. 'But since I've left, he's been following me, turning up at the same places, and he even bugged my friend's flat. When I went out with another guy, my ex-husband deliberately damaged his beautiful car!'

The policeman's steely grey eyes studied her. 'How long have you been separated?'

'Six weeks.'

He raised his eyebrows. 'And you're already seeing some-one else? You didn't waste much time, did you?'

His contemptuous look infuriated Laura. 'I just went out for dinner with a friend. I hope you're not condoning what my ex-husband did to me?' she said angrily.

'Don't put words in my mouth,' the officer warned.

Laura tried to keep her face expressionless and concentrated on the wall behind him; otherwise, she was in danger of climb-ing across the desk and throttling him. And that wouldn't help her case at all. 'So you think I should stay with a violent man?'

'See, there you go again!' the policeman said, frowning. 'That's not what I said at all. I just think that young people today don't give enough thought to their marriage vows.'

Laura stood up. 'He's a violent thug and he's not my hus-band any longer – '

'Ms Thornton. Sit down, and let's talk about this sensibly.'

Laura sat down again, aware that she was on the verge of losing her temper, and knowing that such behaviour wouldn't work in her favour. She made a valiant effort to put a non-threatening and pleasant expression on her face.

The officer became more interested when she told him about the writing on Steve's car, and about the listening device that had been planted in Kerry's living room. She even produced the device for the officer to see.

The officer nodded as he looked at it. 'Okay, I'll look into your claims. But it would be impossible to prove that your ex-husband planted the bugging device – I could have it dust-ed for fingerprints, but I suspect you and your flatmate have already handled it?'

Laura looked crestfallen. 'I'm afraid so. And we dropped it into water to stop it working.'

The officer grimaced. 'The perpetrator probably wore

gloves anyway. Nevertheless, we'll send an officer round to
Mr Jones's apartment to speak to him.'

Laura nodded, relieved. 'Thank you, officer,' she said gratefully. She was glad she hadn't walked out earlier, although
she'd been strongly tempted to do so. Now she was actually
hopeful that a visit from the law would quickly cool Jeff's ar-
dour. But she was also aware that it could increase his volatil-
ity. She just had to hope that Jeff would regard the police visit
as a turning point, and decide to leave her alone.

That night, in Kerry's flat, Laura brought her friend up to date
with what had happened at the police station.

'It didn't start off very well,' she admitted. 'but things began
to improve when I produced the listening device. It was as
though he suddenly started believing me!'

'Does he think it's any help?'

Laura shook her head. 'But he's going to send an officer
round to talk to Jeff.'

'That's great,' Kerry said, opening a bottle of wine. 'Hopefully, that should bring an end to Jeff's antics. If he has any
sense, he'll calm down and realise that it's pointless to keep
hassling you. And if he tries anything else, it'll be easier to
make the police listen next time.'

Laura nodded. 'I hope so – but my problem must seem very
insignificant to the police, given the horrendous situations they
have to deal with on a day-to-day basis.'

Kerry looked at her sharply. 'I'd consider a mental ex-
husband to be rather serious! Anyway, I'm sure the police will
give your situation the attention it deserves.' Looking at the
strain on Laura's face, Kerry proffered a suggestion. 'Maybe
you should visit your doctor, and get something to help you
sleep,' she said. 'I've heard you wandering around the flat in
the early hours of the morning.'

Laura grimaced guiltily. 'Sorry. I hope I haven't disturbed you? But you're right – this business with Jeff is causing me a lot of stress. I'll make an appointment tomorrow.'

Kerry nodded approvingly, pouring them each a glass of wine. Then, as they clinked glasses, Kerry proposed a toast. 'Here's to a Jeff-free life from now on!'

Chapter 45

*A*s the days began to get longer, Kerry cycled over to Greygates to play with her friend.

'When did you learn to ride a bike?' Laura asked with surprise.

Kerry reddened. 'Oh, a friend taught me.'

Laura looked at her suspiciously. 'What friend, and when did they teach you? You never said anything to me about learning. If you'd told me you were getting lessons, I could have come along and learnt to ride, too!'

'Oh, it was just someone Mum knows,' Kerry said dismissively. 'And he only gave me a few lessons. I didn't need any more.'

'And who bought you the bike?'

Kerry coloured as the lie formed on her tongue. 'Mum did.'

Laura felt hard done by. It was as though Kerry had moved on to a different level, and she was being left behind. She was always acutely aware of the three-month age difference between them – it always seemed to give Kerry an advantage. And now that Kerry could ride a bike, Laura was suddenly afraid that she might move on to other friends, people who could ride bicycles and therefore could cycle to the woods or to the park on picnics.

'Will you teach me to ride?' Laura asked anxiously.

Kerry nodded. 'Okay, but I don't want you falling off and damaging my bike.'

'Huh!' said Laura, annoyed now. 'I can see you're more concerned about your bike than about me.'

Kerry grinned. 'You're right – because once you've learned on mine, your parents will buy you a brand new one, and I'll be left with the old one that you've wrecked!'

Although still annoyed, Laura could see Kerry's point of view, but she was still determined to acquire this new skill.

'Okay, I'll strike a deal with you. If I damage your bike, I'll let you ride my new one when we go out cycling together. But I can't let Mum know, because she'd kill me!'

Grinning, Kerry nodded. 'You've got a deal. Come on – let's get started!'

'And while you're here, could you fix my skateboard?'

Kerry nodded. 'Of course. What's wrong with it?'

'I don't exactly know, but one of the wheels is definitely stuck.'

'It's probably rusted up since last summer. I told you to oil the wheels before putting it away, didn't I? But I'll bet you didn't.'

As she watched Laura's cheeks turn red, Kerry didn't need any reply.

'Dad, Kerry is teaching me to ride a bike,' Laura said proudly, as she joined the family for their evening meal.

Alan felt a pang of guilt, realising that he should have been the one to do it.

'That's great, love,' he told her enthusiastically. 'Would you like me to help?'

Laura shook her head. 'No, thanks. I've nearly mastered it already. But you can watch me at the weekend – I should be able to do it perfectly by then.'

'So I guess you'll be wanting a bike for your next birthday?' Alan said, smiling.

'You're not bad at all,' Kerry conceded grudgingly, as they finished Laura's latest cycling lesson. 'I think your dad was impressed, too.'

'Thanks,' Laura said, blushing. She was delighted with her progress, and thrilled that her father had come along to watch her ride successfully around the lawn at Greygates the previous afternoon.

Kerry and Mr Thornton had also shared a knowing wink, and Kerry knew he was grateful she hadn't told Laura about the secret lessons he'd given her. Kerry liked sharing a secret with Mr Thornton – in a way, it was almost like having a secret father of her own.

As Laura climbed off, Kerry inspected her bicycle. 'You don't seem to have done any damage,' she declared magnanimously, 'so I'll let you off our deal. Just as long as you give me one go on your new bicycle when you get it?'

'Hmmm…' Laura murmured pointedly. 'But what if you damage my new bike?'

'You catch on fast, don't you?' Kerry said, grinning, as she leaned her bike against the wall. 'Anyway, I wasn't really going to hold you to it. And I've fixed your skateboard, too – it's in your shed.'

'Oh, thanks – that's brilliant!' Laura said, smiling.

'No problem,' Kerry said gruffly, embarrassed by Laura's obvious admiration. 'It only meant adjusting one of the wheel nuts where it had rusted.'

'Come on, let's go and get some juice from the kitchen,' Laura suggested. 'Riding a bike is thirsty work!'

'Okay,' said Kerry and, arm in arm, they headed across the lawn towards the house.

After Kerry had gone home, Laura joined her mother in the living room.

Sylvia put down the newspaper she'd been reading. 'So you can now ride a bike – that's marvellous news, darling!' she said. 'Before Daddy left to check on something at the factory, he was telling me how clever you are! I'll come and watch you tomorrow, if you like? It was good of Kerry to teach you.'

Laura nodded, sitting down in an armchair opposite her mother. 'Mum, is Kerry's mother very rich?'

Sylvia laughed. 'Good heavens, what a strange question! No, Kerry and her mother aren't rich – but they're not exactly poor, either. They're just not as well off as we are.'

'But Kerry's mother has the most amazing ring – with a diamond that's much bigger than any of yours,' Laura insisted. 'It sparkles in the light – it's amazing.'

For a split second, Sylvia had felt that old, familiar jolt of anger that rose up inside her any time diamond rings were mentioned. But instantly she chided herself – there was no point in allowing herself to become continually riled by it. She was never going to know what had become of the ring Alan had bought, and it would serve her best to forget all about it.

'Have you eaten your supper, darling?'

Laura nodded.

Sylvia kissed the top of her daughter's blonde head. 'Well, then, run along and get ready for bed. You've had a busy day – cyclists need lots of rest, too, you know!'

CHAPTER 46

A week of relative peace ensued after Laura's visit to the police. There were no more phone calls from Jeff, and she was feeling upbeat about life again. Although Kerry was insistent that she could stay as long as she liked at her apartment, Laura had taken a day off work to search for a new place to live. It wasn't fair to her friend to have to share such a small and cramped space indefinitely.

As she sauntered along the street, surveying estate agents' windows, Laura felt happy and confident about the future. She'd made a dreadful mistake by marrying Jeff, but hopefully that was all in the past now and, if he'd just leave her alone, she could get on with her life.

She'd also been to visit her doctor, and been given sedatives to help her sleep. She hadn't actually taken any yet, but the mere fact of having them in her possession seemed to have acted like some sort of placebo – she'd been sleeping like a baby ever since.

She was also toying with the idea of actually buying a flat – although she'd inherited a huge amount of money when she'd reached twenty-five, she'd never touched it because of the guilt she felt over her parents' and brother's deaths. Now she was beginning to see the sense of owning her own place. It would make her feel secure, and beholden to no one. But it was a big decision, and she was scared of tying up so much money in a property she might later realise wasn't suitable for her needs.

She was also greatly relieved that she'd never told Jeff about the money – she had Kerry to thank for that. Although Jeff didn't seem to have any financial worries, he did like to spend, so he might have been very happy to access her money. He might even have tried pursuing her in the divorce courts for a substantial share of it.

In one of the estate agent's offices, Laura explained her indecision about buying to Avril, the young woman who'd elected to answer her queries.

'Well, we have a luxury apartment at the corner of Green Street – it's available for rent, but the owner is intending to put it on the market next year. If you rented it and decided you'd like to buy it, you'd be in pole position to make an offer.'

'That sounds interesting,' Laura said enthusiastically. 'I like the Green Street area. When can I see it?'

'I can take you there now, if you like. It's got a concierge and is dual aspect, so I think you'll really like it. The concierge is a security feature that many people like, especially single women.'

Laura was pleased. It sounded perfect for her, especially in her present situation with Jeff. She also liked the idea of being able to live somewhere before having to make any decision about buying it.

The second-floor apartment in Green Street was bright and airy, and had extremely high ceilings, which Laura instantly loved. She was captivated by the sense of space they engendered, and even though it was only a two-bedroom unit, it had a wide hall, a large living space and two very large bedrooms.

She was also intrigued by the unusual layout – the entrance

hall, kitchen and living areas were over the large bedrooms, luxury bathroom and built-in storage units downstairs. Access to the bedrooms below was via a beautiful staircase.

'What an unusual layout – I'll bet the architects have won prizes for this design!' Laura said, gazing around in awe.

Avril nodded. 'This building was a major restoration project some years ago. The whole interior was gutted and redesigned. It's quite spectacular, isn't it?'

The rent was also high, and there was a hefty annual service charge, but Laura felt that the extra facilities were well worth it.

'I love it,' she said happily. 'But is it okay for a friend to see it before I decide?'

'Of course.' Avril smiled. 'But I get the feeling you've already made up your mind!'

Laura nodded. 'It's just that I'd feel better having a second opinion – I've a tendency to rush things, and it's already landed me in lots of hot water!' She smiled. 'How soon would I be able to move in?'

'I can have the paperwork done within the next two weeks. Then it's all yours.'

Laura nodded happily. She had a good feeling about the apartment, and she just knew Kerry would love it, too.

Kerry was just as impressed by the apartment as Laura.

'Wow!' was her immediate reaction as she stared up at the high ceilings and the large living room, flooded with light. 'This is amazing!' Kerry whispered. 'The layout is so airy and spacious. It's fantastic!'

Laura grinned. 'I just needed your opinion first.'

Kerry gave a mock gasp. 'Have you had a personality transplant? Where's the impetuous woman I used to know so well?'

Laura grinned. 'I guess Jeff taught me a few valuable lessons.'

'Well, he's gone now, and it's the start of a whole new life for you, love – congratulations! Let's go out tonight and paint the town red!'

Chapter 47

*T*he afternoon sunlight shone through the closed curtains, il-luminating the slick of sweat that covered their naked bodies. Both of them were dozing, made sleepy by lovemaking. Sudden-ly, a sound interrupted their post-coital afterglow.

'What was that?' Ellie asked anxiously, sitting up and check-ing her watch. 'It couldn't be Kerry – it's far too early for her to be back from tennis.'

Alan smiled at her. 'Stop worrying! It was nothing.'

Ellie lay down again, and he took her in his arms.

'I hate living like this,' she whispered. 'Always afraid of be-ing discovered, afraid of every little sound.'

He silenced her with a deep kiss. 'It won't be for ever, love – we'll find a way to be together soon. I promise.'

For a while, they lay together in silence, each listening for any other unfamiliar sound. But all they could hear was the sound of each other's breathing.

Ellie was the first to break the silence. 'I think she should be told the truth. Kerry deserves to know that you're her father.'

'Not now, love – she's still too young. When we're finally a couple, and can be together all the time, we'll tell her.'

'I wish I could have you with me all the time,' Ellie said wist-fully, pulling the bedclothes over her naked body.

'So do I,' he whispered, kissing her nose playfully. 'and you will *have me, very soon. But we can't afford to rock any boats just yet.'*

'That doesn't stop me wishing,' she replied, brushing a tear from her eye. *'I wish I'd been the one who met you first. Then we wouldn't have to go through this charade all the time.'*

'Let's not spoil the little time we have together. I want it to be joyful – I want to show you how much I love you!' Alan replied, stroking her face and tenderly kissing her nose. *'Now, I'm going to make love to you again, and that will let you know just how much you mean to me!'*

Groaning, she surrendered to his tender ministrations. He knew exactly how to excite her. Every touch, every look, turned her on. And she knew it was the same for him – they just couldn't get enough of each other. It had been like that for years, yet they'd never grown tired of being together.

Afterwards, they lay in silence, exhausted but still savouring their delight in each other.

Eventually, he looked at his watch. *'It's time for me to go, love,'* he whispered. *'Kerry will be home from tennis within the hour.'*

After a final kiss inside the front door, and having checked that the coast was clear, Alan stepped outside. As his eyes adjusted to the strong sunlight, he thought he saw a sudden movement over near the outhouse, but when he looked again, he could see nothing. It was probably just his overactive imagination – Ellie's fears were making him jittery, too. His visits to her were always fraught with the fear of being caught. He strode quickly to his car, which was, as usual, parked behind the house, well hidden from the road. He checked his watch again. With luck, he'd be home in time to join the family for dinner.

CHAPTER 48

Kerry awoke from her dream, her forehead clammy. She'd gone to bed early and fallen asleep quickly. Now she felt disoriented as she looked at her watch. It was just before midnight. The streetlights outside provided backlighting for the trees as they blew in the wind, throwing bizarre shadows onto the glass of the window. She suddenly realised that a phone was ringing somewhere in the distance. It had to be her own mobile phone, since Laura had gone to a movie with her colleague Maria, and was staying overnight at the other woman's house.

Leaping out of bed, Kerry hurried into the kitchen, feeling a chill of apprehension running down her spine. A late-night caller was never the bearer of good news.

'H-hello?'

There was no reply, although Kerry knew there was someone on the other end of the line. Breaking her own rule never to respond, she shouted angrily at the caller.

'Whoever you are, go to hell!'

Then she banged the phone down on the table. She was furious at being woken up just after she'd managed to drift off to sleep. She briefly wondered if she should be worried about this latest call: was it part of some frightening scenario orchestrated by Jeff or his drug-dealer colleague? Quickly Kerry dismissed the idea and accepted that it was probably just a wrong number.

Kerry had seen the strange man again several times outside her place of work, but now she didn't let it bother her. He seemed completely harmless and he never bothered her, just stood watching her. She was also relieved she hadn't told Laura about him. Laura would have made an even bigger deal of it. Yet again she'd proved the value of keeping her own counsel. Deciding to make herself a cup of tea, Kerry turned on the kettle. She was wide awake now, and unlikely to get back to sleep any time soon. If she couldn't drop off quickly, she might even help herself to one of the sedatives Laura had been prescribed but never used. There was an important meeting at Sea Diagnostics in the morning and she needed to be alert. Damn the caller, whoever he or she was.

Although she was no longer frightened, these random incidents had, nevertheless, brought back long-forgotten memories from her childhood. She'd never told anyone – not even Laura – about the man who used to hide in the shadows of Treetops's driveway and watch her as she played. Even as a child she'd refused to let it bother her, believing that by telling anyone she'd only make it worse, and there was also the distinct likelihood that her mother would restrict her freedom and insist she play indoors instead.

She'd never been able to see the man clearly, since he'd always stayed hidden among the trees. At times, she had convinced herself that this man in the shadows was her long-lost father. She became adept at weaving stories in which this father of hers had a starring role. Sometimes, he'd just returned from overseas, or from bravely fighting in some war or other, and he was unable to resist seeing how his daughter was getting on. But since he seemed unable to visit her openly, she eventually changed her story to one in which he'd been in prison – wrongly convicted, of course – and that her mother had banished him for ever from their lives. Desperate for a father of her own, Kerry had relished that particular story, and for a while she'd even unfairly resented her mother for keeping this noble man at bay.

Sighing, she rinsed her cup and headed back to bed. It was time to forget about men hiding in shadows and silent phone calls. Sea Diagnostics was about to tender for yet another big project, and it needed her full attention the following morning. Within minutes of climbing into bed, Kerry was fast asleep again.

CHAPTER 49

A week later, Laura decided it was time to return to the local police station. She was actually looking forward to her visit this time, since she was hoping they might have some news about their visit to Jeff. Hopefully, her ex-husband would leave her alone now that the police had been in contact with him.

In the police station, Laura waited eagerly as the duty officer on the front desk searched for the report and then, having found it, hurried off to confer with a colleague.

Shortly afterwards, Laura was ushered into the office of a different police officer from the one she encountered on her previous visit. This one was a detective sergeant, and he acknowledged her presence with a nod, thumbing through the stack of papers in front of him, extracting several sheets of paper. 'Hmm, yes, it says here that one of our officers went round to Mr Jones's apartment last week.' The DS looked up. 'But according to this report, your ex-husband says you're making it all up.' He looked down again at the wording in the report and read it aloud to her. 'He says you're a vindictive woman who's determined to wreck his life. According to him, you're out for revenge because he kept some of your wedding presents.'

While Laura sat open-mouthed, the police officer read from the papers again. 'It says here that he offered them back to you, but you wouldn't accept them. He maintains that you refused to take them because you wanted to be able to keep hassling him.'

Laura was aghast. 'But that's exactly what he's doing to me! Can't you see that he's hijacking *my* story and using it against me!' she shouted.

'Calm down, Ms Thornton. All shouting at me will do is prove the man's point – he said you've even been screaming down the phone at him, too.'

'That's untrue – he's been the one hassling me!'

The DS looked at his notes. 'Well, he's got a sound alibi for the time you claim he damaged your friend's car, and he's given us a recording of you on the phone to him and, I have to say, it did sound as though you were the one hassling *him*.'

The DS stood up, left the room briefly and returned with a small tape recorder. As he pressed the button, Laura could hear her own voice, strident with tension. *'You bastard, Jeff! I am sick to death of you – don't make me do something I'll regret! You're nothing but a pathetic loser!'*

Laura was speechless. 'So you obviously didn't hear the bits where I begged him to leave me alone,' she said quietly.

'You were angry. I can hear that. But it takes two to tango. Now, I suggest you calm down and look at the situation rationally.' Before Laura could answer, the DS spoke again. 'Your ex-husband has also filed a complaint against you on the grounds that you're the one who's making his life a misery – that he's moved on, but you just won't let him be!'

Laura exploded. 'My ex-husband is from a violent, dysfunctional family – his father killed his mother, then hanged himself – yet Jeff saw fit to model our marriage on theirs! He's told me he works for MI5, but I've no way of knowing if that's true or not. I'm also fairly sure he's killed someone!'

The DS's eyes narrowed, and he made a quick note on the report. 'Things tend to get nasty when couples break up,' he said noncommittally. 'And people have been known to make false accusations against each other.'

'I'm not making this up – '

He rose from the table. 'Ma'am, I don't think there's much more I can do to help you. If you don't want to see your ex, then surely you can just stay away from him?'

'That's what I'm trying to do, but he keeps turning up everywhere I go!'

The DS looked exasperated. 'Ms Thornton, I can see you're very worked up about the situation. And maybe you're reading more into it than it warrants? But, by all means, call us if there are any further incidents – '

In tears of frustration, she stomped out of the police station. Yet again, Jeff had foiled her attempts to get help by pre-empting her claims. He was even more devious than she'd thought.

CHAPTER 50

'I've just been to Kerry's parent–teacher meeting,' Ellie told Alan as they prepared to shower after an afternoon of lovemaking. 'The teachers are really pleased with her progress over the last year, particularly in maths and science.'

Alan nodded. 'That's great. But then, I'm not really surprised – we have a very bright child, you know!'

'Kerry's also been doing brilliantly on her tennis course,' Ellie added. 'She's reached the junior finals in the end-of-season tournament that's being held at the club next Friday afternoon – it would mean a lot to her if you could be there.'

Alan nodded, moving over to allow Ellie to step into the shower beside him. 'Of course I will! But it's probably best if I go there on my own – I mean, this will be the first time I'll be seen publicly at an event where Kerry's taking part – so there's no point in rocking any boats.' He inclined his head. 'I presume Laura won't be turning up to support her friend? That would be a disaster –'

Ellie shook her head. 'No, Laura's not keen on tennis and, anyway, she does ballet classes on Friday afternoons.' She nudged him playfully in the ribs. 'Shouldn't you know that already?'

Alan grimaced. Ellie was right. He was inclined to forget who was doing what sometimes.

'I'm glad the girls have at least a few different hobbies, and get to spend some time apart from each other,' Ellie added. 'Because most of the time, they seem to be stuck together like glue!'

Alan smiled down at her and kissed the top of her wet head. 'Tell Kerry I'm looking forward to seeing her play next Friday.'

Ellie smiled at her daughter as the child returned from tennis, looking dishevelled, in need of a bath and a change of clothes. 'You've been putting a lot of effort into this tennis lark, haven't you?' Ellie said, brushing a stray strand of hair from Kerry's damp forehead.

Kerry nodded. 'I'm good at it,' she replied, with no sense of modesty. 'There's a mean girl on the course called Harriet, and she thinks she's better than anyone else at tennis. But I'm going to thrash her in the tournament next Friday – then she'll know who's the best!'

Ellie smiled. 'I have a bit of news for you – Mr Thornton is coming to watch you play in the tournament!'

Kerry looked wary. 'How do you know? When did you see him?'

Ellie coloured. 'Oh, he – er, he was just passing by and dropped in to say hello. And when I told him about your tournament, he said he'd love to attend!'

Kerry smiled shyly. Inside, her heart was jumping for joy, and she wanted to shout out with glee. It was the most exciting thing that had ever happened to her!

Ellie smiled as she helped her daughter out of her grass-stained clothing. The regular loads of washing over the summer period were a small price to pay for the free time it allowed her to be with Alan.

'Come along and let me run a bath for you – you look like a scarecrow!'

Without demur, Kerry allowed herself to be propelled upstairs. She simply couldn't stop smiling at the thought of Mr Thornton watching her play next Friday. She'd make him proud of her by beating nasty Harriet and claiming the junior prize!

*As the week progressed, all the pupils who had won their pre-
liminary tennis matches were spending extra time on the courts,
as they prepared to demonstrate their burgeoning skills to their
doting parents on Friday afternoon. Each final match had been
arranged on the basis of age and skill, with Kerry and her opponent being from the youngest age group in the competition. Theirs
would be the first match played. The winner of each match would
receive a small trophy.*

*Kerry was secretly thrilled as she waited eagerly for Friday to
arrive. As she continued to hone her skills against any other pupil
willing to take her on, her coach was confident that she could
beat her opponent easily. 'You're doing really well this week,' he
told her happily. 'I don't know what's happened, but you seem to
have developed a real urge to win. Keep it up, and you'll definitely be taking home the junior trophy on Friday!'*

*Kerry grinned her thanks, basking in the extra confidence that
his words inspired. Right now, she felt invincible. She was going
to wipe Harriet off the court while Mr Thornton watched! Having
him present would be almost like having a dad of her own! On
Friday she'd be just like all the other children, whose dads would
be turning up to cheer them on.*

*As Kerry prepared to leave the clubhouse after practice, her
nemesis was lurking outside the door to harangue her.*

*'You won't stand a chance on Friday,' Harriet said, sneering at
her. 'You're poor, and you haven't even got a father!'*

*Kerry struggled to keep her emotions under control. 'And you're
just a big bully!' she told the older girl, her eyes blazing. Kerry's
heart was pounding as she stepped into the abyss. 'Besides, my
father is coming to the tournament on Friday – to see me win!'*

Harriet was left with her mouth momentarily open.

'You really have a father?' she asked at last.

*'Yes,' Kerry said. 'But he's away most of the time, on very im-
portant business.'*

'*I don't believe you!*'

'*Well, you'll just have to wait until Friday, won't you?*' Kerry retorted, shoving a surprised Harriet aside as she headed off home.

At the Friday morning breakfast table, Sylvia raised an eyebrow and looked at Alan frostily. '*Don't tell me you've forgotten? We're going to Laura's parent-teacher meeting this afternoon! They want to report on her progress this year, and discuss her options for next year.*'

Alan shrugged. '*I can't make this afternoon, Syl. I've got an important meeting on.*'

'*Well, you'll just have to cancel it,*' Sylvia said acerbically. '*You missed the last parent-teacher meeting, and I absolutely refuse to attend another one on my own! It's important that Laura sees we're taking her education seriously. Besides, if the teachers can make the effort to see us before the new school year starts, then I think you should be able to show some interest in your daughter's future, too!*'

As they arrived for the tennis tournament on Friday afternoon, Ellie found herself a good vantage point on the sidelines while Kerry strode confidently into the clubhouse where the coaches and the other pupils were gathered. Some were chatting in groups, while others were getting last-minute tips about their serves or their backhands.

Harriet was instantly at Kerry's side. '*Where's this father of yours then?*' she whispered nastily, giving Kerry a sly dig in the back.

'*Don't worry, he'll be along shortly,*' Kerry said smugly.

As the two girls waited to be called onto the court, Kerry scanned the sidelines, searching eagerly among the other parents for Mr Thornton. She caught her mother's eye and Ellie waved *encouragingly, but Ellie's presence was of secondary importance to her. The only person Kerry wanted to see was Mr Thornton.*

As Harriet and Kerry took their positions for the preliminary knock-up, Kerry took a last look around the sidelines. There was still no sign of Mr Thornton anywhere. She hoped he wasn't going to be late.

'I thought you said your father would be here?' Harriet hissed, as she made her way to the other side of the net. 'You've been lying – you haven't got a father at all!'

'Yes, I have!' Kerry muttered.

'Liar!' Harriet said, laughing maliciously. 'From now on, I'm going to call you Kerry-no-dad!'

Kerry was selected to serve, but she was so blinded by anger that she put the first serve straight into the net.

As she served again, Kerry put the ball wide this time. Harriet's taunting was seriously upsetting her, and Alan's absence was breaking her heart. Why would he say he was going to attend, then not turn up? Was she so unimportant to him that he'd simply forgotten?

Kerry's third serve was successful, and for several minutes the ball went back and forth between the two girls. Kerry began to feel more positive about her performance, but then she made the fatal mistake of averting her eyes to search again for Mr Thornton, enabling Harriet to send a forehand low across the net, too fast and too far away for Kerry to return it.

Kerry's confidence took a nosedive. She couldn't think of anything but the fact that Mr Thornton hadn't bothered to turn up. Blinded by tears, Kerry missed Harriet's next return as it thundered past her and landed just inside the base line.

'First game to Harriet!'

As the two girls stood together beneath the umpire's chair, waiting for the start of their second game, Kerry longed to pour her juice over Harriet's head, since the bigger girl was using every opportunity to further undermine her.

'*Any sign of Daddy yet?*' the other girl whispered maliciously. '*What a pity he can't be bothered to turn up for his daughter – who's in real trouble right now!*'

With Harriet's peals of laughter ringing in her ears, Kerry's shoulders slumped as she made her way to the opposite side of the court for the next game. By now, she had lost all concentration and all belief in herself. Mr Thornton didn't care, so what was the point of caring about anything?

In the second and subsequent games, Kerry was no threat to her nemesis. She'd lost her fighting spirit and, by the end of the match, she'd lost all six games disastrously and ignominiously to Harriet.

As she left the court, smarting from the shame and feeling the weight of other people's pity, she felt overwhelmed by grief. This was just the most devastating thing that had ever happened to her. As for Mr Thornton, she hoped she'd never see him again. Why had he told her mother he'd be there? He was a liar, and she hated him!

Her situation was made even worse by having to wait on the sidelines while all the other matches were played. Harriet insisted on sitting beside her, continuing to needle her with snide comments about her absentee father all afternoon. Kerry longed to hit Harriet over the head with her racquet, but she knew how important it was to appear outwardly sanguine about losing her match. Despite her humiliation, Kerry wanted to be seen as a good sport.

After the matches and the prize-giving, Ellie was waiting outside the pavilion for her daughter. She was still puzzled that Alan hadn't turned up, and she cast a final futile glance around the court. She hoped that nothing was wrong. He'd seemed so keen on seeing Kerry play...

Kerry strode angrily out of the clubhouse, pushing aside other pupils and their parents as she joined her mother. '*I thought you said that Mr Thornton was coming along today?*' she said, her face red with rage.

'Yes, Al – er, Mr Thornton said he'd be here. I wonder what happened to take him away? I'm sure it must have been something very important,' Ellie said soothingly. 'I know he was really looking forward to watching you play!'

Kerry said nothing. She wasn't able to speak any more, since she was holding her jaw rigidly in an effort to keep her unshed tears under control. She didn't want her mother to see how upset she was, in case she told Mr Thornton. And Kerry would rather die than let him know that she'd cared about him being there.

'Never mind, there'll always be another time!' Ellie said cheerfully. 'What does it matter that you lost one match? Even top players lose sometimes. Come on – let's head back home. I've made an apple pie for after dinner – your favourite!'

CHAPTER 51

The following week, Laura got the keys to her new apartment. She didn't have many possessions other than her clothing and the precious photographs of her parents and brother. When she left the apartment she'd shared with Jeff, she'd taken only the minimum of items with her, since her prime concern had been to get away to safety.

The new apartment came complete with beds, a lavish kitchen and two beige sofas in the large living room, but everything else Laura would need to supply herself. On the day she moved in, she and Kerry spent several enjoyable hours traipsing around the shops getting the remaining items she needed.

'Shall I stay with you for your first night?' Kerry asked, as she filled a kitchen cupboard with packets of food. 'I mean, it's bound to be a bit lonely until you get settled in. We could get a takeaway…'

'Thanks, but there's absolutely no need,' Laura replied cheerfully. 'You must be sick and tired of me by now, and I'm sure you're dying to have your flat to yourself again!'

'Well, if you're sure…'

'Of course. I'm quite looking forward to being here on my own. Not that I'm not grateful for all your help, and for putting up with me for so long – '

Kerry dismissed her thanks with a wave of her hand. 'All

for one, and one for all – isn't that our motto? You'd do the same for me.'

Laura nodded. 'But you'd never be so stupid as to get involved with someone like Jeff.'

Kerry patted her arm. 'What's done is done, so forget about him. Anyway, I'm much too cautious to rush into anything – maybe that's a fault rather than a virtue. At least you followed your heart.'

As Laura stood alone in her new apartment, she felt a surge of joy. The apartment was hers and she loved it! Right that minute, she wanted to buy it, lock stock and barrel. So it was probably just as well that she'd have to wait until next year, because she was being her usual impetuous self again. Living there would enable her to find out if the apartment truly suited her. But in her heart she knew it would.

A sudden wave of sadness swept over her. She'd never expected to be buying a home on her own. She and Jeff had planned on eventually buying a big home in the country, and she'd always imagined it would look similar to the house where she'd once lived with her parents and brother. There would be trees for their children to climb, and acres of garden where they'd learn about nature and have lots of space to let their imaginations run riot, just as she, Pete and Kerry had done all those years ago.

Sighing, she shook her head, as though to dislodge the memories of her past. She hoped she hadn't seemed too eager to get rid of Kerry. She owed her friend a huge debt of gratitude, and she wouldn't want to hurt her feelings. But she was really excited at being alone in her new home.

As she walked from room to room, Laura made a list of all the things she'd need. Since she was already planning to stay in the apartment long term, she intended making it look exactly the way she wanted it. Looking around the apartment, Laura made a vow to start spending some of the money she had stashed away in banks and investments. Rationally, she knew that the guilt she felt over her family's deaths was pointless, and whether she spent the money or not, nothing was ever going to bring her family back.

She could also assuage her guilt by giving some of the money to Kerry. And she'd do it just as soon as she and Jeff were divorced. The legal ending of her marriage seemed the perfect time to reward her friend for all her help and support over the years.

Checking her watch, Laura was astonished to discover that it was already quite late – how times flies, she thought, when you're enjoying yourself! Drinking a cup of tea before heading downstairs to bed, she settled back into the comfort of one of the large cosy couches, and contemplated her future in the apartment.

Climbing into bed, Laura was still smiling. She felt that at last she was entering a new and exciting phase of her life. No sooner had her head hit the pillow than she was fast asleep.

Laura awoke suddenly. Her befuddled brain had registered an unusual sound somewhere in the apartment. She reached for her watch, and its luminous dial told her it was just after 3 a.m. In the dark of the room, she was unable to see anything. Listening carefully, she heard nothing, so she assumed it had just been her imagination going into overdrive. It was probably just one of those creaky sounds that buildings made – she wasn't yet familiar with the Green Street building's quirks. All the same, she now wished that she'd accepted Kerry's invitation to stay the first night with her. Her heart was thumping and her mouth was dry. She'd locked the front door, hadn't she? Stop it, she told herself crossly. You're behaving like an idiot.

Anyway, there's a concierge on duty downstairs, so nothing bad can happen. That's why you took this apartment – so that you'd feel safe.

She was just dropping off to sleep again when she heard it. It was a faint scraping sound that she couldn't identify, and it was definitely coming from somewhere upstairs. Someone was in her apartment! Terrified, she glanced around the dark downstairs bedroom. But there was nowhere for her to hide. There was no key in the door either, so she couldn't lock herself in. What was she going to do? Did she wait in bed for whatever was going to happen, or did she try to escape?

Leaping out of bed, she dived behind the bedroom door and crouched down, listening all the while for sounds of anyone coming down the stairs. If only she had some kind of weapon! Her heart was beating so loudly that she felt sure that whoever was in the flat must hear it. She felt as impotent as a small child, recalling all the times she'd been terrified of the monsters beneath her bed, whose tentacles might reach out and grab her leg if she tried to climb out. And she remembered how her father would get down on his hands and knees and confirm with a shake of his head that there were definitely no monsters lurking there.

Laura felt tears filling her eyes as she remembered the father she'd loved so much. How she wished he was there now, to protect her! Angrily she brushed aside her tears – this was no time for self-indulgence and maudlin thoughts. She needed her wits about her if she was to deal with the present situation.

As the minutes ticked by with no further sound, Laura began to relax a little. Maybe she'd just imagined it? But she was still too terrified to leave the bedroom and investigate. By now she had cramps in her legs and one arm was numb from hanging tightly onto the doorknob for support.

Eventually, the cramp proved too much to bear any longer,

so Laura stood up as quietly as she could. Straining to hear, she waited anxiously but could make out no further sound. She could hear the noise of occasional traffic outside, and it lent an air of normality to things. Had she simply imagined the scraping sound? After all, the concierge down in the foyer wasn't going to allow anyone up to her apartment without good reason, and certainly not in the middle of the night. She was just being silly once again.

All the same, she was still too scared to check any of the other rooms. Sitting down on the bed, her head now resting wearily against the headboard, Laura stifled a yawn as she pulled the duvet around her. A wave of lethargy swept over her. She'd need to let each of the three concierges know about Jeff, and ensure that he was never allowed anywhere near her apartment. She'd do that in the morning. Right then, she was feeling unbelievably tired – all the drama of the last half-hour was proving exhausting. Her eyelids began to flicker, and she was having difficulty keeping them open.

Gradually, Laura's grip on the duvet relaxed, her eyelids gave up the fight to stay open and she fell into a deep sleep.

CHAPTER 52

*A*lan was turning his car into Treetops's driveway just as Kerry and her mother arrived home after the tournament.

'Mr Thornton, what a surprise!' Ellie said, smiling, as she and Kerry stepped out of her car. 'Would you like a cup of tea?'

Alan nodded. 'Thanks, Ms Beckworth, that would be lovely.'

While Ellie went inside, he turned to face the child, looking contrite. 'I'm so sorry that I missed your tournament, Kerry – but I had a really important business meeting that I simply had to attend.'

Kerry shrugged her shoulders. 'Don't worry – it didn't matter,' she told him stonily.

Only then did it dawn on him that he'd hurt her badly. He felt chastened, but there wasn't much he could do. Sylvia had cracked the whip, and he didn't dare defy her on those few occasions when his mild-mannered wife actually asserted her will.

'I'll come to your next tournament,' Alan said, desperately wanting her absolution.

'I said it doesn't matter,' Kerry told him firmly, refusing to look at him. 'It was only a stupid tennis tournament anyway – nothing like as important as your *meeting!*'

'I'd like to get you something nice, you know, to make up for not being there,' Alan said softly, knowing that he was wheedling, but unable to stop himself. 'Would you like a new bike, or an even better tennis racquet?'

Walking off, Kerry pretended not to hear.

The following morning, as Kerry climbed up the big tree at Greygates to join her friend on the platform, Laura was all smiles. 'How did your tennis tournament go?'

Kerry shrugged her shoulders. 'It was okay. But I was beaten in the finals.'

Laura squeezed her friend's arm affectionately, knowing how much Kerry always wanted to win. 'What bad luck – but I'm sure you'll win the trophy next year!'

Kerry looked bored. 'It doesn't really matter. I think I might give up tennis anyway.'

Laura looked startled. 'You don't mean that – you love tennis! I'm the idiot who can't hit a ball straight, but you're brilliant at it!'

Kerry quickly changed the subject, not keen to discuss her humiliation any further.

'How was your day yesterday? Did you do anything exciting?'

Laura grimaced. 'I was really looking forward to telling Mum and Dad how well I'm doing at ballet, but when they came home from the parent-teacher meeting at the school, I knew by their faces that I was in trouble! Apparently, my end-of-term maths test was a disaster – '

But Kerry was no longer listening. 'Your parents were at the school yesterday afternoon?'

Laura nodded. 'You're lucky that your parent-teacher meeting was last week! Now Mum is furious with me. Dad is being a lot nicer about it, but he said I might have to go for a maths grind this year – '

Rage filled Kerry's heart – Mr Thornton had lied to her. He'd told her that he was attending a business meeting, whereas he'd put Laura's school visit before her tennis tournament. Which wasn't really surprising – inevitably, Mr Thornton would choose

Laura over her. She had no claim on him, other than the fact that she longed for his attention. But why did he say he'd attend her tournament if he knew he couldn't? Didn't she deserve even the tiniest bit of consideration?

Tears filled her eyes. Not having a dad of one's own was the most awful thing that could happen and, as always, Kerry felt the loss acutely.

'Are you okay?' Laura darted a concerned look at her friend, even though she knew Kerry would never willingly acknowledge her own vulnerability.

'I'm fine,' Kerry snapped. 'I'm just a bit tired.'

Laura nodded, at a loss to help her friend who was obviously hurting, and the two girls sat together in silence.

Laura was the first to feel the raindrops. 'Looks like we'd better go indoors,' she said quietly, and began scrambling down the tree as the rain started to get heavier. 'Let's go back to the house – we could try finishing that jigsaw I got last Christmas. And I could show you the new antique figurine that Dad's recently added to his Lladró collection. It's a really valuable piece, and he's so chuffed to have found it.'

Kerry's eyes narrowed. 'Okay,' she said.

It was late, but Alan wasn't ready for sleep. As he headed for his study, he kissed Sylvia's cheek as she stood at the bottom of the staircase. 'I'll follow you up later, Syl. I've one or two reports I need to read first.'

Sylvia smiled tenderly at him. 'You work so hard, darling – don't you ever take a break? I hope you realise just how much I – we – all love you. And appreciate your efforts.'

Alan nodded, feeling overwhelmed by guilt. Thank goodness Sylvia had no idea about his other life. The hair on the back of his neck rose at the mere thought of her discovering his duplicity. He loved Ellie, but juggling both lives was proving inordinately stressful. He was also riddled with guilt over poor Kerry – he'd genuinely intended being present at her tennis tournament. But he was only one man – maybe it simply wasn't possible to keep two relationships successfully running in tandem.

In the peace and privacy of his study, Alan sat down at his desk in his big leather swivel chair. There was a certain comfort in having a private space of one's own. Especially since the rest of his life was monitored so tightly by all the other people around him. Here, at least, he didn't need to answer to anyone.

Idly he spun around in his chair, allowing his eyes to rest briefly on the things he loved as he viewed the room. Leather chairs, shelves full of books – most of which he'd never read – a built-in bar, with cut-crystal glasses and a selection of whiskies. He smiled ruefully to himself as he poured a single malt, enjoying the intense aròma before taking his first sip. As he relaxed over his whisky, Alan allowed himself the supreme luxury of thinking about nothing at all.

After topping up his glass a second time, he allowed the chair to circle once again, his eyes alighting on his precious Lladró collection, which stretched along the top shelf of the bookcase. It gave him a thrill when he came across a rare piece, especially if he got it at a knockdown price. He'd discovered such a piece on a recent trip abroad, and he hadn't hesitated to buy it, since he knew it would cost twice as much if he'd acquired it in London.

Now, he swung his chair round to enjoy the delights of his most recent purchase. It was entitled 'Spring Birds', and he'd carefully placed it alongside his other acquisitions.

His eyes were by now slightly glazed from the whisky, but he didn't think his eyesight was sufficiently affected as to render his new 'Spring Birds' figurine invisible. Urging his chair to make another circuit, the only conclusion he could reach was that his newest acquisition wasn't on the top shelf any longer. Yet he definitely remembered putting it there – he was certain of it.

As he hoisted himself up out of the chair, he heard a crunching sound underfoot. Looking under his desk, he discovered his new figurine lying shattered on the carpet. As he studied the pattern of destruction, he noticed a small indentation in the wood of the desk that signified the figure had been smashed against it. It had been broken on purpose and in anger, and the culprit hadn't even bothered to disguise their actions. Presumably they'd wanted him to know how angry they felt.

Upstairs in the bedroom, Alan began undressing in the dark. 'Are you still awake, Syl?'

'Hmmm,' Sylvia mumbled sleepily, turning round to face him.

'You know that new Lladró piece I bought recently? Well, I'm afraid it's broken.'

'What?' Sylvia sat up in the bed and switched on her bedside light. 'What happened?'

Alan hesitated. 'I seem to have knocked it off the shelf,' he lied. 'A pity – there aren't many editions of that particular piece.'

Sylvia was immediately sympathetic. 'What rotten luck, darling! I know you were so pleased to have found it, and at such a great price, too! Never mind, I'm sure you'll eventually track down a replacement. That's the fun of the chase for you collectors, isn't it?'

Alan nodded, climbing into bed beside her and pulling the duvet over him. 'By the way, has Kerry been here recently?'

Sylvia nodded before turning off her bedside light again. 'She and Laura were doing a jigsaw puzzle on the kitchen table earlier today.' Sylvia paused for a second. 'Why did you ask about her?'

In the darkness, it was easier to lie. 'Oh, no reason. I just wondered, that's all.'

CHAPTER 53

Laura awoke to find the sun streaming in through her bedroom window and, for a moment, she forgot about her late-night intruder. She'd fallen asleep with her head still resting against the headboard, and her muscles now felt stiff and sore from lying in such a cramped and unfamiliar position. Then she remembered the terror she'd felt the night before but, in the daylight, things didn't seem quite so frightening. Jumping out of bed, she left the bedroom and tiptoed up the staircase onto the floor above, finding a bundle of keys for the various rooms resting on the console table in the hall.

She also discovered what had been making the scraping sound the night before.

Lying on the floor just inside the front door was a large envelope. Clearly it had been stuffed through her letterbox with difficulty, and had been bent in the middle in order to get it through. Laura instantly felt rather foolish. But who would be delivering a letter at around 3 a.m.?

Tearing off the top of the envelope, Laura drew out a large *Good Luck in Your New Home* card. When she opened it, her heart sank. It was signed: '*Jeff*'. Then her annoyance turned to anger. Jeff had cost her another night's sleep! And how on earth had the card reached her apartment? There was no stamp on it, so clearly it had been hand-delivered. Surely Jeff didn't have access to the apartment complex?

Dressing quickly, Laura left her apartment clutching the card and its envelope, and headed downstairs. She needed to catch the night-duty concierge before he finished his shift.

In the hall, the elderly concierge greeted Laura warmly, but she was in no mood for pleasantries. Quickly she told him her name and apartment number and showed him the card.

'Oh, yes,' said the concierge, beaming. 'A very nice, tall, blond man called here last night. He begged me to let him deliver the card to your apartment, but naturally I couldn't allow him to do that. So he asked me if I'd deliver it.' The concierge smiled at her. 'When things were slack, around three o'clock, I managed to go up and push it through your letterbox. It was a bit on the large size for the slot, so I had to bend it a bit to squeeze it through – I hope the noise didn't wake you? But the guy was adamant that he wanted you to get it first thing this morning – to celebrate the start of your first full day in the apartment.'

The concierge looked pleased with himself, thinking he'd done her a favour, and clearly expecting her to be grateful. But the smile was quickly wiped from his face when Laura explained the situation.

'Please – don't ever let him near my apartment,' she begged him, 'no matter what he says – believe me, I don't want my ex-husband within a million miles of me. And I'd be grateful if you could tell the other concierges – or do you want me to have a word with them?'

'No, it's okay – I'll let them know,' the elderly man told her, looking concerned. 'I'm sorry about the card, but please don't worry any further. We'll make sure you're safe here – that's our job.'

Bleary-eyed, Laura returned to her apartment. She had no doubt that Jeff had deliberately chosen to have the card delivered during the night, and he'd selected a large card so that the noise of it being stuffed through the letterbox was bound to frighten her. But, more worrying, was the fact that he'd discovered where she was living. Was she ever going to be rid of him?

Laura phoned the estate agent's office.

'Avril, it's Laura Thornton. Did you let anyone know that I'd moved into the Green Street apartment?'

The woman thought for a moment. 'Oh, yes, now that I think of it – a man phoned yesterday, looking to rent an apartment in the same block, and I explained that we'd just let one there. He asked if it had been let to a Laura Thornton, and I said yes. I assumed he was a friend of yours? I told him I'd let him know if another apartment becomes available...'

'Do you remember his name?'

'Let me check for you...'

Laura heard what sounded like a desk drawer opening and the rustling of paper, then Avril was back on the line.

'Jeff Jones was his name.'

Inwardly, Laura was screaming. But outwardly she tried to appear calm. 'Please – I'd be grateful if you'd let me know if he ever intends moving in here – because I'll be moving out.'

'Why on earth – ?'

'He's my ex-husband, and a man I hope never to see again!' Laura told her.

Avril was immediately contrite. 'Oh, God – I'm so sorry! I'll make sure he doesn't rent anything in Green Street through us – in fact, I'll take his name off our list this very minute. I'll also leave a note here in the book, and explain the situation to the other agents when I see them.'

'Thanks,' Laura said. 'And I'd really appreciate knowing if he contacts you again.'

Turning off her phone, Laura sat staring into space. Jeff was ruining her life! He was orchestrating a slow campaign of terror, yet she was powerless to do anything about it. Now she'd end up leaving the apartment she already loved, since she wouldn't even contemplate staying there if Jeff had access to the building. The idea of seeing him on a regular basis was more than she could cope with.

Laura sighed. Already Jeff had robbed her of her peace of mind, filling every moment with fear. Everywhere she looked, she saw his face – in trains, buses, on the street, in shops. She had to stop letting him be such an all-powerful force in her life. He was only one person – although she was well aware that his money could buy him extra eyes.

Resolutely, Laura decided that the only way to cope with Jeff was to adopt a different attitude. She'd be the one to change. She'd stop letting Jeff dictate how she lived her life. She'd ignore his petty behaviour, and when he got no response to his actions, he'd get tired of playing games and go away. She wasn't going to let him drive her out of the apartment she loved. All the same, she was glad she hadn't actually bought it yet. Hopefully, by the time that option became available, the situation with Jeff would have resolved itself, and she could make it her permanent home.

CHAPTER 54

*A*lan wiped his brow. He'd just stormed out of a heated meeting with his father-in-law, where he'd had to ask Dick Morgan to bail out the factory for a third time. But the old man was refusing, claiming to be worried about tying up his capital in such a precarious business venture, and having to wait too long for a return on his investment.

'But how can you call it precarious?' Alan had bellowed at him. 'This is one of the most viable businesses in the area. We just need to update some of the machinery – otherwise, we'll go under!'

They'd parried back and forth all day and, finally, Alan had seen red and walked out of the meeting. Now he'd have to approach the bank for a loan instead and, even if they were to agree, their conditions would be more than stringent. To hell with Dick Morgan!

The only advantage was that most of the previous loan had been repaid. Sylvia's father had been rewarded handsomely for his earlier investment – in fact, if he hadn't demanded such a high rate of interest, the factory might not now be needing to ask for another loan! Alan was livid. The only benefit – if he could call it that – was that it was now the ideal time to ask Sylvia for a divorce.

In a way, asking her now would be a way of punishing her father for his refusal to reinvest.

All day at work, Alan preoccupied himself with planning just how to bring up the subject of divorce with his wife. His stomach was churning and he was developing a stress headache. At lunchtime, instead of his usual visit to Ellie, he rang her, pleading a business meeting, and went out for a walk, hoping that the fresh air might clear his head. But he returned to the office feeling just as stressed. Every ten minutes he looked at his watch, wanting the work day to be over, yet perversely dreading it.

As he sat daydreaming, there was a knock on his door.

'Mr Alan, production's stopped on Number Three conveyor belt.' Tony Coleman, the factory manager, stepped into his office. 'We've already sent for Maintenance, but that order for Superbuys is going to be delayed by an hour or more...'

Alan sighed. Sometimes he was sick of his responsibilities. Everyone seemed to want a piece of him. Sylvia wanted him, Ellie wanted him, and he was charged with the responsibility of keeping hundreds of workers in their jobs. Sometimes he just wanted to run away – perhaps to a desert island, where no one could find him.

Alan got to his feet. 'Okay, Tony – I'll be with you shortly.'

He'd have to ask the workers to stay late, since Superbuys was an exacting client, and likely to impose a penalty for late deliveries.

As he left his office and headed downstairs to the factory floor, he wondered how it would feel when he was going home to Ellie after a day's work. Would his life with Ellie become as boring and predictable as it currently was with Sylvia?

It would feel odd living with his eldest daughter. He'd grown very fond of her, although he didn't see her as often as he'd like, since his visits to her mother always took place when she wasn't around.

He was also considering, for the first time, the effect his divorce would have on Pete and Laura. How would they feel about seeing him living with their friend's mother? Would they still call to play? Would his relationship with Ellie drive a wedge between him and his two other children?

Alan's stomach was still churning, because he also knew that as soon as he and Ellie went public about their relationship, she'd insist on letting everyone know that Kerry was his child, and that would have a devastating effect on poor Sylvia. Divorcing her was bad enough, but having her know that his affair had produced another child three months before she'd given birth to their own daughter – well, that would be the ultimate humiliation. How could he do that to her? She loved him, and she'd never done him any harm, so how could he destroy her in that way?

Then he thought of his father-in-law, and his blood ran cold. Even though Sylvia would undoubtedly behave with dignity, Dick would probably punish him by demanding back the balance of the money he'd already ploughed into the factory. Even though there wasn't a huge amount still owing, it was enough to tip the balance precariously, possibly leading to closure of the factory, with the loss of hundreds of jobs. He simply couldn't do it – the price was too high for everyone concerned.

By the end of the day, Alan was physically and mentally exhausted. His headache was pounding and his skull felt as though it was about to split open. In truth, he was beginning to wonder if a divorce would be worth all the hassle; it would be at the expense of so many other people's happiness and livelihoods, and that would ultimately ruin his own peace of mind.

By the time he got home, he still hadn't made up his mind about what he was going to do. He was relieved to discover that no one was home. He decided to go upstairs to his bedroom en suite, and have a shower that would hopefully relax his aching muscles and soothe his thumping head.

When he entered the bedroom, he was surprised to see Sylvia sitting at her dressing table. She was just putting down the phone extension, and she looked up happily when he entered the room. He felt a rush of remorse. How could he bring such devastation to this genuinely lovely woman? He cared for her very much, and if he hadn't met Ellie, with her sparkling eyes, luscious lips and voluptuous, accommodating body, he'd have been content to spend the rest of his life with her. Sylvia didn't deserve what he was contemplating.

His wife's eyes were twinkling, and he was momentarily worried. Had he forgotten some event they were going to that evening? Was it their anniversary? That would be ironic.

Conspiratorially, she turned to face him. 'I'm not supposed to tell you, darling, but Daddy's just been on the phone, and he's had second thoughts about investing in the factory.' She looked at him shyly. 'You know, he thinks you're a wonderful businessman. He says you have a natural flair for business, and he doesn't want to see that flair limited by lack of capital. He told me confidentially that he's reconsidered his earlier decision, and has decided to be your backer for as long as you need him. Isn't that great news, darling?'

Alan nodded, relieved that the factory's future was assured, but knowing that now he couldn't possibly ask his wife for a divorce. In a way he was relieved, since he genuinely cared about Sylvia. She was the mother of two of his children, and he didn't want to hurt her.

'You'll pretend you don't know, won't you, darling?' Sylvia asked anxiously. 'You know how Daddy loves to play his little power games. Let him have his fun first, then look surprised and grateful when he tells you.'

Surprising even himself, Alan suddenly leaned forward and placed a kiss on the top of his wife's head. She, too, looked surprised at this spontaneous gesture of affection – he could see that her cheeks had blushed crimson. She looked so pleased that he felt guilty at ever having considered hurting her so badly. She'd done absolutely nothing wrong – he was the one who was guilty of cruelly deceiving her. And Laura and Pete – how on earth would he have been able to tell them he was leaving?

As he stared at his reflection in the mirror, Alan saw a stranger looking back. What had he been thinking of? How could he leave his wife and children? He sighed. Ellie would just have to accept that there could be no marriage – now or ever. But he'd ensure that she and their daughter wanted for nothing.

Alan stood in Ellie's kitchen. He hadn't dared initiate any sexual contact, as he usually did on arrival.

'I really did intend to do it,' he whispered. 'But I can't leave now, love – I'm sorry, it's out of the question. I need her father's investment in the factory – but I love you, too. Can you please accept the situation as it is, since I'd rather die than lose you?'

Ellie bit her lip. For years, he'd dangled the carrot of marriage in front of her, although she'd known in her heart for a long time now that it was never going to happen. And marriage to Alan might create far more problems than any joy it would bring – he wouldn't be the successful businessman without his father-in-law's money, and his father-in-law wouldn't invest unless Sylvia was happy. And without the factory, Alan couldn't financially support his children. So they were all trapped in a spiral of need. A penniless husband would be no picnic and, slowly but surely, she and Alan would gradually annihilate each other. So, she was willing to sacrifice the legal niceties in order to keep Alan's love, since that was all she'd really ever wanted.

Ellie looked down at her beautiful diamond and gold ring. She knew how much Alan cared. He'd taught Kerry to ride a bike, and made a point of including her in his family's events whenever he could. They'd both come to accept that the two girls had become firm friends, and they'd managed to structure their own lives to accommodate it. In fact, it was astonishing and wonderful that they'd managed to maintain their secret lives together for all these years, without ever hurting anyone else.

Instinctively, Ellie rushed into Alan's arms. 'I love you,' she whispered, reaching up to kiss him.

Gratefully, Alan kissed her back. 'We'll grow old together,' he promised. 'I know the situation isn't ideal, but we'll make it work for us. I'll never stop loving you'

CHAPTER 55

The duty concierge beamed at Laura as she returned home from the university. 'I hope you're settling in okay?' he asked.

Laura smiled. 'Yes, thanks, Jim – I can't believe that I've been here two weeks already! I really love the apartment. But there are still a few things I need to get, like a rug and some lamps…'

The concierge nodded. 'Yes, it takes a while to turn a place into a home, doesn't it?' He smiled cheerfully. 'At least you've got your TV working now. So you'll be able to – '

Laura turned sharply. 'Hold on – I don't have a TV. What do you mean?'

'Oh.' The concierge looked puzzled. 'I thought – I mean, the guy said he was here to fix your TV. He said you couldn't get any reception, and he was going to sort it out for you. He knew your name and apartment number, so I assumed – '

'What did he look like?' Laura asked, her heart pounding.

The little man looked contrite. 'Well, he was a tall, blond guy, wearing a dark grey uniform with a red and yellow logo.' Momentarily he looked confused. 'Are you saying – ?'

'Yes!' said Laura angrily. 'You let my ex into my apartment!'

The concierge blanched. 'Oh my God, I'm sorry! Since the guy knew all about you, I guessed you'd probably booked an appointment with his company and forgotten to let us guys at the desk know…'

'Would you mind ringing the police?' Laura asked frostily.

'Well, ma'am, if you're sure nothing is missing…'

'No, officer, everything seems to be there,' Laura said dully. 'And you're certain that no listening devices or cameras have been installed in the apartment?'

The police officer looked mildly amused. 'At your request, our people have checked thoroughly, madam, and we've found nothing.' He looked at his notebook. 'But we'll certainly be contacting Mr Jones, to see if he can throw any light on the matter. I believe one of our officers has visited him before?'

Laura nodded, her voice shaky. 'Yes, I've already reported my ex-husband for stalking me – he's been making my life a misery ever since we broke up. And it looks like he's determined to continue his campaign against me.'

The officer gave her a sympathetic nod.

She appreciated the police presence, and she was grateful for their attention to detail. But she was well aware that Jeff would probably have a sound alibi for the time her apartment was broken into.

The policemen looked at her closely. 'Are you absolutely certain this couldn't be a mix up?' he asked. 'Isn't it possible that the TV man asked for your flat by mistake, but went to another apartment instead?'

Laura shook her head. 'No, the concierge opened the door of my apartment for him. And, before you arrived, the concierge checked with all the owners of the other apartments. No one else had booked, or was visited by, a TV repair man today.'

The police officer looked puzzled. 'It seems a little odd that someone would break into your apartment, yet steal nothing,' he remarked. But seeing Laura's thunderous expression, he decided it was safer to say nothing more.

After the police had gone, Laura sat in her kitchen staring at the walls. She felt sick at the thought that Jeff had been snooping around in her apartment. She still wasn't convinced that he hadn't hidden a listening device or camera somewhere, although the police had assured her there was nothing present.

Laura shivered. Despite the police's assurances, she no longer felt safe and secure in her own apartment. Looking around fearfully, she wondered if Jeff could have inserted a tiny camera into the light overhead. Or inside a picture frame? Was he watching her, at this very minute?

Mentally shaking herself, Laura decided that she wasn't going to let Jeff dictate how she lived her life. This was precisely what he wanted – to drive her mad. He might have done nothing to the apartment, but he'd have known that the mere fact of him being there would be enough to set her nerves on edge.

Feeling very emotional, Laura went downstairs to her bedroom and sat on her bed. Then she opened the drawer of her bedside cupboard. This was where she kept the precious photos of her parents and brother. Like a comfort blanket, she always reached for them in times of stress; connecting with her lost loved ones helped to calm her – looking at their smiling faces always helped her to dispel the loneliness that often threatened to overwhelm her. It confirmed that she'd once been part of a loving family.

Reaching into the drawer, Laura expected to feel the familiar plastic folder beneath her fingers. But it wasn't there. Frantically pulling out the drawer, she gaped inside. The precious photos of her parents and brother were gone!

Staring into the empty interior, Laura was unable, for several seconds, to fully comprehend what could have happened. Then it hit her like a ton of bricks. Jeff had taken the photos! He knew how much they meant to her, and he'd have known exactly where to find them – she'd always kept them in the drawer of her bedside table, even when she and Jeff had lived together.

As the enormity of what had happened began to sink in, Laura sat down on her bed and began to weep. She felt as though she'd lost her beloved family for a second time. Jeff had won yet again, because he knew how much the loss of the photos would hurt her.

Some time later, when Laura had dried her eyes and washed her face, she made two phone calls: one to the police, to report her missing photos, and the other to Kerry, who promised to come over immediately.

A little while later, a red-eyed Laura opened the door to her friend. On seeing Kerry, she burst into tears again.

'My life is a total mess, isn't it?' she wailed as Kerry embraced her. 'And I always seem to be calling on you to get me out of one bad situation after another.'

'Don't worry,' Kerry soothed. 'You've just had a run of very bad luck lately.'

'This isn't about luck, Kerry – this is Jeff, trying to unhinge me!'

'And you're certain you haven't mislaid the photos?' Kerry asked tentatively. 'If you like, I'll help you do a thorough search of the apartment – '

Laura looked distraught. 'Surely you, at least, believe me? I've already been through this scenario with the police on the phone. They thought I might have mislaid them, too. But it's Jeff – I know he's the one who took them!'

Kerry hugged her friend tightly. 'Look, I know it's awful, but that's what Jeff wants – to make you miserable. Please don't let him get to you – he'll have won.' She handed Laura a tissue. 'Here, wipe your eyes, love. I know you're devastated, but at the end of the day they're only photos – you'll never forget your family. You have them stored where they're most important – inside your heart.'

Laura refused to be placated as she wiped away a fresh batch of tears. 'But they were the only photos I had left of them!' she sobbed. 'Sometimes, when I can't remember their faces, I panic, but then I always had the photos to remind me – now I have nothing left!'

CHAPTER 56

'*Syl – are you ready?*'

'*Coming, darling.*'

They were on their way to a prestigious business awards dinner – Alan had already been tipped off that he'd be receiving an award himself.

He looks so handsome, Sylvia thought. I'm a lucky woman, even if our relationship has become a little tarnished over the years.

She'd sensed a change in Alan around the time her father had re-invested heavily in the new machinery for the factory. Perhaps it was simply because her husband's money worries had been eased, but all she knew was that her husband had suddenly become more affectionate. She'd also wondered if it could be because his affair had ended, and he'd finally realised the value of what he had at home.

Sylvia was still mortified by her moment of weakness all those years ago, when she'd blurted out her fears about Alan's infidelity to Ellie Beckworth. No wonder the woman had kept her distance ever since – she must have been deeply embarrassed at being drawn into the lives of her former boss and his wife! Nevertheless, Ellie's words of advice had proved invaluable, and clearly she hadn't betrayed her trust either. Sylvia had been terrified that Alan might get wind of her confession – he'd have been very angry at having his relationship with his wife discussed with a former employee.

It was ironic how, years later, their two daughters had become close friends. Sylvia had hoped that as their daughters' friendship grew, it might somehow bring herself and Ellie together more. But apart from an occasional foray into the village for provisions, Ellie didn't seem to go out much. Years before, Sylvia had seen her in Tony Coleman's company one evening but, other than that, the woman seemed to be incredibly private.

Over the years, Sylvia had made a special effort to show Alan how much she loved him, by looking nice and being enthusiastic in bed. But the passion of their early years had never been rekindled. Clearly, the passing of time dulled such feelings – perhaps it happened in all marriages and long-term relationships.

'Do you think this tie is okay?'

Sylvia dusted a fleck of fluff from his shoulder. 'It's perfect. You look very handsome, darling.'

'Thanks. The taxi should be here shortly. Are the kids okay?'

Sylvia smiled to herself. 'Yes, Alan, the babysitter's with them in the games room. Of course, Pete is objecting to having a babysitter at all – he thinks he's too grown up to need supervising!'

Alan nodded. 'Well, I can see his point of view – he's thirteen now, and Laura's almost eleven.' He grinned at his wife. 'Where on earth have the years gone? They seem to be flying by!'

In the taxi, Alan conversed with the taxi driver while Sylvia sat back and contemplated their situation. It amused and saddened her to think that she was the only one in the relationship who realised that anything had ever been wrong. Alan was probably still living under the illusion that she'd never suspected anything about his affair. At times like today, when they were operating well together as a successful couple, she liked to think that the affair had never happened. Since she'd never given voice to her feelings, it was easier now to put it all behind her. But she still wondered.

'We're here, Syl – you okay?'

'Yes, of course,' Sylvia said, stepping out of the taxi. 'Silly me, I was just daydreaming. Here, let me straighten your tie – we can't have you looking anything less than perfect tonight, can we?'

As she reached up, Alan suddenly hugged her. 'Thanks, Syl – for everything,' he said softly.

Sylvia blushed, embarrassed and pleased all at once. Was it a hug that silently begged her forgiveness? Or a hug that simply meant he cared? Whatever it meant, Sylvia was not going to query it. Not today, of all days. This was a good day, and she intended making the most of it.

CHAPTER 57

Laura was in the middle of a tutorial when Darren knocked on her door.

'Sorry to disturb you, but I need to speak to you. Privately.'

Smiling apologetically at the five students seated around her desk, Laura rose to her feet and left the room. Her heart was thumping, since she knew it had to be bad news. Darren had never interrupted a tutorial before.

'Laura, there's been a fire at your apartment,' he told her without preamble. 'I think you'd better get back there straight away. Don't worry about your tutorial – I'll get Maria to fill in, or I'll take it myself.'

'Thanks, Darren,' Laura mumbled and, apologising to her students, she left the room and closed the door.

Outside, Darren was still standing there, and he hugged her sympathetically. 'I've already organised and paid for a taxi for you,' he told her. 'It's waiting for you outside the main door.' Taking her hand in his, he led her down the corridor. 'Let me know what's happened, won't you? If you need somewhere to stay, you're always welcome to crash at my place.'

'Thanks, Darren,' Laura muttered again, grateful for his comforting presence. She wondered how much damage had been done, knowing in her heart who was to blame for this latest disaster. Was it always going to be like this?

In a daze, Laura sat in the taxi and contemplated this latest outrage. How could Jeff have got into her apartment again?

As the taxi reached Green Street, Laura looked up. She could see that the side wall of the building, where her apartment was located, was now blackened, and the window frame completely charred. Her heart was in her mouth as she contemplated Jeff's latest attempt to punish her. As least she didn't have to worry about her family photos, because he'd stolen those already.

As she rushed into the entrance hall, Laura was assailed by a variety of people, all waiting to speak to her. Laura brushed them all aside, spotting Avril, the estate agent, on the other side of the vestibule. She headed across to her, towards a familiar face.

Avril's face lit up briefly. 'Laura! This must be an awful shock! You poor love – if you like, I can find you somewhere else to live. Obviously it's going to take a while to get the damage repaired. But the insurance company will probably cover those rental costs for you…'

Laura gulped. She hadn't even considered having to leave the apartment she loved.

Avril looked worried. 'You must have left in quite a hurry this morning!' she added. 'You obviously forgot to turn off the cooker after you'd prepared your breakfast.'

'W-what?' Laura was bewildered. Since moving in, she'd never bothered cooking in the mornings – she'd simply grabbed a bowl of cereal and boiled some milk.

Avril gave her a sympathetic smile. 'I'm afraid that most of your possessions are in a fairly bad condition – I suspect they'll all have to be dumped. Luckily, the fire brigade got here quickly…' She shuddered. 'Otherwise, who knows what might have happened!'

Laura felt the colour drain from her face. This was even worse than she'd expected.

'Fortunately, Albert, one of the concierges, was just arriving for duty, smelled the smoke, heard the fire alarm ringing and called the fire brigade,' Avril continued. 'Thankfully, the sprinkler came on, otherwise it could have been a lot worse. People might even have *died*.'

Later that evening, when Laura had bought a few essentials and settled in her new, temporary apartment, she phoned Kerry. She hadn't wanted to do it earlier, since she knew her friend would invite her to stay, and she didn't want to impose on her any more than she'd done already.

'WHAT?' Kerry screeched when told what had happened. 'Oh my God! Where are you now? You're welcome to stay here, of course – '

'I'm fine – I've moved into a temporary apartment,' Laura informed her. 'But I'm going to go to the police tomorrow. I can't let Jeff get away with any more of this – someone could have been killed!'

Kerry sighed. 'Look, I know we'd love to blame Jeff, but you can't really believe he could have done it, can you?' she said gently. 'All the concierges are aware of who Jeff is, so they'd never let him near your place.' Her voice softened. 'Tell me exactly what you did this morning.'

'Well, I got up, heated some milk on the cooker, poured it over my cereal – '

'You see?' Kerry said. 'Do you think you could have turned another ring on by mistake? It's easy to do when you're not fully awake. Was there anything close by that might have caught fire?'

Laura bit her lip. Her chip pan, full of cooking oil, had been sitting on an adjacent ring of the cooker...

'Well, the chip pan was there, but I *know* I didn't turn it on – '

Kerry sighed. 'Laura, I hate to say it, but I don't think you can blame Jeff this time. If you contact the police, you'll just look like an idiot.'

'But I didn't do it! I know I didn't!' Laura shouted, dissolving into tears.

'Look, we're all capable of making a mistake,' Kerry said quietly. 'You're under a lot of pressure right now, so it would have been easy to forget to turn off the cooker – '

'I didn't forget!' Laura screamed. 'Why won't anyone believe me?'

Kerry sighed. 'Okay, Laura, maybe you're right,' she said. 'It's just I'd rather believe it was you, because then we wouldn't have to worry that Jeff was still out to get you.'

'I know it was Jeff!' Laura said stubbornly. 'What the hell am I going to do?'

Kerry shook her head. 'I don't know, love. I'm just worried that the police won't take you seriously. And if it *is* Jeff, then he'll just try some other stunt once the police come after him again.'

'Well, I'm going to them anyway,' Laura said. 'I've got no other choice.'

The police officer looked at Laura sternly. 'Ms Thornton, according to the fire service, the fire was started by a pan of cooking oil left heating on the cooker. It overheated, caught fire and exploded, causing extensive damage to the walls and furnishings. The concierges have already confirmed that no one, other than residents, entered or left the premises yesterday morning.' He looked annoyed. 'How on earth can you consider that Mr Jones is guilty? You're very lucky the fire was caught before it spread to other apartments.'

'But it *had* to be him!' Laura insisted. She was becoming more and more agitated.

The police officer looked at her sadly. 'I think, Ms Thornton, that you'd be well advised to leave the matter to your insurance company. It was an accident. Mr Jones has an alibi, and you simply can't go around accusing innocent people of such crimes. I think it's time to let this issue go now, otherwise you might find yourself in a lot more trouble than you bargained for.'

Stumbling out of the police station, Laura was filled with rage and indignation. How was Jeff still managing to get away with his cruel vendetta? Was he just too clever to get caught?

CHAPTER 58

Alone in her temporary apartment, Laura paced the floor into the early hours. How could she stop Jeff from continuing to make her life a misery? The police didn't seem to take her claims seriously, and Jeff had now neatly turned the tables on her, making the police think she was a demented and irrational fool.

She was beginning to realise that her life could be in serious danger.

Finally, Laura reached a heart-breaking decision. She'd have to leave London and move to a place of safety, where Jeff couldn't find her. She'd ask for a transfer to another university if possible, and beg Darren to keep her new location a secret. Jeff had ruined everything for her.

Where would she go? Having grown up in the outskirts of London and gone to university in the capital, she was going to miss the hustle and bustle of the city – the Underground, the theatres, the markets, the restaurants, the constant buzz of a city that rarely slept. On the other hand, she'd be starting a new chapter in her life, a new adventure that would at least bring her peace. She'd no longer be looking over her shoulder for Jeff, and she'd be able to sleep at night without worrying about a creak in the floorboards.

Jeff was hardly likely to pursue her across the country, was he?

Laura felt apprehensive as she approached Darren's office. She knew he'd be disappointed to lose her, and she didn't like leaving him in the lurch, especially during term-time. But she couldn't risk delaying her departure any longer.

In the confines of his small office, Laura wrung her hands nervously.

'Darren, I don't really want to do this, but I have no choice but to hand in my notice. I'm sorry – I know I'm leaving you in the lurch, but I need you to recommend me for a lectureship at another university. I have no other option!'

Darren looked stunned. 'Dear God, why, Laura? I thought you were happy here! And I've always been pleased with your work – '

Laura bit her lip. 'Thanks, Darren – I love working here, and you know how much I love working with you. Our friendship goes back a long way and I value it greatly. But it's Jeff – he won't leave me alone, and some really bad things have happened. I can't prove it, but I think he was behind the fire at my apartment. I'm afraid of him, Darren, so I've got to get away.'

Darren rose from his chair in agitation. 'Why on earth didn't you tell me?' he asked, his eyes like saucers behind his thick glasses. 'I had no idea you suspected Jeff was responsible for the fire – I thought it was just an unfortunate accident. Is there anything I can do? Do you want to stay at my place?' Laura shook her head as Darren stepped forward and enfolded her in his arms. 'Laura, you can't let him drive you away like this!' he said, appalled. 'I presume you've been to the police?'

Laura nodded. 'Jeff is too clever to leave any evidence that might incriminate him. I just need to get away – I'm hoping that once I break the connection, he'll leave me alone and eventually forget about me. And at that point, hopefully, I'll be able to come back to London again.'

Darren said nothing, gently leading Laura over to a chair and then sitting on the edge of his desk facing her. 'It seems a very drastic step to take,' he said at last.

Laura smiled sadly. 'He's crossed the line too many times, and I think he's only going to get worse. I can't put myself in any more danger, Darren, and I don't want to give him the chance to kill me.' Her voice broke as the enormity of the situation almost overwhelmed her.

Darren picked up a pen, twirled it between his fingers, then put it down on the desk again. He sighed, looking closely at Laura before he spoke, and she felt he was trying to convince himself that what she was doing was truly in her best interests.

'There's a job available at Dorrington University – I only heard about it yesterday from a colleague who heads the department there. Would you mind going so far north?'

Laura shook her head. The further away from Jeff, the better.

'Apparently, the present incumbent had a heart attack and they need someone to replace him immediately. It's a temporary junior lectureship in Sociology, so it won't pay as much as your current job here, but it would get you away from London.' He looked at her directly. 'It would ensure you were safe.'

'Oh, Darren,' Laura said, smiling and throwing herself into his arms. 'I'll take it, thank you so much. You don't know how much this means to me.'

Darren returned her embrace before giving her a regretful smile. 'I just want you to be safe, Laura. And Dorrington will be lucky to have you. But how am I ever going to replace you?' He sighed. To him, Laura was truly irreplaceable, and the thought of her leaving the university was already causing him unbearable pain. 'Well, you don't need to worry about any of that – that's my problem now,' he said, looking at her sadly. 'I'll be sorry to lose you, Laura, but I'll ring Bill Maddison straight away and get the position set up for you.'

While Laura waited, Darren rang his colleague in Dorrington and, based on his assurances, she was given the job immediately. She'd start the following week. Darren also astutely suggested that she might like to leave her job in his department immediately, so that she didn't need to face the other colleagues she liked so much.

'Thanks, Darren – you're the best!' Laura said, hugging him again as she wished him goodbye. She had tears in her eyes – he had always been such a wonderful friend to her. 'I'm going to miss you so much!' she told him.

'I'm going to miss you, too,' Darren said gruffly. He felt bereft and deeply worried as he hugged her solemnly. 'I hope you're doing the right thing, Laura. No one should have to run away in order to survive.'

Kerry's voice shook when Laura told her of her plans to leave London. 'Leave? My God, Laura – where will you go? I can't believe you'd do something so drastic! And you've packed in your job without even telling me!' She looked shocked. 'Are you sure you're not being too hasty?'

'I'm sorry for not letting you know first, but I was afraid you'd try to dissuade me,' Laura told her, tears in her eyes. 'Anyway, I don't feel I've any other choice. Jeff has gone too far this time – I'm not going to hang around until he makes his next move.'

'But Dorrington? It's miles away! I'll never get to see you!' Seeing Laura's eyes fill with fresh tears, Kerry sighed. 'Sorry, love – I'm being totally selfish. I'm only thinking of how much I'm going to miss you. But I see your point – maybe you don't have any other option.'

Laura hugged her friend. 'There isn't any other way – I'm never going to be rid of Jeff otherwise. And because I've no family, I'm in a position to make this a clean break.' She clutched Kerry tightly. 'I never thought I'd be grateful, even for a moment, to be all alone in the world!'

'You're not all alone! You have me, and we'll never lose contact, right?'

'Of course not, but I want you to pretend to Jeff that we're not in touch any longer,' Laura said. 'I want you to be safe too, Kerry. We both know that Jeff is capable of anything.' Laura wiped away a fresh tear.

Kerry looked at her bleakly. 'You've really thought this through, haven't you?' She hugged Laura tightly. 'And to think I assumed you were just being your usual, impulsive self!'

'I've been thinking about it for a while now,' Laura said determinedly. 'The fire was simply the last straw. If I can just break the link with Jeff, maybe he'll eventually forget about me.'

'I hope you're right,' Kerry said fervently.

Laura smiled at her friend through her tears. 'I couldn't ask for a better friend than you,' she said, hugging her best friend tightly.

CHAPTER 59

Sitting on Kerry's bed, Laura swung her legs back and forth, examining them intently. They were definitely getting longer. She'd grown quite a lot this summer and, already, she was two inches taller than Kerry. In just a few more weeks, she'd be eleven! Of course, Pete had grown taller than either of the girls, and that advantage enabled him to make Laura's life even more miserable. Now that he was thirteen, he had assumed that being a teenager automatically elevated him to adult status.

Kerry was leaning out of the window of her bedroom, looking at the unending rain. 'I hate being stuck in here when we've only a week left,' she said. The long summer holidays were almost over, and neither of them relished the prospect of returning to school.

Laura liked being in Kerry's house – Ellie was always welcoming and there was an endless supply of juice, and gardens almost as big as Greygates to play in. Most important of all, she was safe from Pete's endless tricks. At home, he was always doing something to irritate her, and he'd become even worse this summer.

'At least I have something to look forward to,' Laura said. 'Daddy's taking us all away on a holiday!'

'Us all?' For a moment, Kerry allowed herself to dream.

'Yes, Mum, Dad, Pete and me,' Laura told her. 'It's going to be such fun! We're going to France, and I'm so excited!'

As Laura prattled on, Kerry was no longer listening. It hurt too much to hear about all the wonderful places they'd be visiting –

Paris, the Eiffel Tower, Montmartre, the Left Bank – places Kerry had only read about in books. She and her mother had never had a holiday abroad, and probably never would. A sense of rage possessed her. Laura took so much for granted. Last year, the Thorntons had been to Spain, and she'd had to listen to Laura regaling her with stories about Barcelona and its amazing Gaudi architecture. All of which was wasted on her friend. Kerry felt that she was the one who could have really benefited from the experience.

Then she felt mean. It wasn't Laura's fault that everything in her life was perfect. Kerry just wished she, too, could be part of a family. While she loved her mother, it just wasn't the same as having two parents. She wanted a father more than anything in the world.

Realising that Kerry wasn't listening, Laura closed her mouth. She realised how insensitive she'd been. But it was difficult not to share her excitement with her best friend.

To take the sting out of her own good news, Laura looked around Kerry's bedroom, hoping to find a topic they could discuss that might cheer her up. Her eyes alighted on the shelves of assorted books, most of them on subjects she knew nothing about. Turning her head sideways to read their spines, Laura could see titles like: Modern Building Techniques, Engineering and its Role in New Materials, *and* Elementary Physics.

'Have you read all of these?' she asked Kerry, who had now closed the window and was rifling through a pile of books beside her bed.

Kerry smiled. 'Not every single one. But I've probably read bits from all of them – they're mainly textbooks, so I just take what I want from them.'

'You're so clever, and you know what you want to do when you leave school.' Laura sighed. 'I'm thinking about teaching, although I'm not really sure. There are probably loads of jobs I'd like to do, but I just don't know anything about them.'

'You'd be a great teacher,' Kerry said gruffly, embarrassed at paying a compliment. 'You like people and you're good with them – I much prefer working behind the scenes. I like materials and what you can do with them.'

As Kerry continued searching the room, Laura wondered if she could help. 'What exactly are you looking for?' she asked.

'Aha – there they are!' Kerry said, crossing to the bookcase, and taking down a sheaf of papers. She rested the pages on her bedside table and beckoned Laura over. 'I found these plans in a book at the library. They show how to make a go-cart, and I'm going to make us one next summer. What do you think?'

She pointed to a series of diagrams, all of which were meaningless to Laura, but the picture of the finished product instantly caught her imagination. 'Really?' Her eyes lit up. 'Could you actually make one of those without adult help?'

Kerry was quick to take offence. 'Why on earth would I need an adult to help me? The diagrams and instructions are all here, and the tools I need are in the outhouse – it's really quite straightforward. I'll scout around for some bits of wood, and we'll need a set of wheels as well. But we've plenty of time to find them – we've got to get through a whole school year before next summer's holidays.'

Laura's eyes were now twinkling. 'We're going to have such fun – I wish it was next summer already!'

'No, you don't – because then you'd miss your holiday to France!'

Laura had the grace to look chastened.

'Paris was amazing!' Laura told her friend, her eyes sparkling as they sat in Kerry's bedroom. 'I even got a chance to try out my French – but it didn't sound remotely like the French they speak over there! And the people speak so fast!'

Kerry was finding it difficult to appear interested and hoped *that Laura would soon tire of the subject of her holiday. She stared sourly at the plastic model of the Eiffel Tower that Laura had brought back for her. While they'd been abroad, Kerry had counted off the days until their return. Her mother, too, had been quieter than normal, and not at all her usual, ebullient self. It was as though the Thorntons' holiday had somehow put both their lives on hold.*

Kerry kicked a pile of books out of the way, and had the satisfaction of watching them tumble all over the floor.

'Here, let me help you!' Scrambling to tidy up the books, Laura began piling them onto the bed, and Kerry felt a sudden urge to kick her friend as well. Laura didn't seem to realise that she'd deliberately toppled them over in anger and frustration. Sunny-natured Laura always saw the best in everyone and, just then, that just made Kerry furious.

'Don't you ever feel the urge to hurt anyone?' she asked, curious as to Laura's answer.

Her friend grinned. 'Yes, I do – Pete! Of course, I don't mean I want to injure him – just get my own back on him. But he seems able to read my mind – he can always figure out what I'm up to, and he's one step ahead of me, no matter what I try to do. He was such a pain while we were in Paris – always poking me in the back, or trying to trip me up, when Mum and Dad weren't looking.'

Each mention of Paris cut through Kerry like a knife. She'd gladly have put up with Pete's behaviour just to get a chance to see the French capital.

And to be part of a family like the Thorntons.

Chapter 60

On her train journey north, Laura acutely felt the loss of her old life. With every mile the train travelled, she was leaving behind the city of her childhood, where the memories of her parents and brother were most strongly rooted. She was also leaving her best friend Kerry, her colleagues and her career at the university – and the wonderful Green Street apartment. Yet again, she silently cursed Jeff for all the harm he'd done to her, and she wished she could see the shock on his face when he realised she'd foiled his plot to terrorise her.

As the train passed through station after station, Laura gradually began to take stock of her new life ahead. Despite her fears for the future, she was also excited. She had no doubts about her ability to do the job at Dorrington, and there was a certain buzz in being forced out of her comfort zone and into a whole new way of life.

Later that afternoon, Laura approached the magnificent red-brick Dorrington University buildings with butterflies in her stomach. Finding the Sociology Department proved relatively straightforward, and Laura soon found herself knocking on Bill Maddison's door.

Bill was a warm, personable bear of a man – Laura's hand seemed to disappear inside his large one as they shook hands.

'You're very welcome, Laura,' he said, smiling. 'Thanks for

getting us out of a pickle. Darren tells me you're a Londoner?'

Laura nodded, feeling immediately at ease. She surmised that Bill was in his late forties. His tousled, dark brown hair was streaked with grey, and his brown eyes crinkled at the corners when he smiled. She warmed to him immediately.

'I'm grateful for the job, but I'm sorry to hear about your colleague,' Laura said, relieved that he didn't ask her why she'd been able to step into the vacant post at such short notice. She suspected that Darren had explained she had urgent personal reasons for making the move.

'Thanks. If you like, we can ease you in by getting you to mark some of the students' papers,' Bill suggested. 'Then, when I've given you the timetable for first-year Sociology, you can start working out your lecture programme.'

Laura nodded.

'I doubt if you'll have much preparation to do, anyway,' Bill added, smiling. 'Darren tells me you were the bright spark in his department, and very popular with all the students.'

Laura could feel herself blushing. Darren had always been so supportive, and she was going to miss him terribly.

Bill handed her the keys to her new office down the corridor. 'Let me know if I can do anything for you. My door is always open.'

As Laura left the college and headed back to her hotel, she felt a sense of peace gradually flowing over her. She was hundreds of miles away from Jeff, and he'd never manage to find her. Only a few trusted people, such as Kerry and Darren, knew where she was, and Jeff would never manage to extract that information from either of them.

CHAPTER 61

During the first week of the summer holidays, Kerry was busy cutting, shaping and planing pieces of wood in the outhouse at Treetops. She'd found an old crate in the woodpile, and had gleefully set to work converting it and several other pieces of wood into a box-cart. It would be perfect for whizzing down the sloping driveways of both Greygates and Treetops.

In the gloom of the outhouse, Laura watched as her friend hammered different pieces of wood together, then planed them to smooth the surface and remove any splinters.

'Where did you get the wheels?' Laura asked, mesmerised as she watched her friend's clever hands at work.

'I got them off my old baby buggy – Mum had dumped it in the shed. The wheels are exactly the size we need.' Kerry gestured towards the workbench. 'Hand me those axle brackets, would you, Laura?'

Laura gazed uncertainly at the various items laid out before her.

'See those right-angled metal pieces on the left? Yes, that's them.'

Laura handed her friend the items and watched as Kerry nailed them to each end of a long, narrow piece of wood.

Kerry was delighted to have an appreciative audience, and was eager to explain how she was going to attach the moveable steering bar to the front of the car, making it possible for them to change direction when they needed to.

Laura simply gaped in awe, unable to fully understand, but thrilled and looking forward to the fun they were going to have when it was finished. 'Are we going to let Pete go on it?' she asked warily. 'He's so rough, he might damage it.'

Kerry grinned. 'This is going to be very sturdy, so you needn't worry about him! But I think we'll make him really jealous before we let him on it. After all, he wouldn't let us use his skates last summer!'

Laura nodded. She liked the idea of thwarting her older brother.

Finally attaching the front wheels, Kerry spun them to ensure that they moved freely. Satisfied, she turned the box-cart over and both girls surveyed the finished product.

'What do you think?'

Laura gazed at it in awe. It looked very impressive. 'It's amazing,' she said, smiling excitedly at Kerry.

'Did you manage to find some kind of rope?'

Laura nodded, producing a length of nylon washing line from her pocket. She'd no idea what Kerry wanted it for but, when asked to find some, she'd rushed to do her friend's bidding.

'Perfect!' Kerry said, unwinding it and cutting off a segment. Then she tied a knot in one end and threaded the length of clothesline through one of the holes she'd drilled at either end of the front axle.

Urging Laura to sit in the cart, and placing the washing line in her hands, Kerry threaded the other end of the length of the line through the second hole in the steering bar. She then cut off the surplus washing line, and then turned and grinned at Laura. 'Let's take it over to your place for its maiden voyage, shall we?'

Laura nodded, grinning back. She was so excited, and so proud of her clever friend.

As Kerry pulled the go-cart behind her, the two girls headed out of Treetops's driveway and walked alongside the road. As they reached Greygates and hauled the cart up the driveway to the top, Kerry handed the washing-line steering-handle to Laura. 'Go on – you can have first go,' she said generously.

Laura's face lit up. 'Really? I mean – '

'Get into the bloody thing, Laura, and let's start having fun!' Kerry said gruffly. 'Anyway, you're going to be the guinea pig. If anything is wrong with it, you'll be the one to discover it. Ready?'

Laura nodded, grinning happily as Kerry gave the go-cart a shove, and she found herself flying down the driveway. She gripped the washing line, steering herself as she built up speed. 'Wheeeee!' she cried, loving every second of the experience. The wind was making a whooshing sound in her ears as she hurtled past the flowerbeds, barely missing the grocer's delivery boy who was cycling up the driveway. Laura just had time to register his horrified face before his bike wobbled and he fell into the hedge.

Chuckling to herself, Laura continued on, pulling on one side of the washing line to ease the cart around the bend in the driveway – just as her father's car was coming towards her.

Now there was a problem – Kerry hadn't shown her how to stop.

'Aaaaaargh!' Laura tried to avoid the car, but she clipped the edge of its front bumper as she flew past. The cart zigzagged and overturned, and Laura was thrown out onto the driveway. She skinned both her knees and the pain was excruciating, but she screwed up her eyes in an attempt not to cry.

'Laura, are you okay?' Her father came running back towards her, having abandoned his car in the middle of the driveway. He was followed shortly afterwards by Kerry, who was out of breath from running down its entire length.

Having ascertained that she hadn't broken anything, Alan eyed Laura sternly. 'Why on earth weren't you being more careful? You could have seriously injured yourself!'

'Sorry,' Laura mumbled, but then she turned on him accusingly. 'But you're home early! If you hadn't been here, I wouldn't have had any problem!'

'That's because I'm going to collect Pete – he wants to come with me while I pick up my new car from the showroom,' he said mildly. 'Just as well this one is leased, isn't it? Otherwise, you'd be paying for the repairs to the bumper out of your pocket money for a very long time!'

By now, Alan had turned his attention to the box-cart, which was lying on its side.

'Did you make this?' he asked Kerry, who was standing by Laura's side.

Kerry nodded, blushing.

Examining the go-cart, Alan was impressed by the well-designed axles that turned the buggy wheels; the washers and locking nuts that enabled the steering column to move freely, all perfectly in place; and the wood pale and smooth from being carefully planed.

'Well, if you can turn out something this good at your age, you've clearly got a great career ahead of you!' he said admiringly. 'There's just a little damage to the bracket on the steering bar, but I'm sure a bright girl like you will sort that out in no time.'

Kerry blushed again. She was thrilled that Mr Thornton had found a reason to praise her.

'What are you going to be when you grow up, Kerry?'

'I'll probably become an engineer,' she told him shyly.

'Really?' Alan was pleased. 'That's great! You've certainly got the flair for it.'

Kerry blushed again, lapping up the praise. 'I'm interested in how things work,' she continued. 'I want to designs things and find ways to make them work better. That's what an engineer does, isn't it?'

Alan nodded. 'There are lots of different careers in engineering,' he explained, 'but you're right – designing and perfecting products is a big part of it.' He smiled over his shoulder at her. 'You've certainly made a great start with this box-cart of yours – it's just a pity that Laura couldn't keep control of it!'

'It's fine – it's only minor damage,' Kerry said dismissively. 'And it's quite strong, so it can cope with a few knocks.'

Laura smiled at her friend, grateful again for not being made to feel guilty.

'You're an engineer yourself, aren't you, Mr Thornton?' Kerry asked, keen to take advantage of this thawing in their relationship.

Alan nodded. 'Yes, I qualified as a mechanical engineer. Of course, our factory manager, Tony Coleman, takes care of the day-to-day running of the machinery and the timing of production lines. I mainly do the paperwork now, but my knowledge of engineering is a great help to me in understanding what's going on, and in making major decisions.' As Alan began walking back to his car, he suddenly turned around. 'Kerry, would you like to come to the car showroom with me and Pete? They have a big repair department there as well – you might be interested in having a look around while I'm dealing with the finance department.'

Kerry nodded, her heart almost bursting with joy.

'Can I come too?' Laura piped up.

'Okay, come on, both of you,' Alan said, grinning.

The three children stared in admiration at Alan's new car as it stood on the garage forecourt. Its chrome glistened, and its dark red body gleamed with such a sheen that it made them all want to run their hands over it.

Inside, the cream leather seats smelled new and luxurious, and the children smiled at each other as they tumbled inside. They were all chattering nineteen to the dozen, and Alan had to beg for silence so that he could work out which switches had been moved or altered on the newer model.

Eventually, they drove back to Greygates, and found Sylvia waiting on the doorstep to see the new car.

'It's lovely, Alan,' she told him, smiling. 'What do you think, children?'

They all nodded enthusiastically as they stepped out of the car.

'Thank you, Mr Thornton,' Kerry said solemnly. 'I've had a brilliant time today!'

Alan felt a stab of guilt as he patted the child's arm affectionately. 'You're more than welcome, Kerry,' he said softly, aware that she got so much less than his other two children, yet she was pathetically grateful for the little she got.

Sylvia herded them all inside. 'You'll stay for dinner, won't you, Kerry? Maybe you three children can help me peel the potatoes? I'm making chips, since I know you all like them.'

The child nodded shyly. She loved the Thorntons' house, and she wished more than anything that she could have a father like Mr Thornton.

CHAPTER 62

Having settled into a routine at the university, and into her new apartment in Bayside, Laura was relieved to discover that life in Dorrington was proving relatively stress-free. It was great being so far from Jeff, and it looked as though her troubles were finally over.

By her third week Laura had assumed full responsibility for the previous lecturer's schedule. Bill was happy with her work and the students were welcoming and seemed invigorated by the new and different approaches she brought to her lectures and tutorials.

Darren kept in touch by texts and with occasional phone calls, and Laura was always pleased when she saw his number showing up on her phone, or when she opened a text from him. She hadn't realised she could miss him so much, but they had been good friends for a long time and although Bill was an easy-going boss, it just wasn't the same as working for Darren.

As the weeks went by, Laura began to feel secure again, and by the time she'd been in Dorrington for two months, she was feeling confident that Jeff and his antics were now firmly in the past. She was making friends with other lecturers, and before long she was joining them for occasional nights at the pub or theatre, something she hadn't been able to do for ages.

One evening, after an enjoyable night of stand-up comedy in a small city-centre theatre, Laura was still smiling as she bade her colleagues goodnight. She had an early start the following morning, so she'd reluctantly decided against joining them for a nightcap. Living in Bayside meant she had to leave early in order to arrive at work on time, but the coastal location made up for the slight inconvenience. She loved its esplanade, and she'd been fitting in a brisk walk every morning before leaving for work.

Deep in thought, Laura crossed the pedestrian plaza and stepped out onto the main road. The road appeared clear, but some sixth sense seemed to alert her to danger – a car had appeared out of nowhere and was bearing down on her at tremendous speed. Momentarily paralysed with shock, she barely made it to the pavement before the car shot past.

Shaking, Laura stared after the fast-moving vehicle, but it was too late to see the registration or make a note of any other detail. She shuddered. If she'd taken just a second longer to reach the pavement, she'd now be lying injured, or maybe even dead...Her heart was pumping frantically, and she wondered if what had just happened was simply due to her own stupidity. She'd checked the traffic before she'd stepped out, hadn't she? The road had been clear, she was sure of it. It seemed as though the car and its driver had been waiting specifically for her...Laura desperately wanted it to be her own stupid mistake, because if not, she had to face the fact that someone had just tried to mow her down.

She shook her head. She was being paranoid. Then her heart plummeted as a picture of Jeff pushed its way into her brain. Had that been him in the car? Suddenly her peace of mind evaporated, and her eyes began to fill with tears.

Back in Bayside, Laura rang her friend's mobile phone, not even bothering with preliminaries. 'Kerry – are you sure you haven't told anyone where I am?'

'Of course not! Why do you ask? Has something happened?'

Laura bit her lip. 'I don't know – I'm not sure. Maybe I'm just being paranoid.'

'For God's sake, tell me what's bothering you!'

'Look, I guess I'm just on edge, and starting to imagine things. It's probably nothing to worry about – I'm just being stupid, as usual, but I think someone tried to run me down tonight.'

She could hear the gasp at the other end of the phone.

'Oh my God,' Kerry whispered. 'What happened?'

'I was walking back from the theatre – I'd just said goodbye to some of the others from the university – and I was crossing the main road and a car came out of nowhere and headed straight towards me. I barely got out of the way, and I know I wasn't imagining it.'

'Did you manage to see the driver?'

'It was dark and, anyway, I was too busy jumping to get out of the way.'

'Was it a man? Do you think it could have been Jeff?'

'I don't know. It could have been. I just feel sick. I don't know what to do any more.'

Laura's voice was close to breaking, and Kerry hurried to reassure her. 'Look, it was probably just an accident, and completely unconnected to Jeff.'

But Laura wouldn't be mollified. 'You're trying to tell me that I came all the way to Dorrington, and the most dangerous and inconsiderate driver in the whole city just manages to find me?'

'But there's no way Jeff could know where you are. There just isn't, Laura. It must have been an accident,' Kerry replied.

By now, Laura was beginning to calm down a little. 'Yeah, maybe you're right,' she said grudgingly. 'But I got one hell of a fright.'

'I'm sure you did, but just think about it – Jeff must know

you've disappeared, but he won't have a clue where you've gone. Stop worrying, and enjoy your time in Dorrington.'

When Kerry had rung off, Laura threw herself down on the sofa and cried. She didn't know if she was crying from fear or relief, or simply the stress of trying to second-guess Jeff. Kerry was right – he couldn't possibly know where she was.

Could he?

CHAPTER 63

'*Happy birthday, Kerry!*' Laura said, hugging her friend as she arrived at Treetops, and handing over a prettily wrapped parcel.

'*Thanks!*'

Frantically, Kerry tore off the paper to reveal a full-colour book on engineering. Her eyes sparkled with delight – there was no doubt that Mr Thornton had been the one to choose it for her – Laura wouldn't have been capable of selecting such a detailed book on her own.

Ellie appeared from the kitchen and waved a greeting to Laura. Then she smiled fondly at her daughter. '*Before I bring in the birthday cake, there's an extra-special present for you,*' Ellie told her, handing Kerry the gift that Alan had chosen for his secret daughter. '*I'm giving it to you now – before I light the candles – because you might want to use it before I start slicing the cake!*'

As Kerry began ripping the paper off, Ellie urged her to slow down. '*Please be gentle with it!*' she warned. '*This gift is fragile!*'

Thrilled, Kerry uncovered a box containing a top-of-the-range camera.

'*I thought you might like to take a picture of your birthday cake before I cut it,*' Ellie suggested to her daughter, and Kerry nodded excitedly.

'*This is brilliant! Thanks, Mum!*'

Soon the camera was out of its wrapping, and Kerry was loading the roll of film that had been included.

As Ellie re-entered the room, carrying a fresh cream and sponge birthday cake lit with twelve candles, Laura reached for the camera.

'Here, let me take a photo of you blowing out your candles,' Laura said.

'Come on, Kerry – it's time to make a wish!' Ellie said. 'If you don't hurry up, the candles will burn down and melt into the cake!'

As Laura and Ellie stood watching her, Kerry closed her eyes and blew hard. There was only one thing she wished for – so it was just as well that wishes were kept secret.

'Bravo – you got them all in one go!' said Laura. 'That means your wish will definitely come true! And I think I got a really good photo of you, too.'

As Ellie cut up the birthday cake and put slices onto plates, Kerry was now busy taking photos of Laura, her mother, her presents, and even the view of the garden from the window.

'Before you get cream all over your face, why don't I take a photo of you and your mum together?' Laura suggested.

Ellie nodded, pleased at Laura's suggestion. Smiling happily, Kerry surrendered the camera once again and sat down beside her mother, who draped her left arm over her daughter's shoulder.

As the two of them smiled at the camera, Laura looked through the viewfinder. 'Got it!' she exclaimed, after clicking the shutter. 'Although I say it myself, that is going to be a lovely photo!'

'Mum, would you like to see the photos taken at Treetops on Kerry's birthday?'

Sylvia nodded, looking at the two excited faces in front of her.

Both girls had grown so much in the past year, she thought, and soon they'd be on the threshold of womanhood. How had all those years gone by so quickly?

'Of course – I'd love to see them!' Sylvia took the proffered bundle of photos, and was immediately impressed by how sharp and well focused they were. Clearly, the Beckworths owned a high-quality camera. She was also curious to see inside Ellie's house again – she hadn't been there since Kerry was born, and she was keen to see any changes in décor that Ellie might have made.

Flicking through the photos, Sylvia made suitably admiring comments. There were an inordinate number of pictures of Kerry's birthday cake, and of Laura and Kerry together.

'I took that one,' Laura said happily, as Sylvia found herself gazing at a picture of Kerry and Ellie together.

Instantly, Sylvia's eyes were drawn to the hand that Ellie had draped over her daughter's shoulder. It was her left hand, and on her third finger she was wearing the most amazing diamond and gold ring – far more spectacular than the one Janette owned. Sylvia's heart gave a painful lurch. It couldn't be! No, it was out of the question – her mind was going into overdrive as usual. Alan and Ellie? No, it just wasn't possible! Her heart was thumping painfully, and she realised that she hadn't heard a word that the children had been saying to her.

Sylvia tried to smile as she handed back the photos and rose from her chair. She had to get out of the room before the children realised that something was wrong. She knew that tears weren't very far off, and she couldn't let them see her weeping. Her entire world was falling apart, yet she needed to hold herself together, for everyone's sake. If she could just get to the bathroom, then she could cry alone and in peace...

A sob rose in Sylvia's throat. Now she realised why Ellie had always been so distant. What a fool she had been! Her stomach was churning at the thought that Alan and Ellie had been laughing at her behind her back, thinking how pathetic she was, and how easily they had managed to deceive her...

In the bathroom, Sylvia locked the door. Now that she finally knew the truth, she couldn't let it go any more. This time, she was going to confront Alan.

CHAPTER 64

As Laura set off for work, she made her usual early morning detour along the Bayside esplanade, breathing in the salty sea air and revelling in the glorious morning sunshine.

As she left the esplanade and headed up the already busy street to her bus stop, she suddenly felt as though she was being watched. Turning around quickly, she was just in time to see a quick glimpse of a man who'd been staring at her before he melted away into the crowd.

Laura felt a stab of fear in the pit of her stomach. She was positive the man was familiar to her, but her glimpse of him had been so brief, she couldn't place him. Where had she seen him? And why was he staring at her? Had Jeff sent him? Memories of her encounter with the speeding car the previous week now assumed massive proportions in her mind again.

Despite what Kerry thought, it looked as though Jeff had found her again.

As she walked through the centre of Dorrington on her way home from the university the following evening, Laura experienced another prickly feeling running down her spine. She spun around, just in time to see the same man staring again, before he merged into the throng of people crossing the pedestrian plaza.

As she headed towards her bus stop, Laura kept checking

over her shoulder, but the man didn't reappear. It was the second time that someone had been watching her closely, and she didn't like it one bit. While she might have been mistaken the first time, a second time seemed to confirm her worst suspicions.

Laura was now feeling shivery and ill, and kept watching fearfully as she crossed the main road to the bus stop, conscious that this was the exact spot where she'd encountered the speeding car so recently.

She was relieved to see her bus approaching and quickly settled herself inside. She wondered if she was becoming paranoid. Yet within a short space of time, someone in a car had tried to run her down and a man had followed her from the Bayside esplanade to her bus stop. Surely, after these weird incidents, she was entitled to feel paranoid? Or maybe she was simply losing it. This was what Jeff was doing to her. He was twisting the knife, and loving every minute of it.

CHAPTER 65

*S*ylvia leaned her head out the window of the car as Kerry walked up the Greygates driveway.

'Hello, Kerry – I'm afraid Laura won't be able to play today. We're off to get new school uniforms.' Sylvia grimaced, looking at her watch. 'At least we will be, when Laura deigns to turn up. I've been waiting for ages for her to appear.'

Behind his mother's back, Pete was making funny faces at Kerry through the car window.

Ignoring Pete, Kerry smiled politely at Sylvia. 'I think I know where she is, Mrs Thornton – shall I go and find her for you?'

Sylvia gave the child a benevolent smile. 'Would you, Kerry? Thank you so much! We're running late, and I really need to get going.'

Setting off at speed, Kerry ran through the woodland that made up most of the huge garden at Greygates. She knew exactly where Laura would be hiding. Since Kerry had helped her and Pete to build a platform in the chestnut tree all those years ago, Laura spent much of her free time there.

Reaching the tree, Kerry stood at the base and looked up. She could see Laura's legs dangling over the edge.

'Laura!' she called up. 'You'd better hurry up and get in the car. Pete's already in the back, so you've no excuse for delaying any longer.'

'All right, all right,' Laura called down tersely. 'I'm on my *way. I don't need you nagging me as well as Mum.' Laura was annoyed with her friend. 'Where were you yesterday evening?' she asked angrily. 'I needed your help to sort out my skateboard – there's definitely something wrong with one of the wheels, and you're so good at that kind of thing.'*

Kerry kicked the base of the tree. 'I can't be at your beck and call all the time, you know.'

Laura was annoyed, but she said nothing.

Kerry looked up into the tree. 'Since you're not free to play today, I'm going home. But you'd better get a move on – your mum really needs to get going.'

'Yeah, yeah, okay.'

Laura made a move to climb down the tree, but as soon as she saw her friend heading back to Treetops, she sat back on the platform again. She'd brought bread for the injured blackbird she'd found the previous evening – its wing was hanging limply at its side – but it didn't seem interested in eating. Nor did its shiny orange beak look as bright as it had the day before. Laura wondered if it needed water. Why hadn't she thought of that before? It was probably dehydrated. Climbing down the tree, she found an old bowl filled with rainwater. Carrying it up, she placed it in front of the bird, who blinked its eyes warily.

The bird seemed uninterested in the water, despite Laura encouraging it to drink. It made a feeble attempt at flapping its wings, but soon gave up.

'I'd better be going,' Laura eventually told the blackbird apologetically. 'Aren't you lucky you don't have to go to school, or wear a uniform? I'll check in with you later – maybe you'll have managed to fly away by then. I really hope so.'

Sylvia's patience had finally given out but, just as she was preparing to drive off, her husband came hurrying out of the front door.

'Hang on, Syl – since you're still here, I might as well take a

lift with you,' Alan said, settling into the front passenger seat. 'If you can drop me off at the garage, you'll save me the bother of ordering a taxi.'

His wife nodded as she started the engine and began moving off. She wondered if Alan had detected anything different in her demeanour lately. Perversely she hoped so, since a comment from him might create the opportunity for her to raise the topic she'd been dreading, but desperately needed to discuss with him.

Her mind had been in turmoil ever since seeing the photo of Ellie Beckworth's ring. How long had her affair with Alan been going on? Sylvia shuddered. Did Tony Coleman know about it, or were he and Ellie no longer a couple? Now she was glad she and Ellie had never become friends – it would be too painful to lose a close friend as well as a husband. Sylvia stifled a sob. She could no longer live in torment – she'd have to confront Alan soon.

Alan smiled cheerfully at Pete, who was in the back seat, oblivious to the thoughts that were racing around in his wife's head. 'The mechanic said he'd have the heater in the new car sorted out by mid-morning,' he added. 'I can't believe the damned thing has failed already – I only got the car a few weeks ago!' He rubbed his hands together, as if to warm them. 'I'll be glad to have the heater working again – especially since the weather's starting to turn cooler already.' He looked quizzically at his wife. 'I thought you were taking Laura today, too?'

His wife nodded. 'That was the plan,' she replied curtly. 'But she doesn't seem bothered about getting ready for the new school term – so I might as well take Pete to get his uniform anyway.'

Laura ran through the undergrowth and headed in the direction of the lawns outside the front entrance to the house, aware that she'd been gone for ages, and knowing how annoyed her mother would be.

Her breath was coming in gulps as she finally reached the

lawns outside the house, just in time to see her mother's car disappearing down the driveway. Laura sighed, annoyed with herself. She'd missed the trip to town by seconds. There would be hell to pay later.

Chapter 66

'Goodnight, Kerry – see you tomorrow!'

Kerry smiled as she slipped on her coat. 'Goodnight, Norma. I hope you and Jack aren't going to stay too late?'

'Nah – another half an hour and we're both outta here.'

Kerry nodded, wishing that someone else was leaving the building at the same time as she was. Although she'd learned to ignore the old man who lingered about outside, he still made her feel uncomfortable. She'd spotted him twice in the previous few weeks, although she couldn't have described him since she'd never actually seen him up close. But she could recognise his walk by now, and the slight stoop of his shoulders, as though he was a tall man trying to look smaller. At this point, it was embarrassing to remember how terrified she'd originally been, imagining all sorts of scenarios in which Jeff was the protagonist.

As Kerry exited the building, it was starting to rain, and she wished she'd taken her umbrella from her office, but she wasn't going back for it now. She glanced surreptitiously around her, but there was no one anywhere in the immediate vicinity.

Purposefully hurrying along the street, her head down, Kerry walked in the direction of the tube station. She was very conscious that there were few people about at this hour, and there were no crowds into which she could easily merge. The click-clack of her shoes on the pathway was loud and clear, enabling anyone who might be following her to know exactly where she was heading...

Kerry's heart almost stopped as she passed a row of darkened shops. The man was there, lurking in a doorway! As she began to turn away, he stepped out of his hiding place. He raised his hand in her direction, and, for a moment, she wondered if he was holding a gun.

'Wait!' he called after her.

But Kerry didn't hang around to find out what he wanted. Filled with fear, she began to run. Once again, she thought of Jeff and his drug-dealer companion at the hotel. They'd clearly worked out what she'd been up to. She'd been too complacent about her own safety, and now she was about to pay the price. Jeff must have figured out what she'd been doing, and he wasn't going to tolerate her interference any longer...

Stumbling along the rainy street and out of breath, she heard a crack and felt a searing pain, then she was falling, falling, falling...

CHAPTER 67

As Sylvia started the car and headed down the driveway, Alan glanced at his wife. Even after all these years, he still felt guilty for deceiving her. Yet he'd been drawn to Ellie in a way that he'd never been to any other woman. Even now, after all their years of secret trysts and stolen hours of passion, she was still as exciting as ever to him.

And Kerry, his secret daughter – he'd need to ensure that she was provided for financially. He'd promised Ellie that he'd pay for her university education. He'd sort all that out just as soon as he got around to visiting his solicitor. Lately, there was just so much to do at the factory.

Poor Ellie – he felt guilty about her, because he'd made rash promises to her when they'd been younger but, at the time, he'd believed them, too. At one point, he'd genuinely been going to leave Sylvia and marry Ellie, but age and wisdom had made him realise that you couldn't always have what you wanted in life. If you got fifty per cent of it, you were lucky. And he was luckier than most. Anyway, he suspected that Ellie was content to be his secret wife, and to have him maintain his second family in a good standard of living.

'Damn,' Sylvia muttered, and Alan turned to her in surprise.

'What's wrong?'

'I'm not sure, but the car isn't steering properly. It keeps pulling to one side...'

'Well, why don't you drive me to the garage first, and let the mechanics there take a look at it?'

Sylvia nodded, saying nothing more as she concentrated on making her way onto the motorway. But before long, she glanced at him again, her eyes now filled with concern. 'Alan, I can't steer the damned car!'

Aghast, Alan watched helplessly as the car crossed several lanes, heading towards the central barrier of the motorway, while cars all around them slammed on their brakes and hooted their horns angrily. It felt as though the car was on a suicide mission. They weren't going to make it. Alan was paralysed with fear as the central barrier loomed before them.

'Brakes!' he shouted, even though it meant they'd be hit from behind. But it might prove the lesser of two evils. But, oh God, Pete was in the back seat...

'I can't – the brakes aren't working either!'

Galvanised into action, Alan leaned across his wife, trying desperately to pull at the steering wheel, but it wouldn't budge. It was firmly locked in position. He glanced back at his son, who was just beginning to realise the seriousness of their situation. His face was white as he watched his two helpless parents in the front. Alan wondered briefly if he could save Pete by ordering him to jump from the moving car onto the motorway. But just as quickly he dismissed it, Pete would be killed that way. They were in a moving death trap and he was powerless to do anything to save them.

As Sylvia screamed, the car mounted the concrete barrier, then headed directly into the oncoming traffic on the other side. An articulated truck was coming towards them. The last thing that Alan saw was the look of surprise and shock on the driver's face.

After the impact, there was nothing but oblivion.

Since she'd avoided going for her new school uniform, Laura decided to make the most of her free day. She stayed out in the woods all morning, watching rabbits foraging and grasshoppers leaping through the long grass. When she had tired of watching the local wildlife she'd checked on the injured bird again, but it was still sitting exactly where she'd left it.

Realising she was hungry, she made her way back to the house. She let herself in through the kitchen door and made herself a sandwich. It had been a novelty to spend the morning alone without having anyone telling her what to do. The silence of the house was a new experience too, and she was enjoying the solitude.

As she chewed her sandwich, Laura decided she could use her remaining free time to play a trick on Pete. He was always the one who was playing tricks on her – this time, she'd give him the surprise of his life! If she dug a trench between the two big sycamore trees down by the stream, and camouflaged it with twigs and leaves, when he next ran after her, she'd skirt the trap but Pete would fall straight into it! She chuckled at the thought of getting one over on her brother. She'd have plenty of time to dig the trench before the family got back from town.

Briefly, she thought of cycling over to Kerry's house and asking for her help with the digging, but Laura quickly changed her mind. Her friend had been in a grumpy mood earlier that morning and, anyway, she was enjoying being on her own for a change.

After spending the afternoon laying her trap in the woodland, Laura returned the spade to the shed and headed back towards the house. She had no idea what time it was, but it felt late, and she was beginning to feel hungry again. Inside the house, she looked at the kitchen clock, and was surprised to see that it was almost six.

A niggle of worry furrowed her brow. Where was everyone? Surely it didn't take all day to buy a school uniform? Debating whether or not to check on the injured bird again, Laura finally opted for the half-mile walk to Treetops, instead. She'd check on the bird later. She wasn't annoyed with Kerry any more, and was actually looking forward to some company. She was smiling as she started walking along the road.

Chapter 68

As Kerry pitched forward and fell to the ground, her heart was beating so fast that she feared it would burst out of her chest. Initially, the stab of pain she felt in her shoulder made her gasp. She'd heard a cracking sound at exactly the same time as she fell, and she wondered briefly if she'd been shot. Tears filled her eyes and she gritted her teeth as her knees scraped along the ground.

Fearing for her life, she scrambled to her feet again and continued running as fast as she could. Somewhere in the back of her mind, she realised that her body was still functioning normally. Was the sound she'd heard perhaps more like the smack of something – or someone – hitting the wet cobblestones? Besides, she only knew the sound of gunshots from movies and TV. She began to feel rather foolish. Fear had been putting her mind into overdrive.

Risking a quick glance behind her, Kerry could see that she was no longer being followed, and that there appeared to be something lying on the ground. But she wasn't going to hang around to find out who or what it was. By now, she could see the main thoroughfare ahead, where people, cars and buses were visible once again. She allowed herself to stop for a moment to catch her breath. She was seriously winded from her exertions.

With a sigh of relief, Kerry reached the crowded and well-lit street and, without a backward glance, she joined the throngs of people who were heading in various directions – some to the theatres, others to shops or the Underground. Never had she felt so grateful for the company of other human beings...

In the office the following morning, Norma was highly amused as Kerry told her about her nocturnal adventure the night before. She was still laughing when Jack arrived and joined them at the coffee machine.

'Well, from now on, I'm not leaving here after hours unless there's someone to accompany me,' Kerry said resolutely. 'I thought you said the guy was harmless? He almost frightened the life out of me!'

'Look, I'll walk you to the Underground in the evenings, if you're that worried,' Jack offered. He, like Norma, found the incident highly amusing.

Now, in the light of day, Kerry was also beginning to see the humour in the situation, and she felt stupid for behaving in such a panic-stricken way the night before. But she'd felt certain that Jeff was behind an attempt to harm her, and she'd panicked like some lily-livered idiot. She really needed to get a grip.

CHAPTER 69

When Laura arrived at Treetops, Ellie was in the kitchen. She gave Laura her customary warm smile. 'Hello, love,' she said. 'I was just going to take a glass of juice out to Kerry, so you can save me the job.'

Laura nodded, waiting as Ellie filled the first of two glasses with juice from the fridge. When the phone rang, she'd only filled one of the glasses, so she gestured for Laura to wait. As she answered and listened to the caller on the other end of the line, Laura was instantly alerted by the change in Ellie's tone of voice.

'W-what?' Ellie whispered, her hands gripping the landline phone until her knuckles were almost white.

Laura instantly knew that it was bad news, but she had no idea just how bad it would be. Lurking by the kitchen table, she pretended to be absorbed in pouring the second glass of juice, but instinctively she knew that Kerry's mother was too preoccupied to even notice that she was eavesdropping.

'Yes, she's here. How did it happen?' Ellie groaned.

By now, Laura was listening intently and, after a brief interval, Kerry's mother spoke again, her voice quivering with pain.

'Oh my God. Is there any hope?'

Clearly the answer from the other end was negative, because Ellie burst into tears, sinking to the floor, having forgotten that Laura was still in the kitchen.

'What is it? What's happened?' Laura cried, running to Ellie

and throwing her arms around her. She'd never seen anyone in such a distressed state before.

At first, Ellie seemed oblivious to Laura's presence – it was as though a mantle of pain had suddenly surrounded her, cutting her off from everything else. Then, realising that Laura was there, she crushed the young girl to her chest, her eyes brimming with tears.

'Oh, Laura, I can't believe it!' she sobbed, cradling the confused girl in her arms. 'It's bad news, and we'll all have to be brave.'

Laura looked confused. 'Bad news?'

It seemed an eternity before Ellie spoke, and her voice shook as she whispered the words. 'Yes, I'm afraid so, love. There's been an accident...'

In trying to soften the blow, Ellie was actually making it worse for Laura.

'Tell me, please!' Laura screamed.

'Your mother's car crashed, and she, your father and brother – '

'Are they okay? Are they in hospital?' Laura realised that in her anxiety, she was digging her nails into Ellie's hand, but Ellie didn't seem to notice.

Ellie dissolved into heart-rending sobs again. 'No, love, I'm afraid they're all – oh my God, how can I tell you?'

'Please!' Laura screamed, terrified now, clutching at Ellie's arm.

Not even feeling the pain of Laura's grip. Ellie turned her tear-stained face towards the child. 'I-I'm afraid they're all dead. I'm so sorry, Laura!'

Her words momentarily winded Laura, and initially the young girl was unable to speak. Then she broke free of Ellie's embrace and ran screaming out of the house. If she didn't listen, it wouldn't be true. It couldn't be true! Everyone she loved couldn't possibly be dead! It was all a dreadful mistake. Everything would be fine when Mum, Dad and Pete walked back in Greygates's front door. She was going straight back to the house, and she felt sure they'd all be waiting for her there...

As Laura ran into the garden screaming loudly, her eyes blinded with tears, Kerry rushed from the outhouse and looked at her in astonishment. 'What the – ?'

Laura stopped, her eyes red and streaming. 'I didn't go for my school uniform, and now they're all dead!' she wailed.

'What? Who's dead?' Kerry's face was white.

Laura gulped. She was so emotional she could hardly speak, but Kerry grabbed her arm and shook her angrily. 'For God's sake, tell me who's dead!' she screamed.

'They're all dead!' Laura whispered at last. 'Mum, Dad, Pete – they've all been killed!'

'Oh, God, no!' Kerry croaked, now crying too. 'All your family? I don't believe it! Even your father? Why would he be in your mother's car?'

'Because I was late!' Laura screamed. 'It's all my fault!'

She was devastated. Her heart was thumping and her head was spinning. This couldn't be happening. Soon she'd wake up and find it was all a bad dream. Maybe the message had been meant for some other family, not hers...

'I should have died too,' she whispered, fresh tears streaming down her face. She was riddled with guilt that her brother had travelled alone with her parents, simply because she'd gone to check on the injured blackbird. If she hadn't delayed them, they'd have left earlier and might have avoided the cause of the crash.

She desperately wished she'd been in the car with her family, since she couldn't envisage a life without them.

Suddenly, Kerry began running towards her own house, desperate for confirmation from her mother. Distraught, Laura wasn't sure whether to turn back to be with her friend but, more

*than anything, she wanted to be back in her own house with her
family around her.*

*So she ran down the Treetops's driveway and out the gate, and
began running along the road towards her own home. Pete would
be alive when she got there – she had to believe it – and she'd fill
in that stupid trap and just hug her brother tightly...*

*Blinded by tears, Laura ran along the side of the road, hardly
aware of the traffic, except when a car tooted its horn when she
veered too far off the pathway. She didn't actually care if she was
killed because it would ease the pain in her heart, which was
unlike anything she'd ever experienced before.*

*Behind her, in the distance, she could hear Ellie calling her,
but she ignored her entreaties and ran on. She had to get back to
Greygates, because her family would be waiting for her. It was all
a lie – they couldn't possibly be dead...*

*At last, she staggered up the Greygates driveway, running
past the house and down into the woodland beyond. Any minute
now, she'd see Pete's mischievous face peeping out from behind
one of the trees. And if she filled in the trap she'd laid for him,
everything would be all right...*

*Scraping around in the dirt, her tears mingled with sweat and
mucus, Laura tore at the twigs and leaves with her bare hands.
Crazed with grief, she began dragging the clay that she had dug
out earlier from its hiding place behind the tree, packing it back
into the hole she'd finished only hours earlier. Her nails broke
and caked with dirt as she tried desperately to fill the void.*

*Strong arms suddenly grabbed her and, as she tried to free
herself and continue digging, Laura found herself being pinioned
by an equally distraught and out-of-breath Ellie.*

*'Laura, stop!' Ellie cried, her own tears running down her face
and now mingling with Laura's own. 'There's nothing you can do
to bring them back – whatever you think you're doing, it won't
change anything!'*

Collapsing into Ellie's arms, Laura finally gave up the struggle, all the fight gone out of her. Smoothing Laura's hair, Ellie cradled her, and the two clung to each other. In between bouts of tears, Ellie began softly singing a lullaby.

It was there, a little while later, that they were found by the police.

CHAPTER 70

As the weeks went by, Laura began to feel more settled and secure. There hadn't been any further incidents, and she was beginning to accept that it had simply been an incompetent driver who'd almost knocked her down. Her rented apartment was comfortable and in a lovely location, Bill Maddison seemed happy with her work, and all seemed well in her world.

As she left the lecture hall one morning, Laura was feeling in exceptionally good form. She loved it when her students were genuinely interested in the subject, instead of regarding it as something to be regurgitated at exam time.

As she stepped into her office, she turned on her phone and noticed that there was a message in her inbox. The screen said 'Number Withheld', and Laura's heart gave a little, downward jolt. She was disappointed that it wasn't from Darren, since his regular calls, texts and newsy emails allowed her to feel that she was still part of his department. Since Jeff hadn't bothered her for quite a while now, she was a lot calmer when her phone rang or she received a text.

But as she opened the text and scrolled down, Laura wondered if she was about to have a heart attack.

Hello Laura – I really did enjoy your lecture today. You know your subject so well! I was sitting in the back row, so I don't think you saw me. You didn't see me either when you were crossing that busy road, did you? I'm disappointed you left London, but glad to know where my dear wife is now living. J xx

Frightened, Laura threw her phone across the room, feeling that it was now contaminated. How on earth could Jeff have got this latest number, and found out where she was working? Was he here in Dorrington? Had he arranged for that man to follow her?

Laura shuddered, although she was trying to think things through sensibly. She couldn't just up and leave a job every time Jeff managed to find her. Surely he couldn't think she'd ever go back to him? While it was clear he hadn't wanted their marriage to end, surely he had to accept his own role in its demise? Once again, Laura wondered where this would all end.

Laura felt bad about ringing Kerry again, but there was no one else who'd understand how scared she was feeling.

'I've just received a text from Jeff. He said he'd attended my lecture today.'

'Jeff? But how on earth – ?'

'I don't know,' Laura said miserably. 'I've already changed my phone number three times. How could he get this latest number?'

'What exactly did it say?'

Laura read her the wording of the text.

'Look, he's just trying to scare you. He probably wasn't there at all, but I think you should go to the police, anyway.'

'What's the point? They weren't very receptive before.'

'Well, the Dorrington police might be more proactive,' Kerry reasoned. 'Look, just because he texted you, doesn't mean he knows where you are. He's just trying to unnerve you.'

'Well, he's succeeding,' Laura said dryly.

Kerry was beginning to sound exasperated. 'Can't you just try and forget about him? Leave him in the past, where he belongs. He can't possibly find you in Dorrington!'

'Can't he? I wish I could believe you, but I know Jeff. And

what about that guy that's been following me? I can't help but think Jeff is behind it all.'

'What? You never told me about a guy following you! Are you sure you weren't imagining it?' Kerry asked. 'You are rather jumpy at the moment, so it wouldn't be surprising if you read more into situations than was really there.'

'No,' Laura said firmly. 'I caught this guy looking at me, and turning away quickly. Give me some credit, Kerry – Jeff hasn't caused me to lose my mind just yet!'

'Listen, I've got to go,' Kerry told her. 'Norma, Jack and the gang are meeting up to discuss the progress of our star project. But call me if anything else happens, okay?'

As she rang off, Laura had the distinct impression that Kerry was losing sympathy with her, and she couldn't blame her. She had her own life to live, and who needed a paranoid nutcase for a friend? Laura made a vow to take more interest in Kerry's work – that way, she might be able to support her friend, and repay a little of the kindness that Kerry had shown to her over the years. Kerry had been there for her through thick and thin, and it was time she got her own life in order. And somehow banish Jeff for good.

Chapter 71

Laura woke early. For a brief moment, she managed to forget the tragedy of the day before. But realising she was in the spare bedroom at Treetops, the horror of it all came flooding back.

Creeping out of bed, her eyes once again filled with tears, she tiptoed past Kerry's room, then Ellie's room, and down the stairs, where she left a note in the hall explaining that she was briefly visiting Greygates again.

Not surprisingly, she'd completely forgotten about the injured bird. Now she felt guilty for neglecting it. Hurrying down the road, Laura entered the big, metal gates that gave Greygates its name, then made her way to the tree platform in the wood, praying that the little bird's wing would have repaired itself and that it might have managed to fly away. Somehow she felt as though its recovery would indicate that something good, no matter how small, might be garnered from the awful events that had occurred the day before.

But as she climbed the tree to the platform, her heart plummeted as she spotted the little bird's body. It lay stiff and unmoving exactly where she'd left it – it hadn't even attempted to fly. Seeing it tiny, lifeless body seemed to open the floodgates once again, and Laura wept until she had no tears left.

Unable to see because of her tears, Laura caressed the bird's shiny feathers, wishing she had the power to inject life back into the little creature and into all those she loved, or to turn back time so that they could all still be together.

Eventually, she climbed down from the platform and, using a stick, dug a small grave in the soft, damp earth beneath the tree. She cried again as she placed the tiny body in the trench. The bird had represented something wild, beautiful and untamed. But now, along with her parents and brother, it was no more. All the beauty, all the hope, had been destroyed.

Laura was filled with guilt – clearly her delaying tactics the day before had been responsible for her father's change of plan. If she hadn't kept her mother waiting in the car while she tended to the bird, her father wouldn't have been able to take a lift with her. It was all her fault, and she'd never be happy again as long as she lived. And she hoped that wherever her beloved brother was, he wouldn't know that she'd been planning to play a mean, stupid trick on him.

Tears trickled down her cheeks. How could she not have known? Why hadn't she felt something at the moment of their deaths? What had she been doing at the precise moment that the lorry had ploughed into their car? She'd heard murmurings about what had happened, but adult conversations ended abruptly as soon as she appeared. She knew that people were only trying to protect her, yet she had a perverse need to know exactly what had happened. She wasn't sure if that was to punish herself, or to simply understand the enormity of it all.

Later that afternoon, when she returned to Treetops, Laura found a gaunt and sad-faced Dick Morgan sitting at Ellie's kitchen table.

'Laura, let's go upstairs. I'll help you pack,' Ellie told her gently. 'You're going to live with your grandfather.'

Laura was bereft. 'But I don't want to leave here!' she sobbed. 'Oh, please, don't make me go!'

Ellie tried to shush her as they climbed the stairs, not wanting her grandfather below to hear her cries. 'Come on, love – you *can't stay at Greygates on your own. You'll have a lovely time at your grandfather's place, and you'll be going to a new school. Won't that be exciting?'*

'No, it won't, and I don't want to go!' Laura howled, resisting Ellie's efforts to keep her quiet. 'And I don't want to leave Kerry – she's my best friend!'

'You and Kerry can phone and write to each other,' Ellie told her soothingly. 'And you can see each other during the school holidays. That'll be something to look forward to, won't it?'

But Laura wouldn't be mollified. 'I've lost everybody, and now I'm losing Kerry, too!' she cried.

Upstairs, Laura watched tearfully as Ellie packed her few possessions into a holdall. She wondered vaguely how her T-shirts, socks and shorts had got there, but clearly someone must have brought them back from Greygates the day before.

'Why isn't Kerry here?' Laura whispered plaintively. 'Does she know I'm going? She won't want me to leave either!'

'By the time Kerry woke up, you'd already left for Greygates. She's gone for a walk into the village – she's very upset about what happened yesterday,' Ellie said softly, her own eyes filled with tears. 'We're all devastated.'

'Well, I can't go until she gets back,' Laura said firmly, trying to gain a modicum of power over a situation that was already spiralling out of her control.

But at the bottom of the stairs, Dick Morgan was waiting, car keys in hand, as Ellie and Laura descended the stairs.

'I won't go without seeing Kerry!' Laura screamed, clinging to Ellie and refusing to follow her grandfather, who was now walking out to his car.

'Believe me, it's better this way,' Ellie whispered, gently propelling her out of the front door, her own eyes now red from crying. 'I'll tell her you said goodbye.'

As Ellie pushed her firmly towards Dick Morgan's Mercedes,

Laura looked around herself wildly. Where was her best friend when she needed her most? Now that her family had died, Kerry was the only person left who truly cared for her. Rage filled her heart. She'd just lost her entire family, and now they were dismantling the only support system she had left.

But there was no sign of her friend and, numbly, Laura allowed herself to be guided into the front passenger seat, beside her grandfather.

Fastening Laura's seatbelt, Ellie gave her a quick hug. Then the car door was closed, and her grandfather instantly applied the central locking system. Laura felt as though she was suffocating in a prison from which there was now no escape.

As they drove out of the Treetops's driveway and onto the main road, Laura spotted Kerry walking home dejectedly, her face sad and tear-stained. Even though Laura screamed for her grandfather to stop the car, he didn't seem to hear her and, despite banging loudly on the window and gesticulating wildly to Kerry, her friend seemed lost in a private world of her own.

CHAPTER 72

A week later, Laura had an afternoon free of tutorials, so she'd decided to visit an antiquarian bookshop in Dorrington. The bookshop, tucked away in a little side street in the city centre, was renowned for its range.

As she headed for the bookshop, she made a point of walking through the pedestrian area as much as possible. She didn't want to give Jeff any chance to make another attempt on her life. Thankfully, there hadn't been any further texts from him, so she had to hope he just intended to unnerve her from time to time.

Suddenly, she had an uneasy feeling that she was being followed again. Her heart in her mouth, she spun around, and her jaw dropped in surprise. Was that Darren? Before she had a chance to offer a surprised and delighted greeting, he'd disappeared down a side street.

Hurrying back the way she came, Laura stared down the side street where he'd turned off, but it was completely empty. Had she imagined it? She must have, since Darren would never avoid her like that.

Puzzled, Laura walked on, still uncertain as to whether she'd seen him or not. Common sense told her to accept what her eyes had seen, yet she couldn't think of any reason why her former boss would be in Dorrington. Then it crossed her mind that he could be there to see Bill Maddison. Of course, that made perfect sense. But she was still puzzled as to why he'd hurried away when she'd spotted him. She and Darren got on really well, and had always been really good friends. Why wouldn't he want to say hello? Then a horrible thought struck her. Was Bill unhappy with her work, and had sent for Darren to discuss getting rid of her?

Confused and bewildered, Laura no longer felt like browsing. Her whole world seemed to be disintegrating around her. Despite all of Jeff's antics, she'd still had her career, and it had given her an identity and security. Was she now about to lose that, too?

Laura found it impossible to deal with all this uncertainty, so she vowed to tackle Bill straight away. She couldn't bear the thought of Bill and Darren discussing her, and of her being unable to defend herself. If they'd something to say to her, she wanted it said to her directly. Abandoning her trip to the bookshop, Laura hurried back to the university.

When Laura entered Bill's office, he smiled warmly at her, and she was suddenly filled with misgivings. He didn't look like a man who was about to sack her.

'Bill, has Darren been to visit you?'

Bill looked surprised. 'Darren? No, why do you ask?'

'I'm sure I saw him in Dorrington town centre today.'

Looking puzzled, Bill shrugged his shoulders. 'I can't imagine why he'd be here – we talk on the phone from time to time, but rarely in person. Are you sure it was him?'

'Well, I thought it was,' Laura said, now wondering if her imagination had gone into overdrive. Since she was clearly still stressed over Jeff's last text, perhaps in an effort to comfort herself, she'd conjured up an image of someone she knew would always be there for her. But if it *was* Darren she'd seen, why would he hide from her? Surely he'd say hello? But the person she'd spotted earlier had clearly been trying to avoid her.

Suddenly, Laura felt overwhelmed by loneliness and sadness. She didn't think she could stand it if Darren turned against her. He was someone very special to her, someone she'd always been able to count on in the past…What did other people know that she didn't?

'You okay, Laura?'

Waking from her reverie, Laura smiled. 'Yes, of course, Bill. Obviously, I made a mistake about seeing Darren.'

Bill grinned. 'Darren on your mind a lot?'

Laura blushed. Darren had been on her mind a lot more than she cared to admit…

'Sorry, I couldn't resist teasing you,' Bill said, chuckling. Then his expression turned to one of concern. 'But you look worried – is there anything wrong?'

Laura nodded, suddenly feeling overwhelmed by everything and deciding to tell him the truth. 'I'm not sure how long I can stay here, Bill…'

Pulling up a chair, Laura told him all about Jeff, and about everything that had happened since she'd moved to Dorrington.

Bill said nothing while she talked but, when she'd finished, he let out a long, low whistle. 'Wow! I'd no idea things were so bad. Is there anything we can do here at the university?'

Laura shook her head.

'Then I think you need to go to the police – I've always found the Dorrington police to be very helpful. I'll come with you, if you like.'

Laura shook her head. 'The trouble is, I've nothing concrete to show them,' she explained. 'To an outsider, Jeff's text would just read like a message from an admirer. He's too clever – only I know the menace behind the message. As for the out-of-control car, and the man who seemed to be following me – it's all rather tenuous, isn't it?'

'Well, we'll bump up security around the campus – make sure no outsiders can gain access to the lecture theatres,' Bill told her kindly. 'I'll have a word with our security team straight away. Don't worry, Laura, we won't let this guy get near you.' He looked at her sympathetically. 'Promise me you'll go to the police?'

Laura nodded.

Thanking him, she left his office. But, as she made her way down the deserted corridor, she couldn't help shivering. It was all very well to be protected while doing her job, but what about at other times? Was she going to have to stay on full alert for the rest of her life? And now that Jeff had managed to track her down again, was there any point in staying in Dorrington? There seemed to be eyes watching her everywhere, and she wondered if she really was losing her mind.

Laura angrily brushed away a tear. On the other hand, if she'd really spotted Darren and he'd avoided speaking to her, it didn't augur well for returning to her job in London, either. But more than that, she couldn't bear the thought of never seeing or working with him again. What was happening, and why did she feel that everything in her life was spiralling out of control? Bill was right – it was time to talk to the Dorrington police. And she'd do it right away.

CHAPTER 73

Ellie lay alone in her room, the blinds drawn. This was the only place where she could cry in peace. But how could she go on, without her beloved Alan? Her heart was breaking, and she pressed her pillow to her mouth to prevent Kerry from hearing her crying. She wished she could die and be with Alan, but young Kerry still needed her mother.

Ellie stifled a sob. With Alan's death, they'd become penniless. While he'd been alive, she'd been assured of her monthly stipend and could pay her mortgage comfortably. Now she and her daughter only had the miniscule pension John had left her – she'd already had to apply for social security.

Of course, Kerry didn't know why their financial situation had deteriorated so rapidly. Ellie had made up a story about investments that had taken a nosedive, but Kerry had developed a bitterness that surprised and worried Ellie. Undoubtedly, the child was traumatised at losing her best friend so suddenly and at having to leave her expensive private school and start attending the local comprehensive.

They'd also have to sell their beloved Treetops, and move to a much smaller house or flat. Ellie was heartbroken at the thought – all the memories of her beloved Alan were tied up in the house's bricks and mortar. By leaving, she'd be abandoning the place where their love had been nurtured. It would almost be like losing him all over again. Ellie dreaded telling Kerry, but there was no alternative. Alan's tragic death had altered their lives on so many different levels.

Now, she fingered the gold and diamond ring that Alan had given her all those years ago. She'd loved Alan too much to blame him for leaving them unprotected. He hadn't expected to die, had he? And she'd never given a thought to suddenly finding herself without him.

She'd loved him more than life itself and, despite all her blustering, she'd been content to be the woman he loved in secret. In fact, being his secret wife had given her a special joy that had appealed to her sense of the dramatic, and had always kept their passion on the boil. Now, there was no one with whom she could share her special brand of pain.

'Oh, Alan,' she whispered. 'My heart is broken, and it's so hard to live without you...'

Idly, she wondered if Alan and Sylvia were together in the next life. She doubted that there was an afterlife anyway, or that she'd ever see Alan again. But, right then, the pain of loss was so great that she longed for the oblivion of death so that she didn't need to feel this gut-wrenching pain ever again.

She wiped away her tears. Now, at least, her secret didn't matter any more. And it could no longer hurt Alan. His death had freed her from the guilt at last, although she'd have borne it willingly just to have him back again.

She'd never told anyone what had happened on that awful night all those years ago, and she'd done her utmost to block it from her mind. That way, she hadn't needed to face a possible, unpalatable truth. Because once she did, everything would change, and she refused to let it. But, sometimes, as she'd watched her sturdily built young daughter, her dark head bent over some toy she was dismantling, feelings of guilt and regret overwhelmed her. But now that her beloved Alan was dead, it didn't matter any more.

She'd managed to keep everyone happy, while doing the best she could for her daughter.

A tear ran down Ellie's cheek. Try as she might, she'd never managed to totally obliterate that night from her memory, even though she'd made a decision then and there to deny it space in her head. But, sometimes, the memories invaded her dreams at night, or caught her unprepared during the day. Then she'd feel physically sick as she tried to quell the tide of revulsion that rose up inside her.

It seemed that the more she longed to forget something, the more her mind wanted to remind her of it.

'Oh, Alan,' she whispered tearfully into her pillow. 'I hope you knew how much I loved you – and it was only a small deception, anyway...'

CHAPTER 74

Having visited the local Dorrington police station that very afternoon, Laura wasn't quite sure how she felt. While the police officer had been courteous, he obviously didn't hold out much hope of nailing Jeff.

'Your ex would have used a throwaway phone,' he told her gently. 'And the SIM card will have been destroyed by now.' He gave her a sympathetic smile. 'I'm sorry we can't be more helpful, but these situations usually settle down over time. By your own admission, he isn't hassling you quite as much as in the past, so it sounds like he might be getting tired of bothering you.'

'So that's it?' Laura asked in frustration. 'He just gets away with it? He can try to run me down, hassle me any time he likes, yet nothing happens to him?' She glared at the officer. 'And what about the man following me? The same guy has followed me several times – and maybe at other times, too, for all I know – and I'm positive it's not a coincidence!'

The officer looked contrite. 'I'm sorry, Ms Thornton, I'll make a note of it in the logbook, and if anything else happens, don't hesitate to let us know – '

'A note in a logbook won't help me if I'm dead!' Laura told him, flouncing out of the door of the station.

When her mobile rang later that evening, Laura checked the number. It was one she didn't recognise, and at first she didn't bother answering it, as she didn't think she could cope with any more hassle. But when the same number rang again later, she felt so angry that she grabbed the phone, took a deep breath and risked pressing the answer button.

'Hello?'

'Ms Thornton, this is Detective Sergeant Andy Sheeran, from Islington Police station in London.'

Laura's heart began to thump uncomfortably. Was he really a police officer, or was this just another trick that Jeff had thought up?

'The police in Dorrington have been in touch with us about some incidents you reported – '

'Yes?'

The man's voice was curt. 'We'd like you to come here, Ms Thornton, as soon as possible. I have some information that may be of concern to you.'

Laura sighed. Why couldn't he just say what was on his mind, rather than dragging her to London, to be told something he could probably have said over the phone? 'Look, if it's that important, why can't I just go to the local police station? I'm rather busy at the moment – '

'Ms Thornton, what I have to tell you is best said in person. I'd rather you came here, and please – make it as soon as possible.'

Noting the gravity in his voice, Laura made a snap decision. Better to get it over with, whatever it was. 'Okay, okay – I'll get to London for tomorrow afternoon.'

'Thank you, Ms Thornton. See you then.'

Ringing off, Laura arranged cover for her lectures and left a voice message on Bill's phone explaining that urgent business required her to take the first train to London in the morning.

Before she left Dorrington, Laura checked with the local police station, and they confirmed that Detective Sergeant Andy

Sheeran really did exist, and that it was genuinely urgent she visit the Islington police station as soon as possible.

As she sat on the train, Laura gazed pensively out of the window. Something else was definitely wrong. She'd expected to stay at Kerry's apartment while in London, but when she'd rung her friend, she'd been decidedly evasive, fobbing her off with excuses. This offhand treatment was making Laura feel decidedly uneasy – why was her best friend giving her the brush-off? She was also still reeling from having seen Darren in Dorrington, yet he'd deliberately turned away when she spotted him. It made her feel sad and worried that the people she cared about most were now avoiding her. What on earth was going on?

At Islington Police Station, Laura was ushered into Detective Sergeant Andy Sheeran's office as soon as she arrived.

'Ms Thornton, please sit down.'

Laura dropped into the chair facing the detective's desk, still annoyed at being dragged away from Dorrington, especially since her earlier experiences at the police station hadn't been particularly helpful.

'Would you like a cup of tea?'

'No, thanks.'

The officer shuffled some papers on his desk before eventually looking straight at her. 'I'm sorry to have to tell you this – but your ex-husband is dead. He died two months ago.'

Laura's jaw dropped open. What? No, it wasn't possible! Then her eyes began to fill with tears. 'Oh my God! W-what happened?'

The police officer cleared his throat. 'Obviously, you knew about your ex-husband's allergy – well, unfortunately, while he was on remand in prison, he was inadvertently served a trace of peanuts in one of his meals, and the wardens couldn't locate his adrenaline pen in time.'

Laura looked stunned. 'In prison? What was he doing there?'

Momentarily, the officer's expression softened. 'On your previous visit here, I was particularly interested in what you'd said about your husband's parents, and his claims of being in MI5.' He twirled his pen between his fingers. 'After you'd left the station, I looked up the files and discovered that there were a lot of question marks over his parents' deaths. I talked to the officers who'd worked on the case, and they all felt that Mr Jones definitely had something to do with his father's death, although they hadn't been able to prove it.' The police officer looked grim. 'Thanks to you, we got the case reopened – and, this time, the advances in DNA enabled us to get the evidence we needed to prosecute him. He was in jail awaiting trial for the murder of his father when he was killed.' He looked at her closely. 'Did you know that he strangled his father with his bare hands, then used a rope to make it look like suicide?'

Laura shivered, suddenly recalling Jeff's remark about threatening to kill her 'too'. 'No, I didn't. And I'm glad I didn't know that while I was married to him.'

'Although we only got him for that one murder, we're fairly certain he was responsible for a string of other murders as well,' the detective added. 'Several witnesses who were due to testify at drug-dealers' trials conveniently disappeared, and we believe he was the one who killed them.' He looked at her tentatively. 'The Drug Squad were also running surveillance on your ex-husband, but the people at the top of the supply chain are always the most difficult to put away. Of course, we now know that you weren't aware that he was also one of the country's major drug dealers.'

The colour drained from Laura's face as she shook her head. So his MI5 claims had just been a cover to fool his gullible wife. Kerry had been right all along.

'But you said he died two months ago – why on earth wasn't I told before now?'

DS Sheeran grimaced. 'I'm sorry, Ms Thornton – we had our reasons. When you first disappeared from London, we wondered if your ex-husband had bumped you off. The chap at your university wasn't willing to reveal your whereabouts, but we checked your credit-card usage, and discovered that you'd been using it in Dorrington.'

Laura gasped. 'So that was *you* who was following me?'

DS Sheeran nodded.

'You scared the hell out of me!'

The officer gave an apologetic smile. 'After Mr Jones died, we wondered if your original complaints to the police had been part of an elaborate plan to distance yourself from your husband's drug empire, with a view to taking it over after his death.'

Laura's eyes were like saucers. 'What? You mean you thought *I* might have planned his murder?'

DS Sheeran shrugged his shoulders. 'Stranger things have happened. That's why I followed you to Dorrington – we had to find out whether or not you were involved. Obviously, we know now that you had nothing to do with your husband's death or with running his business.'

Still in shock, Laura said nothing.

'But when you levelled further accusations against your ex-husband while you were in Dorrington – after he was dead – alarm bells started ringing, and we began to wonder what on earth was going on.'

Laura slumped in her chair.

He closed the file on his desk and looked at her closely. 'Do you realise what that means?'

Laura shook her head, looking blankly at him.

'It means your husband couldn't have been the person you claim was targeting you.'

Laura's mouth dropped open. 'W-what?'

'Someone else must have been trying to harm you. Do you have any idea who it might be? If you're prepared to register a complaint, we'll investigate this person or persons immediately.'

The colour drained from Laura's face. If not Jeff, who else could it be? Her mind was rapidly racing through all the recent events that had happened, and the people she'd trusted to keep her whereabouts secret. She still didn't understand why Darren had been in Dorrington, but he wouldn't have any reason to harm her...

Then her eyes filled with tears. No, no – it couldn't possibly have been. No, definitely not. How could she even think such a thought? No, no, no – on the other hand, who else would have known all the personal details of her life...? Laura shook her head angrily. How could she think such a thing, even for a second?

The police officer looked at her astutely. 'I can see that you've someone in mind,' he said gently.

Laura shook her head. No, she couldn't bring herself to mention this person's name. Because if she said it, she'd be admitting that she'd actually given consideration, however briefly, to the ridiculous notion...

Jumping up, Laura grabbed her coat and rushed out of the police station, with the detective in hot pursuit.

'Ms Thornton, please come back – !'

Tears now blinding her, Laura hurried along the road. Her mobile rang, but she didn't answer it, guessing that it was probably the police officer begging her to return to the station. She heard a man calling her name, but she ignored him. She had to find out the truth, and there was only one way to do it.

Just as she reached the corner of the street where Kerry's apartment was, Avril, the estate agent, was coming out of a building on the other side. As usual, she was clutching her portfolio of leaflets and teetering on six-inch heels. Waving goodbye to the clients who'd been viewing the property, she crossed the road to where Laura was now approaching.

'Well, hello! How nice to see you, Laura! I thought you'd moved abroad somewhere? What brings you to this part of the world?'

'I'm just on my way to Kerry's place,' Laura explained.

Avril looked confused. 'But she doesn't live here any more. Have you forgotten?'

Laura's jaw dropped. 'What do you mean?'

'Well, she's taken over your old apartment in Green Street –'

'When did *that* happen?' Laura asked tersely.

Avril suddenly looked worried, sensing a potential problem. 'Oh, dear! After the fire, when you gave notice that you were leaving, your friend contacted me and said she'd like to rent it when it had been repaired and refurbished. And that she'd be interested in buying it when the vendor was ready to sell…' Her voice faltered. 'I assumed you knew…you're saying she didn't tell you?'

'No, she didn't,' Laura said. 'Sorry, Avril, I've got to go.' Laura smiled apologetically as she turned to leave, hoping that Avril wouldn't think she was in any way responsible for her ill-humour.

As Laura hurried down the street, once again she heard a man calling her name, but she ignored him and kept on running towards the nearest Underground station.

CHAPTER 75

In the lobby of the Green Street apartments, Laura rushed past Albert the concierge before he had time to react, waving to him and banking on the fact that since she'd once lived there, he'd remember her and would let her through without a fuss.

When Laura knocked at the door of the apartment, Kerry looked shocked as she opened her door.

'Laura! How did you – ?'

'How did I find out you'd moved in here? It doesn't matter – aren't you going to invite me in?'

Kerry gave a weak smile, but it was obvious that she'd been caught out.

As she stepped inside, Laura could see that the apartment was already looking very different from when she'd lived there. The fire damage had been completely repaired, and Kerry's style was already evident in the different range of furnishings. It looked as though she'd been working on one of her projects at a big desk in the corner of the living room, which was piled high with books and papers.

'You didn't waste any time before putting your own stamp on it, did you?'

Kerry rallied. 'Well, you were right – it's a fabulous flat,' she said. 'The amount of light it gets is wonderful, and I envied you so much when you moved in here. Why shouldn't I take it over when you left?'

'It would have been a courtesy to let me know – I'd have been pleased for you. But it never crossed my mind that you could afford the rent and the service charge, much less buy it.'

Kerry smiled malevolently. 'Well, I wanted to stake my claim, because I expect to have the money *very* soon.'

As the two women stared at each other, Laura licked her lips. Her mouth was dry as she tried to find the words she wanted to say, but no sound would come out. As she stood there, Kerry went into the kitchen, returning with two glasses of juice. It was just the kind of thing that Kerry usually did, and it lent an air of normality to a very bizarre situation.

At first, Laura ignored the drink, but her throat and mouth still seemed unbelievably dry, and she wanted to be able to articulate her case clearly, so she took the glass and gulped the juice down rapidly. The whole situation still seemed unreal, but her mouth felt fresher and her tongue now seemed able to form the words she wanted.

'Jeff is dead – he died two months ago,' she said. 'He was on remand in prison – they finally nailed him for killing his father and making it look like a suicide. And you were right, he was also involved in drug-dealing.' She took a deep breath. 'So you know what that means, don't you?'

One look at Kerry's face told Laura all she needed to know. Kerry shrugged her shoulders. 'It looks like the game is over,' she said, giving a rueful smile. 'I'd hoped to have fun with you for a little while longer, but it looks like you've worked out what I've been up to...'

Laura's heart sank. She'd been desperately hoping that Kerry wouldn't be the one who'd been targeting her. She'd been positive her friend could offer some logical explanation for what had been happening to her.

'But how – I mean, Jeff *was* hassling me, wasn't he? So I don't understand – '

'Oh, make no mistake, your husband was a violent, nasty thug,' Kerry said, finishing her own juice. 'At first, I was really worried about him, but I soon realised that Jeff was the icing on the cake – I loathed him, but he served my purpose admirably.' She smirked at Laura's incredulous expression.

Laura's voice was barely a whisper. 'What do you mean? I thought you were my best friend! I don't see why you'd want to – '

Kerry didn't answer, and Laura longed to hit her. Instead, she lashed out with her hand and sent all the books and documents on the desk flying.

'Answer me!' she screamed, as both women surveyed the mess of papers now spread all over the floor. Simultaneously, their eyes were drawn to a pile of photos lying among the debris, but neither of them seemed able to move or speak.

At last, Laura found her voice, although it only came out as a squeak. 'So *you* were the one who stole my family photos!'

She bent down and picked up a photo of her father, which had now been put into a frame. In it, he was smiling at the camera, looking carefree and happy. Laura stared at it, mystified. 'Why did you put the picture of my father into a frame?'

'Because he's *my* father as well!'

'W-what?'

Kerry sneered. 'Poor Laura – you thought you had the perfect family, didn't you? But all the time, your dad was doing it with my mum – and I was the result!'

'I don't believe you!'

Kerry shrugged her shoulders. 'It doesn't matter what you believe. How do you think I could go to the same posh school as you? Because your father – *our* father – paid all my school fees. And he was planning on leaving you all, to come to live with Mum and me!'

'My father would never have left my mother!' Laura said

angrily. She was finding it difficult to reconcile all this new information with what she remembered of her parents' lives. They had always seemed happy but, back then, at not quite twelve years of age, what child could understand the nuances of adult conversation, gestures and glances, the heartbreak that could lie behind smiling faces?

Kerry sighed. 'You may well be right. But I actually heard him tell Mum he was coming to live with us.' She looked triumphantly at Laura. 'Do you remember Mum's ring?'

Laura nodded. She'd often admired the beautiful diamond and gold ring that Ellie always wore on the third finger of her left hand.

'When Mum died suddenly, the undertakers returned it to me – and do you know what? Inside was an inscription that said: "Alan and Ellie forever". That confirmed for me what I'd always known anyway.' Kerry's face suddenly crumpled, and Laura thought she detected the glint of tears in her eyes as she continued. 'You had a father every day of your life – I didn't! Why should you have had everything? He was my father too, but I was never recognised. I was just his dirty little secret!'

Laura was experiencing a complex range of emotions. On the one hand, she hated what Kerry was saying about her parents, but she was desperate to understand, even if it meant learning unpalatable truths.

'H-how did you find out about this supposed affair?'

'It was easy enough. One day when I was about nine, I came home early – tennis lessons had been cancelled – and I discovered your father's car parked behind the house.' Kerry looked steadily at Laura. 'I could hear my mother and your father in her bedroom, so I crept up into the loft above her room, and was able to peep down through a crack in the ceiling – and I saw what they were doing.'

'B-but what made you think you were his child?'

'I heard them talking about it,' Kerry said triumphantly. 'When they were lying in bed, Mum said that it was time I was told who my real father was. But he begged her to wait – he said the time wasn't right yet, and that they'd tell everyone I was his daughter once he'd left your mother. He promised Mum he'd do it very soon.' Her voice trembled. 'I crept back outside, and watched from the outhouse as he drove off afterwards. Then I pretended to come home at the usual time, and Mum never suspected a thing.' Her voice rose. 'I waited day after day, week after week, for him to make a public announcement about it. But when nothing happened, I figured it was time to help things along myself.'

'W-what do you mean?'

Kerry's face contorted in anger. 'You were always impulsive and emotional, weren't you, Laura? That's why you weren't in the damned car when you should have been! You went off to save that injured bird – so you escaped the death I'd planned for you, and I lost my father instead!'

Laura was bewildered. 'What are you talking about?' She suddenly felt as though the ground was giving way beneath her feet. No, it couldn't be true – no, no no!

Kerry grimaced. 'I thought I could create the perfect family. I figured that if you all died, my father would come to live with Mum and me, and we'd be a real family at last.'

The colour had drained from Laura's face. 'But I remember you crying your heart out when you heard about the crash!' she said, bewildered. 'We cried together – were you acting then, too?'

Kerry gave a thin-lipped smile. 'I didn't need to pretend – I *was* devastated! Your father – my father – wasn't supposed to be in the car that day!' Kerry glared at her. 'So you see, I was genuinely crying because I'd lost my dream of a real family – yet somehow *you* managed to survive!'

A tidal wave of rage welled up inside Laura. She longed to

use her fist to wipe the smirk off Kerry's face, but there was more she needed to uncover first.

'What did you do to the car?'

'I tampered with the steering the night before.' Kerry smiled triumphantly. 'Remember that afternoon when we all went to collect your father's new car from the showroom? Well, I learnt everything I needed to know from one of the mechanics in the workshop there!' She grinned. 'He thought I was just a nosy kid, but I got him to answer some very pertinent questions! That's why you couldn't find me to fix your skateboard – I was in your garage, underneath your mother's car!'

'You merciless bitch – how could you!'

'Do you think I cared about you? I wanted a family of my own!'

Laura stared at her incredulously. 'All the times that you were crying, I thought it was out of concern for me! And your poor mother – she must have been heartbroken, too!'

Kerry's eyes narrowed. 'That day when we got news of the crash – my mother ran off to Greygates to comfort *you*! Even though my heart was breaking, there was no one there to comfort *me*!'

Laura said nothing, thinking how devastated Ellie would have been if she'd known the lengths to which her own daughter had gone in pursuit of her dream family.

Kerry's voice rose in anger. 'We were left penniless after my father died – despite all his protestations of love for my mother, he made no financial provision for us! So I've had years of poverty to keep my hatred on the boil. While you went swanning off to live in luxury with your grandfather, Mum and I were left with nothing! I ended up attending a comprehensive, and we had to sell the house I loved because we couldn't survive any other way!'

'Well, my father wasn't exactly expecting to die, was he?'

Laura retorted. 'We'll never know what he intended to do, because you killed him! And you destroyed your own mother's life, too.'

Kerry suddenly laughed. 'Remember that hideous plastic Eiffel Tower you brought back for me from Paris? Well, I hated it, and I hated you, with all your expensive family holidays! But I kept it to remind me every day of how unfairly I'd been treated – and to make sure I never forgot that you'd inherited the Thornton millions, whereas I'd got nothing! Since then I've just been biding my time, and waiting for the day when all that wealth would finally be mine.'

Laura's mind was reeling. It was all too much to take in. And she was beginning to feel very weak...

'Then, of course, you had to meet Jeff.'

Laura stared at her uncomprehendingly.

Kerry cocked her head to one side. 'By the way, how did your ex-husband die?'

Laura's lip quivered. 'The prison accidentally served peanuts in his food, and they couldn't locate his adrenaline pen in time to save him.'

Kerry grinned. 'Aha! So his allergy finally caught up with him! It seems a fitting end to a thoroughly nasty person. I just wish *I'd* been that lucky when I tried to bump him off...'

'Y-you tried to get rid of Jeff, too?'

Kerry laughed. 'Oh, Laura, you're such an innocent! I needed to get him out of your life – otherwise you'd probably have changed your will in his favour! How do you think the peanuts got into his food at the restaurant? And did you really think that his missing adrenaline pen was an accident?' Kerry grimaced. 'After that damned do-gooder saved Jeff's bacon that night, I had to hope that you'd eventually divorce him. But I was terrified that you'd tell him about the money before then, or that he knew already, and had latched on to you in that pub, knowing you'd inherited a fortune.' She grinned triumphantly. 'But now that he's dead, I don't need to worry any more.'

In the silence that filled the room, Laura felt as though her heart would break. Everything she'd believed had suddenly been taken away from her, and she felt as though a giant rug had been pulled from beneath her feet. A wave of nausea swept over her, and she leaned against the desk to steady herself. She was suddenly feeling very woozy. 'But all those years we were friends, all those times you were so kind to me – were you really pretending?' she asked at last.

Kerry shrugged her shoulders. 'You really *were* my best friend, up until the day I found out I was his daughter. Then everything changed.' Tears formed in Kerry's eyes, but she wiped them away angrily. 'There were lots of times when I actually forgot how much I hated you, and I genuinely found myself caring about you. But, at the end of the day, it's hard to forget how unfair it was that I was never recognised as Alan Thornton's first-born daughter.'

Thoughts were tumbling through Laura's brain, in no particular order. Her head was spinning, and she was feeling increasingly dizzy. There were so many things she wanted to find out. Surely this was all just a terrible mistake?

'You still haven't answered me about Jeff – it *was* him stalking me, wasn't it?' Laura pleaded. 'I know he made all those phone calls, and I had to change my number...'

Kerry looked exasperated, as though she was dealing with a particularly stupid child. 'Oh, Laura – you really are a dolt, aren't you? If you'd looked properly, instead of reacting so emotionally, you'd have seen that it wasn't actually Jeff's number. I got a pay-as-you-go sim card, and entered it into your phone under Jeff's name. So every time I phoned, using that number, Jeff's name appeared on your screen.'

Laura felt winded, as though Kerry had punched her in the

gut. She felt as though she'd stepped into some strange world where nothing was as it seemed.

'What about the "*Good Luck in Your New Home*" card? Surely that was Jeff?'

Kerry laughed. 'No, it wasn't. I paid an out-of-work actor friend who looked reasonably like Jeff. I knew that the concierge would describe him to you as tall and blond, and you'd jump to the conclusion I wanted you to.'

'And the TV repair man?'

'Same guy.'

'But Jeff *did* phone the estate agent – '

Kerry chuckled. 'What a fool you are, Laura – you almost deserve to be deceived! No, my actor friend made the call and gave Jeff's name.'

Laura was shocked, and another wave of nausea swept over her. 'So Jeff never wanted to live in the same apartment block?'

Kerry sniggered. 'No, he didn't. I think Jeff actually got over you quite quickly. You've always had a tendency to over-estimate your pulling-power.'

Laura gave a jolt as another thought entered her mind. 'The listening device under the coffee table – who put it there?'

Kerry smiled, pleased at her own ingenuity. 'I did, of course! I bought it and installed it under the table – I just pretended to find it there, to scare you.'

Laura's mind was still doing somersaults. 'But the fire in my apartment – Jeff started that, didn't he?'

'Wrong again. It was clever old me! I used my out-of-work actor friend to set the scene. With his hair darkened and dressed as a barista, he arrived at the concierge's desk, offering Jim a free coffee of his choice, courtesy of a new, fictitious café opening shortly. Needless to say, I'd made it my business to find out Jim's favourite coffee in advance.' She grinned. 'I crushed one of those strong sedatives you got into the coffee –

remember those sedatives you got from the doctor, but never took?–so Jim was soon fast asleep. I was able to sneak past him, enter your apartment with the spare key I'd borrowed, turn on the cooker and place the pot of cooking oil on it. Then I sneaked past poor comatose Jim again, and the rest is history.'

'So I need never have gone to Dorrington.'

Kerry nodded angrily. 'You caused me a lot of hassle by your impulsive decision to move so far away. I had to take time off work to go after you – '

'So that was you in the car that tried to run me down?'

Kerry smirked at her. 'I scared you, didn't I?'

'Oh God. Why would you do all that?'

'Why?' Kerry's lip curled. 'Are you a total fool? Because you've always got everything you wanted – '

'Like my parents and brother dying?' Laura retorted. 'You destroyed my life all those years ago! What can you possibly want from me now?'

Kerry grinned. 'Your money, of course. When you're dead, it'll all be mine!'

'If you felt so strongly about the situation, and for so many years, why didn't you try to kill me before now?' Laura asked, bewildered. 'Why wait?'

Kerry gave a harsh laugh. 'Since the money was frozen in a trust fund until you reached twenty-five, there was no point in killing you before you'd actually *inherited* it!' Kerry's face now wore a sneer. 'Do you remember the scuba diving holiday two years ago? You thought I was saving your life, but I'd dissolved a sedative into your juice that morning, and I intended letting you drown. Unfortunately another diver came along, so I had to pretend I was saving you instead!' She suddenly grinned. 'Anyway, if I'd got rid of you earlier, I'd have missed all the fun of taking revenge. Everything's actually worked out for the best. Back then, all I wanted was a father. Now, all

I want is the money that's rightfully mine.' She gave a twisted smile. 'It's ironic, isn't it? Because of me, you inherited the entire proceeds of the sale of the factory and your magnificent family home – you didn't have to share it with anyone!'

At this point, Laura could barely contain herself any longer. 'You nasty, vicious bitch!' she screamed. 'I'd have gladly shared the money with Pete – and with you! If you'd told me you were my father's daughter, I'd have given you an equal share, too! I'm not obsessed with money like you are!'

'Easy to say when you have so much, eh?' Kerry inspected her nails. 'And you were left your grandfather's estate, too. How lucky can one woman get?' Then her mood darkened even further. 'You inherited all that money several years ago, but you never even offered me any!'

'Believe it or not, I'd actually decided to give you a chunk of the money just as soon as my divorce became final,' Laura told her angrily. 'You knew I couldn't bear to touch the money earlier, because I felt so guilty! I thought I'd killed my family, whereas *you* were the guilty one all along!' she said bitterly. 'You killed my family, and now you're planning on getting rid of me. But how do you intend getting your hands on my money? How do you know that I haven't left it all to a charity?'

Kerry looked pleased with herself. 'Oh, I've already sneaked a look at your will – I know you've left everything to me. You even gave me the idea for your death yourself, when you told me that Jeff had killed his father, but arranged the scene to look like a suicide.' Kerry wrung her hands in mock horror. 'I'll tell the police that you've been very depressed lately. That the deaths of your parents and brother have been weighing heavily on your mind, and that you've mentioned suicide several times.' She gave a sigh. 'Jeff's death was probably the last straw – I mean, getting news like that would clearly unbalance your mind, wouldn't it? You were very upset when you arrived here, but I eventually managed to calm you down – or so I thought. Then I went off into the kitchen to cook us dinner, and you repaid my kindness by hanging yourself from the banisters as soon as I'd turned my back. I'll sob and tell the police that I feel responsible.' She smirked again. 'And I'll be distraught when I ring for help.' Putting on a sorrowful voice, she mimicked calling the police. 'Oh help, please – my friend has just hanged herself!'

'But what have I done to you? I don't deserve your hatred!' Laura screamed. 'It was our father and your mother who created this situation! They're the ones who had an affair! Why do you have to avenge yourself on me?'

Kerry gave a bitter laugh. 'Because you were born with a silver spoon in your stupid mouth, that's why! I should have been the daughter who had everything – I was born three months before you! But because my mum was only the mistress, you got all the attention! I knew he was my dad, yet I still had to call him "Mr Thornton"!'

Laura's eyes filled with tears again as she remembered her father and, for the blink of an eye, she could empathise with Kerry's loss before the rage returned. Kerry's very existence confirmed that her father had had another life, a secret life. Briefly she wondered if her mother had known about the affair, and if she'd been aware that Kerry was her husband's daughter? She felt an urge to cry, hoping that her poor mother had been oblivious to the situation.

Laura felt her eyes closing. Why was she feeling so tired just when she needed to be alert? 'You're out of your mind...' she managed to say.

'Maybe I am, but you probably didn't realise that I slipped a sedative into your juice, and I can see that already you're beginning to feel drowsy. When you're comatose, it'll be easy for me to get a rope around your neck and throw you over the banisters.'

Laura's eyelids were fluttering, and she was finding it difficult to keep her eyes open. 'But the police will discover that
you've filled me with sedatives – '

'Don't worry, I've thought that through as well,' Kerry said,
smiling. 'I'll volunteer the information that you've been taking a lot of medication lately, to cope with all your stress. I
nicked those sedatives from you ages ago. I'll be able to produce the box from your handbag – with your name clearly on
it – and show it to the police. I'll remove most of the tablets
first, of course – proving that you've previously dosed yourself heavily.'

Laura tried in vain to move towards the door, but she was
already beginning to feel the effects of the tablets. She found
herself struggling to remain standing, as though a terrible
weight was pressing down on her, and she was finding it difficult to keep her eyes open. Although she willed herself to stay
on her feet, she was overwhelmed by the desire to sleep, even
though her very life depended on staying awake…

As Laura struggled feebly, Kerry laughed. 'You're fighting
a losing battle – those pills are pretty strong. Of course, I'll
weep and moan when you're gone – that's what you'd expect
from your best friend, isn't it?'

Kerry seemed possessed of inhuman strength just when
Laura felt at her weakest. Even though drugged, she tried to
call out, but no words would come. Somewhere in the deepest
recesses of her brain she realised that she was falling into a
deep sleep. And if Kerry had her way, it would be a permanent
sleep…

'Laura! Are you in there?'

Unable to speak, Laura could only make a gurgling sound
in reply. Dimly, she was aware of a banging sound. Was it
coming from the entrance hall?…Perhaps she'd imagined that

someone was calling her name.

By now, Kerry was wearing gloves and had managed to tie a length of rope to the banisters, slip the noose around Laura's neck and tighten it. The banging and the shouting seemed to be reverberating in Laura's brain as Kerry redoubled her efforts to get Laura over the banisters.

'Goodbye, Laura!' Kerry whispered, as she heaved the top half of Laura's helpless body over the rail. Leaning down, she grasped Laura's legs, intending to dispatch her headfirst over the banisters.

Although she tried to grip the banisters, Laura felt like a rag doll, unable to move her limbs, and all she wanted was the oblivion of sleep...

'What the fuck – ?'

'Jesus Christ! What's going on – ?'

There was suddenly a lot of shouting and pushing, followed by a piercing scream and a thud. Someone pulled her back from the abyss. Laura felt the rope being removed from her neck and found herself in Darren's strong arms, as he whispered endearments to her and held her tightly. Laura smiled sleepily. She must be dreaming, but it was such a lovely dream...

CHAPTER 76

Tony Coleman had insisted on driving her home after the cin-ema, although Ellie had assured him she was more than able to make her way home by herself.

'I insist!' he said gallantly, 'Otherwise, I'd worry in case any-thing happened to you.'

'Oh, all right,' Ellie had replied, grateful for the company on the journey back. The movie they'd seen had been forgettable, but she'd enjoyed having someone with whom to spend a pleas-ant evening. Alan was away on a business trip, so the days were dragging more slowly than usual. Being on her own for days on end wasn't a very pleasant experience, so when Tony had turned up on her doorstep and invited her to the cinema, she'd gladly accepted his invitation. She'd also felt that Tony might prove a useful decoy – if people saw her out and about in his company, it would never cross their minds that she could be involved with someone else.

'Thanks, Tony,' Ellie said, as they reached her doorstep and she prepared to go inside.

'Don't I get a cup of coffee?'

Ellie sighed. She was tired and longing to go to bed so that she could dream about her beloved Alan. But it would seem churlish to deny Tony such a small indulgence, especially as he'd gone to the trouble to make sure she got home safely.

'Okay, come in.'

But, once inside the door, Tony grabbed her roughly by the hair. 'You've been leading me on for ages,' he whispered, his breath rasping. 'Do you think you can keep playing games with my feelings? You're nothing but a tease, Ellie!'

'Leave me alone!' she replied, her eyes blazing with fury.

But Tony was undeterred. 'I like it when you're angry,' he said smiling malevolently, still holding her by the hair. 'You think you can put out those signals all the time, but never deliver? I'm not waiting any longer, Ellie.'

'Tony, I never led you to believe – '

'Oh, yes, you did, but right now I don't care whether you believe that or not. I won't take "no" any longer – '

Grabbing her hand, he pressed it against his erection.

'That's what I'm going to give you, Ellie – '

'Tony, please – !'

Tony grinned, his breathing laboured. 'I love when a woman begs for it – it's such a turn-on!'

'I'm not begging, you fool! I just want you to go!'

'I'll go when I'm finished with you,' he said, his face too close to hers. 'Come on, Ellie – you've been married, so you're no vestal virgin. You can't tease a man and not expect him to respond!'

Roughly he pressed his mouth to hers. Retching as she inhaled his stale breath, Ellie tried to pull away, but he was too strong for her. She was now very frightened. What had been a pleasant evening had suddenly turned very sour.

She looked around wildly for something she could use to hit him with, but there was nothing in sight. Silently, she cursed the isolation of her house – it was ideal for conducting an affair, but no one would hear her if she cried for help. If only Alan would arrive and save her! But of course he was away, and knew nothing about her spur-of-the-moment trip to the cinema with Tony that evening.

Tony realised that she was looking for some kind of weapon,

and his desire turned to fury. Still gripping her by the hair, he slid across the bolt on the front door with his free hand, closing off any escape route.

'We don't want any visitors, do we?' he whispered menacingly in her ear.

'Get off me, you bastard!'

Dragging her into the drawing room, he lowered her unceremoniously onto the large rug in the centre of the room, knelt down beside her and began pulling her clothing off. As she resisted his attempt to remove her bra, he momentarily raised her up and deftly flipped open the hooks at the back. Then he bit her nipples as she cried out in pain and fear. How had she ever thought Tony was a nice man?

'Come on, Ellie – you know you want it!' he panted.

In a frenzy of lust, he pulled off her panties and spread-eagled her, using his knees to keep her legs apart while he quickly opened his trousers. Bucking and screaming, Ellie tried to push him off, but he was far too strong for her. Without preliminaries, he entered her, and Ellie cried out as she felt the searing pain as he thrust deep inside her. How different it was from when she was with the man she loved! Then, her body was always ready for him.

With a final heave, Tony reached his climax and lay spent on top of her. Ellie struggled to breathe, fearing that he was going to fall asleep on top of her. But instead, he opened his eyes and smiled at her.

'How about that cup of coffee, Ellie?' he asked, his eyes glinting knowingly.

'Go to hell!' she said, her voice low and disgusted.

'Didn't I satisfy you?'

Her face contorted with disgust, Ellie pushed him off her and rose to her feet. Throwing on her clothes, she marched to the front door, unlocked and opened it. 'Get to hell out of here!' she screamed. 'And never come near me again!'

'Dear me, you do have a temper, Ellie!' Tony muttered as he sat up and rearranged his clothing. 'Calm down – it was hardly a big deal, was it? Why don't we just forget about it?'

'Get out.'

This time, the tone of Ellie's voice didn't brook any argument. Smoothing down his hair, Tony buttoned up his trousers and left without a backward glance.

As soon as she'd locked the door after him, Ellie hurried to the shower. She felt sore, violated and unclean, and she desperately wanted to wash away any lingering connection to Tony Coleman. She'd always believed him to be a dull but essentially mild-mannered man, but tonight he'd proved that she should never have trusted him.

In the shower, she scrubbed her body until it was almost raw, feeling that by doing so, she was obliterating every atom and molecule that might have come from contact with Tony Coleman. At last, she felt cleansed and caressed by the hot, cascading water, and her anger gradually began to fade. It was then that she came to a decision. Today was a day she'd wipe totally from her mind. She'd pretend it never happened. Only she and Tony would know what had transpired, and he'd hardly have the nerve to come near her again. If he did, she'd threaten him with the police.

In the silence of her bedroom, and in the loneliness of her situation, Ellie wept until she'd no tears left.

CHAPTER 77

When the police arrived at the Green Street apartment, they readily accepted Darren and Albert's explanation that Kerry's death had been a terrible accident, resulting from her own attempt to kill Laura. Darren informed the police about Laura's earlier visit to Islington Police Station, and a quick search of the apartment soon located the pay-as-you-go phone that Kerry had been using to pose as Jeff. The police also took away the rope for forensic analysis, but since the protagonist was already dead, there didn't seem to be any case to answer.

Nevertheless, the police had been unhappy about Laura's semi-comatose condition, and had insisted that she be taken to hospital for a check-up. Due to the sedatives, she hadn't fully registered what had been happening in the Green Street apartment. But, in the ambulance, with Darren holding her hand, she was beginning to realise how near she'd come to dying at Kerry's hands, and how Darren's intervention had saved her with only seconds to spare.

Darren explained how he and the concierge had struggled to pull Laura and Kerry apart, and that Kerry had stepped backwards and tumbled headfirst down the stairs, breaking her neck as she hit the floor below.

Yet despite what Kerry had done, Laura didn't want her late friend's name to be vilified. And she was relieved when Darren confirmed that the newspapers were unlikely to find any kind of worthwhile story in what had happened.

'Although it's tragic, it's better for your sake that things ended this way,' he whispered. 'If Kerry had lived, your former friend would have been put on trial, and your whole life and hers would have been sifted through by both police and press – I don't think you'd have wanted that.'

Laura nodded. Although still a little woozy, she did her best to fill him in on Kerry's secret vendetta, and how the death of her parents hadn't been an accident after all.

It was also beginning to dawn on her that Darren's presence in the apartment was both unexpected and out of context, and Laura looked at him quizzically. 'But how did you happen to be there? How did you know where I was?'

Darren smiled as the ambulance pulled into the hospital grounds. 'It's a long story – let's wait until you're home again.'

Laura nodded, suddenly wondering where home actually was.

As though he'd read her mind, Darren took her hand in his. 'Come and stay at my place when you're discharged,' he said softly. 'I promise to take good care of you.'

As she lay alone in her private room, Laura recalled the last time she'd been in hospital, and how her miscarriage had been the catalyst that had ended her marriage. Now, in the space of just a few months, so many of the people she'd once loved were gone – her baby, Jeff and, finally, Kerry.

And, of course, there was the loss of her parents and brother all those years ago. Since that fateful day when she was almost twelve, there had never been a day when she didn't desperately miss them, or feel remorse for her part in their deaths. Now, in the light of Kerry's confession, she was free of the crippling weight of guilt that she'd carried with her since childhood.

Knowing it wasn't her fault meant that her loss was no longer coupled with self-reproach. Her parents and brother had finally become real to her again, not simply reminders of her guilt. It was as though Kerry had given them back to her, releasing her from the pall of sorrow that had defined her relationship with them since they died.

On the other hand, she was now sadly aware that all hadn't been ideal in her parents' marriage. Would her father have left her mother for Ellie? It seemed unlikely, since he hadn't done so during all the years they'd been lovers. Had her mother known about the affair and tolerated it, or had she been totally unaware?

Laura sighed. There was little point in dwelling on what might, or might not, have happened. All the protagonists were now frozen in time, their earthly relationships over. It was all out of her control, and she had to learn to let go.

Wiping away a tear, Laura thought about dear, mischievous Pete who, because of Kerry's jealousy, had been denied the chance to grow up. For eternity, he would always be fourteen. She remembered Kerry with mixed emotions – her father's death would have been devastating for her, too. And Ellie would have had to hide her own pain in order to keep Kerry from guessing about her relationship with Alan. Of course Kerry had known already, and this must have added to the young girl's distress.

Laura sighed. How Kerry must have smouldered with resentment – all her plans had gone awry, her father accidentally dead by her own hand, so her private grief would have been overwhelming.

Laura pulled herself up in the bed. Despite all that had happened, she didn't want to hate anyone. When people were at the mercy of their emotions, reason flew out of the window. Nor could she blame people for falling in love with the wrong person – she'd been the victim of an unwise and unsuitable relationship herself. How had she ever thought that Jeff was the man for her?

She had also been told that since she and Jeff had never got round to divorcing – and he'd never been formally charged with drug offences – his flat and all his possessions would eventually revert to her. Since she wanted nothing to do with them, she decided to have everything sold and the money given to charity. It seemed only fair that it should go to a charity aimed at helping the people whose lives Jeff's business had destroyed.

Laura looked at the clock. It was almost visiting time, and Darren would be in to see her shortly. As she thought of him, a warm feeling pervaded her entire body. Darren was someone with whom she could always be herself. He'd never wanted to change her, unlike Jeff. Darren had also been the one who'd made all the arrangements for Kerry's upcoming funeral. He'd been a tower of strength since Kerry's death, visiting Laura each day since she'd been admitted.

With a regular parade of doctors, nurses and visitors popping in all the time, Laura still hadn't managed to discover exactly what had happened in the Green Street apartment, and how Darren had managed to be there exactly when she'd needed him. He'd smiled shyly when she'd expressed her frustration at not knowing the details, urging her to wait until she was discharged from hospital. Then, he'd promised, he'd tell her everything. The doctors had opted to keep her under observation for an extra ten days, but now they'd decided that all was well and she was free to leave hospital the following day.

'Hello, Laura – how are you feeling?'

Darren had suddenly appeared at her bedside, and Laura's

heart did a tiny somersault. He smiled at her warmly and sat down on the bed, leaning forwards to kiss her cheek.

'I'm much better, thanks,' she told him. 'They're letting me out in time for Kerry's funeral tomorrow. But I'm dreading it.'

Darren squeezed her hand. 'Don't worry,' he said softly. 'I'll be there beside you.'

Chapter 78

As the graveside service ended, Laura, supported by Darren, began moving away from Kerry's grave. She'd gone through all the motions, sprinkling earth onto her erstwhile friend's coffin and behaving as though they'd been close right up until the end. Laura felt a fraud when Norma, Jack and Kerry's other colleagues from Sea Diagnostics approached her, offering their shocked condolences at the accidental death of her dear friend. Nevertheless, she was genuinely heartbroken – despite what Kerry had done to her family, she'd been a major influence in her life.

Just as she stepped from the grass onto the pathway, an elderly man, leaning on a walking stick, approached Laura and extended his hand.

'Ms Thornton? My name is Tony Coleman. I used to be the factory manager when your father was alive.'

Laura smiled. 'Nice to meet you, Mr Coleman,' she said, wondering why he'd bothered to seek her out, and why he was attending Kerry's funeral. Perhaps he was saying hello for old time's sake. Or was he lonely and simply wanted to talk to someone?

As Darren stepped back and made way for him, the older man fell into step with Laura as she began following the other mourners through the graveyard and out towards the main gate.

'I was a friend of Kerry's mother,' he told her, glancing quickly at her. 'She was a lovely woman.'

Laura nodded in agreement.

He hesitated. 'I'm glad she didn't know what happened to her daughter,' he said, his expression bleak. 'It's tragic when someone dies so young, isn't it?'

Laura nodded, still posing as Kerry's friend. Darren was right – it seemed pointless for anyone else to know the truth.

Suddenly, Tony Coleman stopped walking and gripped her arm as his eyes stared unflinchingly into hers. 'Did your friend Kerry ever tell you who her father was?'

Laura gave an involuntary shiver. Surely this old man couldn't know about her father's affair? And if so, why would he bring it up now? She shook her head, preparing herself for the worst.

'Well, Ellie and I...' The old man looked embarrassed. 'We once had what – ahem – I think you young people call a one-night stand. And exactly nine months later, Kerry was born.' His lugubrious face softened as he reached into his jacket pocket, extracted his wallet and took out a picture. 'This is my mother,' he said, handing it to Laura.

She gasped when she saw it. Kerry was the spitting image of the woman in the photograph!

The old man seemed pleased by her reaction. 'Kerry was like her, wasn't she?'

Laura nodded, her eyes filling with tears as she handed back the photograph. She felt overwhelmed by sadness. Poor, disillusioned Kerry – because of a chance remark all those years ago, she'd let her resentment grow out of all proportion. Now it seemed certain that there had never been any basis in fact for her lifelong resentment. Or for the destruction she'd wrought on Laura and her family.

Tony Coleman smiled at her wistfully. 'Your mother approached me at the staff Christmas party the year Kerry was born, making veiled references about my "responsibilities" to Ellie. The penny didn't drop until weeks later, when I realised that Sylvia thought or maybe even knew, that Ellie's child was mine. I tried asking Ellie, but she always cut me off, and made it clear that she didn't want me having anything to do with the child.' Momentarily, he looked embarrassed. 'So I used to watch Kerry when she was small – I'd sometimes hide in the bushes at Treetops and watch her play. Even after she'd grown up, I'd still follow her from time to time. I liked to see where she was going and what she was doing. It confirmed for me, as I noted her mannerisms and discovered the things she was interested in, that she was definitely my daughter.' He grimaced. 'It was silly of me, I know, but I got her mobile number through her office, and I'd taken to phoning her recently, just to hear her voice.' He looked sheepish. 'Of course, I stopped doing that when it dawned on me that by not saying anything, I might be frightening her.'

He paused. 'After Ellie died, I thought that Kerry might be pleased to know that she still had a parent. But although I was still checking on her from time to time, I could never pluck up the courage to speak to her. A few weeks ago, I finally decided that I had to tell her the truth, so I waited outside her office one evening. But I bungled it and she ran away. Clearly, I'd frightened her, so I left her alone after that.' He gestured ruefully to the walking stick. 'I tripped and fell, and broke my leg rather badly. It hasn't really healed, so it's become a constant reminder of that last time I saw her.' His eyes filled with unshed tears. 'Now, of course, I wish I'd made more of an effort to contact her.'

'I'm so sorry for your loss,' Laura told the old man.

Nodding, he accepted her condolences, shook her hand

again and turned back the way they'd just come. Turning to watch him, Laura saw him hobbling slowly down the avenue again. Then he stepped off the pathway, kneeling with difficulty in front of his daughter's grave.

Chapter 79

'Are you okay?' Darren asked, as he helped Laura out of the taxi that had taken them back to his flat.

She nodded, unable to speak. She was exhausted, but relieved that the funeral was over at last. She'd never forget Kerry, her one-time friend, or the extraordinary circumstances that had led to the build-up of so much hatred. But it wouldn't rule her life any longer.

As Darren paid the taxi driver and opened the door into the apartment block, Laura smiled her thanks. It was nice to be able to rely on someone to do all the day-to-day things that needed doing because, right then, all she wanted to do was rest.

In Darren's large but cosy apartment, Laura sank down onto one of the sofas gratefully. There had been little opportunity to talk while she'd been in the hospital. But now, at last, she was longing to fully understand what had transpired that fateful day in the Green Street apartment, and how Darren had materialised just when she needed him most.

Having made a pot of coffee and brought it to the coffee table, Darren sat down beside her and poured the hot liquid into two mugs.

'Now, you'd better tell me everything,' Laura said.

Darren smiled. 'It's a long story, but I'll try to condense it as best I can. After you'd gone to Dorrington, I asked Bill to keep an eye on you, although I didn't tell him why. I was worried in case your ex found out where you were and started hassling you again. Then some police officer rang me, trying to find out where you'd gone. I refused to tell him, but the call got me worried. Why would the police be looking for you? So I decided to pay a quick visit to Dorrington, just to make sure that you were okay. I wondered if I'd done you a favour by telling you about the job there, or if I'd just made you more vulnerable. I decided to see who, if anyone, was tailing you – just anyone who might be hanging around you more often than they should be.'

Laura tightened her grip on his hand, her coffee forgotten.

'But all seemed fine when I got there,' Darren confirmed. 'I discovered that your friend Kerry was staying at the same hotel as I was, but I deliberately kept out of her way, since I wouldn't have wanted you to hear that I'd been in Dorrington without bothering to say hello. I found it odd that she wasn't staying with you, but I assumed your new accommodation wasn't big enough for guests. Then I saw her collect a hire car outside the hotel one day, and I surmised that the two of you were going off sightseeing. I was pleased for you – how wrong could I be! After that, I went back to London.'

'All I saw of that car was the bonnet heading towards me!' Laura said wryly.

Darren gave her hand a sympathetic squeeze. 'Later, I decided to pay a second visit to Dorrington. That was when you spotted me!'

'I was really upset when you didn't want to speak to me – I thought I must have done something to offend you,' Laura said accusingly.

Darren smiled. 'You could never offend me, Laura. But how could I explain to you what I was doing there? I'd have been embarrassed to let you know I was checking up on you.' Darren smiled, keeping a tight grip on her hand. 'When you finally told Bill about the incident with the car, and the man who was following you, he rang me straight away. Then I remembered Kerry hiring the car. That was when I realised you could be in real danger.'

Now it was Laura's turn to squeeze Darren's hand comfortingly, as he fished out his handkerchief, took off his glasses and wiped his eyes.

'Thankfully, Bill discovered that you'd left a voicemail on his department phone, saying you were heading to London by train the following morning. So we agreed that I'd be on it, and that I'd find you and warn you about your so-called friend.' He grinned ruefully. 'I had this stupid idea that I might get a chance to save your life – then you'd be grateful to me forever more. Pathetic, isn't it?'

'No, it isn't – you *did* save my life.'

Darren looked at her shyly as he put on his glasses again. 'I searched for you on the train, but I didn't manage to find you until we arrived back in London. I spotted you getting off, but somehow I lost you again in the crowds. Then I saw you heading for the Underground and I could only hope that I'd got on the same tube as you. When we got to Islington, I saw you get off the train and race into the police station. I was hoping that you'd gone there because you'd already found out about Kerry. But then you shot out of there like a bat out of hell, and I almost missed you – I called to you, but you were too focused on where you were going to pay any attention to me. Luckily, that nice estate agent was able to tell me where you were heading, and give me the number of the apartment.'

Laura nodded, remembering the voice she'd ignored in her haste to confront Kerry.

'Not surprisingly, Albert refused to let me up to the apartment,' Darren continued. 'But I pushed past him and headed

for the lift. Thankfully, he came running after me, because I'd
never have been able to open the door to the apartment myself
– he has a master key, and when he heard the strange noises
coming from inside, he agreed to open the door.' He shivered.
'If we'd been a minute later, Kerry would have had you over
the banisters…'

'The sad thing is – I'd left everything to Kerry in my will,'
Laura whispered. 'I'd also decided to give her a sizeable chunk
of the money just as soon as I'd divorced Jeff.'

Trembling, and still finding it difficult to understand, Laura's
eyes filled with tears again, and she was glad to feel Darren's
comforting arms around her. Even though Kerry had professed
to hate her, she couldn't feel that emotion herself. She had
genuinely loved her friend. Yet Kerry had been a murderer,
harbouring hatred that had grown like a tumour, multiplying
out of all proportion.

'I'm not very good at picking friends or husbands, am I?'
Laura said earnestly, turning to face Darren. 'I thought both
Kerry and Jeff actually cared about me.'

Darren smiled ruefully. 'I'm sorry, Laura – I know it
mightn't be the right thing to say, but I was so glad to hear that
you'd left Jeff. It allowed me to dream that somehow, one day,
I might have a chance with you.'

Laura felt a frisson of delight as he looked at her. Since
that day when he'd saved her life, she'd come to appreciate
his kindness, his generosity of spirit and his bravery. In fact,
she suspected she'd had feelings for him for much longer than
that.

'But why didn't you ever say anything?' she asked curiously. 'We've known each other for years!'

'How could I? If you'd told me to take a hike, it could have
made things very awkward for both of us. Apart from my personal feelings, you're a damned good lecturer, and very pop-

ular with the students. The university wouldn't want to lose you. And if I'd declared myself, you might have found it too embarrassing to stay on – then I'd have lost you twice over. At least if I said nothing, you'd stay on and I'd be able to see you every day.'

What a sweet, wonderful man, Laura thought, her heart brimming with affection for him. Darren was totally different from the kind of man she'd have chosen before – thank goodness. Now when she thought of Jeff, with his blond hair, good looks and suave demeanour, she felt sick to think she'd actually believed she'd loved him. She hadn't understood the meaning of the word back then. Jeff had never cared about her – he'd only wanted her on his terms. And Steve's vintage car had been more important to him than helping a woman in danger. Why had she always chosen such losers?

Now, she was seeing Darren in a totally different light. And with his glasses off, he had the most beautiful soft brown eyes. His black hair was thick and luxuriant, with just a few flecks of grey around his sideburns, and suddenly she longed to run her fingers through it. He had such strong, manly hands, and she felt a delicious shiver run down her spine at the thought of those fingers touching her body. While he wasn't conventionally handsome or tall like Jeff had been, he had a heart as big and brave as a lion. Why had she never noticed how totally gorgeous he was, or how wonderfully secure he made her feel?

Laura leaned forward and kissed him affectionately. 'You're a wonderful man. I think I've always known there was something special about you – I just didn't realise how much you meant to me until you came to rescue me. If that wasn't an extraordinarily decent and generous thing to do, I don't know what is.'

Darren grimaced. 'You're probably feeling a bit emotional right now,' he said kindly, 'so I'm not sure that you'd really want to settle for a plodder like me, in the long run. I'm never going to do anything out of the ordinary, or set the world on fire.'

Laura chuckled. 'I've already come through one attempt at setting my world on fire, and it's not a trait I rate very highly! Besides, *you'd* be taking on a fool – why didn't I realise what a disaster Jeff was?'

Darren looked at her critically, as though he found it difficult to believe her. Then he smiled shyly, taking both her hands in his. 'Well, it was me who had the daft vision of myself as a James Bond-type character, arriving in some souped-up, spectacular car, and pulling you inside just before the baddies were about to harm you. Then we'd drive off, and you'd be so grateful that we'd immediately begin making love.'

'How could you drive and make love at the same time?' Laura asked in mock disapproval.

Darren grinned. 'Ah, but you see, my James Bond car would be able to drive itself. I'd have already put it on automatic!'

'Hmm, I suppose we *could* try making part of that scenario come true,' Laura whispered, her heart beating much faster than usual.

'Well, okay. You could start by kissing me,' Darren said reasonably.

Laura was tingling with excitement. 'And what happens then?'

'Well, I might totally lose control and have my wicked way with you.'

'Sounds wonderful,' Laura murmured breathlessly, marvelling at the fact that she no longer felt lethargic. 'How soon can we begin?'

'Right now is fine by me.'

'What a wonderful idea,' Laura whispered, slipping into his arms.

He grinned. 'And now that you've moved into my apartment, why don't you stay?'

Laura nodded, smiling back. 'I'd like that, very much,' she replied, feeling safe within Darren's embrace.

As Laura thought back to the events that had happened to her, she couldn't believe that she had found happiness again. The past was over and it was time to look forwards now, maybe to starting a family of her own with Darren. She had visions of a large country house like Greygates, with lots of space for children to play.

'I hope you don't mind me being very rich?' Laura added, holding her breath.

Darren grinned. 'Why would any man object to a wealthy wife?' But then his expression turned serious. 'But even if you had nothing, I'd still feel exactly the same about you. I love you very much, Laura, and I'll never let you down.'

'I can't wait for the future – our future,' Laura whispered fervently, as she held him to her heart.

* * * * *

'FANS OF *GONE GIRL* WILL EMBRACE THIS' —LISA GARDNER

Mia Dennett can't resist a one-night stand with the enigmatic stranger she meets in a bar.

But going home with him will turn out to be the worst mistake of her life.

An addictively suspenseful and tautly written thriller, *The Good Girl* reveals how, even in the perfect family, nothing is as it seems.

HARLEQUIN®MIRA®
www.mirabooks.co.uk

Sometimes, one small mistake can have life-changing consequences...

One blistering summer's day, Ellen Moore takes her eyes off her baby.

Not for very long, just for a few seconds. But this simple moment of distraction has repercussions that threaten to shatter everything Ellen holds dear.

Powerful and emotionally charged, *Little Mercies* is about motherhood, justice and the fragility of the things we love most.

'Totally gripping' —*Marie Claire*

'Her technique is faultless' —*Sunday Express*

A family given a second chance at life

A world where nothing—not even death—is certain

All over the world, loved ones are returning from
the dead. Exactly as they were before they died.

As if they never left.

As if it's just another ordinary day.

'Fantastically readable' —*The Times*

'Gripping' —*Shortlist*

HARLEQUIN®MIRA®
www.mirabooks.co.uk

*A chance to uncover the secrets
of her past. A truth that will
change her future forever.*

Early on the morning of her eleventh birthday, Daria
Cato found an unexpected gift—an abandoned baby.
Unable to leave the child unclaimed, the Cato family
adopt Shelly, but the secrets of her birth continue
to haunt Daria.

As closely guarded secrets and sins begin to unravel,
piece by piece the mystery of the summer's child
is about to be exposed. A mystery no one
involved is prepared to face.

HARLEQUIN®MIRA®
www.mirabooks.co.uk